Generation Stone

Revelation Light Calling

Written By: Misty D. Tackett

GENERATION STONE: REVELATION LIGHT CALLING

Dedication

For my mother

Carol Lynn

With all my heart

I love you

The Father's light

Has called you home

Into Heaven's embrace

You left behind

A Legacy

Compassion

Strength and Grace

Amongst Flora

And Beauty

In this story

I give your name

A place

Acknowledgments

To my husband, Charles. I thank you for sponsoring all my crazy endeavors. Thank you, Helena and Autumn, for helping me with my book cover and creating the tree illustration. Robert, I thank you for listening to me read my story. To my family, I love you all so much.

I thank all my friends and family for being my beta readers and giving feedback. Your encouragement has given me what I need to see it all through.

A big thanks to 105 Publishing for all their help through the editing process and for adding the finishing touches to my book's cover. Thanks for always being available when I needed help getting through the most difficult part of this journey.

Table of Contents

Chapter 1 6
Chapter 2 13
Chapter 3 19
Chapter 4 31
Chapter 5 46
Chapter 6 58
Chapter 7 72
Chapter 8 91
Chapter 9 111
Chapter 10 131
Chapter 11 150
Chapter 12 171
Chapter 13 192
Chapter 14 215
Chapter 15 235
Chapter 16 257
Chapter 17 276
Chapter 18 296
Chapter 19 314
Chapter 20 333
Chapter 21 356
Chapter 22 378
Chapter 23 394
Chapter 24 416
Chapter 25 436
Chapter 26 457
Epilogue 479

Chapter 1

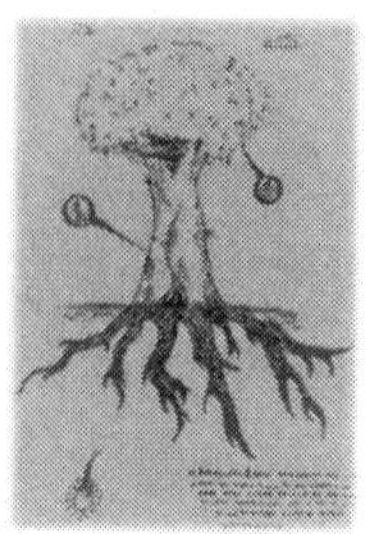

“Jasper, wake up!” I shook my brother frantically. “Jasper,” I pleaded.

Jasper moaned in protest. He responded in a deep groggy voice, “What, Krystle?” Frustration was evident in his tone.

“Listen! I wouldn’t have disturbed you if it wasn’t urgent,” I said.

“Huh?” Jasper yawned and slowly rose on his elbows.

“Dad is outside yelling. He sounds terrified,” I cried.

Jasper's sudden movements knocked a stack of books from the side table to the floor. The noise made our youngest brother Rhodin stir.

“What’s going on?” Rhodin’s small body shifted.

“Don’t worry, Rhodin. Lay back down and try to rest,” I tried to soothe my little brother. My calming attempt was of no avail when we all heard our dad once again.

"GEMMA!!!" Dad's voice echoed out in the night. His calls grew more distant with desperate intensity.

Rhodin sat up and asked, "Where's Mom? Why is Dad yelling for her?"

Jasper was already up and dressed. "Krystle, stay here with Rhodin. I'm going out to help."

"No, Jasper, I'm coming too!"

"Me too!" Rhodin declared.

"You two just STAY!" Jasper demanded.

"G-E-M-M-A-A!" Our Dad screamed in utter terror.

Jasper froze. My eyes widened, and fear trickled down my spine. Rhodin screamed, "Mommy! Daddy!" Tears trickled down his small, reddened cheeks. Jasper took off in a flash. I followed swiftly with Rhodin gripped tightly in my arms. There was no time to think; we were in flight mode.

Jasper sprinted toward the beach. On sheer adrenaline alone, I kept pace a few yards behind. I ignored the pain of each twig, shell, and rock beneath my bare feet. I had hoisted Rhodin into my arms, and I pressed past my limits as I moved with a life-or-death purpose.

"Dad! Mom!" Jasper called out.

"The Cave!" he yelled. "Over by the cave!"

"Jasper!" I cried out.

My lungs were on the verge of bursting. The muscles in my arms and legs burned trying to keep up with him.

"JASPER!" I screeched. My feet were sinking into the sand, slowing my pace. I collapsed to my knees and released Rhodin to his feet. He continued to sob as he held on to me.

"Mommy...Daddy!" Pleas continued from his lips like a haunted, skipping record.

Jasper stopped abruptly. He finally acknowledged me. The moment was so quiet in our solitude. The tide ebbed, and gently it lapped in the background. Jasper had begun turning frantically in place. The sand kicked up from his feet with each twist and turn. His movements jerked while his eyes looked about in all directions.

"I don't hear them anymore!" I declared. Tears streamed down my face. "Why is no one else out here? Surely the entire resort heard us screaming!"

Jasper approached the cave. "DAD...?! MOM...?!" The only response was his voice echoing back to him. It was too dark to go inside. In our haste, we had forgone grabbing anything essential. A flashlight and footwear would have made a big difference.

Jasper walked toward the jungle forest. A big sign marked a trail entrance: GUIDED TOURS BY RESORT STAFF ONLY! HOURS 7 a.m. – 7 p.m. Warning signs are visible before the pathway to the cave. Jasper started to abandon all logic as he walked past the signs. My protective instinct kicked in.

"Jasper!" His name whipped out of me in a sharp crack. I had to get his attention. I would not stand back and allow him to go any further by himself. I knew he was desperate, but Rhodin and I didn't need to lose him too.

Jasper turned back to look at me. Sweat soaked his hair and trickled through his brow. He gave me a stern look with serious blue eyes. “Krystle, we have to do something! I just heard Dad here moments ago. They can’t have gone far. They may be hurt, unconscious,” he cried.

“We need to alert the resort staff! I still don’t understand why no one has noticed?” I looked back up to the ocean blue fabric on the luxury tents as it rippled in the light breeze down the beach. No illumination came from within them. The lanterns flamed from the grand porch of the large white plantation-style house with its stately columns. Many guests and staff were residing here. Still, we saw no one.

Dawn brimmed on the horizon. Small waves started to wash ashore. Jasper fell to his back in exhausted defeat, “AAAAHHH!” He yelled out. He fisted and pulled at his dark blonde hair in frustration.

Mom and Dad would know what to do if the situation was in reverse. After all those lessons they taught us on survival and first aid, we felt at a loss right now. We can’t do this on our own. We have a responsibility to Rhodin. I wouldn’t let Jasper go out on his own, just as I couldn’t leave Rhodin behind to follow Jasper.

We laid exasperated on the beach as precious time ticked along. It felt like we were being held in place by some unseen force. It took everything in me to push my body upright. I noticed Jasper had the same issue. Rhodin must have been affected as he fell asleep as if under some spell. The sun rose ever so slightly. It sent the moon to rest as we lifted to our feet. Something caught my periphery, and I turn to see a luminescent light emanating from the cave. It had a drawing call, strange and otherworldly. There was a pulling sensation I couldn't explain.

"Jasper," I started. My eyes squinted toward the cave as I pushed my long blonde hair away from where it had stuck the side in my face.

"Yes, Krystle, I know!" He responded tersely. He was looking toward the resort. "We need to go get help!"

"No! Jasper!" I tried to get his attention on the cave. He looked at me with a confused expression. Just as I was about the mention the cave, a voice caught us both off-guard.

"Genstone Family! Enjoying the sunrise? I don't usually see children out so early in the morning. Where are your parents?" Mr. Lattimier, the resort owner, approached us with an easy smile. He had greeted us when we first arrived at the resort. He was tall, with olive skin and dark features. He wore a blue polo with Sol Palmera Oasis's resorts logo along with crisp white pants and casual sandals.

Jasper spoke forcefully. "Our parents are missing!"

"Missing? Since when?" Lattimier asked. His voice indicated doubt. "Surely, they are just walking the beach or in the dining hall for breakfast."

I no longer saw the light. My mind must have been playing tricks on me. Perhaps it was how the sunlight played off the rippling water at the cave's edge.

Jasper continued, "No, Sir, we heard our Dad screaming for our Mom. We came running. He had sounded close. By the time we got down here, they had vanished. There was no response from either of them."

Mr. Lattimier looked perplexed. He gazed around. I noticed how his eyes landed on the cave for a long moment. My mind started to scream with suspicion.

He simply looked back at each of us like we shouldn't be here. He lifted a walkie-talkie off his belt and brought it up to his mouth. "Attention, crew! I need all available staff for a Missing Guests Search. Flint and Gemma Genstone," He went on to give a brief description of our parents.

"How did you remember all of that?" Jasper asked.

"I make it my business to know all my guests. The resort staff will know who they are looking for," Lattimier explained.

Mr. Lattimier motioned us to follow him. "Let's go to the main house, Genstone family. We will move you to the house's in-suite accommodations. A staff member will bring belongings to you as soon as possible."

I could see the look on Jasper's face. He wanted to be out there looking, as did I. Mr. Lattimier assured us his staff was capable of handling this type of situation. He would notify mainland authorities if our parents did not turn up in the next three hours.

Mr. Lattimier insisted we stay secured in the main house with a chaperone in the event of our parents' return. He was so sure it was a simple explanation. Although he was catering to our legitimate concern, he probably thought we were overzealous. I didn't trust the way he seemed so casual about the situation. Like this is something that happened often and is solved in three easy steps.

We started to walk back up the hillside dune. Jasper noticed my struggle with Rhodin in my arms. Graciously he took over on big brother duty. I dragged along, ready to collapse. My throat was dry, and my stomach growled. Mr. Lattimier had me sit down while he called and requested a jeep to retrieve us from the beach.

When the Jeep approached the main house, people in uniform spoke in authoritative tones on walkie-talkies. They loaded supplies on all-terrain quad runners; some had already passed by us in Jeeps.

I looked back down toward the beach near the cave. It was a wonder to me how we made it down there so quickly. It seemed so much farther away to my tired eyes. How long were we searching? I wondered how Mr. Lattimier had come upon us so quickly without our notice. But then I realized how taken down I felt and how fraught my mind consumed with worry.

I didn't take note of the time when it all began. I had dreamt about Dad calling playfully to Mom on the beach. No doubt they took a romantic midnight stroll. Dad's voice must have echoed into my subconscious. I woke to Dad calling out Mom's name for real. Along the way, something mysterious happened to them. I had that feeling in my gut. Flint and Gemma Genstone would never abandon their children.

Chapter 2

Mr. Lattimier opened the door to our new accommodations. Jasper laid Rhodin down on a queen-sized bed. I took in the room's décor. I could see the stunning beach view through the French doors.

"I will have breakfast sent to your room," Mr. Lattimier stated. "Please eat and rest. Be assured we are doing everything we can to find your parents. Do not hesitate to ask for anything you need. You may dial the front desk with the phone on your bedside table. You will not be able to make international calls in here, but you may use the phone in my office."

"My phone?" I inquired. I needed to contact my lifelines: Aunt Cassie, Uncle Garreth, and my best friend, Taylin.

"Yes, Miss Genstone. I understand," Lattimier responded. "Your belongings will arrive shortly. You will have an appointed chaperone, Mr. Victor Mehla. My apologies, but being minors, we cannot allow you to go about freely till your parents return."

"Of course, we understand," I stated. I gave Mr. Lattimier a weak smile, which he returned with a look of sympathy. Jasper stood and glared back; his face was red with frustration. He would be turning eighteen next week, and I was turning sixteen the week after. It felt somewhat insulting. We were not small, incapable children. But our parents taught us to be respectful to adults in the most crucial circumstances.

Mr. Lattimier was only trying to help, but as pleasant as he seemed, there was something off. I felt it since the moment I saw his gaze lingering toward the cave. My intuition told me he knew something. He curtly exited the room, closing the door with a gentle click behind him. I turned to Jasper. He returned my look like he knew what I was thinking.

Since we were little, Jasper and I were like two peas in a pod. We had this shared intuitiveness with one another, "I still do not understand how in the hell no one heard us!" Jasper fumed. "And, as for Mr. Lattimier!" Jasper's sarcasm spewed out in detest for our sudden savior. "Showing up so casually like there's nothing wrong with three kids sprawled out on the beach, beaten down by excruciating panic."

I had no response other than to acknowledge and agree. "Jasper, before Lattimier showed up, I noticed something strange. The cave..."

Jasper's eyes shot up in question.

Just at that moment came a knock on the door. "Breakfast for the Genstone Family," a man's voice declared from the hallway outside. "I am your appointed chaperone, Victor Mehla" Jasper went to the door and looked through the peephole, then slowly opened it with caution.

A man with short dark hair and amber eyes entered, pulling a cart behind him. The smell of fresh eggs, bacon, and maple syrup pancakes wafted in and filled my senses with drool-worthy desire. My stomach made its demands known once more.

I immediately grabbed a bottle of water and cracked it open. I started to chug but then had to stop myself. I didn't want to make my stomach upset. The cool water eased the burn of my raw throat. All the yelling from what was now over an hour ago had taken a toll. Jasper grabbed a bottle and took slow sips. Rhodin was still out, so we would let him rest for now.

Mr. Mehla smiled, "I see; I am not a moment too late. Poor kids." His concern sounded sincere. "I am here to help with whatever you require. Within reason, of course!"

"Why haven't we gotten our belongings yet?" Jasper asked. "Mr. Lattimier told us they would be here."

"My apologies," Victor stated. "Sorry for the delay. We had to do a full sweep of your tent to make sure we didn't miss anything. Including any message your parents may have left behind to tell of their whereabouts."

That seemed to appease Jasper for the moment. They could have left us a note before the incident took place. My father's voice screaming "GEMMA!!!" reverberated in my head, and I shivered.

"I am here for your safety as per our resort's protocol," Victor insisted, "I am not here to babysit. I just thought I could be an ear for any concerns you have. Would you like to make a call?" he asked. "I am happy to take you to do so after you have something to eat."

Jasper was not taking kindly to being told what to do by this strange man and started to say, "How about you go eat..."

I didn't want Jasper to finish his snide retort, so I intercepted. "What my brother Jasper is trying to say is, thank you for breakfast, and yes, if we could make a few calls A.S.A.P., that would be great."

"It's my pleasure," Victor smiled and nodded. He knew full and well my brother's words of intent but blew it off with understanding. "I have kids of my own, you know. Maria is fifteen, and Tobias is twelve. So, it's Jasper? You and your youngest brother?" Victor looked at me in question.

"I'm Krystle, soon to be sixteen, and our little brother Rhodin is six."

I look over Rhodin's small form. His light brown hair was disheveled. I wondered what dreams presided through his mind as he held closed his hazel green eyes.

Victor smiled over at our little brother. "My wife and I tried for another, but it just wasn't meant to be." A smile pulled at his lips; his eyes held sadness.

"What happened, if you don't mind my asking?" I was suddenly curious about Victor. He seemed like a decent person.

"My wife, Lee, she had a miscarriage and was no longer able to conceive after that," said Victor.

Jasper suddenly looked sorrowful for being so abrupt. "I'm sorry for your loss, Mr. Mehla."

"No need to apologize, Jasper. I understand you are feeling scared for your parents right now. I figured if I shared a bit of my personal history with you, you'd see that I'm not here to impede. Sometimes we need to see that each of us goes through tough situations in life. I'm here to help in any way I can." Jasper and I both nodded in understanding.

We sat in solemn silence as we tried to eat. Another knock came at the door, and Victor got up, "I've got it. You kids finish up. It is most likely your belongings."

He went and opened the door. "Hey, Darius, my brother! Bring it on in here!" Darius pushed the luggage cart inside with a big smile on his face. He and Victor fist-bumped and shook hands.

"Victor, my brother," Darius returned in a Jamaican accent. "I see you got de kids." Darius held his hand out to Jasper for a sideways hand slap.

"What's up, man?" Jasper smiled and returned the offered gestured greeting.

"Ah, Mon Cher," he turned to me and bowed in a gentlemanly manner. "I bring you your things. I know the kids can't live without phones these days."

I smiled at him. Darius's easy-going demeanor was infectious. "Thank you, Darius." I retrieved my bag from the cart and dug out my cell phone. I tried to turn it on, but it was dead. I found my charger and went to plug it in. The little drained battery symbol popped up.

"Victor, could you please take me down to the office so I can make a few calls?" It had been at least two hours by now, and I needed to let Aunt Cassie and Uncle Garreth know what was going on.

I turned to Jasper. “I’m going to call them and Taylin if possible.” Victor and Darius were making light, cheerful conversation. Rhodin stirred and moaned.

“Oh, man! I did not realize de little one was resting. I’ll be going,” Darius said as he made his way to the door. “Catch you later, Victor, my brother!” Before closing the door, Darius looked at me, then Jasper, “T’will, be all good children. Your parents will be found. Till den, be easy on Victor.” He closed the door gently. I heard him whistle a cheery tune as his footsteps traveled down the hallway.

“I will take you to the office now, Krystle,” Victor stated. I looked to Jasper, and he nodded. “Go! It’s okay. I’ll take care of Rhodin.” Jasper motioned with his head to the door.

Chapter 3

Lattimier was not in his office when Victor led me over to a chair in front of a desk. Victor turned the phone in my direction and proceeded to dial out with the international code for the U.S. "You dial whoever you need to from here," he said as he handed me the receiver. I dialed Aunt Cassie's number first. She picked up after four rings.

"Hello? Who is this?" Aunt Cassie answered, probably confused by the phone number.

"Aunt Cassie, it's Krystle!"

"Krystle? Is everything okay?"

"Mom and Dad are missing!"

"What?! How long, Krystle?"

"Going on three hours now. Aunt Cassie, I'm scared. We heard Dad screaming for Mom. We tried to find them, but it was dark out. They just disappeared!"

"Oh God, Krystle," her voice turned panicked. "Are Jasper and Rhodin okay?"

"Yes, the staff here is taking good care of us. A full search party is looking for Mom and Dad. They assured us they would've found them by now. There's something wrong. Mom and Dad are survivalists. They wouldn't just take off into the night and get into such an easily avoidable predicament." Tears started down my face again. I was trying hard to hold it together.

"Krystle, I'm coming," said Aunt Cassie. "I'm going to catch the first flight! I'll be there as soon as I can. Stay strong, honey. Tell the boys I am coming."

"Okay, Aunt Cassie. I need to call Uncle Garreth too!"

Aunt Cassie sighed, "I understand, Krystle. Please tell him I'm coming, and I don't want any arguments with him. We are in the midst of a family emergency. I don't need him to be his usual obstinate self with me!"

"I will," the sob I was trying to hold in escaped me.

"Oh, sweetheart," Aunt Cassie said with deep sincerity, "We are going to find them, okay? I love you."

"I love you too, Aunt Cassie," I hung up the phone. Victor stepped back into the room from the hallway. I didn't even realize he had left. He handed me some tissues to dry my eyes and blow my nose.

"You are very brave, Krystle." He sat in the chair next to me. "Is there anyone else you'd like to call?" Indeed, he heard my conversation with Aunt Cassie, but he was considerate of my privacy.

"Yes, I need to make two more calls." He simply nodded and lifted the receiver again. He dialed once more then let me take over. The phone rang several times, and I was about to hang up when Uncle Garreth answered.

"Krystle!" Uncle Garreth shouted. "I'm sorry. I was on the other line with your brother. I heard baby girl. I'm working on booking a flight as we speak."

"Oh, okay," I said with a sense of hesitation. Jasper must have gotten enough charge on one of our phones to make the call. Confident I'd call Aunt Cassie first, he took the liberty and contacted Uncle Garreth. "Uncle Garreth, I already talked to Aunt Cassie, and she's on her way too!"

Uncle Garreth sighed. "I figured as such. But, when she gets here, she better not give me any grief. That woman has a penchant for pushing my buttons." For some reason, unbeknownst to me, since I was old enough to take notice, those two were always bumping heads. Aunt Cassie was Mom's sister. Uncle Garreth was Dad's brother.

"Hang tight, kiddo. I got a flight just now, but I won't be there till sometime tomorrow morning, if there are no delays. I've got to throw a bag together. I love you guys. I'll see you tomorrow."

"I love you too, Uncle Garreth," and I placed the receiver back.

By this time, I knew all the numbers I needed to press as I had watched Victor the first two times. My third call was to my best friend, Taylin. She usually joins our family vacations, but this year she went with her family to California. She picked up on the first ring.

"Girl...That had better be you! I've been trying your cell forever! Are you in a dead zone or something?"

Hearing her voice made me smile. "Yeah, it's me. Taylin..."

"So, are you having fun? What's it like in paradise? Tell Jasper there's a girl here that wants his number. I showed her his picture, and she was so in love..."

"TAYLIN....!" I had to cut her off. She would go on and on if I didn't.

"KRYSTLE...What's got you so uptight? Maybe you need to sneak one of them special coconut mixed drink concoctions to chill your nerves. I saw the pics you posted. I wish I were there instead of here."

"Yeah, I wish you were too."

"Krystle, what's going on? You never sound this serious."

"It's my parents, Taylin. They're missing."

"Oh no...Are you serious?"

"Yeah, Taylin. They went missing this morning before sunrise. Dad was screaming for Mom, and then they disappeared!"

"Krystle, your folks know more than them naked-ass people on those survival shows. You know they are going to be okay, right? Remember, I taught them everything I know!"

"You're right!" I laughed. Taylin always had something to say to ease my nerves in any situation. She had my back in every circumstance. I had to pull myself together and stay strong. "Taylin, I have always loved you like a sister."

"Krystle, we are sisters. I am your sister from another mister. Don't be like this, like it's going to turn into some disaster situation," Taylin's voice was full of her signature attitude. "You know I'll come over there and start kicking ass and taking names. If Mr. and Mrs. Genstone don't come back safe in one piece, I'll be over there swinging."

I laughed again. "Taylin, I can always count on you. I've got to go. I need to get back to my brothers. They moved us to their deluxe in-house suite and are treating us like royalty. We even have a butler and everything."

"See, there you go, girlfriend! Your folks are just being players," said Taylin. "They're just out there hiding and getting busy while ya'll score some independence and free upgrades."

"Oh my God, Taylin! You really had to go there!"

"Just telling it like it's real, my friend!" she stated. "Call me and keep me posted. I know you're worried. I'll say a prayer for you, my sister."

"Thanks, Taylin. Love you. Bye."

"Love you too, girlie! Bye."

I leaned back in the chair and took a deep breath. Victor appeared once more. This time he didn't hide the fact he was listening. "You have a good friend. You ready to head back up?"

I put on my brave face. "Yeah, I'm sure Rhodin's awake and driving Jasper bonkers by now."

Victor chuckled, "I hear the same thing from Maria and Tobias every day. Come on, girlfriend, let's go!"

I shot Victor an incredulous look, "Okay, Pops!"

"Pops!" Victor exclaimed. "Oh, I see now how it's gonna be!"

I smiled as I got up from the chair and followed him out of Mr. L's office.

"And I'm your butler too, huh?"

"Nosey much?" I asked.

"All the time." Victor grinned.

As we made our way by the hall leading to the great room, I glanced down and observed Mr. Lattimier talking to a couple of police officers. Both men were wearing suits with badges on their front chest pockets. It was enough for me to pause because I knew it had been past three hours.

Lattimier was so engaged in conversation that he didn't notice me at first. Victor paused and looked in the same direction. I saw how he swallowed hard and placed a hand on my shoulder in support.

"This is not looking good," I stated. My bravery started to take a sidecar to fear once more. My pulse was racing. I had to know what was going on. It was my right. It is about my parents, after all. I was fraught with worry, but I would not give up hope. I turned to head their way. Victor, ever-supportive, followed closely behind.

I looked to Mr. Lattimier in question. He and the two officers turned their attention to me, "Yes, Officers Oliveira and Santos. I would like to introduce you to Krystle Genstone, Flint and Gemma's daughter."

I looked up to the two men in question, “My brother Jasper needs to be here, as well as our youngest brother Rhodin. I know my parents are still missing and still alive. I can tell you whatever you need to know to help find them.”

Office Santos turned to me, “You are very bright and perceptive, Miss Genstone. We were indeed on our way to speak with you and your brothers. Is there anyone else we may contact, family, and friends?”

“I just got off the phone with my Aunt Cassie and Uncle Garreth. They are coming but won’t arrive until tomorrow. I spoke briefly with my best friend Taylin, but she wouldn’t know any more than I told her. She’s in California with her family.” *I could desperately use her by my side*, I thought to myself.

“It’s fine.” Officer Oliveira declared. “May we proceed to your room to speak?”

I took notice of a handful of resort guests as they made their way around the great room. Their eyes looked to me and my current unfortunate entourage in curiosity. I could hear their conspiratorial whispers. I suddenly felt very uncomfortable.

“Yes, Officers,” I said respectfully and turned to go.

I knocked despite having my room key. I didn’t want to just barge in with two new strangers. Three if I thought about it. Rhodin had been asleep when Victor first appeared, so he didn’t know him yet.

“Jasper, it's Krystle! There are some people here with me.” A moment later, I heard the lock turn, and Jasper opened the door. He looked to the officers with Mr. Lattimier behind Victor and me.

"Krystle!" Rhodin exclaimed. He squeezed through the door and wrapped his arms around my waist. "Where have you been? You were gone too long. Did you find Mom and Dad?" He looked up and around me, "Who are these people?"

Jasper's face said it all. Rhodin must have been bouncing off the walls as predicted. "Let's go back in the room, Rhodin. These men are here to help, but they need to ask us some questions."

I plied Rhodin's arms from my waist and turned him to walk back into the room. Jasper held the door open wide to let the men inside. We all went to the sitting room. I sat Rhodin down next to me. Jasper's face held a look of determination, but I saw the worry in his eyes. He, too, knew what this meant. Rhodin pressed close to me and looked at the officers with a troubled expression.

Officer Santos led the questioning, "Mr. Lattimier was able to provide us with some information, but we need to hear your account of what happened. It was in the early morning hours when you noticed your parents had gone missing?"

I proceeded to tell them everything that had occurred from the time I woke till the officer's arrival. They listened intently and took notes. "What is it that your parents do for a living?" Officer Oliveira asked.

Jasper took the lead this time. "Our father owns a construction company, Generation Stone Construction, based out of Dallas, Texas. He and our Uncle Garreth run the company together. Our mother is a physician in family medicine and general surgery. She floats to different hospitals within the Dallas/Ft. Worth area. They both donate their time to 'Worlds of Care Connect,' a volunteer organization that sends aid to countries in need."

"Yes, I've heard of this organization. They do many good things. Is that the reason for your trip?" Santos asked.

"Mostly," Jasper responded, "We were on the mainland working in a favela on the outskirts of Sao Paulo. Mom was providing basic health care, vaccinations, and assisting in surgeries. Dad was donating materials and time to constructing a new clinic. We always go as a family on all these trips and work together. Krystle, Rhodin, and I help Mom and Dad."

All the men had looks of surprise and appreciation on their faces. Victor then smiled like he knew all too well. It felt good to help people around the world. Mostly we were just regular kids.

Back home, it was school and friends as usual. Jasper was on the school track team. He had won a first-place trophy or two. At school, I was a mostly shy art student. Only Taylin brought out the loud, goofy side of me. I helped Aunt Cassie at her floral shop on the weekends. Rhodin was in after-school gymnastics because he had a lot of energy to burn, and he was showing some early talent.

"So, this is how you spend all your vacations?" Mr. Lattimier asked. He sounded quite impressed. "You were undoubtedly here at my resort for a well-deserved R & R?"

"Well, yes," I answered. "We do take a break, usually about ten days. It will be Jasper's and my birthdays. That's why we're here on a side trip to enjoy some family time together and celebrate. We just got here two days ago."

"Okay, that's good to know," Officer Santos noted. "Did you notice anything suspicious, like someone that looked familiar following you to this destination?"

Surprisingly Rhodin spoke up. "Yeah! I saw that little girl on the airplane we got on to get here. I saw her again on the beach yesterday! She kept looking at me strange and blowing kisses at me, all creepy!"

I noticed everyone in the room, including myself, trying hard to suppress a laugh. Rhodin didn't understand that another family being on the same small plane here was just coincidental.

Officer Santos coughed to hide a smile behind his hand, "Is that so Rhodin?" He asked in serious pretense. "And did this little girl say anything to you?"

"Yes, she did," Rhodin stammered out dramatically. "She said she and her family come here all the time, and she wanted me to come explore the cave with her."

That struck me immediately, and I made a mental note. Did this little girl know something about the cave?

Oliveira interrupted my line of thought. "Did she tell you her name?" he asked.

"It was Sinna something. I don't remember." Rhodin stated.

"Oh yes, the Malachite family," Lattimier interjected. "They do frequent our resort each year—very nice family. Cynnica is a very imaginative young lady. You two could play together while you're here, but I wouldn't advise going cave exploring. We provide guided tours for it.

Guests are not allowed to go there without staff supervision."

"That's where we heard Dad screaming for Mom this morning," Jasper stated. "We were close, but it was so dark outside, we couldn't see anything."

The officers took note of Jasper's admission, and at that moment, Mr. Lattimier spoke. "Yes, and we have our people searching the cave and surrounding area as we speak. The cave is not very big. The tide does come in at night, so it's not safe to enter at dark."

Officer Santos began questioning again, "Did you kids see anyone else out there? Any boats out nearby?"

"No!" Both Jasper and I exclaimed.

I knew what they were implying, a possible kidnapping. Mom and Dad had viable skills. Maybe someone from the organization was shady. Maybe pirates! I heard news stories of modern-day pirates stealing people away for ransom. Sure, Mom and Dad made a decent living, but we lived modestly in middle-class suburbia.

Our college funds were a go, but Mom and Dad also donated a lot to charity organizations, mostly healthcare and education. Yeah, I knew it made our family sound like generous philanthropists, but they wanted to instill in us, "be the change we want to see in the world."

We had to admit; our lives were never dull. Our parents' going missing wasn't our idea of living life with purpose. Yes, finding them was our current mission. Losing our parents was a predicament of detriment to our young minds, a trauma unfolding. The what-ifs played in our heads. It was a recipe for breaking down every lesson of strength our parents instilled in us.

Chapter 4

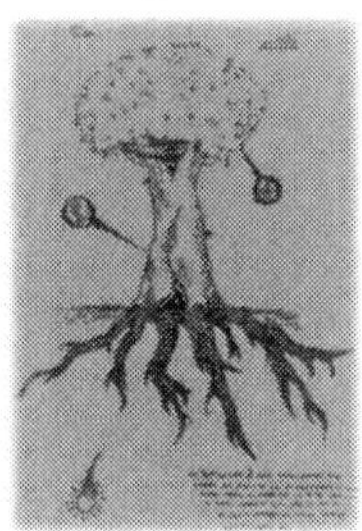

The officers asked a few more general questions and checked recent contacts on our parents' phones. A quick search through their belongings didn't reveal anything out of the ordinary. There wasn't anything suspicious that Jasper or I could see. Santos and Oliveira handed us their business cards and told us to contact them immediately if we thought of anything else. They and Mr. Lattimier made their way out.

Dad always carried a book on rocks & gemstones with him on vacations. It was a small book—old worn around the edges. A keepsake handed down from his grandfather. Since our family name was Genstone, Dad thought it endearing to share this book with each of us when we were little. We would be explorers on our destinations as we searched for and identified different rocks, geodes, and fossils. He was going to go through it with Rhodin on this trip.

He and Mom both kept journals. Mom's entailed places we had been and missions we had accomplished. There were pictures of each of us doing a task with accompanying notes. She always wrote something positive about our accomplishments, no matter how small the task.

Dad's journal kept tabs on us individually. He wrote the meaning of our names along with our growth and milestones. He also made light of our mishaps. He listed all the little boo-boos, scrapes, and bumps that came with uncoordinated toddlers. Small fights over who got more of any particular favorite 'anything' were evident in pictures where one of us pouted while the other enjoyed the spoils.

We were quite often a tag team of mischief. One picture was of me and Jasper outfitted in cookware armor. We wore pots on our heads like helmets with lids as our shields. The wooden spoons we held high in the air were our swords. Dad captioned it, "Jasper and Krystle, Saviors of Genstone Kingdom!"

Rhodin and I sat on the bed together and looked through Dad's journal as we giggled at ourselves caught in our precarious predicaments. It was just the right distraction we needed at the moment. Victor sat across from Jasper and played checkers. "King Me," said Jasper.

"Man, you are whipping my ego!" Victor said with a laugh. "You got to give this old man a chance here. I haven't played this since I was your age."

"You don't play this with your kids?" Jasper asked.

"No, man! You know how the kids are these days, playing video games and constantly on their phones. Their mother indulges them too much when I'm working," Victor sounded somewhat deflated.

"Is it usually your job to watch over the kids here?" I asked.

"My regular job is guest relations. I schedule and organize tours and events and coordinate with the meal planning staff. I order things that are needed here to keep the ship running tightly. I am in and out of the office all day," said Victor.

"Then who is doing your job while you're here watching us?" I asked.

"Well, Darius is my backup when I'm otherwise unavailable. Mr. Lattimier assigned me to you as your chaperone because he knew I was good with kids. I'm chill, you know. I'm good at de-escalating situations. You kids are an anomaly compared to most I see these days. You should take that as a compliment." Victor winked at me with a smile.

"Thanks. You're pretty okay yourself," Jasper said with a smirk.

I checked my phone messages. It was 4:45 p.m. Thirteen hours had passed, and still no good news. I bit at my thumbnail. My heel bounced of its own volition and shook the bed.

"What are you doing?" Rhodin asked.

"Rhodin, it's time for a bath," I stated.

"I'm not ready for a bath! It's too early, and I'm hungry," he whined.

"Hey, little man." Victor smiled. "Do you like chocolate crème pie? I'll go down and bring you all some dinner and dessert if you go hop in the tub and scrub those barnacles from behind your ears!"

That did the trick as Rhodin jumped off the bed and made his way to the bathroom. I heard the water turn on.

"Rhodin cold first, then add hot a little at a time till it's good," I shouted. "And, don't overfill the tub!"

"Yeah, yeah, Krystle, I know!" Rhodin responded in a clipped tone.

"You kids take care of your business, and I'll be back in an hour. I have a few things I need to take care of before I come back with your dinner," said Victor.

"Okay, Thanks, Victor," I responded.

When he left the room, I let out a deep breath. Jasper came to sit on the next bed. "The whole day is gone. Something is wrong. No news about Mom and Dad. Nothing! I feel like I'm about to lose it." Jasper declared.

"Jasper, there's something I've been trying to tell you all day. But I never got a chance till now."

"What is it, Krystle? Do you think Mom and Dad were kidnapped?"

"No, Jasper. It's about the cave!" I wrung my hands nervously.

"Yeah, it's strange nothing's turned up, considering that's where we heard Dad last," said Jasper.

"Not only that, Jasper. I saw something really strange right before Mr. Lattimier showed up."

Jasper looked perplexed. He folded his arms across his chest. He pushed out his biceps like he meant business.

"I saw a strange light coming from inside. I thought my mind was playing tricks on me, but then I noticed how Mr. Lattimier looked towards the cave, too. He had this look like he knew something." I sounded like a mystery sleuth. "The little girl, Cynnica, wanted to take Rhodin there, and Mr. L steered away from the topic or made excuses about it. He mentioned his people were looking there, but are they really?"

How could we know for sure if we're stuck cooped up in this hotel room all day with Victor pinned to us? I was ready to bounce off the walls! Jasper could see it too.

"As soon as Uncle Garreth and Aunt Cassie get here, we're going out there to find out what's really going on," Jasper declared. "I can't take it just sitting here anymore. We need to sneak out and do some recon."

"We can't, Jasper. It'll be dark in a few hours. The staff is buzzing around, and police are patrolling and searching. We'll just get busted and end up right back up here. I say we bide our time and come up with a game plan for when Uncle Garreth gets here."

I watched Jasper as he nodded his head in agreement. "He'll put Lattimier and anyone else in their place. They're not going to bow to a couple of teenagers and a six-year-old," Jasper huffed his frustration.

Rhodin came out of the bathroom with a towel draped over his shoulders and wrapped around his small frame. "Krystle, I need my pj's. And, where is my chocolate crème pie?"

I pulled a pair of pajamas out and handed them to Rhodin. "Victor said he'd be back with our food in a little bit."

"AND....my chocolate pie!" Rhodin wasn't going to let up since he held up his end of the bargain.

Only a few minutes later, Victor delivered our dinner and bid us goodnight. He told us he needed to tie up some loose ends and get some rest. He told us he'd check in the next morning and bring breakfast.

I ate, then took a shower, and got ready for bed. Jasper took his turn in the bathroom then came out in fresh clothes. I climbed into bed with Rhodin and grabbed the t.v. remote. I searched through the on-screen guide till I found a cartoon channel and turned the volume down. Rhodin needed it for background noise to fall asleep.

I watched Jasper walk over to the French doors leading out to the balcony. He stood there and looked out for a while. I picked up my phone and started responding to texts from Aunt Cassie, Uncle Garreth, and Taylin. Cassie and Garreth were on the same flight. They would be here sometime around 10 a.m. tomorrow.

I texted an update to Taylin and let her know I'd call her tomorrow. Rhodin was on the verge of passing out. After the day we had, we needed that one little blessing. I set the phone down and quietly slipped out of bed. I went over and stood by Jasper, "Rhodin is out. I think I need some fresh air."

Jasper slowly opened the door, and we both stepped out onto the balcony. We looked out over the resort. We searched with prayerful pleading eyes. I looked over to Jasper, my strong big brother, my protector. The first show of tears streamed down his face, and I lost it. He turned to me, and we embraced. I sobbed uncontrollably into his shoulder while he held me tightly. I heard and felt him suck in a breath, and then he shuddered. His own body racked in silent sobs.

He held it together all day, but at some point, everyone has to let go. Let go of the pretense. He was the man of the family in our father's absence. He refused to let our little brother see him break down. Rhodin looked up to him, tried to emanate him. They often raced each other in the yard, and Jasper helped Rhodin with his gymnastics practice. They had their goofy private jokes often at my expense, but I had no problem with it as it went both ways.

My thoughts stopped there when Jasper asked, "What are we going to do, Krystle? If Mom and Dad are..."

"Stop," I told him, "We can't think that way. I can still feel they are alive and most likely just as worried about us. We are going to get out there tomorrow and find them."

"You said it yourself," Jasper recounted, "You can feel the lies being fed to us, the false sense of security? I don't think they are putting the effort in that he claims. I know Lattimier is hiding something."

I nodded my head. We were definitely on the same page. I pulled away and used my shirt to dry away my tears. "I think we need to try to get some rest, Jasper. It's been a terrible and long day. Mom and Dad are counting on us, and we need to be ready."

We came back inside, and I kissed Rhodin gently on his forehead before climbing in under the plush cream comforter. Jasper settled in the next bed and started to look at his phone. I turned to lay flat on my back and stared at the ceiling for the longest time. My mind wouldn't let me rest.

I tried my best to move as little as possible, so I would not disturb Rhodin. He could be a light sleeper on occasion, and if he woke, I'd never get any rest. It seemed like over another hour had passed when finally, my eyes started to feel heavy. I whispered a silent prayer in my mind for our parents' safe return and eventually succumbed to sleep.

"Krystle...Krystle...We're here," Mom's voice echoed in my ears, "The Light..." her voice echoed over and over. I felt like I was spinning or more like everything was spinning around me. It was like a bad case of vertigo. I approached a small object on the ground. I reached to pick it up, but it blurred. My hand passed through, unable to take grasp.

Oddly though, I felt water wash across my feet. I could only make out a red color as the object tumbled across rocky terrain. It looked out of place. The object called to me. I chased after it as it tumbled toward a precipice in the wind. It felt like a lure, and I was to take the bait. It tried to pull me over the edge, to my certain death. I continued my reach, and I felt myself begin to fall. Panic shot through me, and I screamed. My body lost all control.

My eyes shot open, and I panted heavily. I grasped the blanket around me. I was awake in bed and covered in sweat. I looked around the darkened room. It had to be some time in the morning. I turned and grabbed the phone off the nightstand. 4:45 a.m. The same as I last looked to note the time the evening before. Was that when they went missing? If so, it's been 24 hours.

I looked to Rhodin and then Jasper. They were asleep. I used the bathroom and wiped my face, neck, and chest with a cool washcloth. I grabbed a bottle of water and took a few sips. I heard the sound of the waves outside. The dream-turned nightmare played through my thoughts. I had a strong feeling that I needed to go to the beach to look for something. I was unable to fall back to sleep. I went to the balcony door and looked out. Resort staff walked the grounds. They were too close for me to sneak out beyond the grassy perimeter. Lattimier intended to keep tabs on us; of this, I was sure. His claim to keep us safe felt more like being restrained against our will.

I paced and chewed on my thumbnail. Different scenarios played over and over in my head. It would be five hours till Aunt Cassie and Uncle Garreth got here. I was sure there would be no guided cave or hiking tours with the search still in effect. Uncle Garreth was probably calling on his resources.

Uncle Garreth had developed more than construction blueprints over the years in his and Dad's business. He made friends with many high-profile clients, clients with connections at Garreth's disposal. All he had to do was make a few phone calls, and people were at the ready.

Rhodin groaned and turned. He took a stuttered breath and resettled. To be able to sleep like a baby, I felt kind of envious. I laid on the sofa in the sitting room, closed my eyes, and just listened to all the combined breathing. Finally, my brain hushed, and I slipped back into unconsciousness.

A knock sounded at the door. My eyelids peeled open. Jasper yawned as he dragged his feet across the room. He opened the door and held a finger to his lips so the visitor would keep quiet. Victor entered with breakfast. He smiled and winked as he continued to the dining table to place out our meal. “Be back later,” he whispered to Jasper, who nodded in return.

“Was that Mr. Victor? I got to pee! I smell breakfast!” Rhodin got up and made a beeline for the bathroom, and closed the door. I took a moment and stretched, then yawned loudly.

Jasper cracked the drapes slightly open and looked outside. “I see guests out walking the beach,” he stated. I came to the door to see. Couples strolled along beneath the beautiful blue morning sky. Seagulls flew around, and a pelican stretched its wings then took flight from a wood post toward the water.

“Another day in paradise!! That is for everyone here besides us,” Jasper stated sourly.

Rhodin exited the bathroom with a barrage of questions. “Have they found Mom and Dad? Can we go to the beach today? When is Aunt Cassie and Uncle Garreth getting here?”

“Mom and Dad are still out there somewhere. Aunt Cassie and Uncle Garreth should be here soon. Yes, we will go to the beach today. Aunt Cassie will take us, I’m sure.” I answered his questions as I made up a plate of breakfast for him.

Rhodin sat down. “I’m really worried about Dad and Mom. I want to go to the cave. I had a dream about it last night.”

Jasper and I were both taken aback. “I had a dream too,” we said at the same time. We looked at each other.

“I heard, Mom,” I said. “She was calling me. She said something about a light. I think she was telling me what I saw at the cave wasn’t my imagination.

“I was flying over a massive forest. I felt like I could see through a bird’s eyes, and it was tracking them. I could hear them talking, but I couldn’t make out what they were saying.” Jasper rubbed his tired eyes.

I pondered the coincidence and meaning of our dreams as we ate. A knock came from the door. I got up and looked through the peephole. “Aunt Cassie!” I exclaimed excitedly. I opened the door and threw my arms around her.

“I’m here. I’m here, sweetheart!” We embraced, and my eyes watered as I struggled to keep myself in check.

“Aunt Cassie!” Rhodin shouted. He sprung up from his chair and ran. I opened a wide breadth for him, and he wrapped his arms around her waist.

“Hey, Rhodi!” Cassie exclaimed endearingly. “We are going to have some fun today, you, me, and Krystle!” We helped Cassie inside with her bags. “This is a very nice room,” she observed. I knew she was trying to keep things neutral for Rhodin’s sake.

“Hi, Jasper.” She pulled him in for a hug. “Things are going to get done today,” she spoke with a low voice in his ear.

“Is Uncle Garreth here?” Jasper asked.

Aunt Cassie grimaced and rubbed her forehead. “Yes, he’s downstairs giving the owner of this fine establishment a good stern chastising. He told me to tell you to get your essentials together. He said we should all come to meet him down in the lobby when ready.

"Rhodin, get your swim gear on, and we'll get some sunscreen on you," Aunt Cassie ordered.

"Finally!" Rhodin exclaimed. "Now we can go find Mom and Dad. I don't think the people here know where to look, but I do!" He pulled his swim trunks out of his bag and went to change. Aunt Cassie had a questioning look at his remark but just went with it. She figured Rhodin was acting his usual imaginative self.

"Aunt Cassie, are you tired from your trip? We've got some breakfast leftover if you're hungry." I pointed to the dining table.

"I am a little bit tired, but I'll be fine. I've been pumping in the caffeine since I woke up from our layover in Rio." She took a pancake and rolled a few sausage links in it.

"Your Uncle Garreth and I snoozed off and on during our flight. He's been on his laptop making connections with anyone who can help while on the way here." She bit into her pancake-sausage roll, and her eyes went back in her head, "Oh, man, that's good! I haven't eaten anything in over eight hours. My stomach was a little off on the airplane."

I went to change into some beachwear and covered up with a bright tye-die t-shirt, cargo shorts, and sandals. Cassie applied sunscreen on Rhodin. Jasper waited patiently by the door with his backpack as we gathered some essentials. He was all geared up and ready. For the first time since early yesterday morning, we were all out the door.

I could hear Uncle Garreth's deep booming voice through the whole downstairs lobby as he faced off with Lattimier and Officer Santos. Other resort guests passed through with concerned looks. They paused momentarily and then hurried along as things seemed to escalate.

Uncle Garreth was a big guy with a brooding nature, and he was tough as nails when a situation called for it, as it did now. People who didn't know him well didn't see the total goofball he could be like he was when around us.

"Well, obviously, your efforts haven't been good enough! I've already got people in search vessels around the island. And, yes, before you ask, they are doing everything by the book! Did you even think to have scuba divers searching these areas?" His finger pointed out to multiple areas on a map.

"We've been using every resource at our disposal, Mr. Genstone. We've been searching non-stop," Lattimier held up his hands in a placating manner. "Please, I implore you to step into my office. We are happy to work together with your resources."

"It's been over 24 hours! My brother and sister-in-law are knowledgeable people. They have been to some of the worst places on this planet. They know how to survive anywhere. My associates have been out on search and rescue missions in torrential conditions. They have found people in no less than 10 hours tops! And, you stand here telling me not one person here has found anything? Not a clue?"

"Uncle Garreth!" Rhodin shouted. He dropped his beach towel and ran towards him.

Uncle Garreth paused amid his tirade and turned, "Hey, What's up, my big man!" He held out his arms to catch Rhodin and lifted him. Mr. Lattimier had a look of relief on his face. He took in a breath.

Garreth turned to us with Rhodin still in one arm. "Bring it in, kids!"

He hugged me with his free arm and kissed the top of my head, "Hey Krystle Burger, you doin' alright?"

I would've objected to his annoying pet name for me, but I let it go for now. I knew he was a man on a mission but always made a moment to show his family affection. "I'm doing alright, Uncle Garreth."

"I know, kiddo," he replied. He let me go and set Rhodin down. He came over to Jasper and gave him a manly embrace with a few back pats. "You ready to go find your folks?"

"I've been ready, Uncle Garreth," he replied. Jasper scowled over at Lattimier.

Uncle Garreth turned Lattimier's way with a look that said, *Just you try and say anything objectionable to my nephew or me.* Mr. Lattimier turned to Officer Santos to avoid our Uncle's wrath. "Please let us escort you to our vehicles. We have two quad runners made available for your use."

Uncle Garreth spoke to Jasper, "You said something about a cave down by the beach. We'll start down there first."

"We have searched the cave twice already," Lattimier claimed.

"It's best to leave no stone unturned. My family said that's where they heard my brother. I'm going to go see for myself," Uncle Garreth stated. He didn't trust Lattimier's word any more than Jasper or I.

"I mean to assist. As a matter of safety, we cannot allow anyone into the cave without a trained staff escort," Lattimier stated.

"Do you have a waiver I can sign?" Uncle Garreth asked. "Cause, if it's a matter of you worrying about me suing your ass for any injury incurred upon my person, I'll sign the damn thing. But we are going, with or without you or your assistance," he stated vehemently. I noticed Office Santos with a wide-eyed look, his lips positioned in what looked like a long, low whistle.

Victor showed up at that moment, "Here is a waiver, Mr. Genstone. Just sign here. One for Jasper as well. I'll escort you into the cave," he volunteered.

As Jasper and Garreth quickly read and signed the documents, Lattimier bit his lips. His face turned red with a look of contempt toward Victor. "Of course, that will be fine," he gritted out. "Just please take extra caution. You must make sure you exit before the tide starts coming in, before nightfall."

"Let's go, kids," Uncle Garreth commanded.

Chapter 5

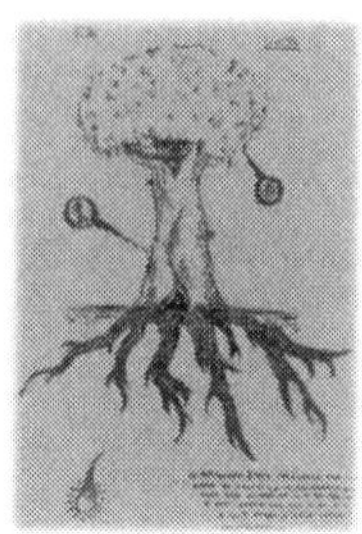

We loaded onto the quad runners. They could fit up to three people each. Uncle Garreth and Jasper got on the first and placed Rhodin between them. I sat behind Victor with Aunt Cassie behind me. Officer Santos approached Garreth. “You know we could use a man like you on our force. Lattimier has been a gracious prick, throwing off his false pleasantries.

“Believe me when I say we’ve been doing our part Mr. Genstone. Unbeknownst to him, Lattimier is a suspect in your brother and sister-in-law’s disappearance. We have our man on the inside.” Santos motioned his head Victor’s way. Victor smiled and nodded at Garreth. “This intel is between us only. We don’t want Lattimier becoming a flight risk.”

Garreth nodded back with a smirk. “Let’s roll. We’ll be in communication, Officer.” He revved up the engine. “Hang on tight, kids.”

We were down to the beach in record time. We parked by the pathway to the cave. It started getting pretty rocky the closer we got to the entrance.

Aunt Cassie took Rhodin's hand. We stopped at a small area, all smooth pebbles and sand. The ocean washed in, cascading over the small inlet, then made its retreat. As it continued its cyclic motions, I removed my sandals and relished in the soft foam spray that tickled over my feet.

We stayed outside as Uncle Garreth wanted to gauge for himself whether or not it would be safe for us to enter. Rhodin protested, but Uncle Garreth told him he had the important job of the lookout. "You've got my back right, big man?" He placated Rhodin's need to contribute as a highly integral part of the team. "I need you to help your sister and Aunt Cassie. Got it?"

"Yes, Sir!" Rhodin saluted like a proud little soldier. Uncle Garreth stood up straight with a stern look and saluted back.

"To your post, soldier!" He then looked up at me and winked. I hid a smile behind my hand.

"Yes, Sir!" Rhodin belted out then walked over to me and Aunt Cassie.

"Let's get into position." I took Rhodin's hand and played along. "We soldiers stick together; no man left behind!" We watched as Victor led the way with Uncle Garreth, and Jasper followed.

Jasper took one more look back at me. His eyes told me, *We've got this*. I knew it meant more than the men headed inside the cave. We were all in this together. He turned back and entered the cave.

They were about 25 feet inside. The glow of their torch lights faded into the darkness as they made their way further. I lost sight of them. Rhodin and Aunt Cassie slipped off their shoes. We set them up on one of the larger rocks so they wouldn't get washed away. Rhodin surveyed the area, taking his job seriously. "Aunt Cassie?"

"Yeah, Rhodi?" she asked.

"How long do you think they'll be in there?" Rhodin looked to her imploringly.

"I'm not sure," she replied. "As long as they can, I suppose. Your Uncle Garreth is good at finding clues. He can see things others miss. That's why he so good at his job."

Wow, I thought to myself. Aunt Cassie had complimented Uncle Garreth. This was new!

"Hey, Rhodin, do you want to help me search for clues out here?" I asked. "And while we're at it, we can find some cool seashells and fossils. Dad would love to see what we find when he gets back."

"Yeah, good thinking, Krystle," said Aunt Cassie.

"Okay," Rhodin agreed.

We searched the shallow waters. We picked up different shells and tossed the broken pieces. "So, who's keeping the shop while you're gone?" I asked.

"Oh, you know, Lynn and Carol," Cassie replied. "Thank goodness for the sprinkler system one of your Dad's guys installed. It's on a timer, so I know the flowers will get watered properly."

"Oh, that's good," I replied.

"Krystle, I have to say, I'm very impressed at how you and Jasper have been handling everything. I also must admit your Uncle Garreth has been top-notch in managing this situation. I can delegate duties around my little shop, but Garreth has taken on this extremely stressful situation like a real admirable bad-ass."

Again, WOW! I thought. It seems times of trouble really can bring people together in unexpected ways.

"I know we butt heads a lot, but it's often about you kids and what we think is best for you," Cassie explained. "He and I both know each other has your best interest at heart. We just have different ideas on the matter. I mean, both of us have, I mean I mostly, helped raise you since you were babies."

"Your mom was so determined to get her medical degree, and your dad was getting the construction business off the ground. My aspirations weren't so high, I guess. But I am so proud of my sister and brother-in-law." She started tearing up. "And, I'm very proud of you kids! I'm so blessed to have you guys in my life." She sniffed and wiped her eyes with the back of her hand.

"I love you, Aunt Cassie," I sniffed as well.

"I love you too, Krystle!" We leaned on one another and continued to watch Rhodin's exploration.

We were wading in the surf coming up mid-calf. Rhodin was starting to go a bit deeper. "Rhodin, back it in toward us," Aunt Cassie called.

"Look what I found," Rhodin exclaimed excitedly. He started back our way with some coral and a small sand dollar.

"Those are pretty cool!" Aunt Cassie exclaimed.

As Aunt Cassie explained to Rhodin his finds, I heard a rock tumbling from somewhere behind. Aunt Cassie had Rhodin handled and was bringing him back to shallower waters. I turned to look for the source of the sound. The tumbling continued to click-clack over pebbles as the water receded.

A stone that most definitely stood out amongst the white broken shells and pale gray pebbles came to a stop before my feet. It was like nothing I'd ever seen before, with bright fiery red blended with molten orange flecks. It was about the size of a large toy marble with an imperfect rounded shape.

I reached down and picked it up as the foaming wash came rushing in back over my feet. Like a sudden electric surge, the memory of my dream slammed into me like a massive tidal force. I wobbled and fell back on my butt. "Oww!" I yelled.

Cassie ran up behind me with Rhodin in tow, "Krystle, are you okay? That looked like a hard fall!"

"Yeah, I'm okay. A little dehydrated, I guess," I said. I clutched the rock in one hand. Cassie took my other hand and helped me up.

"Let's get some water. We've been out here for at least an hour now." Cassie stated.

"Sounds good," I agreed as I rubbed my bum. "I think that's gonna leave a mark." I opened my hand to look at the stone. I had this strong feeling I was supposed to hold on to it for dear life.

"Did you find something?" Aunt Cassie asked. I held my palm out to her for inspection. "That's odd," she exclaimed. "But very pretty. It looks like fire. It doesn't look like it's indigenous to this area, though. How strange!" She wrinkled her brow. "That's a definite keeper. One to look up in your dad's book, I'd say."

"Certainly is," I agreed.

"Can I see?" Rhodin asked.

I held it out to him. "Please don't drop it!" I was suddenly scared to lose it as if my life depended on it.

"Wow, that's really cool, Krystle! Dad would really like that one," Rhodin declared.

"Mhmm!" I nodded in agreement. "Perhaps we'll make a necklace out of it of something."

"Yeah, that would be cool!" Rhodin agreed. He turned it around in his little digits a few more times, and I held out my hand expectant for its return. He handed it back a bit reluctantly, and I smiled at him.

"Thanks, Rhodin!" I looked at it again for a long moment, mesmerized. I put it in one of my cargo pockets that I both zipped and closed the Velcro flap over for safekeeping.

It was another thirty minutes before we heard Uncle Garreth, Victor and Jasper return. They were having a discussion, and Cassie, Rhodin, and I looked to the cave. We heard their voices before we saw them emerge.

"I'm contacting one of my best divers. Spergie can get in and out of tight spaces. He's helped out on our off-shore construction projects and search missions with Worlds of Care Connect. He's just a couple of miles out on one of our search charters." Uncle Garreth held a breathing apparatus in one hand and an underwater diving torch in the other.

Jasper looked forlorn. He held and an article of clothing in one hand.

"Oh no...Is that?" I asked but already knew the answer. "That's Mom's shawl!" I exclaimed. It was her favorite. She bought it on one of our family excursions and now wore it every time she felt a bit chilled. It was from a street vendor in Nepal years ago. It was a beautiful black woven pashmina with an embroidered red and pink floral pattern.

Jasper handed it to me with a sullen look. "We found it in a small pool of water. Uncle Garreth went in and retrieved it. He saw what looked like an opening that may lead to a deeper cavern. He and Spergie are going to see how far it goes."

"You think they could be down there?" Cassie asked with a fearful look in her hazel green eyes. "Oh, dear Lord!" She wrung her hands, then brought them up to rub her arms and shivered.

"We only have about five more hours before the tide comes in. We need to get in and out as fast and efficiently as possible. Damn it!" Garreth cursed. "If I didn't...that Lattimier ass...freaking waste of precious time!"

We heard a motor and saw a boat approaching. It stopped and made anchor just a little way out. "Garreth!" A man with a slim build waved and called out. Jasper stayed with the gear while Garreth and Victor quickly went out into the water to meet up with the boat.

The man had loaded a life raft with scuba gear and was getting in. He started a small motor and came their way. Garreth and Victor grabbed a tow rope and pulled the raft in as the man cut the engine. They pulled the lifeboat the rest of the way into the inlet.

The man lifted the gear and passed it over to Garreth and Victor. They immediately started suiting up. “This is Spergie.” Garreth made quick introductions. “He is an old friend and is the best diver I’ve ever known. He was my instructor when I first learned.” The man was quiet, but he nodded to us as he lifted his oxygen tank onto his back.

“Jasper, I need you and Victor top side, keeping watch on time. We have communication capabilities with these masks. We can talk to and hear you, so you keep us posted.” He turned to Aunt Cassie, “Cassie, if anything happens while we’re down there...”

“I know what to do, Garreth. Just be careful,” she pleaded. I was standing with Rhodin. I squeezed his little hand, and he looked up at me. Uncle Garreth looked to me with confident reassurance. Aunt Cassie took my other hand. Our hands clasped tightly in prayerful aspiration.

The men all turned back to the cave. Jasper and Victor carried large cords of rope on their shoulders. All torches lit as they again made the descent into the darkness.

“See!” Rhodin proclaimed, “I know Mom and Dad are in there somewhere! I feel in my chest.” He put his hand over his heart. He was even braver than I at that moment. I felt like I should aspire to be like my little brother when I grow up. Other than Rhodin's initial panic the morning before, he'd been the essence of calm in the storm. He was at least the calmest one could be, by six-year-old standards.

"Oh ship," Aunt Cassie cursed in her unique way of keeping expletives from Rhodin's young ears, "I hope they have water and food with them if they're going to be in there for hours."

"Don't worry," I told her, "I saw Jasper load his bag with some waters and protein bars. That is something Mom and Dad always reminded us to do before we'd go anywhere." I went to fetch some water and snacks for us. We spread out a beach towel a bit further up the pathway on a softer sandy area. We sat down to eat and drink.

"I hate sitting and waiting," Aunt Cassie stated. "I had to wait for our flights, during flights, on layovers, and here I am, sitting and waiting again."

"I know what you mean," I agreed.

"Oh, honey, I'm sorry. I feel like a jerk. It's insensitive of me to complain. You've been going through all this so much longer. I'm coming off like a total spazz right now!"

"Don't apologize, Aunt Cassie. We're all worried. We all say things in times of stress that come out wrong, at least by our perception," I stated.

"You are becoming a wise young woman, Krystle. You're beautiful and intelligent," she commented.

"There's a difference, you know?" Cassie posed.

"What do you mean?" I asked. I was used to Aunt Cassie telling us how beautiful or handsome and intelligent we were. Jasper and I have tried many times to dispute her need to tell us so often. Aunts Cassie was insistent on saying positive things to bolster our self-esteem.

Aunt Cassie continued, "Intelligence comes with all the knowledge our brains collect and retain. Wisdom, however, is how we grow with that knowledge. It is part of our moral compass and how we learn from our mistakes. It grows our compassion toward others. It drives us to mentor the generations to come."

I considered her words, and I watched as Rhodin started building little creations in the sand a few feet away. He was a little sea sponge, soaking up new experiences every day. This was his second journey with the family as a Worlds of Care Connect aide.

I didn't go on my first volunteer mission trip till I turned six years old. It was the same with Jasper before me. I guess that was the age our parents decided we were old enough to handle these expeditions. Before age six, Aunt Cassie and Uncle Garreth took us on mini-vacations to places like a theme or National Parks while Mom and Dad made shorter volunteer trips.

"How is Taylin doing?" Cassie asked. "Have you been able to talk to her? Does she know what's going on?"

I started to think about Taylin. Besides a few texts, I really hadn't gotten back to her yet, which wasn't like me. Since this whole emergent saga began, I wasn't thinking in my usual manner. I pulled my phone out of my other cargo leg pocket. There was no service down here on the beach.

“She’s in California visiting family. I wish she were here too. But, yeah, I talked to her. She knows Mom and Dad are missing, but I haven’t been able to give her any updates with all that’s been happening.” Aunt Cassie nodded in understanding.

I pulled up my vacation album on my phone. I scrolled through pictures from our mission time in Sao Paulo to our arrival here at the resort. One was a family selfie inside the small biplane to the resort. I made out a bit of the family behind us.

The face of a little girl who looked about Rhodin’s age caught my attention. She was staring at my phone with a look of malintent. Her eyes and hair were dark. She had skin olive with pink lips that smiled maliciously. The sight made me quiver from deep within my bones. I had to look away. It was as if she were trying to take possession of my senses.

“Can I see your pictures?” asked Cassie. She didn’t seem to notice the little girl in the picture. Cassie smiled. “That’s a great selfie!” She scrolled her finger across the screen. She made endearing comments at our usual carefree antics. We were all smiles, heads leaning into one another, typical hand gestures of peace signs and rabbit ears.

There were some photos of us on the beach during the first few days from our arrival. I captured a beautiful moment of Mom and Dad walking down the beach hand in hand. The sun was setting. Mom had her shawl wrapped over her shoulders. She looked so beautiful, with her long brunette locks blowing in the breeze.

Her hazel green eyes looked adoringly into Dad's ocean blues. Dad's blonde hair was tousled like Mom had been running her fingers through it playfully. They looked so in love. It made my heartache. No wonder where one went; the other would follow. She went somewhere, or someone took her. Why did it feel like both? It was why Dad called for her. It was why he screamed her name.

Chapter 6

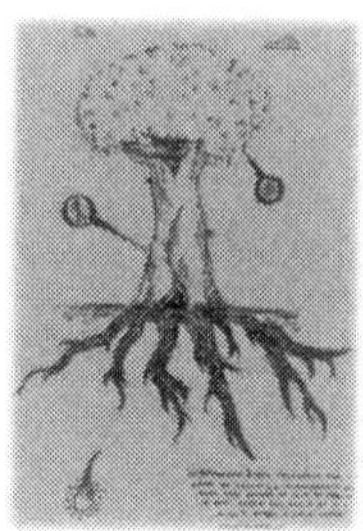

The sun had drifted past high noon as a shadow started to cast from the cave. I was biting my thumbnail and bouncing my leg in that anxious motion again. I wanted to go into that cave. I needed to search and see for myself. But I also felt more and more drawn to it. The later in the afternoon it got, the stronger the feeling became.

Rhodin, Aunt Cassie, and I played in the water, trying to distract ourselves from the guys' anticipated return. We had to keep Rhodin from getting overly bored. I wondered why nobody else came to check on us this whole time. Surely, one of the staff members or the deceptive Mr. Lattimier would have popped in at any moment. But no, we were completely undisturbed. There were the occasional passing boats supposedly part of the search and rescue mission still in progress.

It was approaching 4:45 in the late afternoon when the guys finally emerged. Rhodin had fallen asleep on the towel, and we had placed another one over him. Aunt Cassie and I were in our bathing suits soaking up the warm afternoon sun. We laid back and rested our eyes in quiet contemplation. The guys approached, and I lightly shook Cassie.

We approached the cave entrance to meet them. Uncle Garreth and Spergie were unloading their scuba gear. Jasper and Victor aided them. They all looked utterly exhausted. I looked to Jasper. “Nothing,” he answered solemnly.

“Not absolutely,” Uncle Garreth offered. “There are more ways in and out of the cave, just nothing possible without the right gear and equipment.”

“Either Lattimier didn’t know, or he was lying,” Victor added.

“No other signs of my brother or Gemma,” said Uncle Garreth. “But we’re not giving up. While we have a few more hours of daylight, Victor, Spergie, and I are going into the forest. I’ve got more people diving around the island to look for any other possible entrances. Jasper, I need you to go back to the room. You are tired and need to rest. I’ll bring you back out in the morning.”

Jasper looked like he wanted to protest, but his head dropped as he conceded. He had dark circles under his eyes. We all agreed to head back to the main house and get something to eat. Uncle Garreth mentioned resupplying and heading back out in thirty minutes.

As we entered the lobby, there was blessedly no sign of Lattimier. Uncle Garreth said he would punch him if he saw him, but we didn’t have time to deal with him being taken into custody by the police.

This time we sat together in the dining room surrounded by the other guests. We ate, and Uncle Garreth explained what he saw. There were a few different passageways that a small person could pass through without gear. There were breathing pockets situated in enough places that someone could technically survive if they could tread long enough.

He finished eating quickly and motioned Victor and Spergie to move onward. Uncle Garreth hugged Rhodin and kissed me on the head. As he passed Aunt Cassie, he gave her a gentle squeeze on her shoulder. She placed her hand on his and looked at him with sincere appreciation. Garreth grasped both Jasper's shoulders and spoke into his ear. I didn't hear what he said, but Jasper nodded. The three men exited the dining area and left us to finish our meals.

I could feel the other guests staring, and it started to get to me. "Aunt Cassie, can we please go back to the room now?" I pleaded.

"Yes, I'm exhausted," she exhaled and started to rise.

"Can we please get dessert?" Rhodin asked.

"We'll get some to take back to the room." I told him. We walked together to the dessert cart and made a few selections.

"Hello," a young girl's voice grabbed our attention. "I'm Cynnica. We were on the plane with you." She sounded sweet and innocent; Rhodin and I turned towards her voice. Her dark hair curled up around the ends from being wet and drying into little curly ringlets.

Unlike what I saw in the picture from the plane, her eyes were actually a deep blue. "I saw you coming back from the cave. Did you get to go inside?"

"No," Rhodin said. "My uncle was in there looking for my mom and dad." I put my hand on Rhodin's shoulder. "We waited outside because I had the job of lookout." He puffed out his little chest proudly.

"I'm sorry your parents are missing," Cynnica replied. "But you won't find them in there." Her voice had this eerie edge to it, like one wouldn't hear from a child who looked no older than seven, maybe eight years old.

I bent down to look her in the eyes, "Do you know something?" A feeling of agitation mixed with urgency coursed through my veins. I wanted to grab and shake her for answers.

She looked back at me with sealed lips. A small smile crept up. It looked sinister. She was creeping me out. Why would a child make me feel this way? She reminded me of a childhood psychopath. Was this the vibe serial killers put off when they were children? I took Rhodin by his shoulder and turned him away.

"There's a full moon tonight," Cynnica called out behind us. "Normally, the tide would be high, but the way will be open tonight."

I turned my head to look at her again, but she just turned away and walked back to who I guess were her parents. She didn't look like either of them. They sat at their table and ate like they were on autopilot. Cynnica sat down with her back to us.

Jasper and Aunt Cassie stood just outside the dining room waiting on us. "I told you she was creepy," Rhodin stated.

"Who is creepy?" Aunt Cassie asked.

“Cynnica, the little dark-haired girl sitting in there.” Rhodin pointed, but I quickly pulled his arm down. “She says weird stuff and gives me creepy blowy kisses.” He tugged his arm from my hand.

“Let’s just go back to the room, please.” I hurried us along.

“She’s probably one of Lattimier’s minions.” Jasper half huffed; half grunted. I couldn’t help thinking that perhaps Jasper wasn’t so far off with that statement.

When we got back in the room, Aunt Cassie asked, “Does anybody need the bathroom before I use the shower?”

“I do,” said Rhodin. He went in and closed the door.

“I’m going to try and get hold of Taylin. I’ll be out on the balcony,” I stated.

“Okay, send her my love,” said Aunt Cassie.

“Will do,” I replied.

I sat in onc of the patio chairs and watched the sun descend beyond the horizon.

I dialed Taylin, and she answered, “Are you okay? Have you found them?” The confidence in her voice was gone. “I thought I’d hear from you sooner. But, when I kept trying to call you without an answer, I started to worry.”

“I’m okay, but they’re still missing Taylin! There is something off about everything here.”

"Krystle, I'm stealing my mom's credit card and hauling ass there," Taylin's voice raised, "I'm serious! Nobody messes with mi familia!

"Taylin, Uncle Garreth, and Aunt Cassie are here! Uncle Garreth has been laying down his own brand of justice. He scared the crap out of Mr. Lattimier. We haven't seen him since Uncle Garreth gave him a proper ass chewing."

"You think this dude is responsible?" Taylin asked. "Cause if he is, I'm abought to bring my cousins to go old school on his ass!"

"The police already suspect him. They may have him in custody right now. We haven't seen him since we left for the cave this morning. Either that or he's hiding from Uncle Garreth. I think my uncle put the fear of God in him."

"Righteous!" Taylin stated. "What happened at the cave? Did you see anything in there?"

"Uncle Garreth, Jasper, and a couple of other guys went in to search. They were in there for hours. They found my mom's shawl but nothing else. There was a pool that led down into a small cavern and some small passages, but they couldn't get through."

"Sweet Baby Jesus!" Taylin exclaimed. "I don't want to say what I'm thinking because I know they have to still be kickin'." I knew she was thinking possible drowning, but I put that out of my mind. There was absolutely no way. I will not resolve to believe them dead.

I told Taylin about my dream, finding the stone, and the little girl Cynnica.

“Creepy,” she replied.

“Yeah, she said something about the moon being full and the way being open tonight.”

“It’s time to do of your own recon, girl,” Taylin insisted. “You and Jasper need to sneak out there tonight; go all Sherlock & Holmes! Screw Mr. Lattimier and his ‘Special Trained Staff’! They don’t care about your family. They’re just scared of a major lawsuit.”

I looked behind me inside. Aunt Cassie must have been in the shower. I saw Jasper sitting with Rhodin on the bed. “I need to put a few components to rest first.” Meaning nighty-night for Rhodin and Aunt Cassie.

I didn’t think Uncle Garreth was going to give up looking just because the sun’s going down. We just needed to stay under his radar. We’d be out and back in before things went south. We would investigate near the house and perhaps overhear someone talking.

Taylin and I talked for another twenty minutes. “Stick to the shadows and wear all black if you got it,” she said.

“I’m afraid the only black thing I have is my mother’s shawl.” It was hanging on the back of one of the patio chairs, drying out.

“That’ll work. Just put it over your head,” said Taylin. “And call me back ASAP. Even if it’s at the crack of chickens!”

“Okay, gotta go. Aunt Cassie is out of the bathroom and coming my way. Love you, Tay!”

“Love you too, chica!” Taylin said.

I hung up just as Aunt Cassie came out. “It’s going to be a few for hot water. My muscles needed that. So, is Taylin saying she’s coming now too?”

“Wouldn’t be Taylin if she didn’t,” I replied.

“We’ll be here as long as it takes, Krystle. The Genstone family doesn’t give up.”

“Aunt Cassie, isn’t there a timeframe after which search crews stop looking?” I asked.

“Krystle, your Uncle Garreth is willing to sell the company and pull all resources if necessary. He’d go to the ends of the Earth for this family.”

Uncle Garreth and Aunt Cassie never married nor had any children of their own. They claimed us as their kids. We came first, then their careers. Mom and Dad taught us to reach for the stars. They often mentioned how grateful they were for their brother and sister for all their help.

They let them know they couldn’t do this adventure called life without them. I felt the same about all my family. If I didn’t have Jasper and Rhodin, I definitely wouldn’t be as appreciative as I am. I’d certainly be lost if I were in this situation on my own.

Aunt Cassie yawned, “I need to lie down before I fall over. I think you, Rhodin, and I can squeeze in together so Garreth can crash with Jasper.” She went inside, climbed under the comforter then motioned for Rhodin to hop in next to her. He sprung from next to Jasper and steamrolled over Aunt Cassie to the mid-bed position.

Jasper was on his phone texting Uncle Garreth for updates. I had a feeling he wasn't keeping friends back home posted. He was more reserved when it came to matters of our family. He had people he hung out with but no close friends like Taylin and me.

Jasper once told me that some kids are jerks that enjoyed bullying and teasing people who were "do-gooders." He wasn't embarrassed about how we helped Mom and Dad with Worlds of Care Connect. He just told his friends we went on a lot of vacations, which made them envious. He was popular enough with the girls and dated on occasion but never found anything serious, unlike Mom and Dad, who were high school sweethearts.

Jasper sat his phone down and went to take a shower. He didn't say anything to me as he passed. These past two days have been too much to handle. His mind was probably reeling just as much as everyone else.

I pulled the rock from my cargo shorts pocket to examine it once more. I found Dad's gemstone book and flipped through the pages to see if I could identify my find. The closest thing it resembled was carnelian. The more I held it in my hand, the more I felt a growing tethering bond. The stone whispered to my soul like it had secrets to tell. I secured it back in my cargo pocket once more.

I looked to Rhodin and Aunt Cassie's slumbering forms. Jasper came out of the bathroom dressed in dark clothes. He tossed a dark brown top to me. "Twenty minutes," he said in a low voice. I took that as my initiative to hop in the shower and get ready. I put my same dark khaki cargos on along with Jasper's shirt. I put on socks, and my hiking boots, then slipped out the balcony door. I didn't see anyone out tonight. It was as quiet as the early morning when our parents went missing.

I took Mom's shawl off the patio chair. It was dry and smelled of the sea. I draped it over my damp blonde hair. I looked up to the full moon. It beamed in the late-night sky and cast a pale light over the resort grounds. I slipped inside and gently closed the door. I tip-toed over to Jasper by the door out to the hall and glimpsed back toward Rhodin and Aunt Cassie sound asleep. Silently, we made our retreat.

"Is this what Uncle Garreth was whispering to you?" I asked, "A recon mission?"

"Yeah," Jasper nodded. "First, we look around inside and then a sweep around the building to make sure we're clear of Lattimier. Then, we breach his office to find whatever it is he's hiding."

"How?" I asked. "We're not exactly super-spies with expert lock-picking experience."

Jasper held up a key, "A spare. Compliments of our friend Victor."

"Oh, that will work!" I exclaimed. I wasn't expecting that, but sure enough, Uncle Garreth knows how to get things done. We made our way to the ground floor. We did a sweep up and down the back hallway. Everything was closed and locked up for the night. The lobby was quiet. No one was tending the front desk, so we went straight to the front door. Jasper opened it slowly and looked about.

"Coast is clear," he stated, and we went out. We stayed close to the house and walked around it. We circled a couple of times, and just as we were about to head back in, we heard a jeep and a few quad runners in the distance. "Abort mission!" Jasper declared.

"What if it's Uncle Garreth?" I asked. "He knew we'd be out here."

"Uncle Garreth told me he'd flash his headlights three times if it were him. That could possibly be Lattimier. We need to stay out of sight just in case," Jasper commanded. Geeze, he sounded more and more like our Uncle and Dad when they meant business.

We quickly made our way back inside and swiftly back up the stairs. We were back in our room without any issues. I could see the lights from jeeps and quads pass by, but they didn't stop. They continued on another trail, and both lights and sound faded into the distance.

We both took a breath of relief. We were about to restart our mission once more when I noticed Rhodin wasn't in bed. I looked to the bathroom, but the door was open, and the light was off. I looked in the sitting room then I ran to the balcony door. "Rhodin?" I called his name in question. I opened the door, and Jasper came out behind me.

"I don't see him in the room anywhere, Jasper. Do you think he woke up and came looking for us?" My eyes started scanning the resort grounds. "There!" I declared with urgency. "He's on the beach headed towards the cave! Aunt Cassie!" I yelled.

"Wha..." She said sleepily.

"Rhodin is outside going to the cave," I yelled back as I ran out the door. Jasper was already out and running down the hall.

"Kids…WAIT!" I could hear Aunt Cassie call, but there was no time to wait. Rhodin was in imminent danger.

As we ran, I saw two small figures making a quick pace toward the cave's pathway. *Cynnica*, I thought. Anger and panic fueled my muscles as I kept pace with Jasper this time. Not again! We weren't losing Rhodin too!

"RHODIN! NO, STOP!" Jasper and I screamed out at the same time. Behind us, I could hear Uncle Garreth and Aunt Cassie calling our names. We were now on the beach catching up. I saw Cynnica taking Rhodin's hand, pulling him along faster.

"Hurry up, Rhodin!" I heard her yell. "I saw your parents! They are in the cave waiting for you! Faster before they leave again!"

"Mom! Dad! I'm coming!" Rhodin yelled. "Don't leave!" he cried.

"Rhodin, stop! Don't listen to her! She's lying!" I yelled.

"The way is open, Krystle!" Rhodin yelled back as he continued. "We have to hurry!" They were at the cave entrance.

"Where's the water? The tide?" Jasper asked in confusion. I looked up, and I saw it. The Light! The whole cave lit up from within. My mind paused, but my legs continued to carry me.

Cynnica started to pull Rhodin forward. "Rhodin, NO!" I screamed. Somchow, I pushed past Jasper. I could still hear Cassie and Garreth yelling. Their voices panicked.

"Kids, STOP...STOP," they cried.

Suddenly Rhodin pulled back, and I grabbed hold of him. In the same instant, I pushed Cynnica away. "NO!" She screeched. Her voice didn't sound like a child's. "What are you doing?" She yelled. She sounded like a demonic old hag. "They are in there, I'm telling you! I can take you to them! Just let me guide you!"

"What are you?" I yelled at her. I was seething. I saw Jasper stop right behind her. I looked back to the Light. It was pure white with wisps and waves. I felt its energy. It was calling to me. I held Rhodin's hand. Our Aunt and Uncle ran toward us on the pathway. Jasper grabbed Cynnica from behind.

"No! Let go of me!" Cynnica screeched at Jasper.

"Krystle..." I heard my mother's voice echoing.

"Mom?" I responded. I turned and walked closer.

"Krystle...we're here!" I heard her call to me again. I couldn't see her. I just saw the Light. The waves and wisps started to swirl like a cyclone. I felt warmth on my leg as the stone warmed up in my pocket. I looked down to see a molten glow through the dark khaki fabric. I had let go of Rhodin's hand and put it on my pocket. I looked back up to the swirling white cyclone. I closed the small distance and held my left hand up to the bright swirling mass. My eyes were unscathed. I could see into another world, and it was beautiful!

My palm pressed to the Light, and it felt pliable to my touch. I felt warmth and the soft tingle of energy. The static-like feel climbed up my arm as the pull became stronger. Small hands grabbed my other lowered arm and tugged at me. Bright beams burst out around me.

"KRYSTLE!" A collective of voices screamed.

I was pulled briskly by a powerful unseen force. Fear engulfed me as I felt myself drawn away from my family. I was falling, tumbling, spinning. It felt like my dream. My dream! It was a premonition of this moment. I was inside this void. Flashes obscured my vision. It was like watching an old movie reel starting up before the picture came into view.

I saw my life, my family, friends coming and going. Was I dying? People have described near-death experiences as such. My life was flashing before my eyes, and a bright, white light surrounded me in its ethereal embrace. I felt the wisps and waves brush against my skin like a delicate mothers' touch. Worry and panic faded. The feeling of falling slowed, and I felt peaceful.

I must be, must be. I don't know! I didn't care! I've never felt so relaxed, at ease, untroubled. My eyes were heavy. I started mouthing the words to "Twinkle, Twinkle Little Star." I remembered my mother singing it to me when I was little.

A lazy smile stretched my lips. Endorphins rushed and catered to a natural high. Blissfully, without a care in the world, I closed my eyes and relished this amazing experience. I didn't want it to end. Am I in heaven? I felt my mind start to shut down, but I didn't care.

Chapter 7

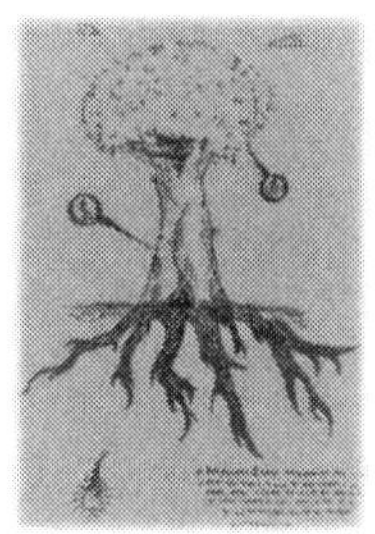

Water was washing around me. I opened my eyes just briefly. They burned with fatigue. I was laid out flat on my stomach. I felt the grains of wet sand beneath my cheek. My lids closed and opened again. I drifted in and out. Feet approached clad in rugged brown boots. I felt myself being lifted and carried by big strong arms.

"Dad?" I felt my mouth move, pushing the word out weakly. There was an earthy woodsy smell, pleasant and fresh. My head lulled. I felt my body being laid down and covered by something weighted and soft. Darkness took me away once more.

I was startled awake by a strange, loud howl. My eyes shot open. It was dark, too dark. It was then I realized I was under something. My hands yanked and flung a covering off my head. I looked up into a night sky filled with billions of stars. I gasped in bewilderment. I felt warmth and turned my head to see a fire burning just a few feet away. My hiking boots and socks were there drying. It struck me that the flames emitted colors in tones of purples, pinks, greens, yellow and blue. Strange?

I rose and clutched the blanket of soft...fur? The hairs were long with whites, browns, and black. What kind of animal hair was this? Oh crap, what kind of animal made that strange howl? I looked around and saw I was alone. But I didn't do all this! Someone was here with me. "Uncle Garreth," I said. My voice was brittle. I could barely speak.

"Here, drink," a deep voice said from behind me. I jumped, and my mouth opened to scream, but nothing came out. "Your voice will come back in a bit. Drink this."

A large hand held a canteen out in front of my face. I reached out hesitantly. The hand shook the canteen, "Go on, take it!" The deep male voice had a rough gravely edge. I took hold of the offered canteen, and both of my hands shook with uncertainty. I tilted the opening to my lips and drank. The feel and taste of cool, crisp, clean water washed over my dry tongue and soothed my throat. It was by far the best tasting water ever.

I drank some more and felt refreshed and awakened. "Thank you," I spoke. My voice already sounded better. I started to pass the canteen back. I looked up for the first time to see the man who came to my aid.

He was a huge, solid mass of muscle dressed in primitive clothing. His hair was long and dark. He had a dark beard and thick brows with intense azurite blue eyes. Although he looked menacing, I sensed kindness about him.

"Uhmm, where am I?"

"You are on Beryl Beach," the man replied.

I looked around again. "What's your name?" I asked as I appraised my surroundings.

"I'm Tovin Otek," he replied. "And you must be Krystle?"

"Yes, how did you know?"

"My shiyava and I came to find you," said Tovin.

I shot up, "You have? My family, my mom, dad, and brothers! I'm looking for them!"

"Calm yourself, young shiyava." He reached toward me with his large hand, and I moved back. "It's okay. I won't hurt you. My Aura and I are here to help you."

"Aura?" I said in question. "What's a shiyava?"

"Aura is my shiyava, and shiyava means child," Tovin explained.

"Oh," I exclaimed, "You're a father; that's good." I felt somewhat relieved. He looked around the same age as my father. "Where is your shiyava, Aura? How old is she?" I asked.

"She is out getting food from the forest. Aura was born on the second amethyst moon before the last two fire moons. If she sees your family, she will bring them here," Tovin stated.

"Okay, I'm confused. First, why is Aura out in the forest alone at night? And, what do you mean by amethyst and fire moons?" I was so out of my element here.

"You'll learn more about our world in due time," Tovin stated. "Also, in terms you may better understand, Aura is seventeen years old. She is very capable of handling herself in the night forest. There's nothing to fear in these parts."

"These parts being?" I questioned.

"We are East of the Aventurine Mountains. Two sols from Unakite Village where we live," he responded.

I was pretty good with geography, and my family had been to multiple countries on our mission trips. These names didn't ring a bell.

Still, my guard began to dissolve, and I started to feel more at ease. Tovin smiled, making his features look less imposing. He had a rugged mountain man kind of handsomeness that a more mature woman would appreciate.

"She's awake," I heard a feminine voice. "I bring food and..."

"KRYSTLE!" I heard Rhodin yell.

"RHODIN!" I cried out. He ran and jumped into my arms, then wrapped his arms around my neck. "Oh my God, Rhodin!" I hugged him tightly. "You're here too?"

"Jasper and me! We came after you, Krystle! I didn't see you. I didn't see Jasper either. I was alone and scared. Aura found me!" Rhodin exclaimed.

I looked up to Aura. Tears streaked down my cheeks. "Thank you," I mouthed to her.

Aura smiled at us. She was a striking beauty with soft olive skin. Big soft brown curls sat wildly atop her head and cascaded down past her shoulders. Her eyes were the same beautiful azurite blue as Tovin's.

She looked like a warrior in her black long-sleeved dress, tied at the waist with a strappy beaded belt. She had that same strange black fur draped along one shoulder that hung down across her body. Her other shoulder had a leather strap crossing the other direction with a large ax sticking out from a holster on her back.

"Your brother, Jasper, is not too far, I'm certain. We will surely find him at sol rise," she said in absolute certainty. She extended her hand in greeting, "It's nice to see you awake, Krystle. Let us sit and eat."

"We have a long journey come morning," said Tovin. "You and young Rhodin will need to rest. You need not worry about Jasper. He will be safe through the night."

I felt I could trust their words. They seemed like people who were proud and honorable. They cast no suspicion my way, and they seemed knowledgeable and confident—no creepy vibes for sure. I was ready to follow them for any answers they could provide. I felt so much better having Rhodin here safe by my side. I wondered, though, if Uncle Garreth and Aunt Cassie came through as well.

Aura pulled what looked like a pear the size of a large gourd out from her satchel. She pulled her ax from the holster on her back. Placing the large pear on a flat stone, she lifted her ax in the air and, in one swift strike, split the pear in two. She dug out some of the seeds with a small knife and passed them around.

I observed the seed that filled my palm. It had a deep purple hue and reminded me of a fig. I watched as Aura and Tovin snapped the tip of the seeds off between their finger and thumbs. They held opened ends up to their mouths and squeezed the seeds, consuming the contents. I followed their action, and Rhodin watched me. I did a test squeeze onto one finger. It looked like light purple yogurt. I gave it a taste and found the flavor light, pleasant, and mildly sweet.

I nodded my head to Rhodin, and he tried it. "Mmm, that's really good. Can I have another, please?"

Aura smiled and gave us each two more. "You won't need more than that. Tanna Fruit is very filling." She proceeded to remove more seeds and put them in her satchel. "The rest will get us through our journey over the next two sols," said Aura.

I found myself taking a liking to Aura. She had a cool, big sister vibe. I could tell she was strong and wouldn't take crap from anyone. That reminded me of Taylin, and I suddenly felt sad.

I pulled my phone out of my pocket and looked to see it was completely dead. I had the feeling I wouldn't have use of it from this moment and onward. Everything here felt different. I had yet to see anything beyond this beach. We were definitely not at the resort anymore. I couldn't recall how I got here or where "here" is exactly.

"Tovin... How exactly did we get here? I understand where we are going, but what is this place?"

"You were called here," Tovin explained, "A passageway was opened for you to enter our world. You are not on your Earth. It is, in essence, like your world but different in many ways. Our ancestors called this world Ki'ichpam Lu'um or 'Beautiful Land'."

"Passageway?" I started to remember the bright white light. "Are our parents here? You knew my name," I said to Tovin.

"Flint and Gemma have been calling to you." Aura said. "They have been looking for you."

"They are here?" I asked excitedly.

"Where are they?" Rhodin asked impatiently. His head turned, and he looked around.

"Yes. Your parents are with my Great Grandmother, Lazula. She explained to them you would be coming soon." Aura smiled. "They came through nearly four sols ago. My cousin Clave found them traveling through the Kaida Forest and brought them to our village. They have been our guests till your anticipated arrival. They are good people."

I felt like I could finally breathe again. Our parents were here, alive and safe. The waterworks started up as I held Rhodin in a tight embrace. "Did you hear that, Rhodin? Mom and Dad, they are here! We will see them soon!"

"I knew they were alive." Rhodin squeezed me back. I wiped tears away from his cheeks and mine.

"We have to go on an adventure, but Aura and Tovin know where to take us so we won't get lost," I told Rhodin, "Right, Aura?"

"That's right," said Aura. She smiled at us, then Tovin. He put his arm around her and gave her a loving hug.

"Let's get some rest. Jasper will show up by sol light, and we will be on our way," said Tovin.

"How are you so sure about Jasper?" I asked.

"A little bird told me." Tovin smiled and looked to a nearby tree. I looked as well but didn't see anything.

"That's an expression we say in our world as well," I stated.

"I know," said Tovin. He smiled. I gave him a quizzical look. He stood to his full stature, and my jaw dropped. Geeze, he had to be close to seven feet tall.

"Rest well, shiyava," Tovin bid. He went to lie on the other side of the fire. Aura lay down at our heads. Rhodin and I huddled up together under the fur blanket. I looked up at the stars once more. Rhodin must have been tired. It didn't take him long to pass out.

I felt too excited to sleep. Mom and Dad were waiting for us. It was hard to believe we were in another world. What were we going to see? Would we make it back home? I prayed that Jasper was alright. I wondered if Uncle Garreth and Aunt Cassie were here. None of us ended up in the same place when we came through the Light.

I watched a star shooting across the sky. It was all so much to take in. I closed my eyes, "Just rest, Krystle," I told myself. Come morning. I didn't want to miss a thing.

I woke to a cool breeze on my face. I sat up and saw Rhodin down near the water with Aura. They were playing hand slap war. The sun was just above the water. The ocean was sparkling, and the sand was pristine. Flocks of bright green birds flew through the air. The sky was the crispest blue I'd ever seen.

A little red bird with lime green wings on the underside flew straight toward me. It landed a few feet away, then turned its head and chirped.

"Hello, little beauty," I said, and it preened. It flapped its wings then hopped onto my knee. "Are you the little bird Tovin was listening to last night?" It chirped back in response. "Wow, you're quite the efficient communicator," I quipped. It chirped twice in reply.

It took off from my knee and flew down near Rhodin. "Oh, what a cute little bird!" he exclaimed. Aura had gotten the advantage and had swiftly pulled her hands from beneath Rhodin's and slapped the tops of his hands. "Hey, no fair, I was distracted."

"It's totally fair!" She laughed. "The point of the game is to pay attention and not let your opponent get you."

The bird chirped at Rhodin.

"Aww, can I pet you, little birdie?" Rhodin asked.

"I think your new little friend is trying to get your attention," said Aura. The little bird took off, flying down the beach.

I watched it as it stayed low and flew with purpose. I got up and watched it. It was flying toward a figure in the distance. Could it be?

"Jasper," I whispered. I started to run, and the figure started toward me as well. "JASPER!" I yelled.

"KRYSTLE!" Jasper shouted back. He started running faster. I heard Rhodin behind me calling out Jaspers' name with excited glee. The bird continued toward Jasper, then made a U-turn and headed back to Rhodin and me. We do indeed have a new little friend. We ran into each other's arms.

"Krystle, I thought I lost you guys for good. I was terrified!" Jasper exclaimed.

Rhodin caught up, and we turned and lifted him in a group hug. "Jasper, they told us you'd be here, and they were right."

"Who told you?" Jasper asked. We looked back to Aura waving in the distance.

"Aura and Tovin," I said. "Tovin found me, and Aura found Rhodin. And, I guess the little red bird found you," I exclaimed.

"That little red bird had been with me since I first got here and then took off this morning. Now I know why," said Jasper. The bird landed on his shoulder and chirped three times.

"Yep, that's all three of us together again. You are a brilliant bird," Jasper laughed. "Thanks, buddy!"

The bird chirped as if saying, you're welcome and took off, now satisfied it accomplished its mission.

"Aww, man, I wish we could keep him," Rhodin exclaimed.

"He probably has his own family he needs to get back to," said Jasper.

I started explaining everything that happened since we arrived here to Jasper as we walked back toward Aura. I saw she was making her way toward our campsite and packing up.

We caught up to her, and I made introductions, "Aura, this is my brother Jasper."

"It's nice to meet you, Jasper," she smiled at him.

Jasper stared back at her, speechless. Jasper swallowed hard. He looked stunned and was obviously instantaneously attracted to her. I nudged his shoulder, and he snapped out of it. I had never seen Jasper react this way to any girl before.

"Uhm, yeah! Uh, hi. It's, uh, nice to meet you too." He swallowed again. I saw sweat trickle down the side of his face, and I laughed out loud.

"What?" he snapped at me.

"Nothing," I said.

A growl came from the forest. Tovin stood outside the tree line behind Aura. Jasper looked up at Tovin and gulped.

"That's Tovin, Aura's father." I supplied this little tidbit of info with a huge smile.

"Tovin, this is my brother, Jasper," I stated.

"Good!" Tovin grunted. "Now we can get going!"

“It...It’s nice to meet you, sir,” Jasper said nervously.

“You too, kid,” Tovin responded, then turned and walked back into the trees.

“Uh, that’s a big guy!” Jasper exclaimed.

Aura smiled. She enjoyed the exchange with delighted humor. “It’s time to move,” she said.

We passed the canteen back and forth. The water was just as crisp cool, and refreshing as the first time. It was then that I remembered, *Oh yeah, I have a bladder!*

“Uhm, Aura! Could we stop a minute? I kind of have to go!”

“Go where?” she asked.

“She has to pee, and so do I,” Rhodin clarified.

I saw Tovin stop in his tracks slightly ahead of us, but he didn’t turn around. He just hung his head and said, “Shiyavas!” with an exhausted breath.

“Oh!” Aura exclaimed in understanding. “If you have to make way, just pick a tree and go.” I’m glad she understood, but that was an odd way to put it.

“Okay, will do! Come on, Rhodin. You go there, and I’ll go over there.”

Aura looked to Jasper. Jasper put his hands up in the air. “I’m good!” he abruptly exclaimed.

“Okay!” Aura chuckled. Tovin just groaned and shook his head.

We seemed to be on a well-worn path. Lush green foliage surrounded us, and rustling noises came from the tree canopies above. Animals hopped from limb to limb. I looked up and caught glimpses of red hair.

“What kinds of animals are in these forests?” I asked Aura.

“Those are forest Yehatis, younglings. They are curious and harmless,” she explained. “We will be fine this side of the mountains.”

“Just this side of the mountains?” I asked. Worry filled my voice. “What’s on the other side?”

“Don’t worry, Krystle! My father and I will keep you safe. There’s nothing out there we can’t handle.”

“Okay!” I swallowed. I had no choice but to trust them with our lives. I mean, Tovin was big and scary. Aura seemed to be very capable for someone as young as us. I only hoped things would get better since we were now on our way to our parents. I had to put a little faith in them. Aura had known Mom and Dad’s first names after all.

As we continued our journey, Aura acted as our tour guide to ease our minds. She told us about the different animals of the forest and the plant life. I listened intently to our new world biology crash course.

I found all the information interesting. Rhodin, on the other hand, was yawning as he trudged along. Jasper was studying Aura more than anything else. Tovin kept pace ahead, trying to make up for lost time.

We had been walking for a few hours. Rhodin started to slow, so we took turns carrying him piggyback. Tovin and Aura carried on like this was just a stroll in the park. Were we getting to a higher elevation? I started to breathe a bit heavier.

I was about to ask if we could stop for a break when I heard rushing water in the near distance. My hope peaked as we approached a river. Perhaps there was a boat or something we could sit in for the next part of our journey. We rounded a bend of trees, and my prayers were answered. The sound of rushing water grew louder.

A waterfall poured into the river below. Tovin approached a large canoe with woven netted seats stretched across the interior. He and Aura unloaded their belongings. Everything was placed for optimal accessibility and tied down. Tovin climbed in and positioned himself in the back while Aura took to the front. Jasper helped lift Rhodin inside. He took my hand, and I climbed in.

It was chillier on the river. Aura got up and unrolled a couple of large fur blankets, and passed them to us. “It’s going to get colder from here. You’ll need these,” she stated. We took them graciously. I bundled Rhodin and myself together.

Tovin and Aura pulled the ropes that tethered our new ride from the grounded anchors. They each pulled out long wooden oars and started pushing away from the shore. The current seemed strong enough as it pushed us along. Tovin and Aura didn’t have to do much paddling. They steered to keep us in the right direction.

Tovin whistled a chipper tune. He looked at me and smiled, “The river is my place of peace," he said. Soon after, Aura began whistling along. Jasper and I joined in. Rhodin was making his best attempt. Mostly little toots and spittle flew from his little puckered lips. I tried not to laugh as I encouraged him along.

We approached a rocky outcropping and floated along underneath. The temperature had dropped a few degrees under full shade. Tovin and Aura started paddling opposite one another, making the canoe steer into a sharp turn. We entered a cavern. Walls of rock rose on either side of us. The natural formations grew higher into the air the further along we went.

The walls started getting narrower and narrower. It began to feel like the walls were closing in on us. Ahead was another rock wall, a very, very high rock wall. Was there a turn ahead that I couldn't see? We began to slow, and it looked as if we were about to crash head-on into the wall. I turned back to Jasper as he also looked around in confusion. I pulled Rhodin to myself a bit more.

"Uh, Aura?" I said her name in question.

"No worries!" Aura turned back to me. "We're just taking a shortcut."

"How is this a shortcut?" Jasper's voice cracked.

The canoe slowed so much that it just lightly bumped into the wall before us. I heard scrapping like rock on rock behind us. I noticed Tovin had just pulled his oar away from the wall. There was a block pushed into the wall. Another giant wall slid out from the wall behind and enclosed us completely. I started to feel like a complete claustrophobe as my breathing picked up.

Jasper's hand shook my shoulder. "Krystle, are you sure we can trust these people?" he asked in a raised whisper.

Tovin started laughing maniacally. Then he mimicked an airline pilot's tone of voice. “Ladies and gentleman, this is your captain speaking. You may have noticed we are currently encased in a watery tomb of impending doom. You’ll also notice that the water will start to rise, but do not panic or try to exit the craft as we begin our ascent. Our attendant will not provide snacks or beverages, but she will provide seat tethers to keep you secure so you will not fly out of the craft to imminent death. Thank you for flying with Crazy Canoe Airlines. Enjoy your flight!”

“What is he talking about, Aura?” I asked in a panic.

“Don’t worry,” Aura smiled. “You are going to love this!” She pulled large ropes from the interior sides across our laps. She placed harnesses around our backs, over our shoulders, and then secured them down to our netted seats with metal clasps.

“When the time comes, just lean back, hold on tight to the rope in front of you, and brace with your feet. And remember to enjoy the ride.” She put a padded life vest and headgear on Rhodin and then patted the top of his head.

I looked at her as if to say; *I’ll need one of those too! Where’s mine?*

Aura tossed Jasper his harness. He repeated the process Aura had demonstrated with Rhodin and me. She winked at him, then returned to her front position and put a rope across her lap. Tovin just started whistling again. Surely enough, the water was rising. We sat in frightful anticipation as the canoe rose higher and higher. Was this thing going to sprout wings as we fell off the mountainside? Were there parachutes tucked into these harnesses?

"Krystle, I'm scared," said Rhodin.

"Don't worry, buddy," I told him with a shaky voice. "Aura said we would be alright, and it will be fun. Right, Aura?"

"Oh, most definitely," she replied. She faced forward and whistled a tune like music one would hear riding in an elevator.

The sky got closer and closer. "Krystle, what the flip is this?" Jasper shouted in desperation.

"I DON'T KNOW, JASPER! I THINK WE BOARDED THE WRONG FLIGHT!" I shouted back.

"Captain to co-pilot," Tovin began again. "We are nearing the top of our ascent. Please check that all passengers are secure. Say your prayers, little shiyavas."

"That's enough joking Dad," Aura replied. "You'll be fine." She assured us.

Tovin laughed again. I was really not enjoying Tovin right now. We reached the height of our ascent. I couldn't see anything but sky from above and in front of us.

"Get ready, kids! You're about to go on the ride of your lives," Tovin shouted. The wind picked up. I braced and called at Rhodin to do the same. The canoe rocked and then slowly tipped forward. I could now see the drop, and it was massive. It looked like one of those theme park log flume rides on megaladonic steroids.

"I don't like this," Jasper shouted. "I'm pretty sure I do need the bathroom! I can't. I can't. DO THIS!!!"

Rhodin started screaming in short repetitive bursts. My heart lodged up in my throat, locked in a strangled hold. My feet dug in with all their might. The grip on the rope in front of me was unyielding. The canoe tipped completely forward onto the accommodating slide of deathly descent.

Water rushed ahead of us and pushed from behind. It was a drop my fear-stunted brain could not calculate. We flew down the mountain at warp speed, and the wind stung my eyes. My scream finally released along with Jasper's in a hysterical frenzy. Rhodin's started morphing into ecstatic laughter.

"Woo Hoo…." Aura yelled at the top of her lungs.

Tovin was laughing like a hysterical mad man. The canoe continued its rushed descent and then curved into a slanted slope. The ride started slowing as we evened out level with the surrounding land. We continued to slow as I saw a river ahead. The slide came to an end, and the canoe dropped gently into the river.

"That was awesome," Rhodin shouted. "Can we do that again?" I gave my little brother a side glance. He was completely elated. Jasper, on the other hand, still had a death grip on his rope.

"Are there any more surprises?" Jasper snapped.

"Are you okay there, little man?" Tovin asked. He patted Jasper on the back.

Jasper's face reddened. "I'm fine!" He clipped. "That was just too intense for Rhodin and Krystle. A bit more heads up would have been appreciated."

"I don't know. Rhodin seemed to enjoy the ride," Aura exclaimed. "How about you, Krystle?"

"I'm peachy, just peachy! But yeah, that was completely unexpected." I took in a deep breath and released.

"Well, you know the expression. Rip off the band-aid," said Tovin. "It's smooth from here on out!"

Chapter 8

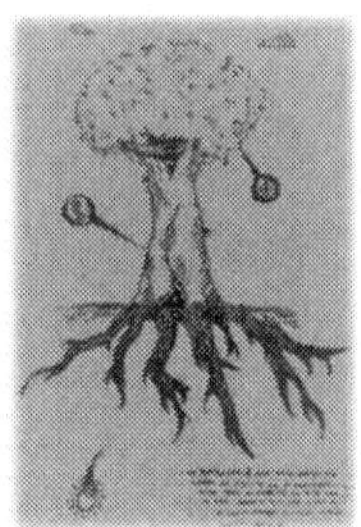

It turns out that shortcut took a whole extra day off our journey. Tovin explained that had we stayed on the river's course, we would've wound around the mountains and through a glacial pass. If we stopped halfway on that route, we would've frozen to death overnight. So, a quick rush down the mountain only rattled our existence for approximately 60 seconds, and we survived.

Aura and Tovin did a lot of traveling like our family. They mainly made tracks for supply gathering as the seasons changed. This time it was for the retrieval of Earthly strays. I could say I felt somewhat like a bewildered kitten unsure of my fate. I had my brothers with me and knew we were another day and a half away from our parents. My mind was at peace. I didn't know what this new world honestly had in store for us.

We followed the sun due west. It was a straight path through mountain passes that let way to the forest. Here and there, we passed open fields of tall grass and flowers. I spotted deer much like our own on Earth with slight variations to their patterns and coloring. There were bushy-tailed squirrels, raccoons, possum, and various birds. Waterfowl grouped along the river banks. Most of the wildlife was comparable to what I'd seen on Earth.

As the sun banked on the horizon, Tovin and Aura turned in toward the shore. "We'll make camp here for the night," said Tovin.

We glided through tall reeds and ran upon the ground. Aura hopped up and out. I heard Jasper grunt as he fell back against his seat. He had forgotten about his harness, which was still fastened. It was kind of comical how eager he was to assist Aura.

It felt good to stand up and stretch. I felt slightly off-kilter as I stepped onto solid ground. My body had to readjust to the stillness after flowing along in the canoe most of the day. We all helped unload and set up camp. We "made way" behind a large fallen log.

Jasper came out from behind with a look of relief. It must be difficult for men to keep up appearances when it comes to trying to impress women. Screaming like a banshee while rushing down a mountain could put a small dent in a guy's ego. He saved face by not exiting the canoe having wet his pants.

We watched in fascination as a new fire was lit using stones. Tovin pulled a pouch from his belt. He poured multicolored powder upon the rocks. He struck one rock against another, and sparks flew out, igniting the powder. Flames arose in colorful hues as I had first witnessed the night before.

"I wish making a fire was that easy back home," I said. "You don't use wood?"

"We do when the need arises," said Tovin.

“What kind of powder is that?” asked Jasper. “It doesn’t ignite like gun powder. And those colors?” He looked on in fascination.

“We have many resources, with many uses,” Aura explained. “Each one you’ll learn about in time. The powder we collect from the grounds where we grow our harvests. There are beetles that produce this powder in a fertilization process.”

All the creatures and plants here are symbiotic to one another. This whole world is a place of mutuality. Its rugged natural richness and beauty have an essence that is so mysterious. I watched as the darkness grew and the stars cast across the sky’s expanse. The moon rose above the trees in the distance. It was blue and looked like a giant round moonstone. It was gorgeous with streaks of pearlescent marble white. It seemed to glow from within rather than reflecting the sun.

“Everything here is so beautiful!” I exclaimed. I looked over to Jasper. He was studying Aura’s features alight by the moon. He looked at her like she was the only beauty to behold in this world. Aura looked to Jasper and smiled, and he shyly averted his gaze. She then looked back at me. I could only hope his heart wouldn’t be broken when we had to return home. That is if we returned!

Aura smiled, “I was born in this world. I couldn’t think of any place else I’d want to be. Though, I have heard your world has many fascinating things. What do you miss?” I found it interesting that she knew more about our world, and we’ve just learned of theirs.

“I miss my friend Taylin. Our Aunt Cassie and Uncle Garreth. We don’t know if the Light brought them through.

It's more about having the people you love with you rather than the place you are. But yes, I can say there are many beautiful places in our world as well. There are also many terrible and tragic things."

"We are not without heartbreak and tragedy," Tovin stated solemnly. Aura put her hand on Tovin's. "I understand what you mean about wanting the people you love with you."

I wanted to ask what he meant. There is love, and there is loss for all of us. Heaviness hit my heart for Tovin and Aura. My chest ached, and I longed for my parents. I would never take their presence in my life for granted again. I felt Jasper's arm come around my shoulder as I hugged Rhodin to me.

I saw Aura really look at Jasper this time. I had a feeling Aura would not be impressed by any display of egotism. Jasper had strength and humility that most boys his age didn't show.

I stared at the full pearly blue moon. I listened to the sounds of insects singing in the trees. The air chilled evermore, and we bundle beneath our blankets next to the fire. The serenity of it all washed over my spirit and bade me to peace and rest.

The next morning, we rose to the sunshine and crisp air. We gathered our belongings and loaded them back on board the canoe. Before we launched ago into the river, Tovin tapped Jasper on the back. "Jasper, I'll need your assistance with something. Come with me."

Jasper audibly gulped, "Yes, sir." He got back out of the canoe and followed Tovin over to the large fallen log. Aura, Rhodin, and I watched as Tovin pointed to the log and explained something to my brother. He had a cord of rope over his shoulder. They placed a couple of large stones behind the log.

He and Jasper walked toward some trees. They picked up larger branches and examined them. Eventually, they came back over to the log with large branches in hand.

I looked to Aura in question, but she just watched the two of them as if this were some normal initiation process. "What are they doing?" Rhodin asked. "Aren't we going to the village today?"

"Yes, we will," Aura said with assurance. "But sometimes there are things we may need to pick up along the way. It shouldn't take too long." She started to get up, but Tovin held his hand up to halt her. She sat back down with a knowing smile. I looked at her, confused. "No worries," she confided again.

"The last time you said that we went down the doom flume," I stated. "What the heck are they doing? Surely, Tovin doesn't mean to have Jasper move that log? It's got to weigh a ton!"

"No, of course, Jasper can't move it on his own," said Aura. "My dad will help move it. He just needs a little assistance with budging it into a roll."

We sat and watched as Tovin and Jasper took the thick, sturdy branches and wedged them under the log. They used them as leverage against the stones. Jasper's face strained red; his biceps bulged.

He used the entirety of his body weight and pulled down on the branch. He then pushed down as it teetered over the stone. Tovin was doing the same on the other end. I heard their loud strained grunts as their weight distribution started to rock the log back and forth, and it began to unearth from its hallowed confines.

The branches cracked under pressure and broke. They stumbled backward, and the log made its first roll. Tovin and Jasper quickly hopped up and started to push the log by hand. Momentum quickened the log as it tumbled toward the water.

"Uh, oh!" I heard Aura say. I soon understood why as the log was rolling downhill headed in our direction.

"Krystle, quickly! Get up front and pull with the oar as fast as you can!" Aura shouted.

"Rhodin sit tight," I yelled. Aura pushed an oar against the shore as I sat up front and paddled swiftly.

"Oh shit!" Jasper yelled. "Look out, guys, hurry!" He and Tovin ran behind the log. Tovin started tossing the rope in the air in a lassoing motion. He let loose and miraculously caught hold around a knotted piece sticking out one end. He dug his feet into the ground and pulled back on the rope.

Jasper took up the rope behind him. The log turned straight, and the two were pulled as dirt piled up in front of their outstretched feet. They were both groaning loudly in what sounded like a painfully earnest attempt to stop the runaway log.

It continued to skid closer towards the water as Aura, and I paddled out of its path. I looked back, and my eyes widened. It looked close to crashing into our canoe at its current rate of descent. “Rhodin, hold on tight,” I screamed in panic. The log splashed down into the river, just missing the canoe.

The wake made us teeter violently back and forth. I dropped my oar and grabbed the sides of the canoe. The force knocked me to my side before I had a full grip.

“Oww!” I yelled. My shoulder hit hard against the canoe wall. I heard Rhodin yell, and I looked at him. He was lying flat across the netted seat, holding tight. He appeared uninjured. Aura was holding steady. Her look first determined, turned apologetic as she looked to Rhodin and then me.

The waves settled. The canoe began drifting toward the current and was pulling us away. The guys were still running toward the water. “We’re going to lose them,” I shouted.

“Catch the rope!” Tovin yelled. Aura caught the rope and quickly tied it off. We jolted backward as the rope pulled taught. The force pitched me forward, and I fell toward the front bow.

"Aaugh!" I felt the wind knocked out of me. I rolled back and forth as I clutched my shoulder and grimaced in pain.

"Krystle...!" Rhodin and Jasper cried out.

"Jump!" Tovin yelled. I lifted my head, and I watched as Tovin and Jasper jumped from the shore to the log floating behind the canoe.

Tovin landed and grabbed hold of Jasper to keep him from slipping and falling into the frigid water. "Hold on, kid!" Tovin shouted. Jasper kneeled and clutched onto the log. Tovin balanced himself and walked the log to the end. He grabbed hold of the rope and pulled it—the canoe backed toward the log. Aura got up and started paddling the oar quickly, one side then the other. I lay still with one arm, useless. My shoulder was throbbing.

I was amazed by both Tovin and Aura's strength and determination. Once there was enough slack, Tovin doubled up the knot on the log and pulled the two vessels close together. He reached out to Jasper and pulled him forward. He swung Jasper around onto the canoe. Jasper flailed as he landed inside.

Aura made a stance for impact and caught him. Their arms went around one another. They both let out an "Umphff" as they collided into an embrace.

"Thank you, Aura!" Jasper said her name like an answered prayer. He pulled away and looked into her eyes.

"You're welcome," she replied. This time she sounded timid and shy despite her act of courage and strength. Tovin then landed onboard behind them. He menacingly cleared his throat. They pulled away from one another.

Jasper came to Rhodin first and helped him upright as Aura bypassed them and came to my aid.

“Are you okay, Krystle? I’m so sorry this happened. We were supposed to keep you safe, and now you’re hurt.” Aura sounded anguished. Jasper came up beside her, and they both assessed my injury before helping me up. “Father, her shoulder is dislocated.” Tovin approached and put a gentle hand on my shoulder. I winced.

“Krystle, I apologize for your injury. This is my fault,” said Tovin.

“You think?” Jasper spoke up. “Why you thought you needed that stupid log is beyond me! First, we could’ve been injured on that ride down the mountain, and now my sister is hurt because you wanted to roll that damn log.” Jasper seethed angrily.

“Listen, kid,” Tovin pointed his large finger into Jasper’s chest. “I have my reasons for doing what needs to be done, and if it weren’t for me and Aura, you would still be wandering that beach right now without a clue where to go.”

“We’re not stupid, you know!” Jasper angrily retorted. “We are Genstones! We know crucial survival skills. And that doesn’t include rolling heavy projectiles toward our family members.”

“Back off, kid, or you’ll be sorry,” Tovin stepped closer to Jasper.

“I am sorry, that we decided to join you!” Jasper exclaimed vehemently.

Tovin's hands balled into firsts. He reached up to grab Jasper's shirt. Aura spoke up, "Father...! Taqa ki ya asha toah ti mehanal!" I don't know what she said, but she spoke the words with passionate ferocity. Tovin released Jasper's shirt, sighed, and stepped back. Jasper backed away and pulled his shirt back down.

"Jasper, please," I said, trying to get my brother back to his senses. "I'll be alright. Just help Rhodin and me out. Okay?" Jasper looked at me, nodded his head, and let out a huff.

"I'll need to reset your shoulder, Krystle. It will hurt. I'm sorry." said Tovin.

"Jasper, please hold your sister steady." Jasper glared hostilely at Tovin but did as he was told. Jasper held me to him opposite my injured arm. I turned my head into Jasper's shoulder and clenched my teeth, anticipating the pain.

"On the count of three." I felt Tovin grasp my upper arm. I squeezed my eyes shut tightly. "One, two... POP!" I screamed when I felt the pull as the ball of my humerus slipped abruptly back into the shoulder socket. I cried for a moment as the shock eased away.

"Are you going to be okay, Krystle?" Rhodin asked. Tears rolled down his cheeks. He sat down beside me and gently brushed my leg with his small hand. "I don't want to touch your hurt arm," he said.

"I'll be alright." My voice was hoarse. "Are you okay, Rhodin?" I asked. He nodded his head. Jasper sat down to my other side, and I leaned on him.

"Here, put this on," Aura said. She assisted me with a sling. She had made it from some material she pulled from a bag. She applied a ruddy clay-like salve to my shoulder. "This will ease the discomfort. Take these, chew them up and swallow them." She handed me some dark blue berries. "These will ease the pain as well." I ate the bitter berries and washed away the taste with some of the cool glacial water. Afterward, I began to relax.

Tovin and Aura took their posts once more and pulled us out to the flow of river current. It was smooth travel from that point on. The log floated along behind us. Jasper moved to the seat ahead, just behind Aura. He kept forward and only looked back to Rhodin and me occasionally.

I wanted to ask Aura what she had said to her father, but I figured it best to wait. Hours came and passed with little conversation. Tovin didn't whistle like he did yesterday. I looked back at him. He looked off to the land, passing one side then the other. His features were contemplative and sorrowful.

This silent drifting made me feel exhausted. I asked Jasper to take Rhodin, and I laid on my good side across the wide netted seat. I pulled the blanket around me. I watched clouds drift overhead for a little while, then closed my eyes.

I must have slept a while. The sun was to my right when I sat up. We passed through wild grasslands that expanded never-ending on either side. The beautiful soft green Aventurine Mountains were now miles away to the East. I looked ahead and startled at the sight before me. Some miles in the distance, massive trees were spaced systematically in circular patterns.

People moved about and tended to animals in the open fields. There were stacks of harvest loaded into wooden carts pulled by adorable miniature burros.

As we drifted closer, dogs started barking, followed by children calling out, "Ahtee, Ahtee!" Aura waved and shouted back in a joyous greeting. She looked back to us with a big bright smile and proudly proclaimed, "We are home!"

Small curious children ran up to the shoreline laughing, smiling, and waving. Rhodin perked up at the sight. A joyful feeling filled me as Rhodin, Jasper and I waved back. The people were beautiful with silky raven hair, smooth tan skin, and strong lean muscles. Men and women both had prominent proud facial features indicative of Indian ancestry.

Giant trees rose around us as we drifted further along. The river banks morphed into high rocky walls of greens and pinks. Stone steps led upward to the large towering trees. Wooden-roped bridges crossed the expanse of the river connected to trees from the upper branches. Children ran across fearlessly, followed by adults carrying full loads in their arms.

Everyone was active in some sort of work or play. Market places sat amongst some open areas where goods were out on display. Crafts and tradespeople worked amongst the market places. Grindstones turned and sharpened tools. Metalsmith forges burned alight and with sounds of hammering. Women sat at large weaving looms. Their dexterous hands worked beautifully, colored intricate patterns into artistic displays. Men pulled large shearing blades across logs propped up on wooden scaffolds. The bark stripped clean away and showed the outlines of new canoes in the making.

Children sat in parents' laps as they helped grind grain with large stone mortar and pestles. Large stone chimineas were alight, and the scent of freshly baked bread permeated the air. Peace filled their demeanor as many sang along with their work. They laughed and joked with one another. It all felt truly utopian in its rugged and primitive beauty.

Aura and Tovin responded to calls from the shores in their native tongue. Further along, people of different ethnicities intermingled amiably in cheerful communication—many used hand gestures like sign language. People traded food and goods with one another. This community was one big happy family.

The canoe had made a turn into a small tributary. Ahead there stood a single giant tree surrounded by extensive open grounds. We were passing under another bridge, and I looked up. A boy with intense gray eyes caught mine and held my stare. He had an athletic build with golden-tan skin and dark layered wavy hair. I turned around and looked up again. Transfixed, we held each other's gaze until the canoe rumbled and bumped up against the stone dock. The motion drew my attention away from him.

"Lazula, Manachaca tahaanee!" Aura shouted jovially.

An older woman appeared from a doorway in the tree, "Aura, Tovin, ycj ohto mi kotayah," she began in their native language. Turning to greet my brothers and me, she said, "Welcome, Genstone Family."

With a gracious smile, she motioned for us to follow her and turned to go back inside. We all stood up and stretched. We gained our footing on the flat smooth rock landing. Curiosity pulled me to look to the bridge once more, but the boy was gone.

Jasper helped me get steady as I was still a bit disoriented. My shoulder still ached, but it could've been much worse.

Aura led us up the stone steps toward the tree. I couldn't help but look up and up. Large, sturdy branches reached up and outward. Lush green leaves with purple and teal tear-shaped fruits the size of large coconuts hung ripe for the picking. Small multicolored lights moved about the leaves and branches, blinked off and on in a beautiful display. Blues, greens, pinks, purples, reds, and yellows twinkled in continuous wandering movements.

We came to the opening of the mammoth tree. Carvings in the trunk depicted the history of the village, much like hieroglyphs or cave paintings. Totems posted on either side of the entryway with four spheres arched across. The carvings ran up, down, and all around the outside. The insides were hollowed-out; everything hand-carved within the tree, from the seating to the shelving that curved along the interior walls.

The space was large and open, with the kitchen and living areas on the main floor. Stairs curved along the interior wall and led to multiple landings above. There were beds, tables, chairs, and storage trunks on each. The center on the ground floor sat a large round bulbous stone chiminea that served to heat the home's interior. It looked as though it could be used for cooking as well.

Lazula guided us to sit on large pillows piled around the fire. Aura went to a large farm-style sink and proceeded to lift and push down the arm of a pumping mechanism. Water poured from its tap into a pitcher. She stirred in some crushed organic fragrant mixture and then set the pitcher to heat on the chiminea. Bowls filled with a variety of foods were passed around to each of us.

"Please eat. I know you are tired and hungry from your journey. My name is Lazula. It's a pleasure to make your acquaintance, young Genstones." Lazula stated graciously.

"I know you have questions and long to see your parents. They await you down the river and are very excited to see you. Much has happened, and much will be explained in time." Lazula smiled knowingly at each of us. I looked at my brothers, and they seemed as perplexed as I felt.

Lazula held a strong timbre of leadership that called for a sincerely held reverence. Authority and wisdom resonated off her very being. It prompted Jasper to speak respectfully, in complete opposition to his current nature, as he felt impatience at having to sit and wait once more.

"I mean no offense, but we were told that our parents were staying here with you, and we had anticipated seeing them upon our arrival."

Lazulas' deep dark blue eyes held Jasper in regard, "Of course, Jasper. Your parents told me about each of you," she smiled. "Krystle, Rhodin." She regarded each of us in kind.

"Your parents are preparing a place for you. They have been working diligently since learning of your arrival to our world. Before such time they were here with me. They were calling to you. I know you heard them as you are now here." She looked at me and then Jasper.

"Yes," I confirmed. "Why are we here?" I asked. It was the most important question, after all, aside from the whole meaning of life. Our lives fell into a new spectrum. How many people can say this sort of thing happens to them?

"The moons choose who to call here, and their purpose is revealed when time comes due," Lazula explained. "Your world's singular moon controls the tides and everything connected. The moons of our world control fate and destiny from the moment of our birth to the time we leave this plane of existence."

Lazula held out her hand expectantly. My brothers and I looked at one another, perplexed. "In your pocket," said Lazula.

My brow creased in confusion, but we all started patting down our pockets. I reached the round shape protruding from my cargo pocket, and it occurred to me this is what Lazula wanted.

I watched as Jasper and Rhodin pulled various items from their pockets, but I knew she wanted the stone. It occurred to me that until that moment, I had nearly forgotten its existence.

I felt a little guarded as I unzipped the pocket on my thigh. I lifted the stone between my forefinger and thumb in front of my face for inspection. It was like seeing an old friend for the first time in years.

"I understand your hesitancy, child, but you have nothing to fear from me." Lazula held her hand out toward me, and I slowly guided the stone toward her, then gently placed it in her hand.

"You see," she continued as she closed her hand around the stone, "There are four moons. The Pearlescent Blue Moon that you see each month. The Amethyst Moon you'll see yearly. The Fire Moon you'll see every decade, and the Grand Glacial Moon comes every century. I have lived through two Grand Glacial moons, and my third is coming this winter's solstice.

"Each moon assigns a purpose to each life as it comes into this world. We all have a purpose, great or small. It works together for peace, happiness, and fulfillment for all our people. I was given the gift as the Four Moons Keeper, and I am the great elder of this village. I have taken my role respectfully and humbly. I serve my people with the wisdom bestowed upon me."

"You are almost three hundred years old?" I asked in amazement.

"Wow," said Rhodin, "You look so young!"

Both Lazula and Aura laughed. "Thank you, Rhodin," Lazula responded. "We tend to live longer and look younger because our world is healthy and strong; as such, so are we."

Lazula looked at me. "There is a calling of great importance, Krystle," she raised her hand, grasped around the stone, and squeezed it tightly. She chanted a few words

I could not understand, and the reddish-orange glow permeated through her skin.

"The Fire Moon has called you, Krystle Genstone," Lazula said in a raised, mighty voice. "You have a great purpose! The Fire Moon rectifies wrongs. It calls to those fierce in spirit. I believe your purpose will be fulfilled when the next Fire Moon rises. Until then, the moons may provide more answers, and you will receive those answers as they are given."

"I am the least fierce person I know," my voice quivered. She says this as though I'm called to be some brave warrior, more like Aura or my friend Taylin. I could see Taylin up for the challenge. I'd be more like the sidekick, only standing in the distant background saying, "You've got this, Taylin, I've got your back!"

Lazula looked at me, "Do not doubt yourself, Krystle." She then pressed the stone against my injured shoulder, and the glow continued down through my arm. I felt heat radiate and grow in intensity, but it did not burn. The pain in my shoulder felt as if it were being pulled away into the stone. The glow retreated to Lazulas hand, then dimmed dormant.

I stared at her hand in shock as I lifted my arm and rotated my shoulder. The pain was gone. There wasn't even the slightest bit of discomfort. I looked to my brothers, who also wore shocked expressions.

"I'm completely healed!" I sat in awe.

"As I said, the Fire Moon rectifies wrongs," Lazula stated matter-of-factly.

"Wait, are you telling me that stone is..." I started.

"Yes, it is a stone cast out from the Fire Moon, and it found its chosen. It chose you, Krystle," Lazula answered with a bright smile. She then opened her hand. The stone dropped down. It hung from a leather strand that had somehow magically fed through a hole that wasn't there before. The stone had a different shape to it as well. It was now perfectly rounded and smoothly polished. She held it, dangling out before me.

"Take hold of your destiny Krystle. Keep it with you always. It will serve you well," Lazula extended it toward me with expectancy in her eyes. I reached out and took hold. I placed the leather strand around my neck and tied it. The stone quickly glinted as it made contact against my skin, and I felt something go through me. It felt like an awakening. I still didn't know all the answers, but I felt confidence rise inside me that wasn't there before. I lifted it between my fingers once again, this time feeling the newly polished finish. A smile curled my lips. I felt empowered yet humbled but mostly honored.

"That's the same stone you found at the cave?" Rhodin asked as he came around to sit in front of me. He lifted it between his little fingers, feeling the new texture for himself. "That's super cool, Krystle. Does this mean you have superpowers or something now?"

I laughed, and I heard everyone else around us chuckle. "Maybe Rhodin, I don't know for sure."

"Krystle, The Fire Moon Princess!" Rhodin declared. Everyone laughed again.

"I don't think it makes me a princess, more like a caretaker," I replied.

"Nope," Rhodin argued, "Princess!"

"If you say so, Rhodin. For you, I'll be a princess," I chuckled and ruffled his hair.

"Cool," he responded.

"May I see it," asked Jasper. He looked upon the stone in fascination.

"Sure!" I turned to him.

He simply lifted it for inspection as Rhodin did. "It really has healing powers. That's amazing!"

I looked around the room with all eyes on me. Lazula nodded at me. She knew I felt the surge go through me, and I suddenly felt a connection to her that traversed her years and mine as well. Our spirits acknowledged each other like old friends, and I knew I could trust her with anything. She would be my teacher, my guide. Peace surrounded me at that moment, and I felt like I belonged in this world.

Chapter 9

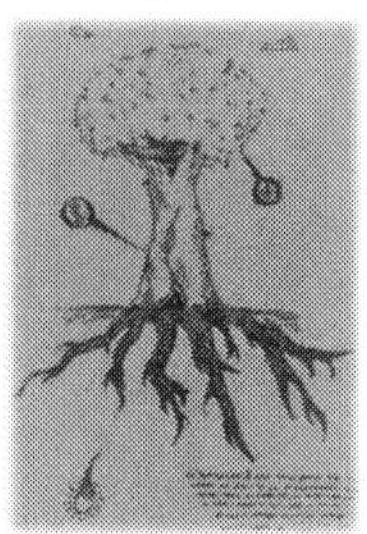

We were led up the curving stairway and shown our guest accommodations. Jasper and Rhodin got a bed on the first landing, and I continued up to the next landing with Aura.

Tovin had gone back outside. He left Lazula on the first floor and mentioned having to tend to something. Aura turned down the bed, and we climbed in and pulled the cool blanket over ourselves. I could hear Jasper and Rhodin's quiet mumbles down below.

"This seems like a dream, any minute now; I'm going to wake up in my bed at home." I turned to Aura, and she turned her head to me and smiled.

"And would you be disappointed?" she asked.

"If you asked me that any time before tonight, I would've said no, but now..." I trailed off. "I do miss my best friend Taylin and my aunt and uncle."

"I understand," Aura said. "I know what it's like to miss the people you love. I'm so happy you and your family that you are here now. I feel like we're going to be great friends, like sisters even."

"I had that feeling too, just earlier." I smiled at Aura. I started to yawn. "It's been a very interesting day."

"It has. Let's rest now, sister." She smiled back at me. "Big day tomorrow."

"It seems that way every day here," I chuckled.

"It is. You'll never be bored. That's for sure," said Aura.

"Aura?"

"Hmm?"

"What did you say to Tovin after the log incident? You know, when he and Jasper were at odds?"

"I told my father not to disgrace our ancestors with ill actions. He can be hot-headed from time to time, but he is a good man. He would not have hurt Jasper," Aura replied.

"I didn't feel he would either, but that was pretty intense. Jasper tends to be hot-headed as well," I said.

"I noticed," Aura replied with a knowing smile. "Men tend to get that way when they are protective."

"Yeah, I guess it runs in my family. My dad and Uncle Garreth are the same."

"It is good you have your brothers and parents here, Krystle," said Aura.

"Thank you, Aura. For you and Tovin getting us here safe." I felt the sincerity swell in my chest as I said those words.

"You're most welcome, Krystle. I know there were a few bumps along the way, but I am most grateful you are all here."

She squeezed my arm and smiled. I smiled back, then closed my eyes to rest.

The next morning, I woke to the divine smell of breakfast cooking. The aroma wafted up through the tree and had me sitting up and putting my feet to the warm, smooth wooden floor.

Today was the day we would reunite with our parents. Excitement had me jumping up. I looked and saw Aura was already out of bed, and I could hear small chit-chat going on down below. I descended the steps down to the ground floor.

Tovin and Aura were sitting at the kitchen table while Lazula pulled the bread from the stone oven. The table was set for all of us with stoneware plates and metal utensils. Clay tumblers and pitcher was ready for pouring some fruit juice. There were cheese, fruit, and nuts ready to grab from the center.

My stomach started to grumble, and my mouth began to salivate. Everything here was made fresh. No grocery store supermarkets. I noticed the shelves were stocked well with various ingredients in jars, bowls, and cloth bags.

Tovin was the first to look up and greet me. “Good morning Krystle. Come have breakfast.”

“Good morning,” I responded with a sleepy smile. I sat down next to Aura. She took the pitcher and poured juice for Tovin and herself, then me.

“Thank you,” I said. I tried the juice that was more like a cider. Lazula set the bread before Tovin, and he cut it into slices with a large knife. I turned as I heard footsteps. Jasper and Rhodin had come down to join us. They each took a seat and looked at the food eagerly. Aura passed the pitcher across to Jasper, and he poured the cider for himself and Rhodin. Lazula then sat down opposite Tovin. She said a blessing in their native tongue, and then we passed the different platters around, making our selections. I took just a little of everything. I had to try it all because nothing in this world had disappointed me so far.

“After you finish eating and freshen up, we will get ready to go see Flint and Gemma,” Lazula said, smiling at each of us. “We are not far. Just a couple of miles further down the river.”

Once I had eaten my fill, Aura showed me to a room that was tucked behind the stairwell. It looked like a primitive bathroom. She referred to the room as the ‘make way,’ and I remembered how she told me to go in the forest. I was thrilled they had indoor plumbing though things functioned a bit differently. She showed the different mechanisms and gave an extended rundown on how everything operated. She then left me to take care of myself.

Rhodin was waiting to go next, so back in, I went with him to give him the quick lesson. I gave Jasper a brief synopsis outside the make way room and left him to his own experience. There was going to be a new learning curve in this world.

It was finally time to go to our parents. We all loaded into the canoe, including Lazula. She was excited to see us reunited. Aura and Tovin took up their oars, and we drifted back out from the inlet toward the opening of the river. We continued down from the way we came the day before. People going about their day on the banks stopped to wave and bow their heads in respect to Lazula. She responded to her people lovingly in words or hand gestures.

A beautiful smile graced her lips at each person. She shouted encouraging words to anyone who appeared discouraged with a task at hand. They would smile and laugh and return to their task with renewed enthusiasm. Lazula was an enigma of positive energy. She brought out the best in everyone she greeted.

It was just a few minutes later; we slowed over to the left bank. We docked and unloaded. Tovin unloaded a few more bags than what we had with us before today.

"These are some more supplies and food for your family," Tovin explained. He passed a few bags to each of us after we stepped out on the stone dock. He and Aura tied off and jumped out with more bags. Lazula led the way up the steps. A grouping of tree homes stood before us.

There was a difference with these dwellings. There were three trees, with two near the river embankment and the third sitting further back inland. In the middle of the grouping was an opening with a large bulbous stone chiminea. The fire pit kept the outdoor picnic area infused with warmth.

Lazula made her way inside the tree to the left, and one by one, we entered. I dropped my bag and looked around in awe. It was beautiful. There was a curving staircase with four large landings above. Each had partially closed-in walls with beautiful ornate columns and handrails. Light filtered in through arched windows from each landing. A pole went from the ground to the top of a very high open ceiling. Two large built-in shelves flanked out from the pole with doors on either side. A slide curved down the opposite wall, which branched off from each landing and merged, ending on the main floor

I turned in circles and took in the open living and kitchen areas. To one side was a large semi-circular wooden couch with colorful cushions. There was a round table in the middle, and a woven patterned rug lay beneath. A stone oven set out from the wall alongside the kitchen sink. Beautiful glass and metal lanterns hung from carved wooden arms that extended from the walls. The glow emanated throughout the home that was both warm and welcoming.

"Welcome home, Genstone family," Lazula opened her arms in a grand gesture with a big smile on her face. I could see Jasper and Rhodin reacting as I had. This was our new home? This was beyond generous!

"The village has pitched in to get your family started with all you need," said Lazula. "Everyone contributes and starting tomorrow, that includes you as well Genstone Family. We love and respect, and help one another. These are the only rules you must follow. Everything else will fall into place.

"This is insane," Jasper muttered. "Uhm, I meant that in a good way," he declared and smiled modestly at Lazula. She just chuckled.

A tapping noise from above had all of us looking up. Suddenly, people were popping up and out from all over, yelling, "Surprise!" We all jumped, completely startled. Then they all started singing Happy Birthday.

The two doors flanking the pole opened. From the left, our Dad stepped out. From the right, our Mom stepped out. Jasper, Rhodin, and I shouted all at once, "MOM...DAD!" We all rushed to meet and embrace. Tears of joy sprung from our eyes as we hugged one another and said, "I love you!" There wasn't a dry eye in the room as everyone around us witnessed our reunion.

My mom could see I had questions. "We will have plenty of time to answer everything. This day is the first of many good things to celebrate. Our family is safe and reunited; we get to live in this beautiful village full of wonderful caring people, and it's Jasper's and your birthday."

My dad spoke to the crowd of new faces. "Our oldest son Jasper is eighteen years old, and we look forward to the man he will become. We've always been proud of his kindness, strength, and bravery. He will be a great contributor in this world as he was in our world."

Mom then continued. "Our daughter Krystle is sixteen years old. In our world, this would be considered a milestone. She is bright, artistic, wonderful, and caring. We are very proud of the person she has grown into, and she too will be a great contributor to this community."

"Shall we continue this celebration outside?" Lazula shouted.

Everyone cheered and proceeded out the door. Each person was carrying something to contribute to the celebration. Platters of food, drinks, and gifts wrapped in a cloth tied with twine. Each person smiled and greeted us with, "Welcome and happy birthday." We smiled and returned our thanks.

Dad put his arms over mine and Jaspers' shoulders and led us out. Mom held Rhodin in her arms; he was hugging her for dear life. It felt like if we let go, we could lose them again. We just got each other back. I suppose this felt too good to be real.

Once we stepped outside, everything was set perfectly in place. My heartfelt gratitude for each person here shone on my face as I looked around at all the smiles. Everyone sat on the benches, and food was passed and served. Lazula stood, and everyone quieted.

"This is a most joyous day. We welcome you, Genstone family, Flint, Gemma, eldest son Jasper, beautiful daughter Krystle, and precious youngest son Rhodin. You are part of our family. Each of you has a gift for the greater good. You may call on anyone here, for we all serve one another in our community. To the Genstones! Our newest family members!"

She raised her drink in a toast, as did everyone, and we all drank. Everyone cheered and stomped their feet beneath the tables. We ate and drank, and everyone conversed. Children played. There was laughter all around. Then Dad stood and asked for everyone's attention.

"Time for gifts," Dad announced. Jasper and I sat on a bench, and the children brought gifts to us. Each child laid a gift at our feet and said from whom it came, then turned and sat cross-legged on the ground before us. We thanked each child.

There were many things, all handmade, all beautiful. We received clothing, bedding, and grooming essentials. Jasper got a set of wood carving tools, and I got a drawing pad made from a thick papyrus and a set of multicolored charcoals. Tovin and Aura presented us with beautiful knives with intricately carved wooden handles with leather sheaths for carrying.

Dad approached Jasper, and Jasper stood up. Dad placed a large oblong cloth-wrapped gift into Jasper's hands. "For my eldest son, this gift I give is befitting for the man who stands before me now. I'm so proud of you, Jasper!"

Jasper opened the cloth, and his eyes widened. Jasper held in his hands a labrys ax with a polished wooden handle and shining green stone inlay.

"Thank you, Dad," Jasper stood tall. I could see he was trying to hold back tears.

"It's okay, son," Dad consoled with tears pooling in his own eyes. He put his hands on both Jasper's shoulders and looked at him intently. Jasper then nodded as a few tears escaped and ran down his cheeks. Dad hugged him then he moved to stand in front of me.

Tears were already running down my face as I stood before my father. A gentle, loving smile adorned his handsome face. “My daughter! Time is a thief! My baby girl has grown into this beautiful young woman.” He placed a small red velvet box in my hands. “I kept it with me so you wouldn’t happen upon it before it was time. Your mother and I picked this out together. Happy Sweet Sixteen, Krystle!”

I slowly opened the box to reveal a gorgeous pair of gold studded diamond earrings. “Oh wow! Thank you, Dad and Mom.” I hugged him.

Mom came up to me. “I can help you put them on.” I took off my old earrings. Mom then put the new diamond earrings on my ears.

“Absolutely beautiful,” Mom said. “And the earrings are nice too!” I laughed, and she hugged me and then Jasper.

“Don’t forget me,” Rhodin yelled playfully. We all squeezed him.

Music started to play, and people began to dance. The music was old Celtic drumming with a fiddle and flute. I looked to the source, and a family was playing. The father played a large drum accompanied by one boy on tandem drums. Another boy played the flute while the mother played the fiddle.

The boys were twins with dark auburn hair and green eyes. They were strapping, tall, lean, and had handsome features. The father was an older version of his sons with dark hair and blue eyes. He had a light peppering of gray in his beard.

The mother was youthful and beautiful with long red hair. Freckles lightly speckled about her nose and cheeks. She had bright green eyes, which had the slightest crinkle of laugh lines around them as she smiled and played.

Everyone stood and joined hands. We formed a circle and leaped around the large stone chimenea. We went around a couple of times, then stopped and changed direction. Laughter erupted as a few people stumbled in haste to keep up. The beat of the drums picked up, and we all doubled our pace.

I could feel the heat rising on my cheeks, which also ached from the contagious smiles and laughter. The music came to an abrupt stop, and all collapsed back in a fit of laughter. It took a moment to catch my breath and sit up. I looked around to see my new neighbors and family in various states of merriment. I noticed Jasper locking eyes with Aura. She saw me looking and turned away and started talking to Lazula, both giddy. Jasper then looked back at me and grinned.

A slower beat and lulling fiddle started a more amorous cadence. Couples joined up and started to sway. Mom and Dad took to each other's hands. Their faces showed tenderness. The knowledge of their family together once again made this dance meaningful. Jasper approached Aura and tapped her on the shoulder. He started asking her to dance, and I could see Tovin scowl. Lazula quickly grabbed Tovin and turned him in distraction to dance with her.

I smiled as Aura nodded, allowed Jasper to take her hand, and then placed his other hand on her waist. They looked at each other, and Jasper's throat bobbed as he swallowed nervously. I could see her mouth, “Happy Birthday, Jasper.”

They continue in a sort of waltz to the music. I felt a light tapping on my shoulder and turned to see one of the twins looking down at me. He was even more handsome up close. “May I have this dance, Miss Krystle?” He had an Irish accent that only added to his attractiveness.

I swallowed nervously but feigned boldness as I asked, “And may I inquire your name before I accept your offer?”

“Benjamin Tucker. Bennigan, me brother, wanted ta dance, but I beat him to it.” He pointed to his twin, glaring our way, still playing the drums with an angst vigor. Benjamin just smiled, waved, and turned to ignore him.

“A lovely young lady should naht be standin’ idle while festivities are goin. Me Da, Eric, is on the big drum, and Mahm, Liv, is playing the fiddle. Our lil’ sis, Hailey, has taken to your young brother.” I looked over and saw Rhodin and Hailey sitting together talking. She held a small brown mouse, and Rhodin cupped his hands to allow the animal to scurry to him.

Seeing as everyone happily occupied, I accepted Benjamin’s offer. I placed my hand in his and felt his hand on my waist. We started to move to the music. I wasn’t the best on my two left feet. Benjamin led well, which put me more at ease. “It’s good to have your family back together. Our family has been here since I was a young kid, probably the same age as your little brother.”

I came out of my shy stupor as I asked, “Wait, where did your family come from? How did you get here?”

"Same as you, I suppose," Benjamin replied. "A light path appeared to us as we were visitin an ancient monument in Meath. Bennigan and me was drawn to the Light. Our family was all pulled through together. Me sister was born here, so this is all she has ever known."

I was mystified. We weren't the first family to come through from our world to this one. Probably not the last either. I wondered in silent contemplation. How many people have come through? Have any gone back? Could we go back?

Benjamin interrupted my thoughts. "I know you will love living here. I was resistant at first, but the way the people here took us in and shared their hearts. Well, it ded naht take long to make friends. The work ethic and values were naht much different from our clan back home. It was easy to fit in. What year is it back on Earth?"

This question surprised me. Lazula's explanation of the moon cycles here should make it easy enough to track Earth years. That is, given there were the same hours, days, seasons, and so forth. Perhaps there was more of a difference in time between our worlds.

"What year was it when your family came here?" I asked.

"1985," Benjamin replied.

My eyes bugged out. "You're kidding, right? It is 2020 now. How old are you?"

Benjamin's eyes bugged out. "2020! Yer pullin' me leg? I'm 17 years old!"

"How can you only be 17? If you were six at that time, you should be 41!" I exclaimed.

Benjamin let out a low whistle. "That'd make me old as me Da, well almost. 2020! Wow! What's it like? On Earth, I mean?"

"Do you mind if we sit down? I'm feeling a bit tired on my feet," I told Benjamin. That and my brain was trying to process this improbability.

"Sure," he said. We parted and walked over to a bench to sit. Music continued to play, more upbeat once more. There were still people dancing with more coming to sit. Children were playing little party games and batting at a piñata. I saw Rhodin standing in line, waiting his turn with Hailey by his side. Mom and Dad were sitting with Lazula and Tovin. Jasper was still with Aura sitting out closer near the river.

Benjamin poured us each a fresh drink, and we took a few sips before resuming our conversation. "Well, people communicate through technology more than they do face to face." I pulled out my dead phone and held it out to him. "It's a cell phone, a telephone, but it doesn't work here."

He took hold of it, "This is a telephone?" He turned and flipped it around in his hand, pushing on the little side buttons. "It's so small. There are no cords or dials. It's strange. How does it work?"

"Well, if it worked, it would first have to be plugged in to charge. Then, I could push this button on the side to turn it on. The screen would light up, and I could dial numbers by pushing on the screen display. Or, I could just push this button and say someone's name, and it would dial them, and we could speak even see each other."

"Woah, that's crazy! I wish it worked, so I could see." Benjamin ran his hand across the smooth blank screen. "I remember talkin' to me Grammy on the telephone when I was little. It is a huge leap from then to now." I smiled and nodded my head in agreement.

Another voice projected over Benjamin's head from behind. "So, what's this now? Movin' in on me, chances are ye Benjamin? I ded naht get a chance to dance with the girl, and you already tired her with your boring self!"

"Aye, brother," Benjamin replied exhaustively, "It's not my fault, you tripped o'er your drum tryin' to get to her. Besides, the music sounded better to dance with the lovely lady with two drums."

"No way, you nit!" Bennigan exclaimed, "Ya know the flute makes for a more ideal couples dance! I should have broke me drum o'er your bleed n' head, and then who'd be sit n' talking with the beautiful girl instead. At least I'd be more entertainin' company!"

I couldn't help the giggles that were escaping me by this point. I tried to hide the grin with my hand, but these two were the cliché comedy act of two jealous brothers fighting over the new girl BBC version. "You two are adorable," I said to calm the storm and appease the duo.

"Ye think so?" They questioned back in unison with big smiles on their faces.

"Certainly," I laughed. "It's nice to meet you, Bennigan." I extended my hand to shake his. He grasped mine, then turned it to kiss the tops of my fingers. I blushed, "It seems it is only fair that I dance with Bennigan as well, Benjamin, for the sake of keeping the peace between brothers."

"Ah, you see, brother," Bennigan started, "Beauty comes more willingly to those who wait."

"Nah, she just feels sorry for ye, ye langer," Benjamin replied with a grin. Bennigan ignored his brother and led me to dance. He held my hands as we jump skipped to the beating drum. The faster pace wasn't conducive to conversation. Bennigan would shout and hoot, and I couldn't stop laughing. He certainly put on a charming display as he flaunted his steps in a jig.

The party started to wind down as the day faded. The Tucker brothers introduced me to their parents and little sister Hailey. She and Rhodin were becoming fast friends. They certainly looked adorable together. Eric and Liv were very welcoming with handshakes and hugs. Their treehouse was straight across from ours.

This was going to make life interesting. Being the new girl next door to twin dueling brothers may cause a few challenges. I didn't feel any spark with either of the brothers. They were funny and cute, but I'd have to make it clear early on that we could only be friends.

People cleaned up and said farewell as Jasper, and I collected our gifts and took them into our new home. Tovin took Lazula back to her home, and Aura stayed behind to help us put away food and supplies. Mom and Dad had already assigned our sleeping quarters. Mom and Dad took the first landing. Rhodin was on the next, followed by mine, then Jasper's at the top.

Rhodin had everything he needed, plus some gifts from the village, which he started opening while Dad sat with him. Jasper went all the way up to his room to get settled. Mom accompanied me to my room.

Two wall lanterns illuminated my room. There was a bed with tall wooden posts. Large pillows in soft blues lined the headboard. A large wooden chest sat under an arched window. There was a desk and chair with an oval mirror hung on the wall.

Mom helped me put my things away in the trunk. "Krystle, I know this is going to be a big adjustment for you."

"I understand, Mom. This is pretty huge for all of us," I replied.

"Lazula was explaining some things to your Dad and me that pertained to you. She assured us not to worry, but evidently, you have a significant role to fill. No matter what, Dad and I will be here in every way possible to help you."

"I know, Mom. It's just so surreal right now. Just a few days ago, we were scared senseless, trying to find you and Dad. I know it's not your fault."

"Krystle, I'm not so sure about that. I mean, I didn't know when I saw the light. I went willingly, but there was a pull that I couldn't seem to resist."

"I felt it too, Mom. We heard Dad yelling for you, and it woke us. Then he screamed, and we panicked."

"Krystle, I'm so sorry you all had to go through everything you did." She had a regretful look in her eyes.

"Uncle Garreth and Aunt Cassie came to help us. They were there when I came through, but I don't know if they made it here or not. Jasper and Rhodin followed me immediately."

"Oh, I wonder if they are here?" she questioned. "Lazula told me she feels it when people come through. That's how we knew you and your brothers were here. I'll have to ask her if she can sense Cassie and Garreth."

She put her finger on my stone necklace. "Lazula told me the Fire Moon called you. I have something to show you." She pulled at something around her wrist. There was an opal stone on a bracelet. I touched it, and it felt smooth and cool.

"The call came to me as well; only mine came from the Grand Glacial Moon."

"Oh wow!" I exasperated. "Do you know why?"

"No, but Lazula felt I'd know why very soon," she sighed. "We've been preparing non-stop for your arrival here today. I'm so happy we've got you all back. I feel relieved, but I am pretty tired."

"I can sense that, Mom. I can finish up here. I think I'm ready to sleep as well," I said with a yawn.

"We'll talk more. I know Dad wants to explain some things too," she said. We hugged, and she kissed my forehead. As she left, Aura was standing in the entryway.

"So, you okay with me sleeping here tonight?" Aura asked. "It's going to be a busy day tomorrow!"

"Come on in, sister," I smiled. I unfolded my new blanket. Aura helped me spread it out on the bed. "Each day here seems even more interesting than the one before."

"I imagine I'd feel the same way if I was in your world," Aura replied.

"True," I said. "So, what's up with you and Jasper?" I asked unabashedly.

"Your brother is a good person. He's easy to talk to and doesn't put on a show like most boys do in my presence."

"Do you like him?"

"I do," Aura said, "But Jasper has much to learn. My father may have a hard time accepting Jasper spending time with me."

It seemed there was more to it than a daddy protecting his little girl. Tovin had confidence in Aura's ability to take care of herself. There was a more in-depth story here.

"So, the Tucker twins," Aura bumped her shoulder against mine with a smile. "I saw you dancing with them."

"I like them. I think we'll be good friends. There's too much competitive sibling rivalry. I know it's all in good fun, but I don't want to be responsible for bruising a brotherly relationship. So, I don't see any romance in the future."

"I understand." Aura nodded. She pulled a large, heavy drapery that gave my new room privacy where there were an open half wall and doorway. Nice to know and better than nothing at all.

Chapter 10

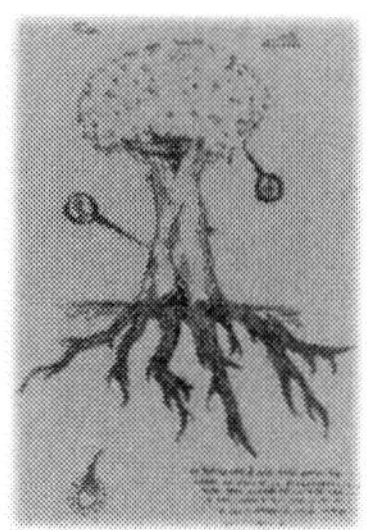

The next morning, I woke refreshed. Daylight was coming through my window. I heard my family talking downstairs, and I smiled. It was a new day and a fresh start. I got up and dressed in my new clothes, which were warm and felt like soft fleece against my skin. I found a hairbrush and a tie to put my hair in a ponytail.

I sat on my trunk and opened my window to breathe in the cool fresh air. I had a view of the river, and I took in the tranquil sound of the water's gentle flow. It was crisp and clear, and I could see fish swimming along the currents. Every person and creature here had work to do today. That included me.

I was about to get up when a small red bird landed on my window sill and chirped at me. It fluttered its wings showing off the bright green undersides. It looked like the same bird from the beach. Could it be?

"Hello there, little beauty," I greeted in a cheery tone, "Haven't we met before?"

"Chirp, Chirp, Chirp..."

"Yes, I do believe it's you, from the beach? You flew all this way to make sure we made it here alright?"

"Chirp, Chirp, Chirp..."

That was enough acknowledgment for me. I held out my finger, and it hopped on. "Are we to be new friends? May I pet you, little one?"

"Chirp, Chirp..."

I gave the little bird a loving head-scratching, which it seemed to appreciate. It then hopped on my shoulder near my ear. The bird began a sequence of light chittering chirps then butted its soft head playfully against my ear. I laughed softly. Then I felt a tug on my ear, and the bird then flew out the window. I put my fingers up to my ear and realized my earring was missing.

"OMG...You little thief!" I put my head out the window. "You better come back with my earring," I shouted. People below stopped to look up at me. Embarrassed, I smiled and waved, then quickly pulled my head back in, bumping it on the window sill.

"Ouch!" I put my hand to my head to rub the throbbing ache, and it felt wet. I brought my hand away and saw a small smear of blood. "Uhg!"

I went over to sit in front of my vanity mirror.

"Krystle, are you okay?" my mother called.

"Yeah, I just bumped my head."

"Let me come take a look at it," she replied.

"It's okay, Mom. I don't have a concussion or anything, just a small bump. I'll be down in a minute."

“Okay, sweetie, we have breakfast ready. I’ll still take a look at it when you get down here.”

“Okay,” I responded. As I tried to inspect my head in the mirror, I caught a flash of the Fire Stone around my neck. I reached up to touch it, and it flashed again. I felt warmth on my fingers. I looked at my hand, and the smear of blood was gone. The ache of my head was gone as well. I touched my fingers to my head again, and the injury was no longer there. My hand came away clean, no blood. *The Fire Stone corrects wrongs. It heals*, I remembered.

I did notice that my diamond earring was missing for sure. The next time that little red bird shows up, it better have a good reason for stealing from me. I know he helped reunite us; I would gladly have given him something more useful for a bird, like seeds or bugs. I took out my other earring and put it away. I didn’t want my folks to ask, and I was hoping to get the match back. I went over and searched the floor for the backing and luckily was able to find it; then I put it away for safekeeping as well.

I got up and drew open my curtain. I saw everyone below sitting down to eat. I turned to take the steps but then noticed two other options. I could slide down the pole or take the slide. The slide landing was closest to the kitchen area, so slide it was. I sat down and pushed off. I felt like a little kid again as I swiftly curved downward and my feet hit the floor. Everyone looked up and smiled.

“I believe everyone made use of the slide this morning,” Dad chuckled. Everyone else laughed along, which was music to my ears.

“The pole is fun to go down, too,” Rhodin chimed in. “It’s the quickest way to get to the bathroom.”

Mom got up from her seat, "Sit here, Krystle. Let me take a look at your head."

"It's not bad at all, Mom… really!" I exclaimed.

"I'm still looking, Krystle, for my peace of mind, okay?" She examined my head, "Huh, I don't see anything. You sure you're feeling alright, though? Your 'ouch' was pretty loud." She gently grasped my chin and slowly turned my head to look at my eyes. "Pupils are good."

"Okay, thanks, Mom! Love you!" I know she worries, but she usually isn't so over-the-top about it. I guess the separation has heightened her concern factor. I looked over and saw Aura sitting next to Jasper. Stolen glimpses and smiles passed between them. They did look cute together. It is the most I've seen my brother smile in his entire life.

Jasper's smile abruptly fell as he looked up and toward the doorway. "Good morning Tovin," Dad greeted, "Come, have some breakfast." Tovin glared at Jasper but quickly turned toward my father and nodded.

"Good morning Flint, Gemma, kids." He sat next to Jasper. Jasper's demeanor changed to stiff, uncomfortable silence. Aura looked at me, covering a smile with her hand, holding a piece of bread. I smiled and looked down at my plate full of food and proceeded to eat.

"So, what are we doing today?" my mother asked.

"Well, I'm taking the guys to work on a little project," said Tovin, as he gave Jasper a hearty pat on the back. Jasper choked and coughed. "You okay there, buddy?" Tovin continued to pat Jaspers back. I could hear the loud thumping of Tovin's hand as it reverberated through Jasper's chest.

"Yeh...Yes," Jasper coughed a few more times, and Aura passed a cup of water to him, encouraging him to drink.

"Good, well, you'll need to bring your ax and wood tools. Flint, you'll be joining us, right?" Tovin asked.

"Wouldn't miss an opportunity to teach Jasper a new skill," Dad smiled. "Rhodin, you can come too. I think you're old enough now to learn to work with some tools." Rhodin's face lit up, and he bounced in his seat.

"Flint, please be careful with what you let Rhodin use," Mom pleaded.

"I know Gemma," said Dad, "I'll bring both our boys back in one piece." He kissed Mom on the cheek. "I'm gonna wash up and get some supplies together. You boys do the same as soon as you're finished eating. Don't take too long."

"What does this little project entail, Tovin?" Mom asked.

"We're just working on a new canoe for your family. You'll need one," Tovin stated.

"Oh, that's very thoughtful, Tovin. Thank you," Mom replied.

"What are the rest of us doing?" I asked.

Aura responded this time. "We have some various harvesting to do. We need certain ingredients to stock up and take to the mill."

"Okay, sounds great," said Mom. "Let's clean up here and pack some lunch to go."

As we were heading out, the Tucker family was splitting up and saying farewells for the day. "Hello, Krystle," both Benjamin and Bennigan smiled and waved over at me. "What're ya up to today?"

"Hi guys," I waved back, grinning. "Off to harvest some secret ingredients," I replied conspiratorially.

"Oh yeah? Whatcha' makin' wi' that?" Benjamin asked.

"Probably repellant for ye, brother," Bennigan retorted.

"Ha, piss off, ye langer," Benjamin sliced back.

"Enough o' that, ye two!" Liv chimed in. "Get goin' wi' the men. Krystle dohs naht need the likes of ya pinin' an fittin' o're her all the deh."

Hearing my name in acknowledgment of their behavior made my cheeks turn red. She pushed the two along then turned her cheek to receive a kiss from Eric. She walked over to us with little Hailey in tow.

"Mornin' ladies. Krystle don't ye go worryn' bout the likes of me sons. They need to show more respect around a young lady. Ye have me permission to smack em' upside the noggin if needs bein'."

"I'll be sure to keep that in mind, Mrs. Tucker." I laughed.

"And, call me Liv dear. No need of formalities round er' love."

"Okay, Liv," I smiled, and she smiled back at me.

"Good morning, Liv," Mom responded with laughter and gave her a friendly hug.

"Mahm, will I get to play with Rhodin today?" Hailey asked, looking up at Liv.

"Aye, surely ya will love. But first, we ladies got some work ta do, so it will be a wee bit later," Hailey accepted this with a nod.

The guys headed down the path along the river. We followed Aura, and she stopped at a tree as the men continued ahead. We proceeded up steps that spiraled around the outside of the tree. We all followed in single file. It led us up to a rope and wooden bridge that crossed the river and connected to a tree on the other side.

I was kind of nervous being this high up, but I followed Aura's confident lead. She walked across without needing to hold on to the waist-high ropes that surrounded us. I held on with a tight grip as the bridge lightly swayed and bounced with our steps. It looked secure; I just wasn't too confident in myself crossing without incident. I've already been hurt twice since getting here, so I wasn't taking any chances.

Once we made it to the ground on the other side, we walked through the openings between more tree homes till we reached an open field full of honeysuckle. Insects buzzed around, and deer fed off in the distance. Fragrance and beauty filled my senses.

We all had burlap cross-body bags. Aura instructed us on what to pick and what to leave to keep everything in balance. We talked and bantered about the guys, much as women tend to do outside their presence. It was fun and relaxing. Other people from the village were doing the same.

There were more small children on this task, so I suppose this was induction day for me—the easy job allowing for the shock factor to ebb away.

Once our bags were full, we emptied them into a cart and repeated the process. We did this until the cart was full. “Baxxy, Sierra!” Aura called and whistled. Two dogs started barking and running our way. Aura pulled some dried meat strips from her satchel pocket, and the dogs lined up in front of the cart.

“Here, Krystle, come meet Bax and Sierra,” she held the meat strips out for me to take. The dogs looked at me, tails wagging, and Aura put a harness on them. She commanded them to sit and waved me on to approach. The dogs licked their chops and gave excited whines. I stood facing the dogs. “Bax is on the left, and Sierra is on the right,” Aura stated. They were both gray and white with soft fluffy fur; only Bax’s coat was darker on his back. They both let out a whiney bark.

“Now listen up, you two,” Aura commanded. Both dogs tilted their heads at her. “This is my friend Krystle, and you will be good for her. She is going to feed you and pet you. You will stay seated and behave like the lady and gentleman I know you’re capable of being!” The two barked back with intelligent comprehension.

“Hi, Bax. Hi Sierra,” I held out my offering, and they took it and wolfed it down quickly.

"Mind your manners," Aura commanded. The dogs whined their apologies. "It's okay to pet them, Krystle. They are well trained and very sweet."

I ran my hands atop their heads and around their ears. They were so soft and smelled like the wild forest. I bent down on one knee, and they both licked at my cheeks.

"Hey, that tickles!" I laughed. I got up before I fell over and received an onslaught of wet kisses. Hailey approached and gave the dogs hugs and praises. Mom even came over to pet them, and she's not much of an animal person. Living here, I guess it was time for her to start.

Aura attached the wooden pull to the harnesses. "Can I ride again," asked Hailey. Aura lifted Hailey onto the cart. Hailey lay back against the flowers and giggled as Aura gave Bax and Sierra the command to go. They pulled the cart at a steady pace as Mom, Liv, Aura, and I walked alongside.

The dogs kept pace with us on the path. We passed more people along the way, and they greeted us with smiles. Everyone was bustling about on their daily task. Traffic picked up as we got to a storage mill. Bax and Sierra sat as people came to help us unload. Aura released them from the cart and gave them another treat.

We finished the task then walked around the market area. There was a booth with clay soap bars. "Let's get some supplies while we're here," Aura suggested. "We have a full trading system. So, you may take what you need. You worked for it," she picked up a few clay bars and passed them to me. One smelled like mint and rosemary, the other like citrus and honeysuckle.

Mom moved ahead, taking notice of a tree from where people were coming and going. We went inside to find shelves fully stocked with a multitude of jars. It was an apothecary shop.

My mother's eyes lit up. "Aura," she said, her name in question, "There are so many things here I could use. I am a doctor. I could trade my services for supplies here."

"That would be great," Aura replied. "We do have a few healers in the village. I'm sure they'd be happy to get more help. There are many remedies here. Lazula would be glad to arrange a place for you to practice. In the meantime, you may take what you need.

Mom started perusing the shelves and taking what she knew would be helpful. "I'm amazed at what is available for medical supplies," Mom stated. "It would be wonderful to get back to practice again. I'd love to help the people here. It's what my family has done since our kids were Rhodin's age. Traveling the world and taking care of medical needs for people who couldn't otherwise access or afford it."

"Perhaps that's why you were called Mom," I stated, "Because you can help people heal."

"Could be!" Mom speculated. "Though the people here are, for the most part, complete pictures of health and longevity. I'm sure I can still help in many ways."

"Certainly so," said Aura. "We're not completely free of illness, injury, and there are expecting mothers. Lazula is an excellent midwife, but sometimes things happen, and assistance is needed."

We loaded the cart with our newly acquired supplies, and we made our way back to the honeysuckle field.

A little later, the guys arrived. Rhodin and Hailey played while the Tucker twins, Jasper, Aura, and I, sat and talked.

“Did you make progress with the canoe?” Aura asked.

“Yeah,” said Jasper, “But, I’m pretty sure Tovin has it out for me.”

“What do you mean?” Aura asked.

“He’s constantly over my shoulder, pushing me to do this, do that, hurry up, slow down. He’s like a drill sergeant. My dad doesn’t interfere; he says it’s good character building, learning how to follow instructions from someone who knows what they’re doing.”

“We know what you mean,” said Benjamin.

Bennigan shook his head from side to side, “Yeah, our Da is the same! He seems to live for whackin’ us upside our heads even tho we’re already workin’.”

I smiled and laughed. “I think that has something to do with your commentary. You two argue a bit much.”

“Nah, we do naht argue! We’re just expressin’ ourselves in a disgruntled brotherly manner,” said Benjamin.

“Quite right, dear brother,” said Bennigan, “Agree to disagree an’ we hadn’t a fistfight in o’re a year now.”

"Violence is never the answer. How about some healthy competition instead? Like running a race," I suggested.

"Sounds like a good option. Winner gets to take Krystle on a date," said Bennigan.

"Wait, what?" I startled. "I wasn't talking about making me part of this."

"Okay," Bennigan agreed, "Loser bows out."

"Excuse me!... I'm not a prize to be won! I decide who I want to date or not," I declared.

"I want in on this race," said Aura. "I win; you both back off. I'm in this to uphold my sister's choice."

Okay, I could use Aura's back up here.

"I'm in too," said Jasper, "Only I want Aura to go out on a date with me if I win, and you two back off my sister." Aura's jaw dropped in shock at Jasper.

"Did you not just hear your sister Jasper? I'm not a prize to be won, and besides, I already want to go out with you."

It was Jasper's turn for his jaw to drop. "Really?"

"Don't be dense, Jasper," I said, "It's obvious you're both into each other. Oops! Sorry, Aura. Am I overstepping?"

"Not at all," said Aura. "I have nothing to hide. I'm an open book. Yes, I like you, Jasper."

"I like you too, Aura," Jasper professed.

"I know," Aura smiled. "Okay, let's do this! Once around the field. Start and finish line is here," she dragged a line in the dirt with her heal. "Krystle, you call start and declare the winner."

"Alright!" I got up and stood to the side. I knew Jasper had this in the bag. He was our high school track star. Then again, Aura was very confident and knew the terrain well.

All four lined up. Jasper got into his stance. The twins mirrored Jasper. Aura stood poised and ready. I lifted my arm, "Ready, set, go!" I dropped my arm, and they took off. Jasper and Aura matched pace, while the twins just kept up.

About halfway around, the twins started pushing at each other and ended up tumbling on the ground. Bennigan pushed up, but Benjamin grabbed his brother's ankle and pulled him back down. Benjamin got up and started to run. Bennigan made it back to his feet and struggled to catch up.

Jasper dropped back a few paces behind Aura. On the final turn, Jasper shifted into his signature turbo mode and breezed by Aura. Aura's face turned determined, and she picked up the pace. She pumped her arms; her feet pounded the ground. Jasper continued to keep his distance, and he crossed the finish line. His body whipped by me, and I felt the rush of wind. Aura finished seconds later.

The twins were head to head, scowling and pushing at one another. They finally crossed; one followed immediately after the other. The twins dropped flat on the ground, huffing.

Jasper barely broke a sweat. Aura approached me only slightly winded. “Your brother is as swift as a Yehati, I’m impressed. I’ve never been beaten in a race before. There are many more things I’m sure I can best Jasper at. I look forward to teaching him,” she smiled.

“Competitive much?” I asked, smiling back.

Aura winked, then walked up to Jasper. “So, when do you want to take me out?”

“Uhm...Yeah...” Jasper was suddenly nervous. He was looking over toward the adults, more precisely at Tovin. “Where is a good place to go around here?”

“Hold on,” said Aura. She walked over to speak with Tovin. Jasper was beginning to sweat now. Tovin looked over our way and said something we couldn’t hear. Aura nodded and started walking back to us.

“What was that about? I asked.

“I told Dad I was going to teach you two how to knife and ax throw tomorrow after we finish our work. He just said he’d send my cousin Clave to help,” said Aura.

“Oh?” Jasper questioned. He let out a breath that sounded like relief. “Your cousin Clave, huh?”

“Aye yah, Clave is a nice fellow,” said Bennigan, “Kind of quiet though.”

He and Benjamin laughed.

“Hilarious, you two,” Aura said sarcastically.

"What?" Benjamin asked. "Clave and us, we're good old friends."

"What are they going on about?" Jasper asked.

"Nothing," Aura replied, "Clave is very nice, kind of shy. But he works well with the children as a teacher."

"Oh, that's nice," I said. "I enjoyed working with the children when we went on our mission trips. I taught them the basics like ABCs and some art lessons."

"That's not a half-bad idea," said Aura. "We've needed a teaching assistant."

"Really?" I questioned. "And, you think Clave would be willing to help me or let me help him?"

"Of course," Aura chimed. "Lazula will be happy to hear this."

Later around our communal chimenea, everyone sat telling stories. The Tuckers talked about the life they left behind on Earth and how they came to be in this world. They had a long family history of musicians. Eric had played drums and electric guitar and traveled with a band in his younger days. He and Liv met after one of his gigs and hit it off. They married, had the boys, then six years later ended up here.

Dad told the story about he and Mom being high school sweethearts and our world travels. He joked about not thinking our travels would take us to a whole new dimension. Everyone toasted to that. But we were all thankful. Dad explained what happened the night he and Mom came through the Light.

They had gone for a late-night walk on the beach and ended up falling asleep after some “snuggle time.” At this, the Tucker twins snickered, and Liv gave me that look of “by all means” and winked. I happily took the liberty of smacking them both on the backs of their head

“Auch, what ded ye do that for?” they both asked with hunched shoulders. They raised their hands to block any further punishment. I just smirked while Eric laughed and gave me two thumbs up.

“Methinks I’m taken a liking to ye, Krystle. Keep me boys in line and teach them some manners,” said Eric.

“We’ll accept this from Krystle,” said Benjamin. “So long as she dohs naht abuse the powers ye have granted, Da.”

“Naht, just me, your Mahm too,” said Eric.

“Geeze, as if we don’t get enough already,” Bennigan complained. He turned and winked at me. “But I won’t complain if it’s coming from you, Krystle. You can put those pretty hands on me any way ye want...”

WACK... “Auch, oh come on, Mahm! I was just playin,” Bennigan was now rubbing the back of his head.

“You mind what ya be say’n to a young lady,” Liv said adamantly. I could hear Hailey and Rhodin whispering and giggling.

“Auch, an’ would ya listen to those two over there,” Bennigan complained. “Thick as thieves they are.”

“You needn’t worry about that, just yerself,” Liv chastised.

Ah yes, our neighbors were a vibrant bunch. Jasper, Mom, and Dad were having a hard time trying to contain themselves from bursting out in laughter. Dad cleared his throat.

"Sorry, Flint, by all means, continue your story," Liv encouraged. She turned and gave the twins a warning glare, and they put their hands up in defensive. She nodded her head with satisfaction.

"Okay." Dad started again. "I woke up and saw that Gemma wasn't there and went to see if she was back in the tent. I looked out and saw her walking down toward the cave. I called to her, but she didn't hear me, so I started after. I kept calling louder and louder, but it was like she was in a trance. I started running, but it seemed the faster I ran, the longer it took me to catch up. I started to panic. By this point, I was yelling her name, but she never looked back."

"That's when I woke up, and I heard you," I told Dad.

He nodded to me in acknowledgment and gave me a sorrowful apologetic look. "I saw the Light at the entrance of the cave. It felt so foreboding. Gemma was reaching out for it, and I was scared out of my mind." Mom reached and threaded her fingers through Dad's.

"Me goodness!" said Eric. "I'd ah behn outta me mind too if it was me wife." He put his arm around Liv and pulled her close, and she put her head on his shoulder. The twins were quiet and transfixed at this point.

"Before I could reach her, she was stepping into the Light, and I screamed for her. I didn't stop running, and before I knew it, I was jumping straight into it without a second thought. It was just after I started feeling like I was falling that I thought about you kids, and the guilt consumed me." Dad's eyes were watering at this point as he looked around at each of us.

"We heard you scream, Dad, and came running, but it was too late at that point," said Jasper.

"We don't blame you, Dad," I said with tears streaking my face.

"You either, Mom." Jasper voiced his agreement, and we all stacked hands together.

"We landed, for lack of a better word, in the forest just west of the mountains," said Mom. "I woke up confused, wondering where I was, with no recollection of how I got there. Your father found me, and then Clave showed up and led us here and to Lazula. She explained what happened to us and from there showed us how to call to you."

"We heard you in our dreams," I said. "Then, the night from the cave when we came through. I could hear your voice."

"I heard Dad in my dreams," Jasper further confirmed.

"Do you think Lazula could show us how to call out?" I asked. "Maybe we could let Aunt Cassie and Uncle Garreth and Taylin know we are alright."

"It couldn't hurt to ask," said Aura. She had just stepped away for a while to get some of the fire-making powder. “Lazula is always willing to help so long as it doesn’t interfere with what is dictated by the moons.”

There is still much more to learn about the moons and how they intergraded into the village's lives. And the Light calling people from Earth was another mystery. Tonight, the blue moon rose in the sky, full and brilliant, along with the dusting of stars. I looked up through the trees where lightning bugs danced and wondered about family and my friend back on Earth. Taylin must be going out of her mind. I needed to find a way to contact her. I missed her so much. Aunt Cassie and Uncle Garreth, if they came here, we did not yet know.

Chapter 11

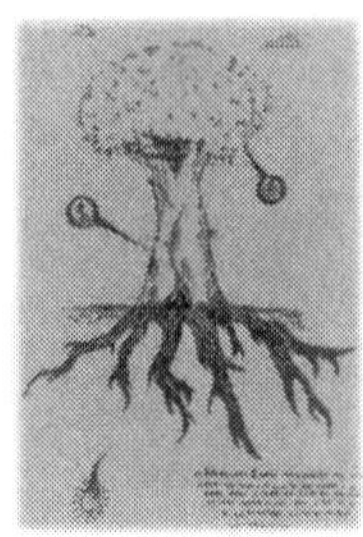

The next afternoon after we finished our daily task, Aura took us out to another field near a forest area. Aura sat behind me and plaited my hair into a loose French braid. Hailey and Rhoden picked flowers and began tucking them in my hair like a floral tiara.

"Ye look quite lovely," said Hailey. "Aura, would ye do me hair like Krystle too?"

Aura smiled, and I moved over and watched. Hailey bunched some flowers in her tiny hands as she sat patiently. Her beautiful red hair was pulled back, sectioned, and braided. Little naturally curled tendrils sprung out from either side of her little rosy freckled cheeks. Her bright green eyes popped more with her hair pulled back. I helped put flowers in her hair. She stood up and held her hand out for me to take. "We be princesses now, Krystle," she declared in her sweet melodic voice.

I stood with her, and we began to walk. Rhodin then shouted out for all to hear, "Make way for Princesses Krystle and Hailey!" All the little children started giggling. Hailey pinched her lips together, trying not to give anything away.

“Okay, what’s the joke?” I asked.

“Rhodin just told everyone to ‘make way’ for us,” Hailey burst out giggling.

It took a moment for my dunce of a brain to pick up the meaning. Then Hailey spelled it out for me. “He told everyone to go to the bathroom for us!”

At this, I burst into laughter. “Oh, very good, you sneaky little booger,” I yelled at Rhodin.

He just bowed and said, “Thank you! Thank you very much, your majesties of the make way!” A way behind Rhodin, I saw the Tucker brothers rolling in the grass, laughing their asses off.

“Oh now, you’ve gone and done it!” I yelled at them. “Teaching my sweet baby brother your wicked ways, I see.” I started to make a run for them.

“Oh shite!” they yelled. The Tucker twins jumped to their feet and started running. I could hear Aura and Jasper laughing as I made chase. “Take cover, brother! Guard your head!” Bennigan yelled.

“Off with their heads!” Hailey shouted. All the other kids started charging and yelling like little warriors. It was a sight as the twins toppled, and all the children piled on them.

“Tickle torture!” I yelled. The children started parroting my words and attacked.

Benjamin and Bennigan began screaming. “Mercy!! Have Mercy on our poor souls!!”

“Serves you right!” Aura shouted. She looked at me, and we laughed.

I turned away to leave the boys to their rightful punishment. I looked up to see a boy approaching. It was the boy from the bridge just before Lazula’s house. His eyes were on me as he approached. He moved with smooth confidence, not once averting his gaze as he came closer. His gray eyes were as intense as the first time I saw them, and I couldn’t help but swallow down the rising beat of my heart. He smiled, and that was it. I was done for!

I stood there, unable to move my feet, and he came right up to me. I watched as his chest expanded, and he seemed to be breathing me in. *Hi, I’m Clave. You must be Krystle.*

I heard him speak, but his mouth didn’t move. Was I hallucinating? Just then, the little red bird I had seen twice before landed on his shoulder. Its flapping wings caught my attention and brought me out of my stupor.

“Oh, yes. That’s me,” I said nervously. Good grief, I’ve never been this nervous talking to a boy before. I was trying to concentrate on getting the loud thrumming of my heart out of my ears.

Oh, he smells good! I bit my lip. I heard him laugh. *That voice! Oh, help me, I’m going to melt!* My thoughts were getting out of control. *Get a grip Krystle! Did I say that all out loud?* I questioned myself.

The little red bird chirped. *You!* I thought accusatorially.

This is my friend Chorus, said Clave. He *has something to return to you and wanted to apologize. Hold out your hand.*

I started to hold out my hand, but wait, was Clave actually talking? I didn't see his lips move once other than to smile at me. Dimples, smooth tan skin, gorgeous face. Am I sweating? How embarrassing! Chorus landed in my hand and dropped something from his beak. My diamond earring!

I blinked and slightly shook my head. "Uhm, I guess you're forgiven, Chorus. Chorus! I like his name. It suits him." I replied.

Thanks... Clave responded, lips still unmoving. Okay, curiosity was getting me somewhat past this attraction spell. Was he throwing his voice like a ventriloquist?

"How are you doing that?" I asked.

Doing what? Clave asked coyly.

"You're talking to me, but your mouth is not moving." I pointed at his gorgeous lips.

That's because I'm not actually speaking with my mouth, he said.

"Huh?" *I must be hallucinating.*

You're not hallucinating, he said.

Am I talking out loud? I haven't felt my mouth move. I put my fingers to my mouth for confirmation. He watched this movement and licked his lips. *Have mercy! Keep your cool, Krystle*, I thought to myself.

No, it hasn't, he agreed and smiled.

"What's going on here?" I finally asked out loud. "How is this possible?"

You have heard of telepathy? Clave asked.

"Of course, I have! I haven't been living under a rock for the past sixteen years. So, you're telling me, that is how we are actually communicating? Right now?" *Geeze, catch up, Krystle!*

Clave continued with that smoldering smile. *That's exactly what I'm saying, Krystle. I only do this with people I choose and only when Chorus is nearby.*

He's my interpreter, so to speak, considering I'm deaf. Kind of funny when you think about it. I have to have a bird around to sing it out.

Oh wow, I thought. "I'm sorry, I didn't know," I stated out loud. *Idiot, he can't hear you out loud*, I chastised myself.

You're not an idiot, Krystle, Clave laughed. *I can hear you out loud, too, with Chorus here. He hears and feeds back to me like a telepathic hearing aid. Plus, I'm good at reading lips.*

"Ohhh," I drug out a bit too long. I was likely to drool if I didn't close my yap. Clave just laughed in my head, but he held one hand to his stomach as if he were laughing out loud.

This is just so bizarre! I just can't believe I'm communicating telepathically, I thought. *Might as well since he can hear me anyway!*

Clave laughed again. *You're really funny, Krystle! I like a girl with a good sense of humor.*

Oh crap, I thought. *So, you've basically heard my every thought since the very beginning?*

Pretty much, Clave replied.

"I'm mortified," I declared. "Uhm, so when Chorus is not around, you read lips and use sign language, right?"

Yes, Clave confirmed, *And when Chorus is not around, I cannot hear a person's thoughts.*

"Well, I know a little sign language, so you may have to send Chorus away so I can stop embarrassing myself," I stated.

At this, Clave bent over, clutching his stomach, and I could hear him laughing riotously. Okay, this was a pretty funny situation, but I was still trying to get my embarrassment under wraps.

You look beautiful when you're blushing, Krystle, said Clave. *We just met, and I already like you.*

My heart skipped, and I could feel the heat rise in my cheeks. I braved looking into those gray eyes. "I like you too, Clave," I declared boldly. From where did this sudden bravado come? I suppose I should thank Taylin for taking me under her wing all those years.

Whoever Taylin is, I'm certain you could let her know; it's all you, Krystle, Clave responded. His smile was gone. That look of intensity was back in his eyes. I gulped.

"Send the bird away quick because I cannot be held responsible for the thoughts that I'm so desperately trying to keep out of my head right now."

Clave's smile broadened.

"Chorus, I like you really but, could you just flit flap away for just a bit?"

Krystle, you're killing me, Clave laughed.

More like the other way around, lady killer, I thought.

I would never hurt a lady! Clave sounded shocked.

"Relax." I laughed. "It's just an expression."

Oh, I see! An Earth expression. What does it mean? He asked.

"That's for me to know and you to find out," I declared saucily.

Fair enough, I suppose I'll let you off the hook, for now, Clave smiled. *Chorus, go find some crickets to eat.* Chorus chirped and flew away.

Immediately the line severed, and I already missed his voice.

"Better?" Clave signed and smiled.

"For now," I smiled.

"I see you've made yourself acquainted with my cousin Clave," Aura stated as she and Jasper approached us.

"Yeah, we did," I said.

Aura started signing. "Clave, this is Jasper, Krystle's brother."

"Nice to meet you," said Jasper extending his hand. Clave put out his in return and shook.

Clave signed, and Aura interpreted, "He said, nice to meet you, Jasper." They nodded and smiled at each other. "So, shall we get started with some target practice?" Aura asked.

"What are ye all goin' on about?" Benjamin asked. He and Bennigan came over, having escaped the tortures of the child hoard.

"By the way, great retaliation tactics," said Bennigan. "We were hopin' you'd pull a full-on personal attack. Well played callin' on the lil' minions, princess."

Clave signed to the brothers, "Karma's a bitch." We all laughed as Aura interpreted. "Plus, those kids are my students, and I taught them to know their enemy's weaknesses!" Clave's face showed a mischievous malevolence.

"Yeah, well, we pretty much had to offer each kid a lift on our shoulders to get them off our backs," said Benjamin. "I think those vicious lil' buggers bruise my ribs." The twins were rubbing their sides and wincing. Big babies!

We gathered up our knives and axes and made our way to the large wood rounds mounted upon a few trees. Clave started showing us how to stand, aim and release. Rhodin and Hailey sat off the side to watch. People have slipped up on the backhand as their dangerous weapons flew behind them. It happened a few times with me.

Clave and Aura competed with one another, closing in on the center. The Tucker twins could handle a blade pretty well. Jasper started to get the hang of it.

My first few tries missed completely. I was excited when my knifepoint finally hit wood; even if it was on the outer edge, it still counted to me.

Throwing sharp instruments that could kill or maim was rather stress-relieving—odd thought for a peace-loving person such as me. We were living in the wilds now, so; it was time to add to our survival skill repertoire. Hearing the sharp 'thunk' as my knife hit its mark was so satisfying.

Aura and Jasper began a spirited taunting and jeering between themselves. Jasper's competitive nature rose to the occasion, and he was determined to hit the center mark. Jasper took a semi-sideways stance and grasped the ax's handle, then lifted his arm. He drew a concentrated breath, arched his arm back, breathed out, and let loose like a pro league pitcher. Head over handle whippcd through thc air in a perfect cyclonic motion. It struck dead center with a loud crack.

Flocks of birds rushed up out of the trees in a raucous trilling cacophony. A collective, "Whoa...!" spilled out of our mouths. Aura smiled and applauded Jasper. She approached him and rewarded him with a kiss on the cheek. He stood there dumbfounded.

I was up again and tried for the stance Jasper had started. Clave came up behind me and guided my body with his. One hand cusped over mine, and his other grasped my waist. I was already finding it hard to concentrate, and he had to pull the ultimate trademark guy move. He had to know what this was doing to me. I mean, come on already! Is Chorus around to hear my thoughts? I couldn't tell at the moment.

The Twins were clearing their throats aggressively and standing with chests puffed out as if to assert some former claim. I glared at them pointedly, and they deflated.

Clave had noticed this transpire and smirked. Oh, he knew what he was doing, as my breath gave pause to his own upon my neck. Shy my ass!

Really, Chorus! Now you show up? I could hear Clave's laughter once again and feel his chest rumble against my back.

Just relax, Krystle. Line up your aim, breath, and let loose, Clave instructed.

If you only knew the multiple implications of those words, Clave, I thought back. *May I please get some space? I'm having a very difficult time concentrating being surrounded by all your alluring manliness!* Clave laughed, then stepped back. This time I was going to show him who was in control of this situation. I aimed true and let my knife fly. It hit just right of Jasper's ax with a 'thunk' and reverberating 'ping.'

"YES!" I fist-pumped the air. Everyone cheered, and I turned and curtsied like a goofball. Jasper came up and high-fived me, followed by Aura.

"That's my girl!" Benjamin and Bennigan shouted. They ran up and sandwiched me in a twin hug. Jasper went to retrieve our blades. When he turned to head back to the group, we heard a whipping and another resounding crack.

We turned around to see a large ax not only struck center, but in the exact same mark Jasper had left behind. Gawking, we all turned back to look from which it came. Tovin stood in a pose with arms folded across his great frame and an amused look on his face.

"You kids are catching on pretty quick," he commented dryly. "Lazula has asked to see you this evening. Rhodin, you are invited to stay over with the Tucker's if you like."

"Yes, Rhodin, please come. We have some games we could play," Hailey insisted.

"Okay," Rhodin agreed.

We gathered our belongings and started walking back home. Chorus had settled on my shoulder. Rhodin noticed and asked, "Krystle isn't that the same bird from the beach?"

"Yes, the one and same, his name is Chorus. He belongs to our new friend Clave." I gestured to Clave, and he smiled at Rhodin.

Tell you little brother that Chorus is my tracker, and he was happy to help you find one another, said Clave.

Can't you tell him the same way you just told me? I asked.

I will open up with your family in time. For now, I only want to talk openly with you, Clave responded.

Are you really so shy that you can't talk with a child? I asked.

No, I'm not shy, but I have my reasons, He winked. *Please, let's keep our special way of communicating just between us for now,* Clave implored.

I figured I'd go along with it. For now! *Okay, fine! But I do expect an explanation sometime soon.*

I promise. He smiled. I smiled back and relayed the hand-signed message to Rhodin.

"Thank you, Chorus," said Rhodin cheerily. Chorus flew and landed on Rhodin's shoulder and fluttered his wings. Rhodin giggled, "He's tickling me!" Chorus chirped merrily.

"Awe, he's so adorable," Hailey cooed. Chorus went to her and started nipping at the flowers in her hair. She and Rhodin were in a fit of giggles. Tovin looked back and smiled.

We made it back to our tree homes and saw Eric, Liv, Mom, and Dad sitting out around the large communal chimenea. They were holding long skewers into the flames.

"We're making s'mores," Dad called.

"They have that here?" Rhodin asked excitedly.

"Not exactly the same, but pretty darn close. Lazula has asked for you, Jasper and Aura, to stay at her house tonight. She wanted to show you how to call out." said Mom

"Really?" I asked. I looked to Jasper. "We could try to reach Aunt Cassie and Uncle Garreth."

"I'd like to do that." Jasper agreed.

"Good," Dad said. "Your mother and I have tried, but we couldn't tell if they received our messages. We couldn't get any feedback the way we were able with you kids. Perhaps you'll have a better chance."

I frowned. "I want to connect to Taylin, but I didn't see her just before. Does that mean I won't be able to reach her?" I asked.

Clave started to speak to me through our connection, also signing for everyone else. "It can be that way sometimes. If you had a strong connection with your friend before you came here, she would most likely hear you. The connection is strongest in our dreams. Your parents may have attempted to call out while your Aunt and Uncle were awake. If they are too consumed with their thoughts, it can be difficult to receive messages as well." Aura interpreted for Clave, and everyone nodded in understanding.

"Ded we naht ever call out to our family or friends?" Benjamin asked.

"Yeh, we ded, a long time ago," Eric confirmed. "We tried for a while, but ne're got anything back. We called out a few more times after Hailey was born to let em' know we had a baby girl. After that, we stopped. It was pullin' too hard on ye mahm's heart not hearin' back."

"We've made our peace and moved on," Liv declared. I could see she still held sadness as she looked down. Her hand rubbed at her chest. Eric took her hand in his and kissed her cheek.

My heart broke for them. The Tucker's had family they left behind. I could relate to the worry and anguish of not knowing. I am sure our family and friends are beside themselves right now. I felt kind of selfish like I was thoughtlessly moving on too soon. That's why I needed to try and call out to them. Whether it worked or not, at least I'll know I tried.

I felt a firm hand on my shoulder and turned to see Clave with that intense look. *Krystle, you are not selfish. Do not burden yourself with guilt. You've been through much while doing everything you could to find your parents. The moons and the Light led you here. Many times, in our lives, there will be things that are beyond our control. The mystery lies in the meaning behind it all. I hope you do not come to resent being here. Perhaps I am the selfish one because I...* he stopped abruptly.

Because you what? I asked between our outward silence.

Tovin broke our exchange, not having heard a word of it himself. "Let's get going. Lazula has prepared a meal and awaits our arrival."

"Go pack what you need," Mom told us.

Jasper and I went inside and gathered our necessities. I opened my vanity drawer and looked upon my cell phone still D.O.A., and sighed. "If only I could just power you up to at least look at pictures," I remembered that I still had my diamond earring in my pocket. I fished it out and put it back with its mate in the box. I grabbed my sketch pad and charcoals. I could still draw from memory. I took the slide down and joined everyone outside. Jasper was getting hugged by Mom. He stepped over to join Aura and Clave.

"I love you, honey," Mom said. She kissed me on the forehead. "Tell Aunt Cassie, 'I call on secret sister society.' Maybe she'll be more determined to get in touch. She could never resist the opportunity to gossip or tell me things she didn't want your Nana or Grandpa to know."

"Okay, I will, Mom." I knew that the "secret sister society" was something they shared growing up. They had to keep secrets between them no matter how desperately they may have wanted to tell others. They called to order on Friday nights in their treehouse.

Dad hugged me and said, "Have a good night, sweetheart. Tell Uncle Garreth not to jump too quickly on any big decisions. Love you, kiddo."

"Okay, Dad. Love you too," I kissed him on the cheek and turned to go.

"Cannae, we go too?" Bennigan asked. "Perhaps we could reach out to our people."

"Sadly, ye were too young to have a tight familial connection. So, I doubt if ye knew who ye was talkin' to. They would probably think they're goin' senile being as old as they are by now," said Liv. "They have more en likely written us off as departed, and you'd scare the shite outta them. They'd think they was hearin' from ghosts. Our family was very superstitious; they was."

"Yer heads are still too far up yer arses to properly concentrate," Eric scoffed. "Lazula dohs naht need ya two around with yer tomfoolery."

The twins hung their heads down in defeat. I felt bad for them. More time had passed on Earth than it had here. Their Grammy probably passed on, and any friends would've long forgotten them. They were so young when they walked the Light's path to this world.

On the ride upriver to Lazula's, I had started sketching a portrait of Taylin. I never wanted to forget my best friend's face. I didn't think I could, but it was nice to have an image to look upon, even if it were not in the flesh. Tovin and Clave were paddling the canoe. Aura sat next to me, and Jasper sat behind us.

"You are very good at drawing people. Is this your friend Taylin?" Aura asked.

"Yes," I replied. "She's so beautiful, inside and out. I was envious of her at one point. Boys would gravitate towards her. But she told me she was envious of me too. She said the only difference between us was that she paid attention to them, and I was too shy to notice. She told me boys were always looking at me but never approached because I'd duck and run. She said I gave them a complex."

"So, you never had a boyfriend or dated?" Aura asked.

I looked ahead to Clave paddling with his back to us. I looked around for Chorus and didn't see him. He must have flown off to find his dinner and settle in a tree for the evening. Clave's lack of body language indicated he couldn't hear what we were saying. Jasper already knew my tragic dating history. I doubted Tovin would care. His concern was for his daughter and my brother's intentions.

"I went to a party one time with Taylin. Some boy approached and started dancing with us. Taylin broke away with another boy. I felt awkward with this boy named Travis. He was nice enough. We talked for a while outside. He was my first kiss, but no sparks. We ended up being friendly acquaintances passing in the halls at school, nothing else."

"I understand," said Aura. "I have no time for boys. They act like young Yehati swinging and grunting. I'm not impressed. I've always been faster, stronger, independent. Tovin insists I was always headstrong since I was a young child. Also, I would never partake in a petty rivalry over a boy."

"Taylin and I always said that no boy would ever come between true friendship," I stated. "Speaking of boys acting like Yehati, I wonder how to broach the subject of the Tucker twins. I've never been in a situation like this before. I must tell the brothers they're strictly in the friend zone. I don't want to be the type of girl that strings them along."

Aura laughed. "Do you want Tovin to put those two in their place? My father is an expert at scaring unwanted suitors away." She came closer and whispered in my ear, "Jasper is the first to stand up to Tovin. He's the first boy to impress me." She winked

I laughed. "No, I don't think that will be necessary." I leaned and whispered to her. "I'm glad you're not completely impervious to all boys. My brother seems entranced by your wild feminine wiles. He is also a respectful gentleman. Our Dad would punish him for behaving otherwise."

"No worries," Aura whispered. "Jasper is not in the friend zone. I have no intentions of stringing him along, nor will I give myself fully until I know his intentions are true. He'll have to prove himself worthy to my father."

"What are you two conspiring?" Jasper whisper shouted. "I want in the loop, especially if it's about those two incredulous numbskulls. They seem incapable of catching on that Krystle is not interested."

Aura and I both laughed. Jasper looked at Aura and smiled. He certainly was entranced by her laughter and beauty.

I looked forward, and Clave was looking at me with a smile. He winked and turned ahead. I felt my cheeks heat up. Aura noticed the exchange and nudged me with her arm. I looked at her and bit my lips, trying to hide the obvious attraction. She gave me a knowing look. I gave her the "don't say anything" stare. She put a finger to her lips. "Your secret's safe with me."

Tovin and Clave did not join us at Lazula's. Jasper, Aura, Lazula, and I sat around the fire inside her home and updated her on our life here so far. She looked impressed with our capabilities and newly acquired skills. Aura mentioned me helping Clave as a teaching assistant. Lazula was delighted and agreed.

I showed her my sketch of Taylin, and her eyes widened. "This is your friend on Earth? She looks like someone I once knew." She cleared her throat. "But that was a long-past memory."

I saw her discreetly wipe away a tear. I wanted to ask her what she meant, but Lazula quickly moved on. "I have everything ready for your calling. Krystle, your connection with the Fire Moon will aid you. You and Jasper will hold hands, so he may also have a stronger connection. The connections between our worlds are stronger when there are people close to us on the other side. Strong emotional connections bridge the way. The receiver needs to be in a dream state or close to it when the Light chooses to appear."

"Do you know when the Light is about to choose when a crossing is due to happen?" I asked.

"I have premonitions, but it's not an exact timing," Lazula responded. "But with you and your brothers, I was anticipating it."

"What was the difference?" I asked.

"Your family is the ninth generation to cross to our world within my lifetime. Every family before yours was chosen and crossed throughout your world's history. I never knew who was coming. I just felt it when it happened. Each generation has contributed positively. When your parents crossed, I felt a strong connection to the Grand Glacial Moon. It was predetermined, but the timing was dependent on something unexpected. Your mother chose a path, a moment that lined itself with a purpose. The pull she described was so strong, unlike anyone else who had crossed."

"Once your parents arrived, they sensed your determination to find them. That's how they were able to call to you so easily. The Fire Moons call for you made the Light's appearance a second time in the same place possible. I felt the Fire Moons plea as well, and for the first time, I knew who was coming and when to expect your arrival."

"The Light had never appeared in the same place twice before?" I pondered this question out loud. "If my mother hadn't chosen some action in the exact moment in time, she wouldn't have been called by the Light? Yet, it was predestined? But then the Fire Moon chose me as a champion to some indeterminable cause? What does all of this mean?"

"I hope not to upset you when I say this, Krystle, but I believe it was only ever supposed to be you," said Lazula.

"Only me?" I couldn't help but feel upset by that implication. Lazula's next response justified my feelings.

"It means that you were the ONLY one who was supposed to be here," said Lazula.

"So, I would have arrived here on my own, without my family?" My heart clenched in my chest. I felt heaviness; the loneliness of that thought felt brutal. A different path would have left my parents and brothers behind, searching for me. I'd be one more face on a poster with no possibility of return. At least no chance that I could see. Would I have found my way to the village? Would I have learned to call to my family?

Lazula, seeing my distress, set my mind at ease, "But it seems the moons had conspired, and a purpose for your family members allotted. If I had control, I would have made it so in their stead. I am most grateful everything worked as it has."

I let out an exhaustive breath, "Me as well."

Jasper squeezed my hand, and I looked at him. “Krystle, you are stronger than you think. And, we would never have given up on you if it were the other way around. You know this. Plus, if Mom’s crossing were predestined, we would have been here eventually anyway.”

“But, can you image Jasper? We wouldn’t have known the timing of such an occurrence. The Tucker twins would be the same age as Dad by now if they were still back on Earth. Yet, here they are only eleven years later by this world’s time and the same age as us. I don't know how that works.”

“Really?” Jasper was stunned. “I didn’t even know that.”

“I will explain this another time,” said Lazula. “For now, let’s concentrate on your purpose for being here this evening.”

I felt myself having to shake my nerves away from the previous conversation. I took a deep breath and focused on Lazula. She took out four stones from a pouch. She explained each came from the four different moons. She laid them out in a line before us. She started chanting in her native tongue.

“Close your eyes and concentrate on the person you want to reach. If they are receptive on the other side, you will feel a pull in your mind. You will be able to see within their dream and send your message. Communication will not be full conversations, just words, and pieces. Concentrate on precise words you want to relay,” she instructed.

Chapter 12

I closed my eyes and concentrated on Aunt Cassie first. Lazula continued her chant. I felt Jasper's hand tighten around mine. My body felt like it was sinking into the ground, but I remained calm. I felt the tug in my mind. My eyes opened, and I was no longer in Lazula's home. I was up in a treehouse.

"Gemma...Gemma...Where are you?" A little girl's voice called. "There you are!" A head full of little blonde curls popped up through an opening from the floor. The little girl shined a flashlight at me, and I held my hand in front of my eyes and squinted. She climbed the rest of the way through then settled cross-legged on the floor in front of me.

"Aunt Cassie?" I asked.

"Gemma, you're acting weird again. Do I need to tell Mom you're not feeling well," she asked? I looked at Aunt Cassie's child form and realized I was in her dream. Of course, she wouldn't recognize me as her niece. She looked to be ten years old. I didn't exist yet.

"Just playing with you," I said.

She handed me a glass soda bottle and opened another for herself. I felt the cold and watery condensation on my hand. She took a swig and released a satisfied, "Ahh..."

"What did you say?" she asked. "Gemma, you know I've been looking for you all day. I was getting worried."

"I'm okay, Cassie," I said. "Try to find the Light again. I'm there."

"The Light?" She frowned. "What light?"

"I'm there; find the Light," I said again. I took hold of Cassie's hand and looked into her eyes. "I'm okay, Cassie, we all are."

Cassie's eyes widened. She looked frightened. "Who are you?" she cried. "Where's Gemma?"

"It's me, Krystle, your niece. Aunt Cassie..."

"I don't have a niece," she yelled. She tried to pull her hand away from mine. "You're crazy. Who are you? What are you doing in our clubhouse?"

"I'm Krystle," I repeated. "Gemma gave me a message for you."

"What?" she screeched. "Let go of me!"

"Girls, are you alright?" A woman's voice came from outside the clubhouse window.

"Mom..." Cassie started to yell. I clasped a hand over Cassie's mouth.

"Shhh! Stop panicking. Let me tell you the message," I whispered. "I'm not going to hurt you, and Gemma is okay. Look for the Light. Oh yeah, and don't tell anyone else, you have to swear it on Secret Sister Society."

Aunt Cassie's eye went round, and then she nodded her head in sudden understanding. "Krystle?" She said my name in question. A look of recognition was dawning on her features. "Wait, where are you going? Come back! Where do I find the Light? Where are you guys? We've been…searching…searching…" her voice echoed away, and everything around me started fading. I tried to shout out to her again, but my voice echoed back to me.

New scenery faded into view. I was sitting next to Taylin in our high school cafeteria. "Taylin, oh my God, I've missed you!" I reached out to touch her, but my hand went straight through her. It was like I was a specter, or she was. I really couldn't tell. "Taylin?"

She didn't turn her head to acknowledge me. Was she awake? Was she dreaming? I couldn't tell either way. Taylin pushed her lunch tray away with its barely eaten contents. She pulled out a notebook and started writing.

Tomorrow will be a month since Krystle and her family had gone missing. I've not heard anything new from Cassie or Garreth as they continue the search. Everyone else has written them off as dead, but I don't believe it. I can feel it in my gut. I've been begging and pleading with my mother to let me go with Cassie and Garreth on their next mission. They said they hadn't seen the Light since the night Krystle, Jasper, and Rhodin went through. I know they are alive somewhere. It's like I can feel some connection to a place unknown. I may have to pull my resources and, lifelong grounding be damned, just go. Life has not been the same since you left, Krystle. I can't eat, can't sleep. People look at me like a social pariah. I look like death incarnate. I can't function without my BFF. I lost my sweet sister, the yin to my yang. I miss you so much, Krystle! I won't give up!

Tears trickled down her face as she closed the notebook, and she tucked it away in her backpack. She madly wiped the tears away from her cheeks. She gave the stink eye to a couple of girls who passed, and they quickly averted their gaze. I looked at Taylin. She did look tired with dark circles under her eyes. Her usual rosy glow had turned ashen.

"Oh, Taylin, I'm so sorry!" Tears started down my cheeks. "I'm okay. I miss you so much! I wish there were a way you could hear me right now. Find the Light."

"Find the Light," Taylin repeated.

"Wait, Taylin, did you just hear me?" I asked with hope risen in my voice.

"Krystle?" Taylin questioned. "I'm losing my mind. I need to sleep."

"It's me, Taylin; I'm here." I watched her rise from her seat and shouldered her backpack. "Find the Light, Taylin," I shouted. She started walking away, and I began to panic. I tried to follow her, but I was stuck in place, now sitting cross-legged on the floor.

"Taylin," I cried out. I tried to reach out and grab her. Everything started to fade away. Just before I lost total sight of her, she turned and looked back directly at me.

"I promise, Krystle. I'll find the Light. I'll find you...."

I felt my body jerk. Darkness surrounded me. I felt hands on my shoulders shaking me. "Krystle, come back to us!" The voice sounded panicked. I blinked my eyes open. A shape was over me, blurred. Then my vision began to focus.

"Lazula?" My voice creaked. She helped me to sit up and handed me a cup, encouraging me to drink. I took a sip. Herbal warmth flowed over my tongue and down my throat.

"I have never seen such a connection before," said Lazula, her head shaking. "Who were you talking to? You were mumbling. It sounded like full conversations."

"I reached Aunt Cassie. I could tell she was dreaming. She was a little girl in her and Mom's clubhouse."

"There was someone else," Lazula observed. "The connection was so strong; I could feel it like waves rolling through my spirit."

"It was Taylin. I think she was awake. She couldn't hear me," I started to shake. "That is, she couldn't hear me until I mentioned the Light."

Lazula's eyes went wide in wonderment. "That's never been possible before."

"What's never been possible before?" I asked.

"If she were awake, she wouldn't have heard you at all," said Lazula.

“She knew about the Light before I said anything about it. She was writing in a journal about Cassie and Garreth not seeing it since the night we came through.”

“Do you think the Light is going to make an appearance somewhere close to Taylin? You did say people can hear a call if the Light is near, right?” I asked Lazula.

“That could very well be,” said Lazula. “If your Aunt and Uncle are still waiting for it to appear in the same place you came through, they will be disappointed.”

“She was at school. That’s over a thousand miles away from where we were. If Cassie and Garreth are home now, we should try to reach them again to let them know,” I cried. “They’d be making an unnecessary trip.”

“Either that or Taylin plans to make good on her intentions to go with them,” said Aura.

“Taylin said she felt a connection to a place unknown. Well, that’s what she wrote in her journal,” I said.

“It could be her strong connection to you, but there could be another reason,” said Lazula.

“What reason?” I asked.

“Another moon calling,” said Lazula. “If it’s so, she will find a piece from one cast out to her. The Fire Moon did for you, and the Grand Glacial Moon did for Gemma.”

“I did get a visual from Uncle Garreth,” said Jasper. “I saw him; he had maps with markings spread out over a table. There were notes and something about moon phases.

He was talking to someone about historical locations and mystical occurrences. He said a year. 1985."

"That was the year the Tuckers arrived," I cried out. "Uncle Garreth is researching past events. He's on to something."

"So, it seems," said Lazula. "Your family is very resourceful. I sense they may find their way. It is only a matter of time. Could you see any kind of pattern of the markings on those maps?"

"I couldn't tell," said Jasper. "I only caught a momentary glimpse. Plus, he was pacing back and forth, which further obscured my view."

"This is a good start," said Lazula, "I can only hope this information gets to the right people."

"Is this world supposed to remain a secret from our world?" I asked.

"Each person who has come through the Light never knew of our world before arrival," said Lazula.

"Have people from this world come through the Light to Earth?" I asked.

"Only a few," Lazula said solemnly. "But that is a story for another day. The night calls for my weary bones to rest. I feel I have dispersed much energy in this calling." She got up slowly and went to lie on her bed. Aura did not say anything but looked concerned. She took a drink to Lazula's bedside and pulled blankets over her great-grandmother.

"Rest well," she said and kissed Lazula's head. I looked at Jasper questioningly. He returned the look. I felt like there was something Lazula was not telling us. Perhaps it was something from which she was trying to protect us or her own heart.

I thought of how Taylin's image struck Lazula and how she wiped away a stray tear. She lost someone, and Taylin's image was a reminder. She hadn't said as much, but she did have a story to tell. I had to know. I looked over to her bed and watched the blankets slowly rise and fall with her breaths. Who did she lose?

The next morning Tovin and Clave returned. Chorus landed on my shoulder. *Good morning Krystle,* Clave's voice rang cheerily in her head. *Ready to come to class with me today?*

Yes, I smiled as I gave Chorus a loving little head-scratching. Chorus leaned into my finger and chittered his appreciation. *We should get Rhodin and Hailey.*

Your Mom and Dad will bring them to us, said Clave. *We should be going. Class meets a few miles up the river. It's close to your mother's new medical practice.*

Oh wow, that was fast! My mom's clinic is already up and running? It's only been a couple of days. I noticed Aura was still sitting at Lazula's bedside.

"Is Lazula okay?" I asked.

Aura gave me a reassuring smile. "I think last night was a bit much for her. She just needs a little extra rest today. I'll be staying with her. No worries."

I gave Aura a pointed look, "You know I get suspicious when you say those two words."

Lazula's voice rose from under the cocoon of blankets. "I'm fine, child. I'll be up and at the day in a few more hours. Go. You have a class to teach." Her arm lifted from the blankets, and she waved me away.

Clave chuckled. *Best not to undermine grandmother's authority. The children are looking forward to seeing you again.*

I followed Clave out. "Okay, I'll see you later, Aura," I called back. "Lazula, feel better."

"Thank you, Krystle. I'll see you later," Aura called back.

Jasper and Tovin were waiting in the canoe. Jasper had a few new accessories for holding his ax and knife, making him look more like a smaller version of Tovin.

"What are you looking at?" Jasper asked.

"Your new leather holsters," I said with a smirk. "Nice!"

"Yeah, well, it helps to have while on the move," Jasper responded.

Clave climbed aboard and held out his hand to me. I took his hand and felt my stomach flutter. I dipped my head to watch my step and conceal my blushing cheeks. Clave sat down next to me and his thigh brushed against mine. The proximity was sending pleasant tingles throughout my body. I looked forward and swallowed nervously.

Trying my best to keep my composure, I asked Jasper, “Where are you off to today?” I hoped the nervousness I felt didn’t project into my voice. Then I remembered Chorus was on my shoulder, and Clave could hear my thoughts. I felt Clave’s thigh muscle tense up beside me. He was quiet. Was he feeling nervous as well? He seemed well composed and confident when I met him just yesterday. He whistled, and Chorus landed on his shoulder.

Jasper spoke up in answer to my question. “Tovin has another project for me.” His voice had an uncomfortable edge to it. “Dad and the Tuckers are meeting up with us.”

“We’ll be dropping you and Clave off on the way,” said Tovin. “Aura will be by to get you this afternoon.”

My uncle is a man of many words, Clave joked. I turned to look at him and smiled. He stared back at me. *If she only knew what looking into her eyes was doing to me!*

Same, I thought.

Krystle, did you just hear my thoughts? Clave questioned.

Uhm, I wasn’t supposed to? I asked.

No one has done that before, said Clave. *They only hear what I want them to hear, and it’s never my personal thoughts.*

Oh! I exclaimed. *Sorry, I wasn’t trying to; I just heard it.*

Don't be sorry, said Clave. *I'm just surprised.*

Well, I suppose it's only fair since you can hear all of mine. Perhaps you have met your match, I spouted back playfully.

Perhaps I have, in more ways than one, Clave responded. His voice sounded smooth and predatory. I opened my sketchbook on my lap and started flipping the pages back and forth quickly to fan the flustering heat rising in my face.

Anyway, what will we be teaching the children today? I asked to quickly change the subject and primitive atmospheric pressure building between us. I trained my focus on the cool, clear water flowing around us. I enjoyed watching all the beautiful fish swimming around in their pleasant environment.

Clave put on that gorgeous dimpled smile. *Most of the kids know sign language and a bit of English, but they are a mix of ages and skill levels. Perhaps you could draw pictures and teach them words by visualization. You can sit in at first and observe while I sign. You, in turn, can brush up on your signing skills as well.*

That sounds reasonable enough, I agreed. *Will you be speaking out telepathically to me while you sign?*

Yes, you and the students, said Clave. *Only one student is deaf, and he doesn't have an animal interpreter connection. The rest of my students are a mix of native and Earthlings. One of which is your brother Rhodin.*

Well, Rhodin is going to be surprised by your gift. Does Hailey already know? I asked.

Yes, and she has sworn to secrecy as well as the other children. There are certain people I want to keep up boundaries around. I'd have a literal headache having to converse with said people if word got out.

Two of said people being the Tucker Twins, I said knowingly. *You mentioned their little sister, so it has to be them.*

You do understand, don't you? I'm not doing it to be a jerk, but I find their company a tad off-putting at times, Clave said this while running his hand down his face like he was scraping off the muck.

No, I understand. I like the Tucker twins, but they can be a bit discombobulating, I agreed.

Clave nodded, looked up, and pointed; *Our pupils await.* The canoe slowed, and we pulled up to the stone dock where ten children stood smiling and waving. I remembered seeing a few of them yesterday. I smiled back at my comrades in the throwdown and torture of the Tucker Twins.

Clave jumped out and helped me up. *You've got all your things?* Clave asked.

I do, I answered. I turned back and waved to Japer and Tovin as they started to pull away. "See later Jasper and Tovin."

"Ahtee Krystle," said Tovin. "Enjoy your day."

Dad came by and dropped off Rhodin and Hailey. "Behave yourselves." He looked to the kids and then at Clave and me.

"You will, Rhodin and Hailey. Right?" I asked.

"I always behave," said Rhodin.

"That's not who I'm talking to," said Dad. He winked, and I glared back at him.

"Really? Are you going to be that kind of Dad?" I thought. I heard Clave laugh.

Co-conspirators, I thought. *Betrayal!*

"Everyone will behave, Dad," I said through a strained smile. My dad laughed and started walking back to Eric and the twins. Eric was grinning at me, and I opened my sketchbook, pretending to be all business. I could hear Benjamin and Bennigan complaining about not being able to attend class. They continued to grumble as they followed their father.

Ahtee and good morning, my minions, Clave's voice came through as he signed. The children laughed, and Rhodin's eyes widened in surprise. *For those of you who are new here, I'd like to say welcome. You can hear me speaking without moving my mouth, thanks to Chorus, my telepathic interpreter. Rhodin and Hailey, please approach.*

Rhodin looked hesitant but stepped forward when Hailey encouraged him. *Now hold up your hands and repeat this pledge in your mind. I'll be able to hear you,* said Clave. Rhodin looked at me, shocked. I smiled and nodded to him in encouragement.

I, Rhodin Genstone, and Hailey Tucker, do solemnly swear...

"Why am I doing this again?" asked Hailey. "I already promised I wouldn't tell a soul."

You're leading by example for Rhodin, Clave explained.

"Oh, okay then," said Hailey. She smiled and held up her hand. Rhodin followed her lead.

You promise not to tell another soul outside our class that I, Mr. Clave Frost, can talk to you in your heads. To reveal this to anyone outside this group will result in dipping in the river. And believe me, you don't want that. It will freeze your toes and finger right off, said Clave.

"You can't do that!" I admonished.

And I haven't had to, said Clave. *The children here understand what it means to hold the trust and what happens when they break it. Right, my students?*

A collective "Yes" and nodding of fists answered.

Just go along, Krystle. I would never touch a hair on any of these kids' heads. Think of it as a mild scare tactic, an initiation to a club. I'm not going to say or do anything detrimental to their young impressionable minds.

"That's debatable," I said. Clave smirked back at me. "Fine, just take it easy on Rhodin. He looks intimidated."

"I swear I won't tell a soul," said Rhodin. He puffed out his chest. "I'm a man of honor."

I bit my lips together. Hailey was looking at Rhodin with dreamy eyes. Too young! Too young! What do they put in the water here?

The Genstones have got it going on, Clave replied. He waggled his thick dark brows at me. I laughed.

Very good, Rhodin, Clave replied. *Now, if you will all take a seat, we will begin our lessons for today.*

I watched in fascination as Clave spoke telepathically and signed along. The kids followed along, and I was learning as well. I started sketching Clave as he went about his lesson. The kids laughed as Clave mimicked the Tucker Twins pleading for mercy.

I drew each of the students' faces so I could learn their names. I lifted the drawings and pointed, and each student would tell me, and I wrote it under their image. Clave gave the kids each some paper and charcoal pencils to practice writing. I encouraged them to try and draw something they liked. There were drawings of family and animals and foods. One boy drew a likeness of me.

That's Shane, said Clave. *Looks like I may have some competition.*

I gave him an incredulous look. He signed spoke into my mind. *Just kidding! But it looks like you have your first student crush, Ms. Genstone.*

Oh really! Only my first? I folded my arms in front of my chest.

It may be too soon to say, but I think my heart got away from me when Chorus first saw you on the beach.

I was frozen. What did Clave mean by 'when Chorus first saw me on the beach?'

Uhm, I couldn't seem to address the elephant in the room at the moment. Instead, I cleared my throat and finally snapped out of my frozen state. *I know I saw you before on the bridge. I never saw you before that. What does Chorus have to do with…*

I can also see through Chorus's eyes, Clave admitted. *That was the first time I saw you, Krystle Genstone.*

My jaw dropped, and I was gawking like a fish out of water. *Uh, Clave? Just how many times before have you seen me? And how much of me?*

Clave laughed, *Don't worry, Krystle, I'm a gentleman. I would never send Chorus to spy on you in such a way. At least not until you ask me to.*

My face must have turned three shades of Fire Stone. *Clave, this conversation is inappropriate in the classroom.* I bit my lips closed.

They can't hear us. Clave motioned his chin towards the kids, all seated and concentrating on their assignment.

Still not the time or place, I said.

Okay. Later then, said Clave. His look was devilish. I groaned out in frustration, and some of the kids, including Rhodin, looked up at me.

"Just having trouble getting my drawing right," I said. Rhodin just shrugged and went back to work.

So, is it a date? Clave asked.

Huh? I heard him just fine, but my heart was beating so loud. I put my fingers in my ears and wiggled. It didn't work the same way on a heart set in chariot as it did to relieve tinnitus.

What are you doing? asked Clave. He looked amused.

I'm just trying to relieve some ringing in my ears, I responded.

Hmm, I've never experienced that before, said Clave. *Can you give me a demonstration?*

Yeah, I guess, I shrugged. *It's like your ears are yelling eeeeeeeeeee...... at you and won't stop.*

That sounds annoying, said Clave.

It is, I agreed.

So, do you want to go out with me later? Clave asked.

Oh, he hadn't let up on that. Uhm, sure, yeah! I slapped my hand to my forehead. He heard that remark.

I did, He confirmed and smirked.

I slapped my hand to my forehead again and groaned out loud. All of the kids did the same. Are they mocking me? Rhodin was the only one who didn't do it but looked around at his classmates like they lost their marbles.

Are we teaching the kids Earthly gestures of frustration? Clave laughed.

Could you please explain to them I didn't mean it as part of their lesson, I pleaded? Clave smiled, then he signed and explained what I had done and what it meant. They all nodded their heads and laughed when they finally understood.

After the day's lessons let out, the kids went out to play. Aura showed up. She had walked here. "How is Lazula? I asked.

"She's back up and bouncing around without a care in the world," said Aura. "I passed by Gemma's new clinic. She asked me to bring you, Rhodin, and Hailey over."

We arrived at a tree and entered. The setup was just like a professional clinic with a small waiting area and some partitions. No one was sitting out waiting. Slow day, I guess. Mom came out from around the partitions, "Oh hey, kids! Welcome to my new practice."

"This is nice, Mom." I looked around, impressed with how 'clinical' it looked. A man and woman came from the back room.

"These are your children, Gemma?" The woman who asked had an accent that reminded me of the people we met in Nigeria on our mission trip. She and the man had gorgeous glowing ebony skin with dark hair and deep brown eyes. The woman smiled, "I can tell this is your daughter. She looks like you. Nice to meet you, Krystle, and you too, Rhodin."

“Krystle, Rhodin. This is Drs. Abeo and Daraja Ibekwe. They have been here since Earth year 1977.” They didn’t look any older than Mom. I’m no longer surprised since I learned about the Tucker’s. I still didn’t understand the timing of how the Light worked. Lazula told us she would explain that. I shook both Daraja and Abeo’s hands. “Nice to meet you, Doctors Ibekwe.”

“How was your first day teaching?” asked Daraja.

“It was fun,” I said. I smiled and looked back at Clave.

“Yeah, I really like school here,” said Rhodin.

“That’s wonderful,” said Mom. “We are about to have lunch. Let’s go outside and eat.”

“How has your day been, Mom? Have you had any patients?”

“A few sutures and bellyaches. Oh, and a birth,” Mom said excitedly. “Though not what I’m used to,” she said. Abeo and Daraja laughed at her statement.

“What?” I smiled and chuckled.

“Your mother was preparing for a human birth but looked confused when Abeo told her the patient was in active labor out back,” said Daraja. Abeo was cracking up and clapping his hands.

“Oh, the look on your face Gemma! It was priceless!” Abeo and Daraja laughed again.

“Who was the patient?” I asked.

"Come, I'll show you," said Mom. "Rhodin and Hailey will love seeing the babies too."

"Babies?" I asked.

"Come on! This way!" Mom waved us to follow her hurriedly. We followed her around behind the clinic. A small mama burro stood nursing two mini versions of herself.

"Awww," cooed Hailey and Rhodin. "They're so cute!"

"I guess I can add veterinary labor and delivery to my resume," said Mom. "It's so strange how being here has changed my perspective on things. I'm broadening my horizons. I realize how all life is important in ways I've never pondered before."

"I'm feeling the same way," I said. "I wish Taylin, Cassie and Garreth could be here with us."

Mom hugged me to her. "I know, Krystle. I miss them too. But I think we are making the best of our situation as is. I am so grateful that Dad and I have you kids here with us."

"Me too, Mom." Rhodin snuggled into us, and Hailey joined. We wrapped our arms around them.

"I am very happy for my new friends," said Hailey.

"Aww, sweetie," said Mom. "We are happy for you and your family too." I heard someone sniffing. We turned to see Abeo with his arm around Daraja. Daraja was wiping tears from her face.

We opened our hug circle to Daraja and Abeo. I realized we had it better than most that came through the Light. They had family left behind. We had room for our new family here. That did some good to ease some of the heartaches from those we missed. We were all in this together.

Chapter 13

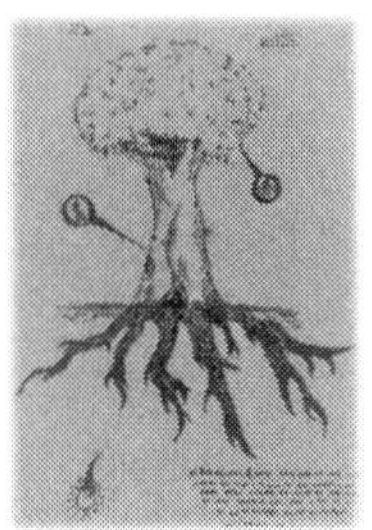

I dressed after having come home and taken a shower. That clay soap was miraculous. My skin was glowing and so smooth, and my hair smelled of citrus and honeysuckle. I let it hang loose freely to dry.

Are you ready? Clave asked.

"Chorus, you better have your blinders on," I told the little red bird sitting on my windowsill.

I promise, only he can see you right now, said Clave.

"And how would I know you're telling the truth?" I asked.

I can only ask you to take my word as a man of honor, Clave stated.

"Where are you right now?" I asked.

Downstairs in your house making polite conversation with Flint and Gemma. Aura and Jasper are coming with us, as Tovin and your father politely requested we chaperone one another.

"And what about Benjamin and Bennigan?" I asked. "Seems unfair to leave them out."

I didn't ask them out on a date, said Clave. *Though, if they don't mind being each other's date, I don't mind if they tag along.*

"That's just wrong, Clave. What have you got against them?" I asked.

Nothing, but I know they like you, Krystle. And they wouldn't be much help in setting the right tone for the evening. I'd like to hold a lady's hand without belligerent background protests, Clave commented.

Nervous energy hummed through me. I tried to divert that energy into an argument for the Tucker's. "I just feel bad for them. They deserve happiness."

They have had many opportunities to be graced by the lovely young women of the village. A few having been my relatives. They have some maturing yet to accomplish if they seek something true. The ladies' words, not my own, Clave included.

The Bens aside. I beg of you to be my savior, as right now, Tovin and your father have teamed up to ground the value of a young lady's virtue into Jasper and me.

I snuck a peek around my curtain and saw Clave and Jasper standing at attention as Tovin and Dad talked to them in stern tones. Aura and my mom sat at the table, whispering to one another.

"Well, at least they are finding something in common. I'll be right down. Hang in there for a minute."

Krystle, please, begged Clave. *If not for me, then for your poor dear brother. I see steam coming out of his ears.*

"Keep your big girl panties on!" I guess I had some immaturity issues of my own to work out still. Mr. Spy Bird Man still had some explaining to do.

Huh? I don't own any big girl panties! Another Earth expression, I take it? Clave asked.

"Ding, ding, ding! Winner!" I announced.

What did I win? I heard the devious smile in Clave's voice.

I grabbed the pole and slid down. When my feet hit the ground, Clave looked over and smiled. Everyone else turned to look. "I'm ready. Where are we going?" Jasper looked relieved at my arrival.

"Not far," said Aura. "We're going to hunt some lightning bugs and hang out."

"Aura, Krystle," Tovin called us and pointed to front and center. "You boys are relieved. You can wait outsidc." Jasper blew out a breath, and he and Clave turned to walk out. "It wasn't that long ago; I was a teenage boy, believe it or not."

"Is that so, Dad?" Aura asked. Tovin glared at her. "Sorry, I'm listening." Aura looked up with a sincere expression on her face. I could see her mouth tremor as she tried to hold a respectful decorum. I was holding my breath just watching her.

"As I was saying," Tovin continued. "I hold you to great expectations as always, daughter, as I know Flint does the same with Krystle. We are putting our trust in both of you to keep those boys in line. Are we clear?

"Crystal!" Aura and I both said. Then we burst out laughing. "Sorry, Tovin. The response was evident to the question. And, well, Krystle, that's my name." Mom was laughing in the background, and Dad was chuckling.

Tovin groaned, "Shiyavas!" He shook his head.

"Just behave, and don't be out all night," Dad said.

"Okay. We won't do anything more than what you and Mom would've when you were teenagers," I stated.

"Uhm, on second thought..." Dad started.

"Flint." Mom put her hand on Dad's arm. "Just let the kids have fun. I trust them."

That was our cue! "Okay. Love ya. See ya. Bye." I grabbed Aura's arm and turned her with me to go out the door.

"Don't worry, Dad," Aura called back to Tovin. "You taught me well." Tovin let out an acknowledging grunt as we passed the thresh hold.

"Time to make a run for freedom, or we'll be stuck here all night," Aura said. We charged off toward the riverbank in a fit of laughter.

At night the honeysuckle field looked like something out of a fairytale. All the lightning bugs were out dancing around the flowers, blinking like Christmas lights. Clave pointed to the ground. I watched in fascination with each step we took.

I was in complete awe. “What causes the ground to light around our footsteps?” One step was green, purple, and yellow-the next red, blue and pink. It reminded me of one of those dance games in the arcades, only this was all part of nature. The colors blended like grainy bioluminescent sand under a black light. An animated movement scurried out from under our feet and surrounded each foot in individual impressions.

“Those are tiny insects that only come out from underground out night. They are fire beetles. Their granules left behind as refuse, we gather for our fire powder,” Aura explained. “They are fast and move out from under our footsteps, creating the colorful patterns around our feet.”

Watch this, Clave signed. I could still hear him telepathically. Chorus was pulling a late shift. Clave signed for Jasper and Aura’s benefit, still keeping the connection between us private. He laid down on the ground, and the beetles scurried out of the way.

A colorful outline surrounded his whole body. He stretched out his arms, and he moved his legs out and in. He looked like Da Vinci’s “Vitruvian Man” making a bioluminescent snow angel. The beetles scurried back and forth, quickly creating a colorful wave effect

“Whoa, man, that is trippy,” said Jasper. Aura laid down with the top of her head, meeting Claves, and started the same motion. “Alright, I’m in,” Jasper exclaimed. He laid out perpendicular to Aura and Clave with his head at theirs.

I started laughing, “Wow, that’s awesome. I wish you could see what I’m seeing.”

Come join us, said Clave. I laid down, and we were four bodies on the ground like North, South, East, and West. Our movements synced up, and I could just make out the glow coming up in my periphery. If someone were looking down from above, they’d see a full circular sweeping light.

Our hands and feet touched and retreated with each full sweep. We were all laughing. Clave stopped on the next connection with my hand. First, our knuckles touched, then our fingers intertwined. I drew in a ragged breath as I felt the warmth of his hand.

I had the feeling the same thing happened between Jasper and Aura because we all stopped moving. All was quiet and still amongst us. I stared up at the stars and breathed in the moment. I relished in the feeling of Clave's fingers stroking mine. The air grew cooler, and the fog of our collective breaths rose above us.

“Perhaps we should make a fire,” Aura suggested. “Jasper, would you help me get some rocks?” She sat up, and Jasper did as well.

“Sure,” said Jasper. I sat up and watched as Jasper and Aura held hands while they walked away. Clave sat up, and we turned to face each other, seated with our legs crisscrossed. Chorus settled quietly in my lap. I smiled and scratched his feathery little head.

I think he’s up past his bedtime. I smiled as Chorus puffed up his feathers. *Will we be able to communicate still if he falls asleep?*

Yes, said Clave. *Are you cold?*

No, I'm okay. I looked around. *I didn't see where Jasper and Aura went off to.*

It's difficult to have a one-on-one conversation with Aura having to interpret for me. Clave reached for my hand once more.

I think Jasper feels like he's in for a battle with Tovin. He and Tovin had a confrontation on our way here.

Your brother stood up to my uncle and is still alive? Clave's eyebrows rose. *That's amazing!*

You've seen my dad, right? He can be rather intimidating, I stated.

You've got me there! Clave chuckled. *I was feeling the pressure as I got the lecture back there.*

My Uncle Garreth is a pretty tough character too. Jasper acquired the ability to stand his ground with our Dad and Uncle as role models.

That's good, considering, said Clave.

Considering what? I asked.

There are traditions with our people in regards to courtship. Jasper needs to be able to stand his ground to prove worthy. Some things have changed a little over time as new arrivals brought modern perspectives with different cultural heritages, Clave explained.

"I've seen many examples around the world in our travels. Where I'm from, people give themselves too freely in more intimate circumstances. There are not many true, long-lasting connections." I looked up at Clave's eyes. He was watching my lips move as I spoke. "Uh, you can still hear me?" I pointed to the side of my head.

Yes, he responded. *But I immensely enjoy watching your lips while you speak as well.* I could feel myself blush.

"Girls in my world would call you a smooth talker," I said. "What about the girls here?"

What about them?

"You must have had a girlfriend or dated before," I suggested.

No, none, Clave stated.

My eyebrows rose, "Really? That's hard to believe."

Is it so hard to believe when a majority of the girls around here are related to me in some way? Plus, there haven't been many more girls my age who have come from your world. None that have captured my interest. Clave smiled at me.

"Okay, I guess that makes sense," I said.

What about you back on Earth? It was interesting to watch Clave's facial expressions as he asked questions. His inquisitive expressions made me want to reach out and touch his face. I felt like I was blinded by my attraction to Clave, and to touch his face would satisfy me. I could mold his likeness with a tangible medium and freeze this moment in time. I could connect with it again and again through my fingertips. I had to take a deep breath and let it go slowly to maintain my composure.

"No one! No boyfriends, no dates, no interests," I said. "I poured myself into art and enjoyed any spare time with my best friend, Taylin. Plus, too many boys only want a girl for her body. I want more than that."

What do you want, Krystle? Clave asked. His thumb brushed back and forth over the top of my hand. My breath stuttered as I breathed in. It had nothing to do with the cold air but everything to do with how intense Clave made me feel.

"I want what my parents have. They fell head over heels for each other in high school, and all these years later, their love has never waned."

Krystle?

I looked up into his grey eyes. "Hmm?"

I want that too…with you!

I couldn't deny that I felt the same as I stared back at him.

Have you ever been kissed? Clave asked.

I wanted to say no. That one and only time didn't resonate. It didn't compare with the feeling I was having now of just hearing Clave ask. Because I knew it implied that he wanted to kiss me. And I wished it was my first with him. I wanted to be completely open and honest with him. What if he was disappointed?

Krystle…?

"Yeah…?"

Remember that one time when we first met? I was completely open and honest with you that I could hear your thoughts? By the way, I'm not disappointed, especially since I make you feel like it should've been me. It can be now and forever after. I told you the first time I saw you was on the beach through Chorus's eyes. Then I saw you from the bridge. I saw you as you danced with the Tucker's. Seeing your joy and laughter, I was there with you. When I finally stole your earring... He stopped and pointed at Chorus; *I was trying to work up the courage to return it to you.*

Then, Tovin created the opportunity by suggesting I meet up with you by way of chaperone for Jasper and Aura. It couldn't have been better timing because I was about to burst in anticipation. The nervousness you feel, I feel it too. It has nothing to do with uncertainty but everything to do with how strongly my heart and soul are drawn to yours.

His admission completely shattered me in the best way. Like the universe broke me down to a molecular level to combine Clave's true essence with my own. His pieces picked up every part of me and put us back together, and I felt complete for the first time in my existence.

Exactly, said Clave. *I couldn't have said it better myself.* His free hand reached up to touch my cheek, and he drew close. *May I have the honor, Krystle Genstone?*

There were no more words as our lips touched, and both our worlds exploded. All senses, physical and beyond, sealed a bond between us at this moment. It was my true first kiss. This kiss resonated through my being. No other lips would touch mine as long as we both should live.

Clave pulled away. *Promise?* His hand cupped my cheek while his thumb brushed over my lips. I couldn't speak, but he knew my thoughts, and he smiled. *I promise as well.* He leaned in and kissed me again. I was so done for! He broke away, and his head lowered and shook as he laughed. *Krystle, you kill me! And I do mean in all the right ways.*

"You are too hot and way too smooth to have a last name like Frost."

Clave fell back and laughed, *By the moons, woman! I'm going to love every second with you.*

"We saw that," Aura said. She and Jasper were walking back hand in hand with huge smiles on their faces. Aura was blushing and aglow.

"I won't tell if you don't," I said. Jasper grinned with a guilty look on his face.

"Deal!" She and Jasper both said at the same time. That fire never got built, but tonight, I didn't think we needed it.

Is it okay if Chorus nests with you tonight? Clave asked. I had bundled him in the loose pocket in my top like a baby joey.

"I think that can be arranged," I declared in a flirty voice. Clave was keeping up appearances by signing in case my folks were watching. I played along with hand gestures and signs I knew. "Shall we do this again sometime soon?"

Most definitely, said Clave. *Shall I see you for class tomorrow morning, Miss Genstone?*

"Yes, Mr. Frost. You shall!" I smiled and fluttered my eyelashes at him. He shook his head and looked at me, his eyes saying more than he dares to say out loud.

I bid you good night, Krystle. Sleep well. He gave my hand a light brush with his own as he turned to walk away. *I know I will be dreaming of an angel with golden hair, ocean blue eyes, and sweet pink lips tonight.*

I turned to walk inside. I felt like I could rocket to the moons. Jasper came in a few minutes later.

"Did you kids have a nice time?" Dad asked. He was seated on the couch drinking something warm. The steam rose from the cup as he took a slow, careful sip.

"We had fun," said Jasper. "You and Mom need to come to see the field across the river at night. It's really cool. Mom would love it."

"Catch any lightning bugs?" Dad asked as he held up his fingers in quotation marks. He smiled knowingly.

Jasper turned away and went to get some of what Dad was drinking. I rolled my eyes and graciously intervened. "Yes, we caught sight of many, thousands." I feigned a yawn. I was too wired to sleep after my time with Clave. I couldn't get him and his kiss out of my head.

"Good," Dad said and smiled. "Be extra quiet going up. Your Mom was exhausted tonight. She wasn't feeling too well."

"Is she okay?" I asked.

"I'm sure it's all a lot with transitioning to this new world and missing Cassie and Garreth," Dad said.

"How are you doing with all of this, Dad?" I watched as Jasper slipped behind me and quietly made his way upstairs.

"I am handling things very well. I miss Cassie and Garreth too, but I'm better than I first was since our little crew is back together. I'm thinking of it as an adventure. Like another one of our mission trips."

"That's a healthy way to think about it," I said. I came over and leaned in to kiss him on his cheek. "I love you, Dad."

"Love you too, Krystle." He stood to hug me.

"Oh, careful! Don't squish Chorus!" I put my hands over my belly pouch.

"Chorus? Is that the little red bird that I saw earlier?"

"Yeah, he's Claves' pet, actually. He fell asleep in my lap, so he's spending the night," I said.

"Okay, sweetheart." Dad gave me a light hug. "Good night!"

"Good night, Dad."

I made a little blanket nest by my window and gently placed Chorus inside. I was having trouble falling asleep in my bed as the fireflies continued to dance around in my belly. Claves words and kisses kept playing on repeat. I closed my eyes and pictured his face. My cheeks hurt from smiling so much. Clave professed his love to me in a way so much better than the actual words themselves. I felt it too.

I pulled my blanket in snugly around me, pretending he was here with his arms wrapped around me. I felt so warm and cozy that I eventually felt myself drifting off. My dreams should be so pleasant. At least, that was what I thought.

I turned my head and looked down. Mom was reaching out for me, screaming my name and crying. She and Dad were being held back by large men with spears. I tried to move but couldn't. I felt restraints around my wrists and feet. I was tied down to some sort of stone altar. A man stood above me. He was tall and dark with amber eyes.

He began to speak out loud as if addressing a crowd of people. "The sacrifice of the Pure Souls is necessary to appease the Dark Spirit," his voice belted out. A feeling of pure dread washed over me. I looked around behind him, hoping to see some savior coming to my aid.

"She is my shiyava; you can't do this." My mother cried. "She is innocent. You give her no chance at life. How dare you!"

"All the more reason for this sacrifice!" The man yelled back. "Guards, take them away."

"No...No..." Mom and Dad yelled and struggled to break free.

I was breathing heavily and sweating. I moved and pulled at my restraints. I started to cry out. "Mom...Dad...No..."

The man placed his hand on my forehead, and I tried to shrug it off. He pet my hair away from my face. "There...calm yourself, shiyava. Your sacrifice is for the good of our people, for your family." I screamed and tossed my body side to side, trying to free myself. The man smiled down at me. His eyes turned black. "Shiyava, it is time to feed the Dark Spirit!" He raised a dagger in the air above my chest.

"No...Noo..." I pleaded. The dagger clasped in both his hands came down swiftly. I let out a blood-curdling scream.

"Krystle...Wake up! You're having a nightmare!" Hands shook my shoulders. My arms flailed out. "Krystle..." I heard Jasper's voice yell. My eyes shot open. Jasper was sitting beside me. Chorus was flying around my room, screeching.

"Oh God, Jasper!" I hugged him tightly. "That was...so real!"

"You're okay now, Krystle. I've got you!"

"What's going on?" Rhodin came into my room, rubbing his sleepy eyes. "Chorus!" Rhodin observed the bird flying around.

"It's okay, Rhodin! Krystle was having a nightmare," said Jasper.

"Rhodin, would you please open my window and let Chorus out," I croaked. "I think he would calm down if he could fly freely outside." Rhodin went and opened the window. A cold breath of air came into the room as Chorus flew out.

I heard moaning. "Mom?" I got up. Jasper and Rhodin followed me.

"I've got you, honey. Here sit up." Dad was helping Mom up. "Jasper, go down and grab a bowl quick. Rhodin, go get a cool washcloth." They took off quickly.

I sat down next to Mom on the bed. I put my hand to her head. "Mom, you're burning up!"

"Ohhh, Krystle, I was having a horrible nightmare," she croaked. "I feel...awful." Jasper made it back with the bowl just in time. Mom retched violently into the bowl. Rhodin held out the cool washcloth to Dad. He took it and rubbed Mom's head and neck. "My medical bag." Mom pointed.

I got up and retrieved it from the end of their bed. "The large bottle with the dropper," Mom instructed. I reached down and felt around till my hand landed on what she requested. I pulled it out. "Ten drops sublingual," she said. Dad pulled her hair back as I administered the liquid and counted out the drops as they released under her tongue.

Mom reached down in her bag and pulled out a jar with some dried herbs. "Brew this. Two tablespoons to one liter."

A knock sounded on our front door, and I went to open it. Clave and Aura were standing outside. "Thank the moons, you're okay..." said Aura. I let them come inside.

You got here quickly, I said. Chorus landed on Claves' shoulder.

Chorus was distressed. He was calling to me, panicked. What happened? Clave asked.

"I was having a nightmare," I said out loud. Mom moaned again from upstairs.

"What's wrong with Gemma?" Aura asked.

"She's really sick. I'm worried," I said.

I'll go get Dr. Ibekwe, said Clave. He took off running. I could hear Mom's continued moans and Dad's soothing voice. Jasper came down, and Aura approached him. They hugged one another.

"Thank you for coming," said Jasper. "I've never seen Mom so sick before. In all our travels, Mom always managed to stay well. It makes no sense that she would get so ill coming to this world."

"I am here for you," said Aura. "I can help. What have you got brewing?" I held up the jar of mixed herbs. "Yes, that will help with nausea. You can add a bit of honey." She came back upstairs and sat at the bedside with Mom. "Here, Gemma, sip." She held a spoon up to her lips.

After a bit, Mom eased back on pillows that Dad had propped up. "Thank you, Aura, Krystle. I think it's already helping. Oh, Krystle, I had such a terrible nightmare. The shadows, my baby girls!" She sounded delirious.

Baby girls? I thought to myself. "Mom, it's okay, I'm fine. It was just a bad dream." I didn't want to tell her about my nightmare. It seemed so similar to what I had dreamt. I didn't need her to worry. She needed to relax and get better.

Dad went downstairs. "Hi, Abeo. Clave, thank you for going to get him."

Krystle! I heard Clave in my head. *I'll be waiting down here. Let me know if you need anything.*

Mom had a nightmare, just like me. I think Lazula should know.

I'll send Chorus to alert Tovin. He'll bring her here.

Thank you, Clave, I said.

I'll always be here for you and your family Krystle, said Clave. *Be there for your mom right now.* He was quiet after that. Dr. Ibekwe entered the room, followed by Dad.

"Gemma, can you tell me what's wrong? Are you in any pain?" Abeo asked.

"Abeo, hey. Yeah, fever, nausea, vertigo, vomiting. Bad dream! Very bad!" She was still delirious and fixated on the nightmare.

"Okay, let me check the patient," said Abeo. He started a series of physical tests. He drew some blood and set her up with an I.V. and fluids from a glass jar hung from a wall hook by the bed. I didn't know they were capable of doing all of that here.

"You're able to run blood tests? I mean, you have the lab technology here?" I asked.

"Of course, many medical pioneers have brought their knowledge through to this world. We have fashioned lab testing equipment and surgical tools with the village's aid and brilliant craftspeople. Your mother has brought new knowledge. So many wonderful advancements on Earth since my time." Abeo beamed. "She told me Earth was amid another pandemic. So very troublesome."

I nodded my head. "Yes, we have been fortunate. I pray we didn't bring it with us to this world. It would be devastating."

"To my knowledge, no illnesses from Earth have traversed through the Light," said Abeo. "I agree and pray that is not the case here. Though I have a gut feeling, the explanation for Gemma's illness is not detrimental. I'll go run the tests and come back with the results as soon as possible." Abeo looked over to Mom. "Rest, Gemma. I'll be back later to check on you."

"Thank you, Abeo." Mom was fatigued. Abeo smiled and nodded, and made his exit. I sat down next to Clave on the sofa, and he put a comforting arm around me. I nestled my head into the crook of his neck. "I'm so tired!" I yawned. "I don't think I can sleep after the nightmares we experienced. I need to know that Mom will be okay."

Do you want me to get you anything? The herbal drink you made for Gemma will help you as well. Before I could answer, Clave was already up. He brought back a cup and put a blanket over me, then sat back down. I sipped the pleasant brew. The anxiety I was feeling drained away. I settled back beside Clave and closed my eyes.

It was daylight when I opened my eyes. Clave was gone; my sketchbook opened on the table. Clave wrote a note in it.

Dear Krystle,

I went to see our students. Keeping the lesson short today. Be back soon.

Yours, Clave.

Clave had drawn a small picture of Chorus. I smiled and closed it. I didn't need my dad going gooey over it and start teasing me.

I went up to check on Mom, and she was sleeping peacefully. Dad was sitting at his desk drawing building plans. "How is she? Did her fever break?"

"Yes, she's doing much better; she just needs to rest. How are you? Jasper told me you had a pretty bad nightmare," said Dad.

"I'm okay. It's just this world, you know? There's meaning to things here, unlike what you'd see or hear back home. People would say we are crazy. We'd all be in the nuthouse. Now we live in a treehouse that grows nuts, or something we've never seen before. And, Mom! She finds out she's been called here by a powerful moon force, and I have as well. We don't know what it means. We have to put what information we get together like some strange alternate dimension puzzle."

"I would've been skeptical to hear of such things," Dad admitted. "Remember, many of our mission trips had various cultures who believed in mystical forces. Earth has become more scientific. This world is still rather primitive. Mystery keeps our minds engaged and opened to possibilities. The people here are more accepting because their minds are open."

"Mystery can feel scary and intimidating when it happens to the person involved," I explained. "It's the not knowing, the lack of control. I've never been a contender in the game of hypothesis. At the same time, I feel more open and alive here. I always felt like I needed to hide inside a shell before. My only outlet for something more was to draw. It felt safe. I controlled the outcome."

Dad looked at me with understanding. "Krystle, you have always displayed a strong presence in ways most people don't define as strength. You're not like your Uncle Garreth. He's always been a charging bull straight into danger's path—a risk-taker. Your Mom has always wanted to save people. I'm the oxy-moron of planner/fly-by-the-seat-of-my-boxer-briefs adventurer. Jasper is a mix of me, Mom, and Garreth. Rhodin continues to surprise me as he rises to new challenges."

"But I've seen you, Krystle. You are loving and peaceful, like your Aunt Cassie. I've watched you take charge in situations when it counts. You've traveled the world and beyond. I never once saw you inside some shell. Call it fate, destiny, mystery. You were called for a reason; something mystical has placed faith in you. Keep your faith, daughter. Faith, Hope, and Love will pull you through."

"Your father is right," Mom said.

"I'll have to write this day down," Dad said jokingly. "I've been wrong before."

"I've told you you're right before, Flint," Mom replied.

"Mom! How are you feeling?" I asked. "Sorry if we woke you."

"It's fine, Krystle. I'm feeling better, just a little weak. I've been listening to my wise husband and my intelligent daughter engaged in a special moment. I'm happy I didn't miss out on this beautiful conversation. It's a moment for posterity."

"Speaking of posterity," said Dad. "Doctor Ibekwe came back with a blood test result you might find interesting."

"What is it? Are you going to be okay, Mom?" I looked at her, my mind filled with concern.

"Yeah! I just have to take a daily regimen to keep the morning sickness at bay." Mom revealed.

"Oh, my God! Mom!? You're pregnant?!"

She smiled broadly, "Congratulations, big sister, you have another sibling on the way!"

I couldn't make full words. "Wha...Uh...Oh! Mom! Wow!"

"How do you feel about this, Krystle?" she asked.

"It's...I'm shocked...but happy! Mom, Dad, this is unexpected but wonderful. Did you already tell Jasper and Rhodin? What did they say?"

"Yes, and they said the same as you," Dad said. I hugged Mom and put my hand on her belly. I felt an instant warmth.

"Krystle, your Fire Stone! It's glowing!" Mom's eyes widened. I touched it and realized that was the source of the warmth. I look down at Mom's hand over mine on her belly. The Opal stone on her bracelet began to glow as well. We looked at each other. Amazement filled our faces.

"Wow! Now that's something I've never seen before," Dad said. There was an insistent knocking on our home's door. "I'll go get it," said Dad. "You two just stay there and keep, glowing?"

Dad came back into the room, followed by Lazula. She looked at us with a bewildered expression. "It seems I have some explaining to do."

Chapter 14

"I have been informed of the joyous news Gemma," said Lazula. "Congratulations to you and your family. It seems with this new development comes a change in some of the information I had explained previously."

I had climbed into bed next to Mom. The glowing from the Fire Moon and Opal Stones had faded and were back to a dormant state. Dad faced his chair toward the bed and motioned for Lazula to sit. Mom and I had our rapt attention on what Lazula needed to convey.

"First of all. I mean no offense, but it seems that while the Light called Gemma, the intention was to bring through the carrier. Gemma, you are the safe harbor and protector of the new Pure Soul inside you. The Light called you, but the Grand Glacial Moon beckons for the child in your womb. This is nothing to fear. It is a good blessing indeed."

Mom's face went from puzzled to relieved to hear this good news. "Do you know what that means for our baby? What should we expect? I mean, I already know what to expect when expecting, but this is a whole new ideation to which I'm not accustomed."

"I was the last born during a Grand Glacial Moon," said Lazula. "It bestowed upon me the gift of the Four Moons Keeper. I have abilities beyond other mortals and have lived longer than my ancestors before. Your precious child is a gift and will be born with abilities to do much good. I cannot say what capabilities this child will have. You will have to learn with your child along the way."

Lazula looked at me. "Krystle and her sibling will be connected pivotally. Together they will accomplish something of great importance. It is important to the balance of our world and links in a way to yours."

"Lazula. I have a question. Though I do not wish to alarm my mother, I feel it is important to reveal." I said.

"Dreams!" Lazula exclaimed.

"Yes! More like nightmares." I held Mom's hand. "Mom, you said you had a terrible nightmare last night."

"Yes. There was a dark shadow. It grew. It was evil and was coming for my baby girls. I was trying to get to my babies, but something was holding me back."

Lazula had a deeply concerned look on her face. "And what of you, Krystle?" Mom turned to look at me with her brows creased.

"I was having a nightmare as well at the same time. There was a man. I was about to be sacrificed." Mom drew in a startled breath. I squeezed her hand, and Dad sat down beside her. He put his arm around her. "The man was telling me the Pure Souls must be sacrificed to the Dark Spirit. Mom and Dad..." I sucked in a breath, and my lips trembled. Tears escaped and trickled down my cheeks.

"Mom was reaching up for me, screaming. They were taken away. Then the man held a dagger over me."

"Oh God, Krystle. That is terrifying!" Mom pulled me to her side.

"You have to remember that not all dreams are literal, but some interpretation of truth," said Lazula. "I will tell you a story of our people's past that may help put your nightmares into perspective."

"Back on Earth, thousands of years ago, our ancestors were victimized. They lived amongst a dynasty with a harsh ruler who believed everything dictated by a high priest. The high priest, Theos, convinced our ruler that human sacrifice was necessary to keep order and bring healthy crops to keep our people fed. Our ruler, Acasos, was under pressure and duress as the yields diminished and the population grew. Acasos acquiesced to the high priest's dictates as prophetic and necessary."

"Ritual sacrifices happened. A call of 'Pure Souls' was needed to feed the 'Dark Spirit' till it was satisfied. The people lived in terror and prayed to the ancestral spirits to send an escape. Exodus came with the first appearance of the Light. Our people took the path unknown over a future fraught with fear of Theos' dark agenda. The sacrifices of hundreds of young children could not be erased, but the hope of a better future pushed our people to escape tyranny."

"Our people rushed to the Light. Theos and Acasos tried to follow but were dispelled. The Light did not allow such darkness passage. Our people were free and made our new home here. Unakite Village was established. The four moons revealed our purpose, and over time we grew stronger. It wasn't till a few hundred years later that new arrivals came. Each new generation brought with them growth and continued balance. Our people overcame their hesitancy and began to embrace each new generation."

"I believe the moons were showing you a representation from our past. Knowledge is power, and we must arm ourselves. It is as I first told you. The moons will reveal information to you at the right time. Use your dreams or nightmares to build your knowledge arsenal. Do not let fear rule your hearts."

"This is why the moons choose who they want. You are the essence of goodness and knowledge. Powerful! Your life experiences up till now have been your guide to your true calling. You are already on the right path. The people placed in your way have a purpose connected with yours. Put trust in this. Your soul can read good from bad. Intuition and the moons will guide you," said Lazula.

Mom, Dad, and I sat in awed momentary silence. Dad finally spoke. "Fascinating. We learned in history about an ancient civilization that seemed to vanish off the face of the Earth. Are your ancestors Mayan or Incan?"

"I have heard of such written in Earth's history. However, we are not Maya or Incan. Our tribe is called, Qinoshotek," Lazula stated.

"What we didn't know was that many disappearances of people and families throughout time are linked," said Dad. "Now we know, as we are part of it. Back on Earth, we are the most current unexplained mystery. We will never be found. Written off as dead. M.I.A."

"But we know Uncle Garreth and Aunt Cassie are still actively looking for us. They saw the Light. Even Taylin knows," I said. "They know the truth!"

"Knowing my brother, he will not give up," Dad said.

"Can we call to them again?" I asked.

"It is within you to do so, Krystle," said Lazula. "You have a strong bond with the Fire Moon. Gemma as well. But I would advise you wait till she is feeling stronger." Lazula nodded to Mom.

"We will." I agreed. I felt a build of anticipation. I needed to take a breath and step back a moment to take in the greater picture. Being shown a flash of the ancestors' terrifying history, it had to mean something more significant.

It seemed it was all building up to some pinnacle. I stood once more on a precipice. Would I fall or stand firm? Lazula was right. I had to arm myself with knowledge. This was a new dimensional puzzle to put together. The first pieces were falling, and I knew I would need everyone in my path to help me put them together. I had to watch in wait for the clues.

Chorus flew into the room. He perched on my shoulder and chirped. *Krystle, I'm here,* said Clave through our connection. *Mrs. Tucker is with me. She brought some food for your family.*

"I will leave you to rest, Gemma." Lazula got up and gave her a soft hug. "You must not push yourself. I know you, child. You can go back to work in a few days." Lazula smiled and winked. She turned and hugged Dad, "Congratulations, Flint."

He led Lazula downstairs. "Oh, Hi Liv!" I heard him say.

"Hello, Flint. Greetings and peace to ye, Lazula," said Liv.

"To you as well, child," Lazula and Liv hugged, then continued in their alternate directions.

"There es the mother to be. Congratulations to ye and yer family. I come to let ye know Rhodin is playing at our house with Hailey. I brought ye food n' some nice soup to soothe a settle ye. Family recipe."

"Thank you, Liv. I greatly appreciate it and you," said Mom. "No need to rush off, though. Care to trade some baby and birthing stories? I'm interested to know what your experience was like here with Hailey."

"Krystle, would ye mind goin' down n' bring yer mother a bowl of soup?" Liv asked. "Clave es wait n' on ye, and I know ye doh naht want to sit and listen in on old war stories and battle wounds. Jus' joke n', but Gemma knows what I mean. Don't ye?"

"I certainly do," Mom agreed. "Go ahead, Krystle, I'll be fine. You should go get some fresh air." I nodded and went to get her some soup. Clave was sitting at the table eating something that looked and smelled marvelous. He looked up and smiled.

"I will be right back," I told him. Chorus flew to the table, and Clave broke off some bread crumbs for him to enjoy. I brought Mom soup and kissed her on her head. She and Liv were happily engaged in conversation. I sat down by Clave. *Did my dad go somewhere?*

Clave continued to chew his food. It looked like a hearty stew and smelled delicious. My stomach growled. *I believe your dad is just outside talking with Eric. Here have some of this stew. It's amazing.* He placed a ready-filled bowl with a spoon in front of me.

You know, it's rude to talk with your mouth full. I teased.

You know, that's the first time anyone has ever told me that. Well, it's a good thing I don't need to open my mouth to talk. Clave teased back.

You have me at an unfair advantage there. But I suppose since we're speaking telepathically, I can eat and talk at the same time too, huh?

True, you can, Clave said. *But everyone else has an unfair advantage over me because they don't have to drop their silverware to talk. You know it usually takes me longer to eat when people are engaging me in conversation. Drop fork, respond. Set down cup, respond.*

Oh! Now I feel so bad for you! I smiled coyly at him while I chewed. *Wow! Liv is a great cook!*

Clave feigned a frown, which just as quickly turned upside down into an I-have-got-to-kiss-those-lips-again smile. His brows wiggled up and down deviously as he continued to eat. I had to cover my mouth with my hand for fear of spitting food out of my mouth from laughter. He was almost finished when a thought occurred to me.

Clave? I'm not the only person you communicate with this way, am I correct? I mean, besides your students, who you've sworn to secrecy? I asked.

Just my closest family. Lazula, my mother, Tovin and Aura. He responded.

Wait! Last night! Aura didn't take off with Jasper to get fire supplies as her own idea, did she? Did you ask a favor? Not that I minded the outcome at all. But still!

I may have! Guess you caught me, huh? Clave threw up his hands in a playful gesture of guilt. *But I knew Aura and Jasper were just as desperate to have some alone time. I believe it was all for the greater good. Everyone benefitted!* Clave winked at me.

I agreed. I pressed my lips to Clave's gorgeous dimpled cheek. He pointed to it again, and I accepted. Instead, I found my lips greeted by his own.

"No kissing at the dinner table!" A male voice yelled. We quickly pulled away from each other. My cheeks were aflame. Clave laughed. I turned to see Jasper standing with his arms crossed over his chest. Aura stood by his side laughing. "Busted!" Jasper laughed.

"Just you wait, Jasper! You'll get your 'busted' moment too! Only you'll have Tovin to face. Practice pleading for your life, dear brother. For I already feel sorry for you when that day comes," I returned in mocked snideness.

"Ooh, she got you there!" Aura laughed.

"What happened to your promise, Aura?" Jasper asked. You said you'd be there to back me up if Tovin catches us." He put his hand to his heart and caved in on himself as if he were being crushed.

Aura huffed. "Jasper, you know I'll be there. It takes two to tango! I'll be just as busted as you. It's not going to stop me or you from being together. My dad just needs to realize I'm a grown woman, and he needs to let me live my own life. He has some past demons to rid himself of, but it's his story to tell."

"Jasper, it's time to man up," I said. "We're all growing up—time to face the wrath that may be. Pay the Piper. How else will civilization continue if not for the rebellion of youth," Clave lifted his cup and called "cheers" in my mind. I laughed.

"What's so funny?" Jasper asked.

Let him in, Clave! Please! My brother can be trusted! I looked at Clave imploringly. He looked back and nodded.

"Jasper, Aura, come sit with us and eat. Liv made this awesome stew." I got up and made them each a bowl and set it on the table. They sat down and joined us.

So, how have you been today? Clave asked. Aura looked up and grinned. She knew what was happening.

"Did you hear that voice?" Jasper asked. "Is somebody else here? Anyone upstairs? It sounded like right next to me. No, more like inside my head. Am I losing it?"

Aura and I busted out laughing.

Not losing your mind, my friend, but I must say you're crazy for dating my cousin, Clave mused.

Jasper looked up at Clave with saucer eyes. "Do that again!" Jasper demanded.

Your wish is my command! Clave smirked at Jasper. Jasper slammed his hands down on the table and jumped up from his seat.

"Whoa, dude! That's insane! Have you been faking this whole time and can throw your voice?" Jasper asked.

No, and no! Sit back down and calm yourself, man. You'll scare off my interpreter! Clave pointed at Chorus.

"What are you saying? Krystle, what is he talking about?"

"Jasper, don't freak out! You've heard of telepathy, right?"

"Of course, I have. I wasn't born under a rock!" Jasper said, astonished.

I laughed. "Funny, I said those same words. Jasper, Clave can speak to people telepathically, but only when Chorus is nearby. And, only to whom he deems worthy of knowing." I told him.

"And I'm just now being let in the loop? Nice, Clave! I see you're into my sister, and I'm staying cool about it. And you're just now trusting me?" Jasper asked.

"Chill, Jasper, it isn't just about you," I spoke up. "You've been inducted into a very small group of people who know this. You can't go blurting it out to anyone else, whether you know if they know or not."

Jasper nodded in understanding, "The Tucker Twins."

Everyone agrees on that note, laughed Clave.

"Wow, man. How awesome. I can appreciate, man, no hard feelings," said Jasper.

None taken, Clave agreed. *But, for this to remain unknown, you must play along when we're around others. You can speak back to me telepathically as well. And watch your thoughts; I don't need to hear T.M.I. with the goings-on between you and my cousin. You'll notice I sign more when I'm out and about.*

"That works for me, man. Just when I thought coming to this world through some weird light, finding out my sister is some supernatural moon catcher, and I meet the woman of my dreams has blown me away. Boom! There goes another bombshell! And, now, Mom being pregnant too! Yeah, this is a lot to take in in one day." Jasper huffed.

"I can say I'm totally with you there, brother," I agreed. If he only knew my whole story. Perhaps, if only we also knew Tovin's full story. I needed some air. "I think we should go for a walk. You and Aura finish eating. Clave?"

He got up and pulled my chair back. I rose and took his offered his hand.

"Such a gentleman!" I stated like a genteel southern lady.

My mother raised me right! And Lazula! And Aura! And especially Tovin! Clave bowed to me. *Shall we promenade, my lady?*

I laughed.

"We shall, good sir!" I chuckled and took his hand.

Dad was sitting and talking to Eric and the Bens. Rhodin and Hailey played with some stones. The Bens got up and saw Clave's and my joined hands. They had a sad, defeated look in their eyes, along with acceptance. "We wish ye congratulations on yer new sibling. May we give ye a congratulatory hug?"

I looked at Clave, and he let go of my hand, assured that I'd return to him after a friendly exchange with the Bens. I hugged each in turn. They each gave me a gentle squeeze. "We'll be good friends, Krystle," said Benjamin.

"Aye," Bennigan agreed. "We know when we've been outdone. It's alright, though. Lazula, encouraging as always, tell us our time will come." They both smiled, and I smiled back.

"You're not upset? I've wanted to say something, but it's been hard to find the right time."

"Don't go frettin' yer pretty head, Krystle. Besides, we're happy for ye. Clave's a good bloke. If he ever dohs anything to hurt ye though, he'd better watch his back." Bennigan gave Clave the "stare"! Clave just smiled and signed while I went along for pretensc.

"He says not to fret your pretty heads. He agrees, he is a good bloke, and he would never hurt me," I repeated Claves' words.

"Very well then," the Bens nodded. I heard Dad and Eric chuckle in the background.

"Dad, Clave, and I are going for a walk," I said.

"Okay, be back before dark," Dad called.

Clave and I walked out toward the field near the forest area where we had first met. "Well, I guess the cat's out of the bag. By the way, a cat is an Earth animal, and that was an expression meaning people know what's going on between us now."

Clave laughed. *Yeah, I've heard that expression before. We do have creatures here that look like cats, but very few are kept as pets.*

"We never had pets back home. We were always so busy with school and traveling. Mom said it would be cruel to leave an animal lonely at home most of the day. The animals here seem to have a healthy balance- my mom pet dogs for the first time. At least the first I've ever seen, when we met Bax and Sierra. And, there's definitely not any birds like Chorus on Earth."

Animals are spiritual and emotional creatures, said Clave. *They are open to human connection. I'm not the only person here that has a spiritual connection with an animal. There are other people connected with all sorts of animals in our world.*

"Is it the 'spirit' connection that makes the way you communicate possible?

Mostly, said Clave. *It's usually related to one of the main five senses, but others have been on spirit journeys with their animal, like a sixth sense.*

"That's pretty cool," I said. "Clave?"

Hmm?

"Not animal-related, but I'd like to try something with you. I guess you'd consider it silly, but..."

Krystle, I'd be willing to do and try any and everything with you, said Clave.

I blushed.

"Okay, stop giving me all those special tinglies and pay attention," I demanded.

Special tinglies? Clave smiled. *I give you 'special tinglies'?* His hands quickly grabbed at my sides, and he started tickling.

"Ahh...ahh...Stop...Please...CLAVE...." I pulled at his hands and slapped at him.

Okay, I concede! For now! He waggled his brows. It took me a moment to catch my breath.

"We will have war if you do that again, Mr. Frost, do you understand?" I admonished.

He laughed and put his hands down by his sides. *I'll behave, I promise!*

"Have you ever lip-synced while speaking to someone telepathically?" I asked. "You know, moved your lips along with the words as you said them in their head? It would seem like you were actually talking."

I've never considered that before, Clave admitted. *I guess I could try. I've lip-read most of my life, so I'll give it a go for you. Okay, Ready!*

"Start with something simple. Watch my lips," I said.

Easy enough, He smiled.

I moved my lips and sang out operetta style, “Me...me...me...mee....”

You have a beautiful singing voice, Clave smirked.

“Quit being distracting,” I complained. I gave him the stink eye and laughed.

Adorable! He smiled.

“CLAVE!” I complained. “Please, concentrate!”

Okay, sorry. For real this time. Here goes. I could hear as he physically cleared his throat as if to vocalize out loud.

“Me..me...me...me...meeeee!” His lips moved in perfect sync with his voice in my head.

“That was good! Now try it with a whole sentence,” I encouraged. Clave moved his lips, and I heard his voice just a beat behind as he continued.

> “Krystle, you make my heart SING!!! I’m so happeee!”

I was cracking up. “You look like a poorly synced foreign movie dubbed in with a bad musical.”

“You think I sound terrible? Now that just hurts Krystle! Now I must continue to SING..., and you can’t cover your EARS...., because you can’t get me out of your HEAD....!” He ended on a low note.

“I can’t, can I...? Chorus, go find some crickets to eat, boy.” Chorus took off.

"Awe, No fair!" Clave moved his lips and signed. "Well, I guess we can talk this way, or…"

I grabbed hold of his shirt and pulled him toward me. "Kiss?" I smiled.

Clave smiled and mouthed, "Yeah!" He nodded his fist enthusiastically. He tenderly cupped my face, and his lips brushed across mine. My palms pressed down onto his solid chest. His fingers slid up into my hair, and he cradled my head. My lips parted, and he deepened the kiss.

We explored the caverns from which taste and touch combined in perfect synchronicity. It stirred emotions and fueled a need for the deepest connection. My stomach burst into fireflies. An electrified current swept through my entire body, and my soul filled with a cascade of beautiful colors. He lightened the kiss and slowly pulled away.

"Wow," I exclaimed.

"Wow," he mouthed back. "Same time, next week?" He signed. I laughed and slapped him playfully on his chest. He wrapped his arms around me and lifted me in a tight squeeze. I could feel his heart beating rapidly against my own. He set me back on my feet and continued looking into my eyes. I stared back into his gorgeous grey depths. Chorus must have returned because I could hear him again.

Krystle, I am completely head over heels for you. I pray you feel the same.

"Consider your prayers answered, Clave, as you've answered mine."

I slept peacefully that night. When I woke to another beautiful day, I saw Mom was looking much better. She was sitting outside with Dad. "I think I should build a swing for us to cuddle together. It would be good for after the baby comes as well. What do you think, my Gem?"

"Mmm, that sounds wonderful, Flint. It would be better than sitting on these benches. We could get some pillows and pile them on. Sip some hot cider as the days get colder and watch my belly as it bulges like a beluga whale's head."

"Off to class, little love bird?" Dad asked. Oh no! Here he goes. Mr. Mushy had been released!

"Dad. I love you. Please don't make me the mean child with your gooey in the center antics." I kissed Mom on the head and gave Dad one on the cheek.

"Eeww, boy coodies!" Dad wiped his cheek and laughed.

"Mom!? Could you help your daughter out here?"

"Flint, behave! Krystle, enjoy your day!"

I started walking away, and Dad began to singing.

"Krystle and Clave, sitting in a tree...K-I-S-S-I-N-G..."

Good grief!!!

Clave was waiting for me on the walking path. *Did you sleep well last night?* Chorus jumped from him to me and snuggled my ear, chittering sweetly. *Hey, don't go getting any ideas; the girl is mine,* Clave stated.

"What's that you say," I asked Chorus? "Oh, really?" I looked at Clave and smiled.

What's he telling you? Clave gave Chorus an admonishing look.

"A little bird told me; someone was spying on me last night while I was asleep. You should already know the answer to your first question" I chuckled.

Ah, come on, Chorus! We had a deal! Clave looked at me. *Do you forgive me? I had to make sure you would be okay since the night before.*

"I forgive you," I turned to him and pressed my lips to his.

He touched my cheek then went to give Chorus a tender head scratch. We held hands until we saw our students ahead. Time to act like the mature professional teachers that we were. The Bens stood waiting with Hailey and Rhodin. She and Rhodin sat at a picnic table, still playing with stones. I was starting to find this odd.

"Top of the morning to ye both," said Bennigan. "We would like to attend class today to brush up on our sign language if that be acceptable to ye."

"We promise to be good students so as not to receive the wrath of Princess Krystle," said Benjamin. Rhodin and Hailey giggled.

I looked to Clave, and he shrugged. “Very well,” I said. “What have you two been working on?” I asked Rhodin and Hailey. “Interesting stones! Have you been trying to identify them?” I looked at the stones spread out over the bench. They all had a smoothness like river rocks, but the shapes were odd.

“Rascal has been bringing them to us,” said Rhodin. “I hear him come in each night, and he drops a new stone off then leaves.”

“Who’s Rascal?” I asked.

“Me pet mouse,” said Hailey. “I thought I had lost him for a while, but then Rhodin told me Rascal has been visitin’ him each night for the past few weeks. He brought me some of these stones as well.”

“Watch this,” said Rhodin. He started moving the stones together. The stones all pulled together with a magnetic force; the shapes interlocked like a three-dimensional puzzle. They made a triangular base with two sides. It looked like half of a pyramid.

“Intriguing,” I commented. I couldn’t put the notion past me that this was a clue to the mystery. Players in my path included the people closest to me. Keys were being laid out on the table. The doors which they opened yet to be found. Clave put his hand on my shoulder. I turned and looked up at him, and he looked at me inquisitively. I hadn’t yet told him about my nightmare and what Lazula shared. He has been my respite from this weight building upon me.

I’m here for you, Krystle. Always. He spoke the words in a loving tone laced with concern in my head. I placed my hand on his, no longer caring what anyone saw and might think.

"Shall we get class started now," I said and signed to the students? All the kids came together, and our class was in session. I watched and took notes as Clave addressed the class in sign language. He signed and presented different words. I drew the hand signs along with each for practice.

Afterward, I displayed a few drawings for the students to copy and make their own reference pages. I had come to find that the Bens were not too shabby at drawing, so I asked them to help some of the students. They obliged graciously, and I found myself surprised at how well they worked together.

You seem to be able to work miracles, Miss Genstone, said Clave. *I've never seen such cooperation from the Bens before.*

Well, this is my dominion, after all. My subjects are loyal and now understand the penalty for insubordination. I joked.

Indeed, your majesty, Clave smirked. I rolled my eyes and smiled. Clave clapped his hands to call the students' attention. *Take your pages home, and be sure to practice with them tonight*. The students were released. Rhodin, Hailey, and the Bens remained.

Chapter 15

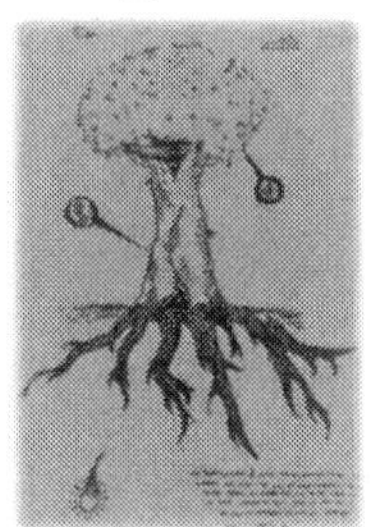

“Hey, guys,” called Aura. “Want to come to have lunch with us?” We all walked down the river and stopped at a workspace. Tovin and Jasper were working on a canoe with a big saw. They both had their shirts off and dripped with sweat.

Tovin was a sight with his vast muscular torso and arms as every one of them flexed and bulged with each back-and-forth movement. I noticed Jasper had put on some muscle as well. Young teen girls passed, appreciating the view. They giggled. Aura gave them a deathly glare and put her hands on her hips. They shut their mouths and hurried along.

Eric called out to the Bens. “When yer finished eating, come o’re here and help out yer old man.”

“Okay, Da.” They both yelled back.

Tovin motioned to Jasper to take a break. They came and sat with us.

“We have finished your family canoe,” said Tovin. He pointed. Down on the river, a canoe had our family name carved into the side. It was a work of art.

"Oh wow, it's beautiful!" I exclaimed. "Thank you, Tovin."

"Your Dad and Jasper did most of the work. I just got them started." Tovin explained.

"What's the one you and Jasper are working on now?"

"A gift," said Tovin.

"For whom?" I asked.

"To be determined," Tovin stated and said nothing more. I didn't press because I knew Tovin wouldn't appreciate playing twenty questions. So, we all sat and ate. Afterward, the Bens got up and went to help Eric. Aura and Jasper kept exchanging secretive looks, and I noticed Tovin catching on. He used his shirt to wipe the sweat off his brow.

"Aura," said Tovin. "I need you to take something to Lazula." He got up and handed something wrapped in a cloth, and he bent down and whispered something in her ear. Her eyes grew big for just a flicker of a moment then she nodded. She started walking back the way we came.

Jasper watched her go with a look of need to be by her side. I saw Tovin look at Jasper and then huff out a resigned breath. "Jasper, it's time I tell you something about my past. I've never talked about it with anyone besides Aura and Lazula. Clave and his mom know a little, but not everything I'm about to reveal. Krystle, it's fine if you and Clave want to stay. But, please, no questions, okay?"

I nodded. Jasper swallowed, and Clave's attention was entirely on Tovin. Chorus sat quietly on my leg. Tovin cleared his throat, then grabbed his canteen and took a swig. The Tuckers were sawing and tapping away with hammers and chisels in the background.

"Some years ago, Aura was but two years old; her mother, my wife, was expecting a new baby. My wife, Solaura, was a strong, beautiful, proud woman. She was my equal in every way. I loved her, and I still love her with all my heart." Tovin drew in a stuttered breath and released. This huge, proud, indiscernible man was allowing a moment of vulnerability with his emotions. I had goosebumps on my arms and legs as I could feel his distinguishable sorrow. Jasper looked like he was holding his breath as he fumbled with his shirt in his hands. Clave took my hand in his, and I saw Tovin look between us and sigh. He continued.

"Late on a storming night, Solaura went into labor. Something was wrong. She was in anguish. My brother-in-law, Mieruss, ran to get Lazula and Zinnia. The storm that night was unlike any I had seen before. Solaura screamed with each roar of thunder. I saw where her water had broken, and there was blood, too much blood. Aura was crying and inconsolable. I was completely distraught as I tried to console her and be there for Solaura. For the first time in my life, I didn't...didn't know what to do!" Tears started down Tovin's face, and it shook me. To see someone so strong and sure of everything brought a realization. Even the strongest of us are breakable.

"Solaura was trying to push. I pleaded with her to try and wait for Lazula to arrive. When Zinnia arrived first,

Mieruss came in behind her and said he sent someone to get Lazula, that she was on her way."

"Zinnia was there as the baby's head started to crown. She instructed Solaura to push. She screamed one last time, and the baby was born. Solaura looked up, and I saw panic in her eyes. Solaura reached out and cried, 'No!'

Zinnia cried out, 'The baby is not breathing," She was wrapping the baby in cloth but had stopped.

"Solaura cried out, 'You will not have my child!' From all the blood loss, I thought she had become deluded. She started to weaken. I was holding her hand and begging her to stay with me. I needed her. The children needed their mother. With her last bit of strength, she reached out and touched our baby. She looked up at me with her last breath and said, 'My soul belongs to our child now.' Then she was.... gone!!!"

I was shaking, and Clave put his arm around me and pulled me close to him. My lips trembled, and tears fell as I felt Tovin's pain.

"Zinnia said the baby had passed as well. I was in so much grief, cradling my wife in my arms. I dared not to look at the baby. It would be so much more than I could handle. Lazula arrived, and the scene in front of her brought her to utter shock. She ran and lifted Aura into her arms and tried to soothe her. It was hours later when I finally let Solaura go from my arms. Zinnia took the baby, and Mieruss helped Lazula take my wife to be buried. Zinnia assured me she would pray to the ancestors for the right of passage into the beyond."

"I didn't want a congregation to be a witness to my grief, bestowing me with condolences. I felt like I would shred anyone to pieces who did so, just so they could feel the smallest semblance of the pain I felt."

"It wasn't until the next day that Lazula returned alone. I stayed behind in my grief, clutching to my Aura. She was all I had left, and I swore I would never let her go. Lazula was confused and had lost memory of what had happened after she and Mieruss took Solaura and our child to be buried. All she could say was they were gone. Mieruss and Zinnia had disappeared. The village had searched for over a year. There wasn't a clue, no trace of them anywhere."

I looked at Jasper. I could see his eyes red-rimmed as he continued looking down. "So, you see now, Jasper," said Tovin. Jasper looked up at Tovin's face. "My Aura is my only and my everything, and I was fighting not to let her go. But I see the way you and Aura look at each other. It is the same way Solaura and I looked at each other. I was afraid for my Aura, for the possibility of what she could lose. But I can no longer be her shield. I can no longer deny her the possibility of what she can gain. So, I give you my blessing to be with her."

Jasper's eyes widened in shock. My hand had a stranglehold on Claves. Jasper spoke with a trembling voice, "Tovin, I am humbled and honored. I will be everything for Aura that she and you expect of me. I will treat her like treasure, above and beyond the most precious of gems. That is what she is to me. I know she will always be your Aura. Thank you for your blessing. I promise to be true to her and her alone. I am in love with her."

"Good," said Tovin. "Fair warning though, son! Her virtue shall remain intact till after there is a bonding ceremony."

"I swear to you, sir, she is still," said Jasper.

"I know," said Tovin. "You are still here and breathing after all!"

Jasper gulped, and Tovin smiled. "Now, back to work!"

Jasper jumped up, "Yes, sir!"

Tovin was putting his shirt back on, and I came up to him. "Tovin?"

"Yes, Krystle?"

I threw my arms around Tovin, and he froze. Then I felt his arms slowly close around me.

"Thank you, Tovin." I squeezed him, and we parted.

"Krystle, I only intended to tell Jasper about my past, but for some reason, with you here...I felt like you needed to hear the story as well."

"May I please ask just one question?"

"I knew you would, Krystle. Go ahead," said Tovin.

"Who was Zinnia?"

"Zinnia was Lazula's twin sister," he responded.

Clave and I walked back to my home. Rhodin and Hailey trailed behind. They were playing rock, paper, scissors.

I was a small child when it happened. I don't remember much, but I knew about Tovin and Aura's loss. Mieruss was my father. I don't really remember much about him. My mom hasn't been the same since he disappeared all those years ago, said Clave.

"I am so sorry, Clave," I squeezed his hand. "What is your mother's name? Can I meet her?"

Her name is Azora. I see her a couple of times each week. She lives with other family members out close to the fields before entering the village. If you'd like, I can take you to meet her the next time I go.

"I would really like that," I said. "Did you know that Lazula had a twin sister?"

I had heard the name before, but I didn't know the association. Lazula never told me. I'm sure it was just as hard on her to lose her sister. She must have shut it out. Or, if she was truly confused after Zinnia and my father went missing, her mind may have suppressed it. Clave had a thoughtful look. *I wonder if they were some of the people who...*

"People who were what, Clave?" I asked.

I don't know, he said. *I've heard people from our world have gone through the Light to your world, and they had not returned, but that was a very long time ago.*

A few hours later, Jasper and Aura showed up at our home. "The new ride is parked out front," said Jasper.

"Sweet," said Dad. "You all feel like taking her for a spin? I know of a few whirlpools down the river," he joked.

"I don't think I can handle anymore spinning right now," said Mom. "Perhaps sometime past my first trimester."

We sat around the warmth of the outdoor chimenea. Everything felt like it was coming together-new family, friends, love. This was our new norm, and everyone amongst our group couldn't be happier.

We had told Mom and Dad how Tovin had opened up and given his blessing for Jasper and Aura as a couple. Mom and Dad looked at them all gooey-eyed and congratulated them. Dad had even told Jasper he'd bring down the hammer if he didn't treat Aura as the precious jewel that she was.

Though it would be some time before we knew when they would progress to the point of being officially bonded by ceremony, we all knew it would happen. As for Clave and me, well, we were in love, but I had just turned sixteen. I wanted to enjoy being together and relish in the innocence and anticipation as we slowly explored more of one another. Clave told me that as long as he got the chance to kiss me every day till our time came, he'd be a happy man. I thought he was the same age as me but had come to find out he was eighteen, just a few months older than Jasper.

Dad was cool about it because he and Mom were the same ages when they had first met. Jasper had complained that it was a reverse double standard in my favor. I had to remind him that he had just gotten off relatively easy with Tovin. Jasper should count his blessings because even Aura could kick his ass. He had agreed she could and would gladly accept anything she'd dish out. If he had done something stupid enough to deserve it, then he had it coming.

I laid in bed that night, replaying the day's events. The blessings, sorrow, and laughter tumbled around in my head like a clothes dryer. Tovin's shared story washed away some pain from his past and gave life to a fresh beginning. But it also left more questions to be answered. What had happened that night with Zinnia, Mieruss, and Lazula? Where had Zinnia and Mieruss gone? Why hadn't Lazula mentioned having had a twin sister?

I wanted to wait for Mom to call out to Aunt Cassie and Uncle Garreth, but I couldn't wait for Taylin. Lazula said I had the ability, so I tried to quiet my mind so I could concentrate. All was quiet in our home, except the occasional snore from Dad. I swore at one point I heard a little scurrying and wondered if it was Rascal making another stone puzzle piece drop off.

I held my Fire Moon Stone in my hand and began to call Taylin's name like a mantra inside my head. It took a few minutes, but then I felt myself slip into a trance. I allowed it to take hold, and suddenly I found myself in Taylin's bedroom. She wasn't there. It was daylight outside, and her curtain was open. I looked out and saw her standing in the driveway talking to a girl. There was a moving truck getting unloaded.

A man came out of the truck carrying a box. This man looked extremely familiar. It was Vincent Mehla from the resort. I couldn't believe what I was seeing. The girl had to be his daughter. What was her name? Maria! I watched as he carried the box toward the house, and my eyes widened. Standing out front talking to, who I assumed was Victor's wife, was Uncle Garreth and Aunt Cassie. It felt too real to be a dream. I felt like I was there. I concentrated and willed myself to be outside with them.

Victor's wife was talking. "I was shocked to hear that Mr. Lattimier had gone missing, and the resort was closed down. We certainly appreciate the new job and lead on finding this house. When you told us it was right next door to your niece's best friend, there was no doubt in our minds. We had to jump on it."

A boy came out and yelled at Maria. "Hey, when are you going to help Maria? I'm not carrying all your junk inside!"

"Be quiet, Tobias! I'm talking to Taylin. Leave my stuff alone," Maria yelled back. "Little brothers, ugh!"

Taylin laughed. "Yeah, I get it. I got my own to deal with." It was so good to hear her voice. No one noticed I was there. Taylin looked right through me. I felt sad she couldn't see me, but I was happy that she and Maria seemed to hit it off.

"I wasn't sure I should say anything, but I want to tell you how sorry I am about your friend Krystle. My dad said she was a kind and genuine person. He thought she and I could've been great friends. When I learned we were moving next door to you; I hoped we could be too," Maria's eyes held a hopeful look.

A few tears broke away from Taylin's eyes. "I really appreciate that. I miss her so much. Her aunt and uncle are still searching," she sniffed and wiped away her tears, "But hey, I think Krystle would approve of you and me being friends."

"I do," I said. I felt the tears springing up in my own eyes. I tried to reach out and touch Taylin. Once again, my hand gained no purchase. I noticed how Taylin rubbed her arms like she was suddenly cold.

"It's like I can still feel her with me sometimes, you know? We knew each other since we were knee-high. She was my sister from another mister," Taylin laughed.

"I'll miss my friends in Brazil, but we still have family there. Dad said we'd visit next summer, so, you know," Maria was conscientious with her words.

"It's okay, Maria. You don't have to feel bad about being happy to see your friends," Taylin reached out and put her hand on Maria's arm. Maria smiled appreciatively. "So, I heard Garreth gave your dad a management position with the construction company."

"Yeah, my dad said he'd be taking on a lot so Garreth could travel more with his search crew," said Maria.

"Maria," Victor called. "Get your butt in gear and help your brother. You'll have plenty of time to socialize once you get your stuff unloaded and put away."

"Coming, Dad!" Maria rolled her eyes then smiled at Taylin. Taylin laughed.

"If you want, I can come help," Taylin offered. "We could set up your room together. We could have fun with it. Plus, I'm just nosey. I wouldn't mind seeing what you bring to the wardrobe table. We look like the same size!" Taylin zinged out in emphasis.

"Ok!" Maria laughed. They started walking to the truck and the scene before me faded. I looked over toward the house just as the last glimpse of the scene passed. I noticed Aunt Cassie looking my way. She was squinting then her eyes widened.

"Aunt Cassie?" I called out.

My eyes shot open, and I was back in my bed. It was already morning, and Chorus was at my window. I opened it to let him in. *Clave, are you close? I have something to tell you.*

Yes, I'm almost there, He said. *Is everything alright?*

I just did a calling; everyone there was wide awake. It felt like I was right there too. I could hear full conversations. I think Aunt Cassie saw me, I said excitedly. *There was a man and his family. I remember him from the place we were when we came through the Light. They were moving in next door to my friend Taylin.*

Wow, Krystle! This is unprecedented. No one has ever made such a strong calling connection before. Did they hear you at all? Clave asked.

I didn't say much. I mostly listened in on conversations. Uncle Garreth is still searching. He hired the man, Victor, to help manage his and my dad's construction company. The resort we were visiting when we entered your world shut down. The owner has gone missing. Mr. Lattimier! I had forgotten all about him and Victor! Clave, this is so much. I don't quite know how to process it all.

Have you told your parents yet? Clave asked.

No. I just woke up. I know it wasn't a dream, Clave, I insisted.

I believe you, Krystle. I'm here at your front door.

I'm coming! I slid down the pole and rushed to the front door. As I opened it, Mom spoke.

"I didn't even hear a knock! Is it Clave?" she asked. "Tell him to come on in and have breakfast with us," she insisted. I hadn't even seen her in my hurry to get to the door. Clave came in.

"Good morning all!" He signed. I turned around, and my whole family was sitting at the table, looking at us.

"Where's the fire?" Dad joked. Clave and I came and sat down. I couldn't eat till I told them everything I just experienced. I explained every detail. Everyone looked shocked.

After I had finished unloading, I took a deep breath and released. Dad spoke. "Well, it makes sense. Garreth has every aspect in perspective. He is good at keeping all bases covered. I'm glad he found someone reliable and trustworthy."

"Victor was good to us, Dad. He is a lot like you. Even has the same sense of humor." I explained how he had helped with the search, and Dad looked impressed and relieved.

"I feel better knowing everything is being taken care of, and the company will be in good hands. It makes being here all the easier. Thank you, Krystle! A weight has lifted off my shoulders." He walked around the table and hugged me.

"So, you think Aunt Cassie may have seen you?" Mom asked hopefully.

"I didn't get the chance to confirm as much, but I had a feeling she may have," I said.

"Krystle, this is so wonderful and...mind-blowing," said Mom.

"I know. Clave and I are going to talk to Lazula about it this afternoon," I said.

After we ate, Clave and I went to teach our lesson and took our students on a field trip. We practiced conversations at the blacksmith forge and with the apothecary. I picked up a few more things from a list Mom provided to help with morning sickness.

“Ahtee, Lazula!” I greeted her with a wave and smile. She was working in a garden off the side of her home. She looked up, and I notice her look between Clave and me at our linked hands. She smiled and stood.

“Ahtee, Krystle, Clave, Chorus.” She held out a handful of seeds, and Chorus leaped to her cupped hand and began to indulge.

“You called out again last night,” said Lazula. “I know because I felt it. It was powerful. The Fire Moon conferred with the other moons. It made passage for you to dream walk. You could project yourself across worlds. The moons must deem your callings to have a great deal of importance. Who was it you visited?”

“I went to visit my friend Taylin. Other people were there along with Aunt Cassie and Uncle Garreth,” I paused. “I think Aunt Cassie saw me.”

At this, Lazula looked surprised. “You believe your aunt saw you?”

“I think so. Just before I felt myself slipping away, Cassie was looking at me, and her eyes had shown recognition. I called out to her, but then I woke up.”

“Your Uncle Garreth? He still searches?” Lazula asked.

“Yes, he does,” I confirmed.

“Taylin seems to be a person of great interest. I can only speculate. The picture would be clearer to me if my sister were here with me. Tovin has finally told you his story. You know now about Zinnia, my sister,” Lazula acknowledged.

"Yes," I nodded.

Lazula pet Chorus. "Just as Chorus links with Clave in his abilities, my sister Zinnia completed the conduit between the two of us and the four moons. We were stronger together. We could decipher more information. I had not mentioned Zinnia before now as it did not pertain to the timeline."

"Timeline?" Confusion filled my voice.

Lazula looked at me and explained. "The Light moves back and forth through time as a sliding ruler. It is not concise as our minds might perceive. The Light travels through your world's timeline to find the chosen generation. When that generation enters our world, it's at the point where the Light facilitates a convergence. So, those chosen can arrive days, weeks, months, or years ahead or behind. It all aligns with the four moon's purpose."

"You are saying that people have essentially traveled both time and dimensions between Earth and this world?" I asked.

"Yes!" Lazula's replied. "I must abide by our moon's dictate what information I reveal. To do so before or after the right time could alter the course. It could present a detriment. It depends on what actions a person chooses in correlation to the information they receive."

It all tied together somehow. There were still some missing pieces to put in place. Was this the reason Tovin felt the need to include me when he revealed his past? It was not only a part of Jasper and Aura's future. It was a revelation for me as well. I needed to know, and now Lazula was free to reveal another key.

It is why the four moons choose her as their keeper. She was an ever-humble servant for which she received power. She never once abused her power. She only sought to serve her people and maintain balance for their world. So, something was amiss!? The Fire Moon called me as its weigh stone. There was something I needed to accomplish to bring a balance. I was set to a scale! A scale that, as of now, was leaning in the wrong direction.

All the while I had been in thought, Clave and Chorus's connection had also reached Lazula's mind. She had given affirmation to my feelings.

I wondered about Mr. Lattimier. How and why did he disappear? He had seen the Light. I know it! It was why he was trying to keep us away from the cave. It made him the villain in my mind. This world beckoned our family to fulfill a need for good, and he was trying to keep us away. Jaspers and my intuition about him felt more affirmed.

All I could do now was wait to see what came next. I felt an ever-growing affinity to the Fire Moon. I had not witnessed it with my own eyes, but I felt its presence within and around me like a protective shield. My Fire Moon Stone glowed, and I felt its warmth on my chest. Unwavering confidence had rid me of fear and uncertainty. I felt Clave's hand take hold of mine. He was my faithful partner and confidant.

Atop my family's tree home, we sat side by side on a broad high branch. Our secure perch brought us closer to the heavens. I felt like I could reach up and trace the stars. We watched as sparkling beams of light shot across the cool, calm dreamscape. Bursts of milky sways stretched through the deep dark expanse as the Pearlescent Blue Moon beckoned lovers in a sweet embrace. It sang of peaceful lullabies to babes wrapped up in their mother's arms.

Clave and I breathed in the cool crisp night air. We traded stories about our lives and our worlds. Clave promised to take me to meet his mom the next day.

There would be some work involved as the majority of the village came together to plant crops. Lazula liked everyone available to pitch in to make the job fast, easy and fun. It had become a tradition, and a means to celebrate unity and the common good. Most other jobs were put aside for the day as this was a benefit to keep all the people and livestock fed through the winter months.

The next morning, we loaded what we would need into our new canoe. Our entire family, alongside the Tuckers, made our way upriver. Everyone headed in the same direction. Laughter and singing filled the air. Several miles, we found a place to dock. We walked the rest of the way to an expansive field. Many were gathering in groups giving hugs and greeting one another.

Clave walked with me to one group where many had turned and smiled at us. A few of them tapped at one another and pointed our way. They were whispering. A few girls giggled.

He approached a woman with long wavy, raven hair and tapped on her shoulder. She turned around. She was a vision of natural beauty. I saw where Clave got his gorgeous gray eyes and plush lips. She had high, proud cheekbones, and she looked young still.

"Oh, Ahtee, Clave." She smiled, and they hugged.

Ahtee, Mother, I heard Clave through our connection. *I'd like you to meet my true heart bond, Krystle Genstone. She and her family are the new arrivals through the last Light. Krystle, this is my mother, Azora!*

"It's an honor to meet you, Mrs. Frost," I put out my hand. She took it and pulled me into a hug.

"Krystle, it does my heart good healing to see my son with you. The honor is mine." She gave me a hearty squeeze and held onto my arms as she back away enough to take me in. "You are a beautiful young lady!"

I blushed. "Thank you! I want to introduce you to my family." My mom and dad stood behind us with their arms around each other. Clave's mother hugged everyone as they made their exchange. She congratulated Jasper and Aura.

"I am so happy Tovin has finally pulled his head out of the chimenea and accepted this beautiful new beginning," said Azora.

Jasper smiled as he held Aura's hand. Tovin came up behind them and pulled Jasper away and pretended to rough him up. "What do you think you're doing with my daughter, boy?" He taunted Jasper.

"Dad, really?" Aura yelled. Tovin released Jasper and punched him playfully in the arm. Jasper mouthed 'oww' and rubbed at it. Tovin put his arm around Jasper and then his other around Aura and squished them together in a group hug. "Dad, we need to breathe." Aura complained.

We were all watching this unprecedented display of affection from Tovin, taking note of renewed joy in his features. It felt safe for the first time to laugh around him.

"This is a joyous day!" Lazula's voice called out from above the gathered village. Everyone quieted instantly to hear what she had to say. "We sow new life into our lands today. We are abundantly blessed as we continue this tradition of coming together. Many hands make fast work. Everyone here knows, and we continue to pass this down through each generation. This is why we thrive. We pay homage to our ancestors, who had overcome atrocity, fear, and division. Today we also welcome new family and friends. Genstone family, please come up!"

We joined her upon a small risen stage. "Some of you have already met the Genstones. I would like the rest of you to know this family. They have already proven themselves a great contribution to our village and have impacted lives here in many positive ways. New bonds of companionship have given birth to renewed joy. I'd like you to meet Flint, Gemma, Jasper, Krystle, and Rhodin. And, there is a new addition on the way."

Aura stood off the side and signed along as Lazula spoke. Shouts of joyous greetings accompanied our names as each was spoken and signed. All shouted out congratulatorily at the news of Moms' pregnancy announcement.

"Let us all bow our head and give thanks for the continued abundance and blessings we receive." Lazula bowed her head, and all followed. She spoke words in her native tongue and ended in English with, "And with thankful hearts, we give utmost gratitude for continued blessings, A-hoa!"

"A-hoa!" All said.

"Let us begin!" Lazula shouted. Everyone cried out joyously. All began forming rows upon rows across the field. Clave demonstrated what to do with a quick scoop of rich earth. He dropped seeds and recovered them with the soil. The people moved through each section quickly. After a few hours had zipped by, the task was complete. We had had so much fun; it didn't feel like hours but mere minutes.

The entire village spent the rest of the day celebrating with a feast, music, and dancing. Aura and I danced alluringly. Our hips swayed, and our arms waved with a come-hither motion. Jasper looked at me and laughed; then, he was caught up with watching Aura mesmerized. Clave looked at me with a predatory stare. Tingles ran up and down my body as I held his hooded gaze.

Jasper and Clave conferred with one another and smiled deviously. They ran at us and swept us off our feet. Clave had me cradled in his arms and pressed his lips to mine. The kiss, playful at first, turned more sensual.

My belly continued to stir with heat. Clave set me down, and we continued to slow dance together. It occurred to me; I no longer cared what anyone around me said or thought. I took Clave by surprise as I pressed my lips back upon his. I closed my eyes and imagined we were the only couple on the dancefloor as all others faded away. Right now, I was sixteen and having the time of my life. I allowed myself the freedom to live in this moment.

Later that night, I woke to the sounds of raindrops. The rain increased, and gentle roars of thunder rumbled across the distant Aventurine Mountains. This was the first rain I experienced in this world. The tranquility had me surrendered under my blanket.

Chapter 16

The following day was overcast. I opened my window and watched the clouds drift west as the sun began to peak out. The blue sky was crisp and fresh. The river below had risen and was flowing rapidly. Our canoe pushed against the higher steps before the top landing. I understood the necessity for the high rope bridges. It would be more challenging to paddle upstream. More people crossed the river this way and walked the paths.

Chorus landed on my windowsill and shook water droplets from his feathers. He jumped into my hand. His little feet felt cold. I bundled him in a soft cloth and brought him in to dry and warm up.

Good morning, Clave, I thought and smiled. A moment later, I saw him make his approach on the path. He had Bax and Sierra with him pulling a cart behind. *What, pray tell, is our mission today?*

Good morning, Krystle! Today, we dig, Clave responded.

What are we collecting?

It will be fun for the whole family. Wear layers and something to swim in. Clave sounded like an excited little boy.

Where can we swim, where we won't freeze our butts off?

You'll see! Tell your family and pack a big lunch. He looked up at me sitting at my window and winked. I waved, then left my room, slid down the slide, and opened the front door. Bax and Sierra barked and whined. Clave gave them a treat and petted their heads. He commanded them to sit with a hand signal then came inside. He kissed me on my lips. *Mmm, you're warm,* he commented.

Your face is cold, I retorted. I put my hands on his cheeks, and he grasped them with his own and kissed each of my palms.

"Aww!" I heard my dad and mom coo at us.

"Good morning, Dad, Mom. We have a fun family outing planned for today."

"Oh, what are we doing?" Mom asked.

Clave began signing, and I repeated what he said to me telepathically. "The rains softened up the clay, so today is a good day to dig. Afterward, we can swim in the hot springs."

"Wait, there are hot springs nearby?" That sounded wonderful on a chilly day such as this.

"That sounds nice," said Mom. "But I may not be able to go in the hot springs being pregnant."

"Many expectant mothers have gone in," Clave explained. "The waters here have rejuvenating and healing magic."

"Okay, no need to convince me any further," Mom agreed.

Dad woke Rhodin and Jasper and went over to invite the Tuckers along. We walked through the forest back toward the mountains. We met Tovin and Aura along the way.

Everyone started digging into mounds of muddy clay. Wet clay plopped down into the cart scoop by scoop. We didn't put in too much so that Bax and Sierra could manage to pull the load. Other people were there doing the same as us. When we had finished, I looked at everyone and myself and noticed how messy we were. This was the same clay used to make everything, including our soap.

I scooped up a heaping handful, walked up to Clave, and tapped him on the shoulder. When he turned around, I plopped it right on top of his head. It ran down his face. The look he gave me promised war. I was cracking up with laughter.

"Fight!" The Bens yelled. I screamed as Clave started charging at me. I turned to run, but he had tackled me into a pool of slop. It was cold, but I didn't care.

Next thing I knew, we were all participating in a mass mud wrestling match. It was couples at first; then Aura stared me down in challenge.

"Bring it on, sister!" I waved her toward me. She smiled with a wild look of carnage and charged at me. "Oh, crap!" I yelled.

She knocked me back with a wet slap on my backside. I struggled, and we rolled. We both grabbed handfuls of slop and plastered one another. We were making the mess of all messes. Clave took on Jasper. Rhodin and Hailey were laughing and throwing scoops at one another.

Aura and I were covered from head to toe and laughing. She had grabbed my arms, rolled on her back, and flipped me over herself with her feet on my stomach. I landed on my back with the breath knocked out of me. Good grief, she was strong! I laid there and called mercy as I tried to catch my breath. She stood over me triumphantly, "Do you concede, sister?"

I made the T-hand motion to call time out. My lungs worked overtime as I nodded my head, "I concede, you win." She held her hand out for me to take and pulled me upright and into a hug. We were completely caked. We laughed at each other.

I noticed the boys had stopped fighting. I turned to see the Bens ogling us. Jasper's attention was on Aura. Clave on me. I looked down at myself. Major wardrobe malfunctions were happening, up high and down low. My top hung low off my shoulders; my cleavage exposed. My shorts had slid low on my hips, revealing a peek of my rear side. Similar mishaps had occurred with Aura. We made quick work of fixing our clothing. Throats cleared, and everyone laughed.

Mom and Dad had given each other a facial. Eric and Liv were caked together in a loving embrace. Tovin had it out with the Bens, Rhodin, and Hailey. He took it easier on the little ones, allowing them to get a few good shots in.

They stood victorious, with heightened esteem in their shorter statures.

Clave laughed as he approached. The clay cracked and wrinkled on his face as he smiled. Clumps had started dropping off. He picked me up and carried me toward the hot springs a short distance away.

Can you swim? he asked.

"Yes, of course! Wait, Clave! What are you doing?" I yelled out in panic. His smile broadened as he picked up the pace. "Clave, no! Don't throw me in!" He jumped in with me still in his arms. I let out a scream before we hit the water.

The water clouded around us as the clay washed away from our bodies. Our heads broke the surface; steam rose all around us. I wiped away small bits still stuck to my skin. Clave turned me around and dipped my head back in the water. He massaged my scalp and worked the rest of the caked clay out of my hair. *Oh, mmm! That feels really gooood!*

Krystle, don't do that! You're giving me the tinglies! Clave mocked in a high-pitched girlie voice. *My turn!* He pulled his shirt up over his head and flung it up on the ground. I turned and faced his glorious smooth tan, muscular chest. Now I had the tinglies. Holy crap! My man was HOT...! Clave threw his head back and laughed.

Oh, my sweet! You have no idea what you did to me, seeing you like that just moments ago. I was ready to beat the crap out of the Bens for staring at you. My hands went to his bare chest, and he shuddered.

Do I detect jealousy? You have no competition! I ran my hands up over his shoulders and turned him quickly, facing him away. His broad shoulders and back were just as enticing. I dipped his head back in the water and started to massage his scalp. My fingernails scratched his head. Clave began to whimper like a dog and jerk his leg under the water. He pulled one of my hands from his head and started lapping at it with his tongue, giving doggie kisses. I started laughing.

He turned around and wrapped my arms around his neck. He pulled me to him. Our chests pressed; my cleavage popped up. The Fire Moonstone floated between us and began to glow. The warmth spread through my body. I was already starting to feel a bit overheated in the hot spring.

Clave and I looked at the glowing stone between us.

Clave?

Yes, Krystle?

I love you!

I love you, Krystle! He kissed me. My head was swimming. Multiple splashes surrounded us. Aura and Jasper, along with the Bens, had jumped in the water. The surface was murkier for a moment before the clay settled.

Clave, I think we should get out. I'm feeling a tad woozy. He helped me out, and the cool air around us was welcoming. He spread out a blanket and pulled out some food. I drank cool water from a canteen, and we ate. I started to feel better. We watched as more from our group got in the water long enough to wash off and relax for a few minutes. Mom wasn't covered. She just dipped her legs in while she sat on the edge and washed her face. She joined us for lunch.

“Hey, love birds,” she greeted. She sat down, and I unwrapped a sandwich for her. “Thank you, sweetheart. You know, Krystle, we should have a little conversation later.” She spoke, not realizing Clave could hear everything she was saying. He pretended not to notice and watched everyone else while he chewed his food.

“Mom, I know what you’re going to want to say. You already went over the birds and bees with me in great detail.” I heard Clave chuckle in my head, and my cheeks flushed.

“Sorry, hun, I don’t mean to embarrass you,” she whispered as if Clave might hear her out loud. “It’s just you and Clave are getting very close, and I know your feelings are getting stronger.”

“Mom, can we talk about this later...please?”

“Okay, sorry.” She sighed. “These pregnancy hormones are messing with me. You know, your Dad and I fell in love at the same age. We got married right out of high school. I had Jasper shortly after I turned twenty.”

I knew all of this already. And I understood what Mom was trying to say. Clave and I were waiting, but I did feel things getting more intense between us.

Little spies were afoot because suddenly Hailey asked, “Ms. Genstone, where do babies come from?” I hadn’t even heard her and Rhodin’s approach.

“Yeah, Mom! Where do they come from?” Rhodin looked down at mom’s belly.

Gemma, the medical professional, would have answered Rhodin open and honestly with all the correct anatomical terminology. Gemma, a friend to Liv, didn't want to overstep with a full explanation for Hailey. So, instead, she did the smart thing and reversed the question. "Where do you think babies come from?"

"Well, me da says one day he fed a stork some birdseed and Mommy's belly started to grow magically," said Hailey.

I heard Clave's laughter in my head, and I snorted.

"What do you think, Rhodin?" Mom asked.

"Well, I know they come from love between a mommy and daddy. But I don't understand how they get put in a mommy's belly," said Rhodin.

"Well, Hailey and Rhodin, you're both right! There is a little bit more to it, though. I'll have to ask Hailey's mom what she thinks."

"But Mom, you're a doctor!" Rhodin declared in an obvious tone. "I thought you knew all these things. Why would you need to ask Hailey's mom?"

"Because Rhodin, I need to make sure Mrs. Tucker is okay with any information I tell Hailey. Different parents have different opinions on how and when to explain the baby topic." Mom huffed. "Could you two please go play? We'll talk about it later."

The duo shrugged. "Come on, Rhodin, I don't think doctors know all the answers either." She pulled Rhodin away by his hand. I snorted, and Clave was shaking with laughter.

"See, Mom? Gets flustering! These kinds of conversations!" I pointed out.

"Okay, Krystle! I understand now." Mom conceded. "I'm just concerned and want what's right and best for you."

"I do as well, Mrs. Genstone," Clave signed at Mom, and I interpreted.

"Very well," she said. "I'm putting trust in your judgment. Just take things easy is all your Dad and I ask."

"No worries, Mom!" I gave her Aura's trademark response.

We were making trails back home when Bax and Sierra froze. They started barking, and everyone turned their attention to them. They were gazing toward the tree line ahead with their hackles raised. Their barks grew more insistent. I looked in that direction and caught a massive flash of white hair. A ginormous figure emerged on the field. Bax and Sierra were barking and whining frantically. Aura held out her hand for them to stay put. The sizeable hairy creature loomed ominously and stared in our direction.

"Dad...that's a yeti...a bigfoot..." Rhodin shouted excitedly. We were all frozen.

"Kids, just remain calm, okay? Don't make any sudden movements!" Dad put his arms out to his sides to shield us.

The Tuckers emerged from the trees behind us, and Eric shouted. "Linger! Yer mine now, ye giant snowflake!" He charged the creature, full speed ahead. The creature threw its head back, opened its mouth, and let out an enormous roar. Its large sharp canines flashed prominently from across the field. It began lunging forward in long fast strides toward Eric. Eric was screaming like a soldier in a battle charge. We watched in terror, unable to move from our position. What the hell was Eric thinking?

But then the Bens followed their dad, whooping and shouting, “Get him, Da!”

There was about to be a crash. My face drained of color as I braced myself to witness Eric’s imminent death. I was about to cover my eyes. I wanted to scream, but my vocal cords had seized up. Eric jumped up in the air. The creature lifted and spread its massive arms, ready to grab Eric and tear him to shreds. Eric crashed into the beast, and it wrapped its arms around Eric’s torso. The Bens crashed into the pair, and the creature fell backward. I heard roaring and yelling. A dust cloud kicked up around the creature as it rolled on the ground with Eric in a wrestling battle. The Bens were pulling at the creature’s arms.

Liv walked fast-paced toward the scene with Hailey in her arms. What the...heck? “Ye all knock it off! Yer scaring our friends!”

The creature sat up and released Eric. Its arms stretched open wide, and the Bens jumped in. It then occurred to me this was not an attack. They were hugging the creature. They were all smiles. Liv lifted Hailey to the creature, and Hailey wrapped her arms around its neck. The creature cradled Hailey and put its other arm around Liv. Were they friends with Big Foot? The Abominable Snow Man? A Yeti?

Then it hit me. Yehati! Aura had mentioned this word several times. What we called a Yehti on Earth was actually the Yehati of this world. I looked at Aura, who gave me a knowing wink as realization dawned on my face.

She, Tovin, and Clave were laughing. “Genstones, you should see your faces!” Tovin held his stomach as it jerked up and down.

“Would somebody please explain what the blazes is happening?” Dad spoke up. My family stood baffled.

“Dad, can we go see it, please?” Rhodin pleaded. Dad looked extremely hesitant. Mom had one hand on her chest and the other on her lower abdomen. Jasper was looking at Aura, waiting for some explanation.

Clave squeezed my hand. *It’s safe, Krystle. That is Linger. He’s completely harmless. A giant teddy bear.* He pulled me forward, but my feet didn’t move.

Just...give me a moment to process all of this! I wasn’t prepared to meet a Yehati today, if ever. All the television shows on Earth depicted a fearsome creature that killed any human that got too close. Yet, there stood the Tuckers exchanging pats on the back and holding a conversation in sign language with the creature. *Linger?* I asked again to confirm its name. Clave nodded and tugged at me again.

“I’m certain he’s curious to meet the new arrivals,” said Aura. “Flint, Gemma, Jasper, and Rhodin, come meet our resident Yehati, Linger. He visits around this time each year to trade with the village.” Bax and Sierra were panting and wagging their tales excitedly. “Come.” Aura encouraged.

We followed behind Tovin and Aura. Jasper walked beside Aura, nervous. Clave and I walked behind them, followed by Mom, Dad, and Rhodin. The closer we got, the bigger Linger grew. We stood mere feet from him and the Tuckers. Tovin hugged Linger. “Welcome back, buddy!” Linger patted Tovin’s back. Aura went next with Jasper standing behind her with his hands tucked in his pockets like a bashful child.

“Linger, these are the Genstones, our new friends,” she signed. “This is my man, Jasper.” She pointed, and Jasper, having been referred to as ‘her man’, stood straight. Aura pulled Jasper closer, and he looked up.

“Uh, I thought Tovin was a beast! Uhm, no offense, Linger! High five?” Jasper held up his hand to Linger. Linger let out a guttural coo and lifted a hand bigger than Jasper’s head. He tapped Jasper’s hand in a high five, and Jasper fell back on his ass.

Aura started laughing, “Sorry, Jasper! Linger forgets his own strength sometimes.”

“I’m okay! Thanks for asking.” Jasper sat up.

Linger signed. “Sorry!” He offered Jasper a helping hand.

“No, it’s cool big guy! No worries! That’s what my woman always says before something big or scary happens.” Everyone laughed, including Linger. We all understood the reference.

“Happy, new bond,” Linger signed to Aura. Aura smiled.

"Thank you, Linger." She went on to introduce Mom and Dad and pointed to Mom's belly, "Baby!" At this, Linger's eyes lit up.

"My mate, Soorah! Baby too!"

"Congratulations, very happy for you, Linger," said Aura.

Liv clapped her hands and wiggled spirit fingers in the air. "Well, it is bout' time you settled down!"

"Yeah, yeah!" Linger nodded. "She says it too!" He signed. We all laughed. Linger had a good sense of humor.

"Hi Linger, I'm Rhodin!" Rhodin jumped out in front of Linger. Linger pretended to be startled. "Oh, I'm sorry, Linger. I didn't mean to scare you," said Rhodin. Linger chuckled and gently put his hand out down low for Rhodin to low-five. Rhodin slapped it, and Linger squinted and feigned pain.

"Strong little man!" Linger signed.

Clave came forward with me in tow. I looked up, and kind brown eyes looked down at me. He smelled like ice and pine. Linger held his hand out, and I placed mine in his. His palms were dark and smooth. I could easily fit six more of my hands in his palm. A soft breath came out from nostrils set flat upon his dark face. His cool breath drifted gently across the top of my hand. "Linger, this is my true heart, Krystle Genstone," Clave signed.

Linger tapped with the fingers from his other hand to his chest. He pointed down to the Fire Moonstone on my chest. "You help. Mighty heart, heal great." Linger placed his other hand gently atop mine. His simple words moved me so. He was a creature so frightful at first glance—a part of this world in its wildest depths. People would describe him as an animal, but his spirit contained the best attributes of humanity. I felt tears on my cheeks. Linger wiped them away with one large finger. He held his hand aloft, and I placed my other hand on his outstretched finger. I held on as a baby would wrap a tiny hand around her papa's finger. After a moments' pause, I let go and backed away.

I looked into his kind brown eyes. "It is very nice to meet you, Linger."

Linger walked back into the woods and returned with a huge sack, stuffed and overflowing. There was hair sticking out through the seams and out the top. There was a mix of brown, red, black, and white.

"What's with the bag of hair?" I looked around for an answer.

"You're wearing it," Aura replied. "Most of our warm clothing and textiles are made from Yehati hair. It is what we trade them for." I remembered the very first time on the beach, the black fur blanket. Or what I thought was fur. It kept us warm all the way here. "The Yehati live in the coldest climate. Their hair keeps them warm. It's better than sheep and alpaca wool."

Interesting! I ran my hands down my long black sweater jacket. All this time, I've been wearing Yehati hair and didn't realize it. We continued our return back home. Linger hefted the large bag over his shoulder. It looked like it weighed a ton. But Linger looked like he could lift several tons, so it seemed no bother to him. As we got closer to the village, people started shouting his name. It seems Linger was quite the celebrity amongst the villagers. He responded in soft guttural grunts.

The people were quite excited to see him. A cart pulled by a couple of burros pulled up, and Linger placed the bag inside. People started gathering around. They rummaged through the bag of hair, making observations about the colors, texture, and quality. People pulled and gathered what they needed and filled their own smaller bags. Linger enjoyed watching all the excitement.

We left the cart and shoppers behind. Linger continued with us; he carried Hailey on one shoulder and Rhodin on the other. They were enjoying the ride. I could see that Linger was going to be a great father to his first new youngling. When we reached our homes. Linger sat down on a log. There was no way he could get through any doorway. It seemed to suit him fine.

"So, ye want the usual?" Liv addressed Linger. Linger nodded, and Rhodin and Hailey slid down off his shoulders. "Okay, shampoo and rinse first. Boys go get the shears and scissors," said Liv. She sent the Bens inside. "Hailey- mint and rosemary. Eric, Tovin, Flint- fetch and heat some pails of water."

Aura had released Bax and Sierra, and the dogs were giving Linger kisses. Linger chuckled and pet the dogs, then waved them off to play out in the field. I watched his every move since his arrival in fascination. "Krystle dear," said Liv. "Would ye mind goin' with Aura to fetch some sacks? We need to collect the hair clippins'."

"Oh, uh, sure!" I followed Aura into the third tree home. It was used for storage. Once inside, Aura handed a few large bags to me and grabbed a couple herself.

"So, Linger?" I asked. "He brings the yearly shedding and clippings, and Liv gives him a haircut?" It all sounded so strange. It wouldn't be if it were any other animal but a Yehati? Yeti? I was still getting used to the idea.

"Liv is the only person he'll allow to cut his hair." Aura said seriously. "He's very particular." I wanted to laugh. Did you ever hear that joke about the Yehti that goes into a barbershop? I had to watch this scenario play out. We came back outside.

It was a full-service Yehati salon. Liv was engaging Linger in conversation as Hailey and Rhodin dipped soapy clothes in buckets and began scrubbing Linger's massive back. Liv was massaging the soap into his scalp, and Linger had his eyes closed. His torso, arms, legs, and feet were soapy wet. The pleasant scents of mint and rosemary filled the air. Linger looked like he was enjoying being pampered. The men lifted the heavy buckets of water and rinsed the soap away.

Liv produced a large comb, and she passed brushes to Aura and me. "Start at his legs." She instructed. I took one leg and Aura the other. It suddenly occurred to me, I was within view of a particular part of male anatomy and tried my best to keep my eyes averted from his 'area'. Come to find out, he wore a loin and butt flap made from his hair woven into buckskin. He was a large specimen, and I was glad not to have witnessed his private area in such close proximity.

Liv passed out towels for us to dry his hair just enough so it wasn't dripping wet. After Linger was all brushed out, Liv proceeded to shear the larger areas first and followed up with the scissors. I had to admit, Linger looked like a handsome Yehati when Liv finished. He had a thick, soft underlayer cropped close all over his body. His loin and butt flaps were more prominent as he stood up. We collected his fresh hair clippings. We filled up all the bags. Liv took them, "I'm goin' to get this all dried and processed into yarn. I have some things I'd like to make for the baby and ye kids. Linger, thank ye for yer donation." That was the easiest part for him.

"How many Yehati are there? That was a lot of hair," I spoke, and Clave signed for me.

Linger started moving his hand in response, and Clave interpreted telepathically. Chorus had been jumping from person to person in our group all day, keeping our connection open. "Yehati are mostly solitary and territorial. Some have small groupings of families. It is hard to determine how many of my kind there are. We come together in larger groups during the coldest time of the year. There are a few communal caves. We all take part in collecting our hair, sheddings and keep them dry in the caves. I have always been the one to make a trade with humans. Most Yehati are frightened to come close to humans."

"Why are they afraid?" I asked. "Did a human do something bad to a Yehati?"

"I don't know of a human harming a Yehati. We are mostly shy. While curious, the Yehati are uncertain how to approach humans. The humans would load a cart of offerings and leave it out near the forest. I would drop off my bag and take what I thought useful. I met Eric and Liv years ago. They showed no fear when they saw me. Benjamin and Bennigan approached me first. They were small like your brother. Liv was kind and insisted on giving me a haircut, and I've been back every year since. The Tucker family established better communications between the humans and Yehati. Now I get more useful things for trade."

Clave's interpretation filled in the gaps as Linger grunted and signed. Clave asked Linger a question, and Linger nodded. *I asked Linger if he would like to join our class tomorrow, and he agreed,* Clave explained.

I smiled and signed, "Thank you."

Linger responded, "You're welcome, Krystle."

Linger brought out a giddy liveliness for all the children. They sat in attention as Linger told them stories. He played out the high-five between him and Jasper. He clapped his large hands together and mimicked his view of Jasper falling back on his butt. All the children were cracking up with laughter. Linger was a very entertaining storyteller. I suppose he was the same amongst his own. It probably got boring during winter, cooped up in a cave.

After class, Clave and I walked around the village with him. Linger always stopped for greetings and hugs. People showered him with gifts and allowed him to take what he wanted in trade. He had several smaller carts filled with full bags of various items. He mentioned the Yehati would be happy with this year's exchange. Some of his brethren have become curious to the point that they may someday come along. For now, Linger was pleased to be the Yehati trade and spokesperson.

The next day we helped Linger load a large cart. He mentioned he'd have help as he approached a point where many would come to his aid. He would return the cart and more things the Yehati liked to trade a little later in the season. We said our goodbyes, and Linger was off. It was like this every year. He came, dropped off, got a haircut, communed with the village, shopped, and left. It sounded like a pleasant trip to a mall.

There was a sadness to seeing him go. I felt like a child having had Christmas day with all the joy and excitement and the day it was over. I leaned my head on Clave's shoulder, and he put his arm around me. We walked back home and back to our small world of love and happiness. I wondered what new surprises awaited. There was only more to learn as my family's adventure in this world continued.

Chapter 17

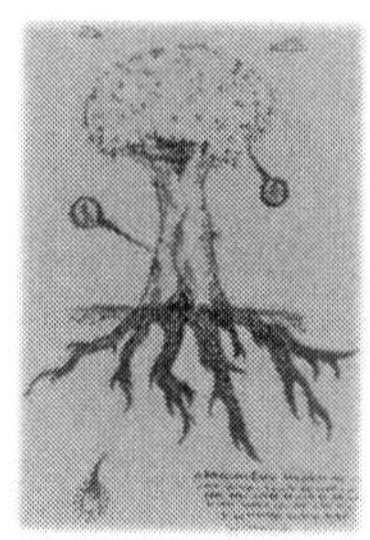

Dear Krystle,

It's been three months! Garreth had gone back to the resort once more, and it is officially deserted. The world moved on from the Genstone Family's mysterious disappearance. You had your fifteen minutes of fame and have been written off. The last two full moons had shown no hints of any strange phenomena.

I met Maria Mehla. She told me you met her father, Victor, at the resort. He saw you, Jasper, and Rhodin go through the light. By the time he had caught up with Garreth and Cassie, it was gone. Garreth ran into the cave after you. He couldn't see or hear anything. He went back to search the next day. All he found was your mothers' shawl again.

Maria has been a great source of comfort, and we have become good friends. When I talked to her for the first time, I swear, it felt like you were there. Cassie thought she saw you. She's been an emotional train wreck and thought her eyes were playing tricks on her.

You know how people say someone must be talking about them when their ears are itching? When I think about you, it feels that way. It's like I can sense you're talking or thinking about me. You'd better be telling people I'm the most awesome bestie anyone has ever had.

School has been mostly boring without you. Maria is only in one of my classes, and we have lunch together. People have finally stopped staring at me and giving me pitiful looks.

I've been helping Cassie and Garreth in any way I can in all my spare time. I research online. I've joined every chat forum for people who have gone missing. I read through everything to see if anything relative shows up. Maria has been helping me with this too. The world has gone mad since you left. I can't stand all the hype and hate going around, so I keep my focus on the search.

Krystle, I hope where ever you are, you're safe. I hope you found your mom and dad and your brothers are with you. I hope you are healthy, strong, and have found happiness. You deserve happiness. I'm trying my best not to hurt so much inside. You'll always be my numero uno amigo!

Love you, girlie!

Taylin

Mom's baby bump had grown significantly, and we had to get some new clothing items. She found a new appreciation for Yehati hair. She loved how soft and warm it felt. It was comfortable and hypoallergenic, so that was a plus in her book.

Dad had built their love swing, and they sat together on it every evening talking about their day and the baby bump. They were trying to figure out baby names and taking polls.

Harvest season came, and there was a Festival. Jasper got down on one knee to propose to Aura. She looked confused and had asked him if he was hurt. He had to explain the Earth custom to her at the moment. When the realization hit, she jumped up and down excited. She shouted out yes again and again. He put a golden band on her finger with an oval-shaped Blue Moon Stone inset. The stone had been given to him by Lazula a few months ago. She had told him that he would know what to do with it.

Lazula made the announcement to the entire village. There was to be a bonding ceremony on the night of the Grand Glacial Moon.

“We will be sisters officially,” I told Aura. “Though, I already feel like we’ve been sisters all along.”

“I’m so excited,” said Aura. “Jasper Otek has a nice ring to it, doesn’t it?”

“I thought it was customary for the woman to take the man’s last name.” Jasper came up behind Aura and wrapped his arms around her.

“Many women on Earth hyphenate their last names. You could go by Aura Otek-Genstone,” I pointed out.

“Yeah, I like the way that sounds,” said Aura.

Jasper kissed her cheek. "I'm happy with whatever you decide, my beautiful thundercloud. You can call me anything you like, as long as you call me yours."

"Ok then, we will be Mrs. and Mr. Otek-Genstone. It's settled." Aura nodded her head. She turned and kissed Jasper on his lips.

"I'm totally cool with that!" Jasper kissed her back.

"My brother is totally whipped! Good job, Aura!" I congratulated her.

"Seems Jasper isn't the only one." Aura's eyes went to Clave.

I deny nothing! Clave shared amongst us telepathically. Chorus chirped in agreement. *Krystle had me the first moment I saw her.*

"Aww!" Jasper and Aura cooed together.

The Twin Bens joined us. "So, that's how it's done now, is it?"

Benjamin fumbled to one knee. Bennigan jumped up and down and squealed like a girl. Aura and I whacked the Bens across their heads simultaneously. It had been a long while since I had to do that, but they don't get to mock my future sister-in-law. That's my job.

The villages' busiest season was upon us. Over the next few months, the whole village worked together in preparation for the winter months.

Everyone was so busy. The days were flying fast. Before we knew it, the first snow was blowing in. Mom was a few months shy of our family's new arrival. We didn't know if the baby would be a boy or girl, but Mom kept referring to it as she or her. Bax and Sierra had had a litter of eight puppies. Rhodin and Hailey begged for all of them. They were relentless and asked every day.

When the puppies were finally old enough, Clave, Jasper, and Aura showed up early one morning with arms loaded. Snowy white and gray puffballs whimpered and whined. Liv and Mom gave in when Eric and Dad talked about how having dogs would be beneficial.

"We will train them," said Dad. "The timing couldn't be more perfect."

"I've just never been used to having pets," said Mom. "I'm agreeing, but they should be outdoor dogs. They are well suited to this environment. You and the guys need to build some shelter for them. Rhodin and Hailey will be responsible for feeding them. I'll have my hands full with our baby girl."

"Ye know ye will have plenty of helpers, Gemma. Everyone is excited for the baby. I got plenty of blankets, hats, and booties for her. She is gonna have everything. Spoiled she will be," said Liv.

"I know," said Mom. "Cassie was a great help with the kids when I was in school. I don't know what I would've done without her and Garreth." She started crying. "Oh, I'm so sorry! Damn these pregnancy hormones!"

"Ye miss them, Gemma," Liv comforted. "I get it. Bein' here without me mahm and sister while I was pregnant with Hailey was tough. It's okay, love, you go ahead and let it out." Mom sobbed on Liv's shoulder. Dad stepped up behind Mom and gently turned her into his arms. He rubbed her back while she continued. I wrapped my arms around them both.

Rhodin came up between them and hugged Mom's belly, "What did you say? Oh, okay, I'll tell her." We broke apart and looked at Rhodin. Was he trying to ease Mom's emotions, or was he really communicating with the baby? I didn't doubt anything anymore. All the experiences I have had in this world so far attested to such a possibility.

"The baby said that everything will be just fine and to pick one of the dogs to come inside. She wants one as a playmate." Rhodin went over and picked up one of the puppies. "I think she would like this one!" It was the runt of the litter. Her coat was mostly white and grey speckled throughout. "We should name her Sienna. Kind of like her mama Sierra."

Rhodin placed the puppy in Mom's arms, and she burst out laughing. "Sienna, it is!" We ran our hands through Sienna's soft plush coat. Sienna gave Mom kisses on her chin. "Whew! Not a fan of puppy breath!"

"Jasper and I can train the puppies," said Aura. "Rhodin and Hailey can help. It will be fun!"

"We can move some things up in the storage tree, and the dogs can stay there till we build something more sufficient. I'll take the kids to get some more food and supplies for them," Dad volunteered.

"So, we're really gonna keep all of them?" I asked.

"Don't you think it would be good to have a whole dog sled team for the upcoming winter?" Dad asked.

"Remember, half of them belong the Tucker's," Mom reminded.

"Yes, but they will all work together as one team," said Dad. "We'll work the rest out."

"May we make use of Bax and Sierra to test out one of the new sleds?" Rhodin asked Aura.

"Of course! The puppies are fully weaned, and Sierra's ready to get back to work," said Aura.

"I understand how you feel, girl!" Mom looked at Sierra. "No offense, kids! I enjoyed being with my babies. I took extended maternity leave with each of you. But when it was time to go back to work, I was ready."

Sienna had settled down in Mom's arms atop the baby bump. It seemed odd that she hadn't put the pup down or passed it off to anyone. She went and sat down on the swing, and Dad joined her. Sienna had fallen asleep, and Mom continued to pet the pup resting on her. She started singing "Twinkle, Twinkle, Little Star." I felt myself sway. My mind was flashing images of me surrounded by white light.

Soft whisps and orbs swirled around me, and I felt so at peace. I remember singing the lullaby to myself. I was in the Light, going in reverse. I heard Jasper and Rhodin scream my name, along with Aunt Cassie and Uncle Garreth. There were a few other people. Some sort of struggle was happening. "She needs help!"

A whisper of a girls' voice came through. "Darkness holds her hostage! You must save her!"

I saw a flash of dark hair and deep blue eyes. "She's mine, and I will have more!" came a sinister voice.

"No!" I shouted. Arms came around me, and I struggled. "No...!" I screamed.

Krystle, my heart! It's me, Clave! Wake up! I felt myself being dragged back through the Light and heard the sound of a door slammed shut. It echoed through my mind. My eyes blinked rapidly, then closed; my body went slack. Strong arms held me up. *I've got you, my love.* My vision came into focus as I was lifted and carried inside.

"Clave?" I looked up at him as he gently laid me down and pulled a blanket over me. I heard the clattering of multiple footsteps, and then Mom and Dad came into view.

"Krystle, honey! Are you okay?" Mom sounded troubled. She was sitting beside me on the couch, holding my hand. I looked at her and shook my head. Dad was kneeling next to me on the floor.

"I don't know...I don't understand what...happened?" I felt my voice struggle for words. Clave brought me something to drink. Dad helped me to sit up and took the offered cup from Clave. I was shaking so hard; I couldn't take hold. Dad held the cup to my mouth and tipped it slowly. I took a few shaky sips. He turned to pass it back to Clave.

"Can you remember anything, sweet pea?" Dad's eyes filled with concern. "You looked like you were having a seizure."

"She was in a trance! Having a vision!" Clave signed. I heard him speak in my head. "Something triggered it."

"Krystle, you scared me, baby," said Mom. "Your eyes glazed over, and you were screaming."

"What...did I...s...say?"

"I don't know...you screamed it twice," said Mom. "What was it? I saw your Fire Moon Stone start to glow."

"The Light...Twinkle Little Star...fighting...save her!" My voice shook. "Oh God...no...Taylin!" I tried to sit up.

"Shh...baby...calm yourself." Dad brushed my hair from my forehead and stroked my cheek. "Garreth wouldn't let anything happen to her. She's safe."

"People we left...b...behind...in...dan...danger," I stuttered.

"Jasper and I will go get Tovin and Lazula," I heard Aura speak. "She will be able to help Krystle clarify this vision."

I watched as Mom and Dad turned and nodded to Aura. "Eric, the boys, and I will watch Rhodin and tend to the puppies," said Liv. "Let us know if there be anything else we can do."

"Thank you, Liv," said Mom. "You are truly the best!"

"Aye, ye know, I'll be lookin' out for me family. That's what ye have become to us, love."

"We all feel the same for you as well, Liv." The two exchanged a kiss on one another's cheeks. Liv directed Rhodin and Hailey out, telling them everything would be alright. I sat up more. Dad moved aside and allowed Clave to sit beside me. Clave put his arm around me, and I leaned into him. I breathed in and released a stuttered sigh. My shaking eased away, and Dad passed my drink back to me. I held the cup securely in both hands and took small sips. The constricted anxiety drained away as I sipped and breathed in the pleasant warm herbal drink. Mom sat back more and held my hand. Dad brought Sienna over and placed her in my lap.

"I always heard petting animals was a stress reliever," he commented and gave the pup a few strokes. He took my cup and put one of my hands on her. She peacefully slept as I allowed my hand to sink into her lavishly soft coat. Claves' hand joined mine. Our hands brushed together. The combined sensations enjoyable. Calm and love replaced fear and dread. This was what I needed.

Dad came over to sit next to Mom. He put his hand on her belly. "Oh, I felt her kick!" He and Mom were smiling.

"Feel this, Krystle!" Mom placed my free hand on her belly. "Oh, there she goes again! Wow, she's excited! She's kicking up a storm!"

"Wow. I can feel it! She's so strong! Hello, baby sis!" I wished Uncle Garreth and Aunt Cassie could be here. "Mom? What if we combined Garreth and Cassie's names somehow? For the baby's name, I mean."

"Hmm, I wonder. Mom played out the combinations. "Nothing comes together quite right."

I looked down at Mom's bracelet and observed the Glacial Moon Stone. It looked like an opal. "How about Garrissa Opal? Or Opal Rose? Aunt Cassie loves roses."

"I think I like that," said Mom. "What do you think, Flint?"

"Garrissa Opal Rose Genstone! I like the way it all goes together," Dad agreed. He put his mouth closed to Mom's belly. "What do you think, little munchkin? Garrissa Opal Rose?"

"Oh, that was a big kick! That either means she really likes it, or she hates it!" We all laughed. Mom placed her hands on either side of her belly. Having a baby sister was going to be fun. I began to wonder how she would look. Would she be as easy as Rhodin, with an occasional bouncy episode? Would she be wild like her environment? Feisty and strong-willed like her sister-to-be, Aura?

Lazula stood at the doorway with Tovin towering behind her. She smiled as she observed the loving scene. She came inside and sat on the low round table in front of me. "You've adopted one of the pups as a family pet? What have you named her?" She gave the pup a few gentle strokes.

"Rhodin named her Sienna," I said. "He told us the baby picked her out as a playmate."

"This is good," said Lazula. "They make the truest, most loyal friends. She will protect the baby with her life. She will be a wonderful playmate."

"Krystle," Lazula pulled my attention to her. "Tovin and I were already on our way here and met Aura and Jasper along the way. I felt the Fire Moon sent you a message! Aura told me you were quite shaken! What did you see?"

"There's something in the way. I felt a heavy door slammed shut. I can't remember everything. I was in the Light. I was going in reverse back from when I came here. There were bits and pieces of what was happening just after the Light took me back on Earth. My brother, Cassie, and Garreth screamed for me. A few others. A struggle. A voice. Help...a girl! Something about helping a girl! I'm afraid Taylin or someone left behind is in danger!" It all spilled out of me. Sienna stirred and whimpered in my lap, and I stroked her head. She left out a stifled huff and settled.

"Did you see Taylin specifically? What did the voice sound like?" Lazula put her hand on my knee and searched my eyes with hers.

"No, I didn't see Taylin. I saw...Oh My God! I saw Cynnica!" I had forgotten about the strange little girl back at the resort. She was trying to lead Rhodin through the Light. She was so insistent. Something was off about her. 'Save the girl!' Could it be Cynnica? I explained this to Lazula. How is Cynnica tied to all this? She knew about the Light, possibly about this world.

"She needed a host to guide her into the Light!" It occurred to me. "She couldn't have gone through on her own!"

"I remember the story you told me; the ruler and high priest tainted by darkness could not go through." The revelation hit me.

Lazula nodded. "This is true. This child Cynnica. Did she act oddly? In what way?"

“She acted like she was in a trance the first time she talked to Rhodin and me. She told us about the Light and that the way is open. She knew and was waiting for an opportunity. She was going to use Rhodin as a host. Before the Light pulled me through, Jasper had pulled her away from us. Me and Rhodin. She was screaming, but she didn’t sound like a little girl. She sounded like she was...possessed!”

“Sweet Heavens, that poor child!” Mom wrapped her arms around her belly.

“I do believe there is a possible danger,” said Lazula. “The Dark Spirit still resides on Earth. The child has become its’ host. It seeks passage here and needs a Pure Soul host to guide it through. I believe it means to finish what it started thousands of years ago. As long as the child gains no host for passage through the Light, we remain safe.”

“What exactly is a Pure Soul? Is it the soul of a child? The souls of the innocent?” Mom asked.

“Pure Souls are new souls that have made their first journey to the world of the living,” Lazula explained. “Pure Souls remain as such throughout the life of the person. So long as the person does not allow themselves to be tainted. The Dark Spirit has always sought to corrupt. It seems Pure Souls are harder to find on Earth or the else the Dark Spirit would have made its way here long ago.”

Our world had become tainted. There was so much animosity, greed, and corruption, war, and bigotry. Another thing occurred to me! I felt like I should whack my head for not remembering this sooner. “Lattimier!”

"The resort owner?" Dad questioned.

"Yes!" I exclaimed. "He said Cynnica came back every year with her family. I think it was the same time every year. She was casing the resort and waiting for the right moment. It means she knew when the Light was due to show up. She needed a Pure Soul to come willingly. Rhodin is a Pure Soul!"

"You are right, Krystle," Lazula agreed. "Rhodin is a Pure Soul. The moons would only choose a Pure Soul. Krystle, you are a Pure Soul as well!"

I looked to Mom's belly, "My baby sister is as well!"

"She is," Lazula agreed. "She has been called by the Grand Glacial Moon. We must make preparations against an enemy that cowers in the body of an innocent child. If she finds a way, we will need to help her, free her from the Dark Spirits' grasp. We must figure out how to destroy it before such time comes."

"Taylin, I need to call out and try to warn her. She, Maria, Uncle Garreth, and Aunt Cassie are actively seeking a way to the Light! She searches chat forums every day. She could be baited and lured. They could all be in danger!"

"Gemma, Lazula, ye must come quickly," Eric stood in our doorway, breathing heavily. "Ye will need to bring yer medical bag!"

Dad helped Mom up. "What's the matter?" she asked.

"Linger!" Eric cried. "It's Soorah, his mate! She's in labor, in distress! I sent Linger back to her and told him I'd bring you."

"Can't the Ibekwe's come?" Dad asked, motioning to Mom's belly. "It's not exactly safe for Gemma in her condition!"

"Jasper and Aura already tried the Ibekwe's. They were not at the clinic or their home. Someone had told them there was another emergency, and they went to see about that."

"I'm coming with you," said Dad.

"I'm coming too, Mom." I stood up. "I'm better! I can help!"

"Tovin and me boys have made a couple of sleds ready. We have more dogs ready to go," said Eric. "Ye can all come, but the men will have to wait back about half a mile. Soorah is already frightened and has had little contact with humans. It could make the situation worse if she sees a group of big men and panics. She met me before, and it took a long time to gain her trust. I will drive the dogs for yer sled, Gemma. You'll be safe with me," said Eric

I'm coming, Krystle, Clave said through our connection.

I nodded, "Could you go up and fetch Mom's medical bag. It's the first bedroom, at the foot of their bed." Clave took off upstairs. We all assembled outside. We loaded the sleds and positioned ourselves. Mom, Lazula, and I sat bundled on one sled manned by Eric. Dad and Clave were on the other sled with Tovin.

Liv stood off to the side, holding Rhodin's and Hailey's hands. "Be careful!" She shouted. The Bens released the lead dogs. Tovin and Eric lifted the leads and shouted, “Hike!” We reared back in our seats as the dogs lunged forward

“We have to go straight Nor-East toward the mountains for five miles, then turn right at the first large boulder before the river,” Eric called out. “It is another four miles North after that.”

I saw Chorus flying ahead, guiding us. *Are you all okay over there?* I heard Clave. I looked over to him and gave a thumbs up.

We will have to do this again, another time when it’s not an emergency. I would say this is fun if not for the dire situation. Sorry, I don’t mean to sound insensitive. It’s just been too much drama already today, I confessed. *I pray Soorah and her baby will be alright.*

It’s okay to feel the way you do, Krystle. Chorus will stay with you. I will be able to see what is happening. If anything is amiss, the rest of us will come to help, said Clave.

The first large boulder was ahead; just beyond it was the river. Tovin and Eric both shouted, “Gee, Gee!” The lead dogs began turning right, and the rest followed. We had to brace ourselves as we hit a few bumps on the way. After one particular hump, we jostled upward from the sled, and our bottoms hit back down with mild discomfort.

“Are you okay, Mom?”

“I’m fine, Krystle… it would take more than a few bumps in the road to cause any concern,” she responded.

I could see the light of fire up ahead. “You’ve got to stop here!” Eric shouted.

"Whoa!" Tovin called out. Their dogs and sled came to a halt.

We continued, and the firelight grew. Linger stood and waved both hands crisscross over his head. We were close, and Eric called, "Whoa!" I could hear the brake dragging before the dogs came to a halt. "Easy!" He yelled at the dogs. Eric came around and helped Mom to her feet. A short distance away, Soorah was groaning. She was in a lot of pain.

Soorah's eyes looked troubled as we approach, but then she saw Eric and Linger, and she calmed. Soorah's belly protruded immensely. She was leaned back against a large rock. Eric began signing to her, letting her know we were here to help her and her baby. Linger sat down beside her. He signed, "Gemma, help baby! Help, Soorah!"

Mom reached out to touch Soorah's belly. Soorah's eyes widened, and she started to screech. Linger took Soorah's hand and tried to calm her. Mom knew what to do at that moment. She removed her coat and lifted her shirt, exposing her belly to Soorah. "I have a baby too!" Mom signed. She reached her hand out for Soorah to take. Soorah extended her hand slowly. Mom slowly guided Soorah's hand to her belly. Mom smiled, "See?" She signed. "I know too! I am here! I can help!"

Soorah's hand expanded across Mom's belly. Understanding came across her features, and she relaxed. Soorah looked up at me. Mom signed, "That is my baby too! She can help!" At this, Soorah nodded. She winced and roared. We all had to cover our ears. The sounds of her pain were deafening.

"I must touch your belly to feel your baby! To help, okay?" Mom signed. Soorah was breathing rapidly. She nodded again. Mom put on gloves and felt Soorah's belly. She moved down to check her. "She's fully dilated. The baby is too large to fit through the birth canal. I'll have to do a C-Section. If I don't, she and the baby could be in big trouble." I watched as Eric translated to Linger and Soorah.

"Krystle, go sit near Soorah's head. I will need you to administer anesthesia carefully. One drop at a time." I did as Mom instructed. Before I held the cloth to Soorah's nose, I looked into her eyes. At that moment, she recognized trust and nodded for me to proceed. After a few moments, Soorah's eyes rolled back into her head, and she had passed out.

Her chest and large belly rose and fell in a steady rhythm. Mom started cleaning Soorah's belly with antiseptic. She instructed Lazula to pass instruments to her. I continued to drip the anesthesia onto the cloth as instructed.

Mom made a lateral incision below the belly button. After the uterine incision, Mom cursed. "Shit! This is one big heavy baby! Eric, I am going to get the baby's head free and clear. I'm going to need your help to deliver this baby. I can't lift this much weight."

Once the baby Yehati's head was out, Mom moved over and instructed Eric on how to proceed. The baby fully emerged then began to cry in a high-pitched squeal. "It's a boy!" Mom shouted.

Lazula rubbed the Yehati youngling down with a towel as he lay upon Soorah's belly. Mom tied off then cut the umbilical cord.

“Congratulations, Linger! You have a healthy baby boy!” Lazula cried. Linger grunted and whooped with excitement. The Yehati youngling had light brown hair like Soorah’s with white patches around its head. The baby continued to cry as Eric lifted the youngling to Linger. Linger cradled his son with a look of joy and pride. He rocked his son, and the youngling settled down. With one hand, Linger signed. “Soorah, okay?”

“Soorah is going to be fine,” Mom responded as she continued to work. She delivered the placenta and began suturing. Once she finished closing Soorah up, she said, “I’m going to need some help up. My legs are cramped.”

She finished cleaning Soorah’s sutures. “Krystle, you can stop the anesthesia. Carefully toss the cloth away. Eric and Lazula helped Mom to her feet and held her steady until she stretched and worked the cramps out.

I heard Chorus chirping and looked up to see him perched on the outcropping over our heads. *You and Gemma did a great job.* I heard Clave come through. I smiled up at Chorus and puckered my lips in a kiss. *Can’t wait,* said Clave.

“What are you going to name him?” Eric signed to Linger.

“Kyan!” Linger spelled out.

“Good name,” said Eric. Linger grunted and nodded. Soorah started to wake. She scooted up and noticed her belly was smaller. She touched tenderly at her stitches. She looked up to see her son in her mate’s arms. Tears sprung from her eyes as Linger gently lay their son Kyan in her arms. Soorah purred and cooed. She looked up at my mom and signed, “Thank you! New friend!”

Mom smiled and signed back, “You’re welcome! Happy for you!” She told Linger about the stitches and how they would dissolve in a few weeks and told him Soorah should move slow and take it easy. Kyan was already nursing.

Lazula signed, “Congratulations!” and gave Soorah a blanket to wrap around Kyan.

“Are you and Soorah going to be okay out here by yourselves?” I signed to Linger.

“Help will come.” Linger pointed back to the forest. I looked and saw curious eyes looking out from the shadows. We gathered our belonging and said our goodbyes to the new family. We started heading back and rejoined Tovin, Dad, and Clave.

Chapter 18

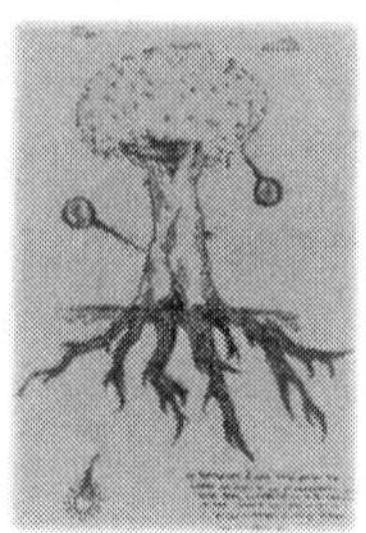

A couple of miles had passed when Lazula shouted, “Stop! Stop here!” The sleds halted. Lazula got up and started walking. “Here...” she said. “It was here.”

“What was here?” Tovin came up beside her. We all followed.

“I’m so sorry, Tovin. I woke up after Zinnia and Mieruss had gone missing in this spot. I feel something. Something is pulling me.” Lazula began surveying the area. She walked toward a cluster of trees, then stopped. She pointed to the ground. “I need to dig here!” She plucked a low branch from one tree and plunged it into the snow.

Tovin retrieved a shovel. He began to dig till we saw the earth. “Just a little more,” Lazula instructed. An object was revealed, but a layer of dirt still obscured its full identity. Tovin reached down to pick it up. Lazula quickly grabbed his arm.

“Don’t...don’t touch it. I need something to wrap it in.” We all stood with our eyes fixed to the ground. Tovin handed a cloth to Lazula. She bent down and placed the cloth atop the object, then lifted it out of the dirt. She held it by an end and shook the loose soil away, and her hand closed around a grip. She slid her other hand beneath the cloth and revealed the object laid across her palms.

A shocked breath escaped me. It was a dagger with a deadly straight blade. The handle held a round diamond embedded near the blade. "That was the dagger from my nightmare!" I was about to be sacrificed!" I felt the warmth of the Fire Moon Stone against my chest as it glowed in confirmation of my statement. "The man in my dream was the high priest! He told me the Dark Spirit wanted Pure Souls. It fed on Pure Souls!"

"Why is it here? How did it get here?" Tovin stared at it with scowling eyes. Lazula carefully wrapped the dagger up in the cloth.

"I do not know the answer," said Lazula. "I am certain it played a part in Zinnia and Mieruss's disappearance."

"Perhaps one of the ancestors brought it over during the exodus," I supplied. "They wanted to ensure the weapon was out of evil's grasp."

"This can't be where it has been all this time," said Tovin. "Someone, either Zinnia or Mieruss, must have found it in its original location."

"The ancestral catacombs!" Lazula declared. "Where most of our first-generation ancestors laid to rest. Someone had it with them when they came through the Light. They had probably hidden it there. Zinnia performed the right of passage. A blessing for those who passed. It may have been she who found the dagger there."

With no more speculations to be made at the moment, we returned to the sleds and proceeded back home. Tovin took Lazula to her home. Everyone was tired from this evening. Dad allowed Clave to sleep on the couch downstairs. I snuggled into Clave, and we fell asleep together.

The next day Clave and I went to Lazula's. I wanted her guidance with calling out to Taylin. Mom wanted to come and try to reach Cassie, but she was still exhausted from the night before. When we entered Lazula's home, she had the dagger laid out on her table and examined it.

"I don't understand. There is no energy of any kind to it. It is an empty vessel."

"What do you mean?" I asked her.

"See here." She pointed to the diamond in the hilt. "It is meant to hold something, a force of energy. It is empty, dormant. I think it was a means of transference. It had been drained. But, into what? Or whom? The blade is how a force is drawn and transferred."

"The sacrifices!" I exclaimed. "This is how the Pure Soul pulls from the body. When the blade made contact with a vessel, the soul was drawn out and trapped in the diamond. The dark spirit fed through contact with the blade. Like a blood transfusion."

"Through the blood enters the spirit," Lazula commented. "It was a quote often mentioned by our ancestors."

"Lazula? Do you think the knife still contained energy when Zinnia found it? She may have come in contact with the blade, and it affected her somehow."

Lazula's eyes widened, and she ran outside. Clave and I followed her. She was searching the carvings on her home.

"There!" she pointed. "My mind is going feeble in my old age. But, it's right there!" An image of a sacrifice. The blade was going into a person on an altar. Hands held a dagger that plunged into the chest. In the next image, over those same hands held the blade out before their own body. They were about to stab themselves.

"I had misinterpreted it all this time," said Lazula. "The person was not sacrificing themselves. They were injecting the Pure Soul into their vessel. Some of the Dark Spirit's essence remained in the diamond. Oh my... no! My poor sister! Zinnia... no!" Lazula began to weep, and Clave put his hands on Lazula's shoulders. My heart felt torn inside. Zinnia may very well be lost to the darkness. She and Mieruss had gone missing on the night Solaura, and the baby passed.

"Lazula? I hate to ask but, do you remember anything from that night? After you went with them to lay Solaura and the baby to rest?"

Lazula's eyes drifted, and she stilled as she tried to recall a distant painful memory. "We had laid Solaura and the babe upon a cart and covered them. It was dark and storming. We came to the resting ground and laid Solaura in the earth. I held the babe swaddled, ready to place her with her mother."

"Zinnia insisted I lay the child upon a stone nearby so she could perform a special ceremony and blessing. I trusted my sister, nothing seemed amiss, so I did as she instructed. I had blacked out right after I laid the child down."

"I woke the next day. Stones set upon the grave. I was shivering cold. I looked around and called out for Zinnia and Mieruss. They wouldn't have left me out there. I was so confused. I stumbled back to the village where Tovin found me just outside his home. He asked what happened. I couldn't recall anything at the time."

"Do you think she and Mieruss were in some plot together?" I asked.

"I don't believe so. It would seem as such since they had both disappeared that night. Speculations have been made. Wild animal attack, kidnapping. No one would have ever accused either of some kind of wrongdoing." Lazula shivered and rubbed her hands up her arms. Clave brought a blanket and wrapped it around her shoulders. She stared back down at the dagger. Looking at it gave me the creeps, but I knew it was another key to the continuous mystery.

"Perhaps you should rest," I suggested. "This seems too much for you right now. I can call out to Taylin and see what comes of it."

"No, child!" Lazula reached her hand out and placed it on my arm. "I am here for you. You have been here for me. Give me a moment, and we shall prepare." I nodded and got up to give her some space.

Clave wrapped me up in a hug, and I breathed him in. His fresh wild scent invigorated my spirit. His strong arms were my anchor. Clave tilted my face up with his finger beneath my chin, and our souls took a moment respite through our gaze. He chastely kissed my lips and continued to hold me. He had become my one constant. The tether between us drew us closer every day.

Lazula rose from her seat and stopped before us. She clasped Clave's head between her hands and pressed a kiss to his forehead. She turned and did the same to me and smiled. "The love and support I see between two kindred souls does my heart good. Let us begin!"

We gathered around the fire, and Lazula pulled out her bag containing the moonstones. One represented each of the four moons. She set down the Fire Moon Stone, Grand Glacial Moon Stone, Amethyst, and Pearlescent Blue Moon Stones. Instantly her Fire Moon Stone and mine upon my chest recognized and acknowledged each other with a flare of warmth and a quick flashing glow. It sent a chain reaction down the other three in line as each flashed in turn.

"The energy grows stronger." Lazula waved her hand across the line of stones. "I can feel their attributes, still separate, yet combining. They sing together like a symphony. Much like the tether between two lovers." She smiled and looked up at Clave and me. "Close your eyes and concentrate. You can hear it. Focus on Taylin. You will have a stronger connection than ever before."

I closed my eyes and eased into the sensation I had felt before when I called. A light flashed. A sweet fragrance enchanted my senses while soothing music played in the background. An adorable little girl with dark hair in a ponytail approached. Her sweet little face, with its soft olive complexion, pink lips, and bluish-gray eyes, came before me.

"Do you want to play with me? My name is Taylin. What's yours?"

"Krystle!" I responded.

I was standing face to face with her. I looked down at my hands. They were the hands of a small child. I touched my face; the proportions were that of a child. I was still me, only me at four years old. It felt surreal being back in my child form. "What are you doing? You're kind of funny. I like funny! Want to be my friend?" Taylin asked.

"Yes!" My voice was small, sweet, and shy. "Can I share a secret with you, and you promise not to tell?"

Taylin's eyes grew wide, and she nodded her head. "Come with me. Let's find a place where no one else can hear us." She took my hand in hers and pulled me along. "Times up!" She told some other kids sitting inside a small pop-up tent. "It's our turn, so move out!" She was so feisty and authoritative. This was the Taylin I always knew and loved. Kids always listened to her. They never tried her authority. She was a born leader, and she had picked me, the underdog, to be her best friend.

We got to our knees and climbed inside the tent. "What's the secret?" Taylin looked at me with a curious expression.

"Uhm, you're gonna think I'm crazy, but here goes. Taylin, we will always be best friends, right?"

"Well, I like you already, so, sure?" She shrugged her little shoulders.

"Okay, so in the future, when we get bigger, I'm going to get lost somewhere."

"Really? Where are you going?" she asked.

"I'll go to another world, and there may be another little girl who is trying to find you to get to me. She has long dark hair and dark blue eyes. Her name is Cynnica. You can't trust her. She's dangerous!" I looked at Taylin, trying to gauge her reaction.

She looked at me. Her eyes squinted, and her lips twisted, then relaxed. "It does sound crazy, but for some reason, I believe you."

I breathed out a sigh of relief. "There's more. You have to find a big bright light. It will be outside somewhere near something like water or a cave or a place somewhere old. That's how you will find me."

"Okay, I promise I will look for you." Taylin held up her hand in a scout's honor gesture.

"It's too late, you know!" A voice spoke to me in the darkness. "She already found her, and your friend has played right into her hands."

"Who are you?" I shouted.

"You know who I am!" The voice was dreadful and resonated malintent.

"Don't you dare hurt her!" I shouted.

"I wouldn't dare. I need her for my plan to work." The words slithered and constricted. It squeezed away at life's breath. "I thought she would be the means to all ends, but I have come to find there is more. So, much more."

"What do you want?" I shouted. "Reveal yourself, coward!"

A wisp of smoke slithered forth, so dark its surrounding paled in comparison. It bolted at me. I screamed and fell backward. My eyes opened. I was back in Lazula's home. Clave had pulled me to him, and I clutched to his shirt.

Lazula sat in a trance. Her eyes moved back and forth rapidly behind her lids. Muttering whispers flew from her lips. She froze. Her back was straight and stiff. Slowly her eyelids peeled open, and she blinked. "We must tell Tovin to head South. He must start to gather supplies and head out as soon as possible."

"What is it, Lazula?" I asked in a panic.

"We have new arrivals! I sense three people."

"I'm going with you," I told Clave. I started to pack, but Clave took hold of my hands and pulled me to him.

It's not safe, Krystle. It's freezing out there. We'll be back in four days tops. You need to be here for your family. Your mom, she needs your support. Clave let go of my hands and turned to go. I followed him downstairs.

"What if the Dark Spirit found its host? What if it's Taylin? I have to be sure. I'm worried, Clave! I don't want to lose anyone else."

The Dark Spirit is a manipulator. It was trying to scare you, Krystle. You know your friend Taylin is capable of defying it. It's in a weakened state, trapped in the body of a child. You said so yourself. Lazula confirmed this.

"What about you, Clave? As you said, it's freezing out there! There's this condition called hypothermia. Surely, you've heard of it?"

Krystle, I've traveled these lands since my youth in the worst possible conditions. Plus, I couldn't get lost if I tried. Chorus will help. The sooner we can leave, the sooner we'll return. I don't want to be away from you any more than you do me.

Clave kissed me. It was fueled with passion and promise. When our lips parted, he leaned his forehead to mine. *You are brave and strong, my love. Nothing in either of our worlds would keep me from returning to you.* His thumbs brushed my cheeks.

He joined Tovin; each of them would drive a sled. Clave pulled up the hood of his coat, and Chorus tucked himself inside. Chorus would fly ahead as needed. Tovin looked at Clave and nodded. "Hike!" Tovin shouted, and both sleds pulled off. I watched as my heart made headway against the wind. The dogs' barking grew more distant till there was no more to be heard but the cold, harsh wind.

I went back inside and closed the door. "Krystle, come sit with me," Mom beckoned. "I need some company, and you need to warm up." I sat beside her, feeling numb both physically and emotionally. She shifted then lifted her arm with a blanket wrapped around it. It draped down like a mother bird's wing, and she brought it around me.

Enveloped in her warmth, I laid my head on her shoulder. I placed my hand on the belly. My baby sister was doing cartwheels. I could see the flutters and ripples of limbs as they poked and protruded beneath Mom's tightly stretched shirt.

"I wish Lazula knew who arrived. She said she sensed three people. It could be anyone." Mom played with my hair. For a moment, I felt like her little baby again. It wouldn't be much longer before I was a big sister again. Everyone was convinced it was a girl.

"Whoever it is, they will need all the help we can supply," said Mom. "This winter has been particularly harsh. It makes me miss the Texas heat."

"Yeah, we went from mild winters with barely any snow to more than we know what to do with." I agreed. "The wind is too cold to go out and play in it."

"All I can say is kudos to the people of this village! All their years here have made them strong and capable of surviving these conditions every year." Mom took a sip of her hot cider, and the baby kicked. She must have been enjoying it too.

"The Grand Glacial Moon is next month. I don't know how Jasper and Aura plan on having their wedding if it's as cold as this," I stated.

Aura and Jasper stayed with her Aunt Azora and her cousins, working on preparations for the big event. Mom and Liv contributed a list of Earth customs and ideas for décor and food.

Liv was working on a dress for Aura. It was a blend of old and new. It was a beautiful creamy-white with a jeweled neckline. The hemline stopped just above the knee in front. It hugged her curves and had a fur-lined hooded long-length overcoat instead of a veil. The coat was open in the front with a fur-lined lapel. The back was long and flowing. A strappy leather belt with white beads and matching knee-high fur-lined boots completed the ensemble. She had tried the dress on repeatedly so Liv could get the fit just right. She looked absolutely amazing in it. I lent my diamond earrings to her for something borrowed. Her Blue Moon Stone ring worked for something blue. She had her mother's gold necklace for something old. Tovin said he had already taken care of something new. He didn't reveal what it was; he just mentioned it would be useful.

"I can't believe my firstborn is getting married." Mom rubbed her belly. "It only seems like yesterday that he was in here. Your father and I were so young."

"You're still young, Mom. It's a good thing too. This baby may end up with nieces and nephews close to her age," I laughed. "You'll be busy as both a mom and grandma."

"It sounds so strange to think about," said Mom. "I guess I've heard stranger family dynamics. I just never thought it would apply here. I always pictured Jasper going off to college. Perhaps meeting a girl there and getting married in his late twenties or early thirties."

"History has a way of repeating itself," I concluded.

"That is so true. Come on, baby girl, let's get up and do some baking. I've already got a bun in the over, and she's craving something sweet," Mom laughed. Once we got started, we couldn't stop. We ended up going a little overboard with veggie pot pies, fruit pies, and a cake. At least we'd be prepared to feed an army once everyone returned. Rhodin was over at the Tucker's nearly every day. Dad and Eric would help with delivering supplies and trades around the village. They were also checking on Lazula while Tovin and Clave were gone.

It was the end of the third day when I heard dogs barking in the distance. I saw two dog sleds approaching. "It's them!" I shouted excitedly. I started running back to the house. "Come on!" I yelled to the Bens. Rhodin and Hailey climbed on the sled, and the Bens pulled them along.

Clave! I yelled. Chorus was flying towards me. He landed on my head. *Clave, I missed you so much! Is everyone alright? Who did you find?*

Krystle, I missed you too. We are better than alright. There is much to celebrate. Go ahead and tell your family, they made it. They found the Light!

I sped ahead. I burst through our front door. "Mom, they're here! Where's Dad?"

"I'm up here, Krystle!" Dad slid down the pole. The dogs barked. People were shouting.

I heard Rhodin scream, "Oh my, God! They're here; they're here!"

Mom and Dad were getting their boots and coats on. I ran back outside. Rhodin had his arms wrapped around a tall figure in an overstuffed blue coat. A woman in a red coat turned and looked at me. "Aunt Cassie!" I cried. I ran into her arms.

"Oh, Krystle! Oh, thank heavens! Sweetie, I love you so much!" She kissed my cheeks and held on. "We found the Light just like you kept telling us too. More like it found us." She squeezed me tight.

"Cassie!" Mom yelled behind us. "Garreth!" Dad was helping Mom stay upright as they hurried toward us. Rhodin jumped up at Cassie, and she picked him up and smothered him in kisses.

"Uncle Garreth!" I smiled at him. Tears were running down my reddened cheeks. "Krystle burger! How are you doing, baby doll? I've missed you!" We embraced, and he kissed the top of my head.

"I'm great now that you're here! Is Taylin with you?" I looked up at his face. He had grown a thick beard. There were a few traces of gray scattered throughout.

"No, I'm afraid not, baby girl. She missed this trip." I looked down. Garreth cupped my cheeks in his hands. "There's still hope, Krystle. We've learned a lot since we last saw you guys. We have someone with us who can explain. He helped get us here."

"Who? Who is it?" I looked up. Mom and Aunt Cassie were holding each other and crying.

Dad had stepped in. "Hey, brother, took you long enough!"

"We had a few delays and a layover, but overwise, it was a smooth trip," Uncle Garreth chuckled. He and Dad hugged it out.

Another man stood in a long gray coat. He turned around, and all I could see were his eyes at first. "Hello,

Krystle Genstone! I hope you've found your time here enjoyable!"

I knew that voice. The man pulled down his hood and a scarf away from his face.

"Mr. Lattimier?!" My jaw dropped. "How? Uncle Garreth! You didn't trust- we didn't trust him!" I pointed at Lattimier. "What makes you trust him now?"

Tovin came over to me and put his arm around my shoulder, "Krystle, I'd like you to meet my brother-in-law and Claves' father, Mieruss Frost."

Clave came and put his arms around me. *Krystle, this is strange for me too. He is my father, and I don't really know him. Tovin always told me my father was a good man. I know you didn't trust him, but he will explain everything. First, we need to see Lazula and send someone to get my mother.*

"I think he owes everyone here an explanation!" I folded my arms across my chest and glared at Mieruss.

Lattimier- I mean, Mieruss approached me apprehensively. "Krystle, I'm so sorry about how I handled the situation when your parents went missing. I had a legitimate reason for my behavior. Please allow me the chance to explain everything. Garreth had already reamed me when I first approached him to help. Your family is so strong. I don't think I could handle any more mistrust toward me. I only want to gain your trust from this day forward. My son, Clave, told me you and he are each other's hearts bond. I couldn't be happier for the both of you."

"I forgive you momentarily on a technicality! But I want to hear what you have to say," I continued to hold him in a scrutinous gaze.

"I'm going to go ahead and get Azora," said Tovin. "We'll meet you at Lazula's.

Mieruss had a look of hopeful anticipation. "Thank you, brother!" Tovin patted Mieruss on the back and walked toward the river.

"My goodness, Gemma! Would ya look at that! I'm going to be an uncle again? Was it mating season when you two got here?" Garreth joked.

Aunt Cassie laughed. "I'm so excited. Another baby! And we made it just in time!"

Sniffling and nose-blowing came from behind. Liv wiped at her nose. "Well, are ye gonna introduce yer clan to me, or aren't ya?"

Mom made introductions, and Liv hugged and welcomed everyone. They met Eric, the Bens, and Hailey. "You are a beautiful little lady!" Aunt Cassie commented to Hailey.

"Thank ye, miss, ye are as well," Hailey replied.

"Oh, my heart, do you hear that sweet angelic voice," said Cassie.

"Dinnae be lettin' that fool ye," said Liv. "Come, ye must be hungry. I've made a stew and bread."

"Mom and I have been baking too much! We need hungry people to help us eat all the food we've made these past few days."

"I can definitely eat," said Uncle Garreth. We all piled inside our house. The Bens brought over their table and chairs. Liv brought her stew and fresh bread. We all sat down to eat. Mieruss was mostly quiet. He wanted to tell his side of the story but was waiting to see Lazula.

After we finished our meal, we thanked the Tuckers and went over to Lazula's. Mieruss was looking around as we walked. "It seems not too much has changed since I've been gone. More tree homes along the river. A few new bridges. A few new faces," he smiled.

We made it to Lazula's and Azora came running out. "Mieruss!" She shouted. She ran into his arms, and they kissed fervently.

"My Azora! My love! Oh, I have missed you so much!" Mieruss poured his heart out between kisses. My heart tugged, and tears sprung. Mieruss was officially forgiven! Seeing a display of love so strong put every misconception to rest.

Clave held me to his side. I looked up at him. Tears were streaming down his face. *My mother has been so sad and lonely since he went missing. To see her with so much joy makes my heart soar. I feel even closer to you, Krystle. Their reunion has freed a part of me that had almost lost all hope that this day would come.*

I hugged Clave to me. *I'm so sorry for holding a grievance against your father, Clave.*

Krystle, you had no way of knowing. There's nothing to forgive. Everything will be better with our families back together once more. This is a joyous day. I love you so much, Krystle!

I love you so much too, Clave! We wiped away each other's tears and kissed.

After the beautiful reunion, Mieruss walked with Azora tucked in close to his side. She clutched to him, unwilling to let go. Lazula stood at her doorway with tears coming down her face. "Mieruss...Oh, bless the moons! You have returned to us!"

"Lazula, I'm so sorry." Mieruss embraced Lazula and cried on her shoulder.

"Hush now, child! I'll hear none of this nonsense!" Lazula admonished. "You have nothing to be sorry for!"

"I tried to stop her!" Mieruss cried. "I..."

"Mieruss, everyone, come in!" Lazula waved us in impatiently. "Let's hear it, Mieruss. What happened that night?"

"Lazula, I've played that moment over and over in my head for so long. I should have warned you- warned Tovin!" Mieruss wept.

"Warned me of what, brother?" Tovin stepped forward.

"Everyone sit DOWN!" Lazula commanded. "Mieruss! Pull it together, son. Start from the beginning."

We all sat down and shut our mouths. We all had our eyes on Mieruss. Azora held his hand tightly. I looked around and saw Jasper and Aura. Things must have been explained to him. He didn't have a look of contempt toward Mieruss. He did look demanding of an explanation as I had before.

Chapter 19

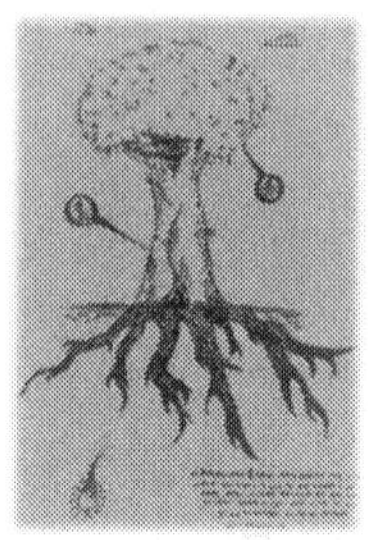

"I have been gone a long time," said Mieruss. "As such, I have a long story to tell."

"Let me begin by apologizing to you, Tovin," Mieruss beseeched. "That terrible night? Does everyone here know?"

"Yes, brother, I have healed much since telling all here, whom I care for and trust," said Tovin. Mieruss nodded his head.

"There are missing pieces to the story, which I have carried with me for a long time," said Mieruss. "That night, I went to fetch Lazula while you waited with Solaura. It was so dark and storming. When I saw Zinnia first, I pleaded her help and sent another young man after Lazula telling him to make haste."

"Zinnia had an off look to her eyes, but I attributed it to the conditions of the night. She sounded herself, and she followed me to help." Mieruss paused. "I did not know, Tovin. I didn't recognize the signs."

Tovin's brows creased in question. Lazula put her hand on Tovin's arm and waved in urgence for Mieruss to continue. "By the time we got to Solaura, I could tell it was too late. All the...blood! Zinnia kneeled to deliver the baby, your daughter."

Tovin gasped and began to cry. Aura came and put her arms around him. They held on to one another. "I'm so sorry, Tovin!" Mieruss cried.

"Continue!" Lazula's voice commanded.

Mieruss cleared his throat. "Do you remember what Solaura said to Zinnia? She said..."

"You will not have my child..." Tovin finished. His eyes grew wide.

"I didn't say anything. I couldn't; it was like my mouth was frozen shut. Something had control over me. It felt wrong. Any intervention I tried was ceased instantly. I tried so hard to fight it, Tovin. I wanted to shout it out to you, but I couldn't."

"By the time Lazula had come, Solaura and the baby had...you know. But, just before Solaura's soul left her body, she said, 'My soul belongs to our child.'

"I saw it. I saw the transference. You didn't see. Lazula did not see. She was trying to soothe Aura, and you were grieving your heavy loss. I still could not open my mouth to say anything. I felt like my body was taken over, though my mind was still my own.

"The soul of your child. It was a Pure Soul! I knew it when I saw it retreat. It was escaping. I didn't realize it at the time. Solaura knew she was fading away; she bestowed her soul to the child. The child remained in a suspended state, an appearance of death. She was frozen by the same force that held me captive."

"Wait!" cried Tovin. "Are you saying that my child is still…"

"Alive! Yes, Tovin, I am!" Mieruss cried. "She had fooled us all. When we took Solaura and the baby to be buried, Zinnia told Lazula to place the baby on a large stone. I was on autopilot as I continue to take care of Solaura. I didn't know what was happening behind me. Not till I had laid the very last stone upon the grave."

Tovin stood, clenching his fists. Anger ruled his features. Aura stood beside him with her hands cupped over her mouth in shock. Jasper stood behind Aura's with his hands upon her shoulders.

Mieruss continued, "I turned around and saw the scene before me. I felt released at that moment. I snapped awake to find Lazula lying unconscious. Zinnia stood before the rock with a dagger held over her head. She was chanting words I could not understand. It was no longer her voice. I heard the baby crying. I ran and knocked Zinnia over. The dagger flew out from her hands. I gathered up your daughter, and I heard a beckoning. The Light appeared before me. It whispered the words "Safe Haven" again and again. Zinnia had gotten back up and was screaming. I lunged for the Light with your daughter in my arms. But, I felt Zinnia's hand catch my ankle."

Every face in the room wore shock as Mieruss took a moment to breathe. "When we landed on Earth. I still had your daughter clutched to my chest. She was full of life. She cried and wailed. It was the most beautiful sound I had ever heard. I looked around frantically for Zinnia, but she was nowhere to be found."

"It took me some time to figure out where I was. Some people approached me. I pleaded for help. They said they were from the Worlds of Care Connect, and they could help me and my child." This time my whole family gasped. The Light knew where to take them.

"I knew I had to hide her to keep her safe. The people helped me with resources. I had to make up a story about how my wife had run away a few days after giving birth. I couldn't afford to take care of the baby. I would've kept her with me if I could, Tovin. I signed some papers to put her up for adoption. I begged them to help her find a family as far away from there as they could get her."

"I learned that I was in the country of Brazil. They took her the very next day. I had prayed for her safety. I remember when I put my name on those papers. They put the date on them, May 21, 2004."

"That's my birthday!" I cried out. I apologized and closed my mouth. This wasn't about me. Lazula looked at me and nodded like it was some kind of affirmation.

"My decision was founded because a few days later, Zinnia had found me. She was so enraged. She had bound me once more and demanded to know where the child had gone. I could not answer her because I didn't know. And as long as I didn't know, she would be safe."

"It wasn't long after that that the Worlds of Care Connect set Zinnia and me up with a job at the resort. Zinnia had played the role of desperation quite well. I was thankful it wasn't the same people who took your daughter. If Zinnia had thought to ask about a baby, they wouldn't have known anything."

"She held me captive for the next sixteen years. She worked her dark magic on the minds of the people coming and going. She took over the minds of the owner and staff. She had everyone convinced that I was the new owner and the previous owner had disappeared. No one remembered his poor soul except me. I could not tell anyone about Zinnia's coup."

"As time passed, something strange started happening to Zinnia. She was rapidly aging in reverse. She became desperate and began leeching off my life force to keep herself from dwindling to non-existence. She would gain control of the minds of some unsuspecting couple to keep up the pretense that she had parents. No one suspected anything. As I grew older, her magic kept me from aging. That is what she stole from me. A year for a year."

Puzzle pieces began snapping into place in my mind. I knew who Zinnia was! Who she had become! "Cynnica!" I cried out.

"Yes, Cynnica!" Mieruss sneered. "Conniving and manipulative! She waited patiently for a Pure Soul to come. She had found the Light again and again but could not get through. It took her some time to realize she would need a Pure Soul to gain access through the Light. While she bided her time, she continued to search for Tovin's daughter. She had gained a lead and not one, but two Pure Souls to get what she wanted."

"I, ever her puppet, struggled with all my might to lead you away." Mieruss looked at me. "I knew where your parents had gone. And in my mind, I vowed, if I could ever escape her hold, I would take you to your parents myself. In the meantime, I couldn't allow Cynnica to get hold of you or Rhodin when the Light was to come. It was unprecedented for it to show twice in the same place and so soon. I knew you were special somehow. The moons called for you."

"I couldn't allow Zinnia to use you. She saw you and Rhodin as a triple prize. Two Pure Souls to lead the way, then consume once she gained access back to this world. She would have been able to rebuild her strength and become a plague to our home."

"By the Moons!" Lazula gasped. Mom and Dad looked at Rhodin and me with worry.

"Why were you not there when the Light appeared? Zinnia was distracted by her plan; she had almost achieved her goal." I said.

"I was arrested and detained for questioning for the disappearance of your parents. I begged them to release me. I found myself able to speak that night, and I would have come. I told them you and your brothers were in danger." Mieruss looked at Uncle Garreth. For the first time, I saw regret in my uncle's eyes. He didn't know! He was just as suspicious of "Lattimier" as Jasper and I.

"What of my daughter?" Tovin boomed. "Did Zinnia find her?"

"She seeks her still. I was close to finding out. I sent letters to anyone who might be able to help. Communication with government agencies is difficult. Response times take months or years. I was taken away and locked up, but I managed to escape. I remembered where the Genstone family was from; I had their information locked away in my mind. I searched and found

Garreth and waited for the right time to approach. I knew when and where the next Light would appear. I had to make sure Zinnia-Cynnica had lost my trail."

"I am sorry I could not find your daughter, Tovin. But, if Zinnia does, the first thing on her agenda is to get to the Light and bring her here. She will not harm her. As of now, your daughter is an unknowing pawn."

"I have to say something," I spoke up. "Mieruss, you are correct in the knowledge that the moons called my family. The Fire Moon called me." I lifted the stone from my chest, and Mieruss's eyes widened. "I have been calling out to Cassie, Garreth, and my best friend, Taylin. My last calling, the Dark Spirit, made contact with me. It threatened to make use of my friend. If all my assumptions are correct, I believe Taylin is Tovin's daughter, and she is in danger!"

"Shit!" Tovin cursed. "What can we do?"

"The next Light will not appear for another four Earth years," said Mieruss. "Until then, we must prepare. Cynnica will bide her time and keep watch over Taylin. She will approach her just before the time comes. If she continues to age in reverse, she will have the appearance of a four-year-old child. She will lure Taylin with her deceitful face of innocence."

"Zinnia was possessed," said Lazula. "You know she wasn't born evil, Mieruss."

"I know this, Lazula," Mieruss confessed. "What I don't know is how she'd become possessed. I tried to speak to the entity that held her captive. There were moments few and far between when it had seemed I broken through.

Zinnia would apologize and beg me to put her out of her misery. She wanted me to help her stop it. My heart broke for her. The entity would regain control. Over time it had seemed she had lost the battle altogether. I didn't know what to do. When the entity resurfaced, I lost control. It must have lapsed at times. I was able to muster enough composure to urge the Genstone kids away from the cave. Even still, it brokered enough control to hold my tongue from explanation."

I felt terrible for Mieruss. I had thought he was the enemy all this time. That he wasn't in cahoots with the Dark Spirit, he was its prisoner; his spirit was in torturous peril. And poor Zinnia! Somehow the Dark Spirit had found its way here. She must have encountered it sometime before that terrible night, and it took control of her.

"The dagger!" Lazula exclaimed. She got up and retrieved the dagger still safely wrapped in cloth. "Krystle, remember? We had figured that the dagger was the way of transference." She unwrapped the cloth and held the pommel.

Mieruss's eyes went wide, "That is the dagger she had. She did not have time to find and retrieve it when the Light appeared. It was left behind. When did you find it?"

"Only days ago," Lazula replied. "I sensed it on our way back home from an emergency Yehati birth."

"I'll have to have you explain that to me later," said Mieruss. "You believe the dagger possessed her?"

"Not the dagger itself, but the Dark Spirit or some essence of it was captured here, in the diamond on the hilt." Lazula pointed it out. "I don't know when or exactly where she found the dagger, but she may have accidentally cut herself with it. The Dark Spirit entered her then."

"You had said one of the ancestors might have brought it through. It had to have been a Pure Soul that carried it. Unbeknownst to them, it contained the Dark Spirit's essence. They hid it in the ancestral catacombs." I explained.

"Yes." Lazula agreed. "And Zinnia must have visited the catacombs to pay homage to the ancestors and found it. It must have called to her..."

"You must save the child!" I exclaimed. "Zinnia. The transference. The dagger is the way! Lazula!" I cried.

"Of course! It is the way to free my sister. I don't know what the repercussions will be. No one outside of this room must know about this dagger and what we've discussed." Lazula insisted.

"This information may cause an uproar, and chaos may ensue. We must keep the people of our village safe. We will all watch out for signs and gather information. We will meet as necessary for further discussion." Everyone nodded in agreement with Lazula.

There was a long silence. Mieruss had exhausted himself. Tovin offered his hand to help him up. He embraced Mieruss and Azora. "None of this was your fault, brother. If you need to hear me say it, I forgive you! I understand it was out of your control. I only wish you would have been able to find my daughter and bring her home. I know the circumstances and hold nothing against you."

Mieruss cried into Tovin's shoulder. "Thank you, brother! I wish I could have as well."

"She is an Otek!" Krystle has described Taylin's personality. "I have no doubt it is her," Tovin declared.

"She drew a picture of her," said Aura. "She is truly beautiful."

"She is!" I agreed. "Beautiful inside and out."

"I would very much like to see this picture," said Tovin.

"I would very much like to show it to you," I replied.

Tovin hugged me. "Thank you for being her best friend all these years."

"That was the easy part. Taylin chose me first. The rest happened naturally." We both smiled in regard to my sentiment.

"Did you know if she was adopted? Has her family there on Earth treated her well?" Aura asked.

"She never mentioned being adopted. I don't think she knew. They have been good to her, though," I said.

"That may have been because of me," said Mieruss. "I asked that her adoptive parents not reveal it till she was eighteen. I didn't want her searching for birth parents she would never find. I didn't want a trail that led back to me. It was for her safety."

"Thank you, Mieruss," said Tovin. I appreciate everything you've done to keep her safe."

"If it were in my power, I would have done more," said Mieruss.

"I know you would have," Tovin gave him another hug.

"Mieruss, my love. We must get home. We have much celebrating to do," Azora kissed his cheek.

"I must be on my way. I can no longer wait for my love's embrace," Mieruss smiled. "Clave, you are a man now! I cannot believe it! You have found your true love with a wonderful, beautiful, intelligent young lady. I am happy for both of you! We must talk in a few days. First, I have some catching up to do of my own." He nuzzled Azora's neck, and she giggled.

Clave smiled. "I understand, Father. I am happy for you and Mom as well. Go, be together and celebrate. I love you both." They gathered in a group hug, and Azora pulled me in. "I have my family again. My joy knows no bounds."

Over the next few weeks, Clave and I visited more with his family. He and Mieruss reconnected, and I was able to see him in a whole new light. Gone was the façade of a pristine resort owner. The real man shined through. Mieruss was loving and funny. I could see why Azora fell so hard for him. She stayed close to him everywhere they went. Their affection for each other was contagious to those around them. Their family celebrated Mieruss' return, and many people had stopped by to catch up.

All of this was happening during the setup of Aura and Jasper's wedding-bonding ceremony. The ceremony would take place in the field behind Lazula's home. The guest list included the whole village.

The night had arrived. The whole village had gathered. A bonding ceremony beneath the Grand Glacial Moon was a big deal for everyone. People paid a blessing to the totems before the bride and groom arrived. There would be a celebration with dancing and food.

Everyone had gathered in the cold crisp night air. Large bonfires roared to the sides. Our families took their seats up front. Lazula came out dressed in a long white ceremonial robe.

Three of the moonstones hung from a necklace. The large opal Glacial Stone was set in a simple gold band upon her head. The Grand Glacial Moon had risen high in the sky. It sparkled like a giant round opal glittering above. It beamed down upon the spot where Jasper and Aura would meet.

Clave and I had already walked down the aisle together. We took our places as Maid of Honor and Best Man. Drums started to beat in a steady, consistent rhythm. All eyes looked behind me, out to my left; Jasper emerged from a tent. He smiled and looked nervous. He looked up, and I thought he was going to fall over from the sight before him.

Tovin led Aura toward the alter with the beat of the drums. She was an absolute vision of a tribal fairytale as her dress, and the rest of her ensemble came together perfectly. Her eyelids and cheeks sparkled as if having been kissed by stardust. Her azurite blue eyes popped, lined in smokey dark gray. Her pink lips were shiny and soft. Dark curls framed her face. Jasper moved forward and kept in step till they stood before one another.

Lazula spoke, “Welcome! It is my honor and humble privilege to bring together this bond. Tovin, I wish you great happiness. For this is no loss, but an even more significant gain. For the generations will continue to grow and honor you as a great patriarch. Kiss your child and let her fly with your blessing.” Tovin had tears glistening in his eye as he bent down and placed a kiss on Aura’s forehead. She closed her eyes, and her lips trembled.

Tovin stepped aside and nodded to Jasper. “To this bond, I give my blessing.”

Lazula continued, “We seal this bond tonight under the Grand Glacial Moon; this is indeed a true blessing! Jasper, take Aura’s hands and speak your vows to her.”

Aura slid her hands into Jaspers, and he looked deeply into her eyes.

“Aura, I vow to you to be the man you deserve. Your beautiful spirit captured mine from the first time I saw you on the beach. You had been our rescuer. You brought us to your haven. You have rescued me in every beautiful way since then. You are my equal in every way. Your heart will always be the beacon that calls to my own. I look forward to a full life with you and the family we will create. I love you, Aura. I give myself to you, body, heart, and soul in a complete unbreakable bond.”

“Aura, speak your vows to Jasper,” said Lazula.

Aura’s eyes sparkled with barely contained tears of joy. “Jasper, I captured you in my arms that day on the canoe. My heart fluttered at our contact. It was a strange feeling I had never felt before. I held onto a lot of pride. I was guarded. I feared getting close and what it could cost. But you followed me around like a lost puppy.” Everyone laughed, including Jasper.

“I let you win the race that day around the honeysuckle field. I had outdone you in every challenge we had partaken. But, Jasper, you broke through my defenses. You made it easy for me to relent. I could see the possibilities beyond all probabilities. You may have lost to me in-game, but you won me over completely. To me, you are my hero. You saved my heart from a past sadness. Your soul breathed new life into my own. I love you, Jasper. I give myself to you, body, heart, and soul in a complete unbreakable bond.”

Lazula stepped forward and placed a long golden chain around them. They exchange rings. “By the blessing of all gathered under the Grand Glacial Moon, all here attest and recognize this union. Jasper and Aura, you are now and forever bonded in body, heart, mind, and spirit. Congratulations. Jasper, you may kiss your bride!”

Jasper placed his hands on Aura’s face, Aura put her hands on his, and their lips met. It was a beautiful intimate moment sealed in time under moonlight’s cast. Everyone cheered and clapped.

“I announce to you Mr. and Mrs. Otek-Genstone,” Lazula called out. Clapping and cheering escalated. Music started, and everyone began helping out to set out food and move tables and chairs. Jasper and Aura shared their first dance. She and Tovin did the father-daughter dance.

It wasn't long before Tovin led our wedding party down to the river. "This is your something new." He pointed down to a new canoe. It was to the same one he and Jasper had been working on the day Tovin told us his story. Only now, it had Otek-Genstone carved into the side.

"Thank you, Father," said Aura.

"I get now why you said it was a gift to be determined." Jasper laughed. "Thank you, Tovin."

"Of course, son," said Tovin. "Please continue to call me Tovin. You already call your father, Dad. It would just seem strange since we all work together most of the time."

Jasper and Dad laughed. "I think that sounds reasonable," Dad responded.

"Are you two love birds ready to embark upon your new journey?" Mom asked.

"Yes!" Jasper and Aura both said excitedly. Every one of our immediate family was taking turns giving hugs.

"Happy Birthday, Lazula!" Aura kissed Lazula's cheeks.

"This is the best gift I have ever received," said Lazula. "Go, enjoy one another." Jasper had boarded the canoe and was reaching up to hold Aura's waist.

"Ahh…!" Mom suddenly shouted and grabbed her stomach. "Flint, my water just broke. The baby is coming."

Aura turned around and pulled Jasper back up with her. “Don’t you say a word, Gemma! I’m not missing the birth of my new baby sister!”

Mom nodded and winced. “Ooh!” She started breathing through a contraction.

“Come, Gemma,” Lazula took one arm, and Dad took the other. They began leading her inside. The music continued as people danced and ate.

Liv ran up. “Is the baby coming?”

“Yeeesss..” Mom said through gritted teeth.

“I don’t need the whole lot of you crowding up this space,” said Lazula. She backed the crowd up and allowed our immediate family and Liv inside. Everyone else stood outside the doorway.

Dad eased Mom down on some pillows while Lazula was giving out instructions. I came to hold Mom’s hand while Dad held her other. Another contraction came, and Mom was groaning. She was trying to get her breathing under control.

“I can feel her! She’s coming, now!” Mom shouted. Dad and I looked down, and sure enough, the head was crowning.

“Oh my, God!” Cassie and I cried together. Aura clutched Jasper's hand as she sat by his side. Her knees bounced up and down in anticipation.

Lazula was down on her knees. “Push, Gemma!”

Mom screamed, and with one blessed push, my baby sister was born. She was a beautiful, squealing bundle with white-blond hair and pink skin. Mom and Dad were crying and laughing. Lazula lay the baby on Mom's chest and finished taking care of Mom.

A soft towel was wrapped around my sister. Mom and Dad were taking her in, kissing her little head and cooing at her. The light from the moon beamed through a window and upon my baby sister.

"She has a birthmark on her head." I pointed out. It was stark white and looked like a ring. The moonlight hit it, and it flashed. The moonstones on Mom's wrist and my chest glowed brightly.

"This is the connection she shares with you, Krystle," Lazula commented. Mom removed her bracelet and tied it around the baby's tiny ankle. The opal stone continued to glow, as did her birthmark.

"Wow," cried Aunt Cassie. "You're going to have to catch me up on the meaning behind all this. What is her name?"

Mom looked at her sister. "Garrissa Opal Rose Genstone."

"I love it." Cassie declared.

"Aura, come hold your new baby sister," said Mom. "You and Jasper still have a wedding night ahead of you."

Aura didn't hesitate. She lifted Garrissa into her arms. "She's beautiful! So sweet! We're going to have a lot of fun together, little Opal Rose! That's what Big Sissy Aura is going to call you." Jasper stood beside her and smiled down at Garrissa.

Garrissa was passed around and loved on. Dad had gone outside and made the birth announcement to the party still going on. We heard the roaring cheer and congratulations. After a few hours, things had quieted down. Jasper and Aura and embarked on their new journey as man and wife. Mom was made more comfortable. She and Dad would stay at Lazula's till the next morning.

Clave and I were the only other two to stay. Mom had nursed Garrissa and was now sleeping. Clave sat with me on the couch as I held my bundled-up baby sister in my arms. The Great Glacial Moon had passed, and it felt like a night of new beginnings.

"Hello, Garrissa Opal Rose!" I spoke low and sweet. "I'm your big sister, Krystle. You and I will go on many wonderful adventures together. This is Clave. He is my true love, but my heart just grew even bigger tonight for my new sister-in-law, your sister Aura, and you. I love you so much!" Garrissa stared. She cooed and squeaked.

She is beautiful, just like her big sister, said Clave. *I can see peace, love, and strength in her. She will hold the hearts of everyone around her, and we will keep her safe.*

I don't suppose we'll be seeing Jasper and Aura for the next few days! Clave smiled and wagged his brows.

"Shh! We don't discuss such things around the baby!" I joked.

Well, consider where she just came from; she may be wiser than we think, said Clave.

"Yes! She knows that her Daddy fed a stork some seeds, and Mommy's belly began to grow magically." I teased.

"Isn't that right, Garrissa?" Garrissa let out a high-pitched squeal followed by a cute little grunt. Clave and I both giggled.

Chapter 20

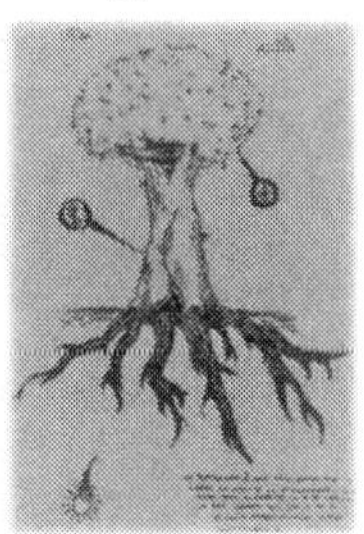

Garrissa Opal Rose had become the center of attention everywhere. Mom was back to work. Aunt Cassie and Garrissa came with her. Aunt Cassie had become Mom's assistant at the clinic. She mostly watched Garrissa until it was feeding time. Cassie also helped Mom's research by making frequent trips to the apothecary. She had acquired a new fascination with plants of this world and their various properties. Cassie's propensity toward making plants thrive had become well recognized.

Uncle Garreth had jumped on board with the men as they hunted, fished, and managed upkeep around the village. He felt like he was on his permanent dream vacation. He was getting his share of women checking him out. A few ladies brought him food and asked him if he'd like to help fix their plumbing. Dad would nudge and tease Garreth. He'd tell him he should make some rounds. Women here loved an excellent handyman.

Uncle Garreth just wasn't ready to be tied down yet. The only little lady who had his heart right now was little Garrissa Opal Rose. He enjoyed spoiling her to pieces. He was the best at making her laugh. Mom told him he'd be a great father someday, and he wasn't getting any younger. He'd just say, "I still have plenty of time."

A new attraction was definitely in bloom. Tovin had come up with so many arbitrary excuses to be within the same vicinity as Aunt Cassie. He would murmur about needing to fix something or was just dropping off a delivery. Aunt Cassie blushed every time Tovin made small talk. His voice had become smooth and pleasant—a significant change from his usual grumbling broodiness.

While Aunt Cassie and I were out on a walk one day, she had suddenly stopped in her tracks. Tovin swung his ax and splintered a log clean in two. Cassie stood gawking at Tovin. There he stood in all his shirtless muscle-bound glory. Tovin looked up and smiled. Aunt Cassie quickly averted her eyes. When she looked back toward him, Tovin purposely flexed his muscles. She blushed and returned a small bashful wave.

"Good morning, Cassie, Krystle," said Tovin.

"Ahtee, Tovin," I returned.

"Hi," Aunt Cassie squeaked shyly.

"What are you two lovely ladies up to today?" Tovin set his ax down and approached us. Aunt Cassie squeezed my arm, and I shook myself free and took a sidestepped. She gave me a look that shouted betrayal. I just smiled.

"Oh, we were just on our way to meet up with Clave and do some target practice." I pulled out my knife and turned it.

"Is that so?" Tovin looked at me like I had some trick up my sleeve. I did, in fact. It's an excellent opportunity to get Tovin and Aunt Cassie alone together. Clave and I had a plan to abandon them. Their mutual attraction was only too obvious. She was brutally shy, and he was dubiously uncertain with his approach.

"If you ladies don't mind, I'd be happy to join you," said Tovin. Fantastic! He was seizing this opportunity. "You two go on ahead. I'll catch up."

"Okay, see ya soon!" I chimed. We walked ahead for some distance. I knew what was coming next. Here it comes!

"Krystle Alexandra Genstone! I can see right through this charade of yours! This man is...is...!" Aunt Cassie stammered.

"Is handsome? Available? Kind? Honest? Loyal? I could go on with all of his positive qualities. I must admit he's intimidating and fierce. A giant, rugged mountain man with grumbling tendencies. But he has significantly improved since you appeared." I prodded my finger at her.

She huffed and looked at me. "I wouldn't even know what to do with a man like him! He's so overwhelming and bothersome."

"You mean, he stirs up feelings in you that you've never thought possible before? Aunt Cassie, now's the time to jump in with both feet. He's Clave's uncle, and Clave sings his praises. Tovin helped raise Clave and taught him how to treat a lady appropriately. He had Jasper standing at attention and made him prove his worth for Aura."

"Krystle, I've never had a real relationship with anyone before. He's a widower. I've heard the stories of his late wife. She was his everything. His perfect equal in every way! How do I even compare or contend with that?"

Aunt Cassie wasn't seeing her worth. She was quite the opposite of who Solaura had been. But perhaps this is what Tovin needed at this point in his life. Someone caring, peaceful and tender.

"Aunt Cassie, I have never seen Tovin this way before. He's always been a good person. He just held the weighted sorrow from his past for so long. He has finally let go; he freed himself from his prison of doubt and fear. You arrived after the storm had passed, like a breath of fresh air."

"You both owe it to yourselves to see what the future may hold. I know you're nervous. So was I when I first met Clave. What Clave and I have now is so beautiful, and it continues to grow stronger every day. I want you to have this same kind of experience, Aunt Cassie. You deserve happiness."

"It's not just that, Krystle. The physical logistics are intimidating!" Aunt Cassie fiddle nervously with her hands.

"If Tovin is everything he has taught Clave to be, then there's no reason to feel that way. For crying out loud, Aunt Cassie! I know you're not a virgin!" I had said this a little too loudly. I saw Clave quickly turn away from us as we made our approach. I could see he was shaking with laughter. I just rolled my eyes.

"Krystle!" Cassie said my name through gritted teeth as a warning. She was behaving like an embarrassed school girl. She cleared her throat and brought her senses back in line. Clave turned back around with a straight face. "Hello, Clave. How are you today?" Cassie politely greeted.

"I'm well, thank you." Clave signed. We hadn't let anyone else in on our secret telepathy pact since Jasper. "How are you, Cassie?"

Aunt Cassie knew he could read lips. "I'm good as well. So, what exactly are we doing today?" We followed Clave to the targets. Clave threw his knife and landed an impressive mark, and I went next. I had gotten much better and could hit the wood knife point each time.

"Wow, Krystle," said Cassie. "I see you've become quite the mountain woman yourself."

"Clave's a good teacher. I've had plenty of practice." Clave handed Cassie a knife and demonstrated his stance and release. She followed and threw her knife.

"I did it! On my first try!" Cassie did a little dance and shook her tush. Clapping and whistling came from behind. She stopped, turned around, and turned beat red.

"That was fantastic!" Tovin applauded.

"Uhm, thank you," Cassie tucked her wavy strawberry blonde hair behind her ears.

"You're a natural," Tovin smiled at her. "Is it my turn?"

"All yours!" I motioned toward the targets. Tovin approached Cassie. He stood over her like a grizzly bear standing over a nervous doe. It was like watching a predator breathe in its prey. Cassie looked up at Tovin. Though his eyes were gentle and kind, she looked like she was facing off with some sort of inevitable doom. She swallowed a nervous gulp.

"Don't worry, timid little deer," he whispered. "You know, I've been told Krystle is much like you, and I admire her very much. She has put me in my place a time or two." He winked at me, and I smiled back at him. I gave a discreet thumbs-up.

Your uncle is smooth, I said to Clave through our connection.

I learned from the best; Clave responded. He put his arm around me. Aunt Cassie's defenses began to crumble as Tovin engaged with her in an easy-going rapport. Clave and I made a break for it as our presence seemed forgotten. We weren't so far away when I heard Aunt Cassie start to laugh.

I think we deserve a medal for our fine achievement today. I leaned further into Clave as we continued to walk away together.

Indeed, my love. Clave turned me toward him, and we kissed. *My uncle and your aunt! Will this make us kissing cousins?*

I'm okay with it if you are, I responded flirtatiously.

Oh, I am most definitely okay with it, he smiled. We found the shade of a distant tree and spent the rest of the afternoon k-i-s-s-i-n-g.

Clave and I made it back home before dinner time. Garrissa was crawling around the room. Sienna followed her around and made sure her baby human stayed safe. Sienna would block and redirect Garrissa every time she'd get close to something unsafe. Mom agreed; having Sienna around made life at home much more manageable. We'd often find Garrissa fallen asleep with Sienna curled around her.

“Did you all have fun today?” asked Mom. Garrissa crawled to me and pulled on my pant leg till she managed herself into a sitting position. She lifted her chubby little arms and squealed for my attention. I picked her up and kissed her little peach blossom cheeks.

“Where’s Cassie?” asked Mom.

“She’s out...with Tovin!” I smiled.

“Finally! How did you manage that one? I thought I was going to go crazy watching all their hormone-infused awkward exchanges,” said Mom.

“I may have, on purpose, walked her by where Tovin was working and mentioned we were going for some target practice. Tovin may have asked to join us. I gave Aunt Cassie a firm pep talk, and Tovin took over from there. Then Clave and I abandoned them.” I sounded like a devious mastermind.

Mom laughed. “Good job, Krystle. I’m proud of your manipulative propensities. You get a big gold star!”

Rhodin came inside, followed by Hailey. “Hey, Krystle. Hey Clave. Asher can do a new trick now. He can play dead.”

“It was pretty easy, considering he lays around most of the day,” said Hailey. “We just call his name, and he lifts his head to look up. We point and say “POW,” and he lays his head back down.”

"Good trick," I smirked. Hailey and Rhodin were seven years old now and had grown a few inches over the winter. They had both gotten stronger from hefting sacks of food for the dogs. When they weren't at school, they would work with the pack.

Garrissa bounced up and down in my arm and reached out to Hailey. Hailey cooed at her, and I passed Garrissa over. Hailey loved toting Garrissa around. She took to calling her Opal and would take her out to see the dogs. The dogs would bark and wag excitedly. Garrissa would reach out for them, and they would instantly calm and sit.

"Any more drop-offs from Rascal, the mouse?" I questioned.

Rascal, the mouse, had resumed his stone deliveries. He must have been hibernating during the winter months. Hailey had been upset, thinking he might have passed away. She was relieved to find new stones showing up each morning after the earth thawed.

"I'll go get them," said Rhodin. He ran upstairs to his room. A moment later, he slid down the pole. He went to sit at the kitchen table. He opened the bag and dumped the stones out. "You have to arrange them a certain way before they come together."

We all gathered around the table and watched as Rhodin quickly dragged the stones into position. I was trying to memorize the shapes and positions. As soon as the last stone was in its correct placement, the magnetic energy pulled all the pieces together. It was now a complete pyramid.

"What is that?" Mom looked at it, fascinated.

"It's a magnetic puzzle," said Rhodin. "Rascal started bringing it to me and Hailey piece by piece. It started before winter. He brought the last of it over the past few weeks."

"Why would a mouse bring pieces of a puzzle?" Mom asked. "What is it supposed to do?"

"So far, this is all we know," said Hailey.

"There are still pieces missing in the middle of each triangle," I observed.

"Rascal hasn't brought anything else. It's been over a week," said Rhodin.

"I think we should take this to Lazula. She may know something about it," I said. "We have our next meeting tomorrow night."

Simple stones, hidden in plain sight, and no one had given them a glance or a second thought. They had been tread over for thousands of years. It was odd that an ordinary mouse knew precisely where to find them. He knew to bring them to Rhodin and Hailey specifically. Rhodin and Hailey knew there was something special about them. They had played with the stones intently. They worked together to solve the puzzle. It had to be an integral piece to the bigger picture.

We had all gathered together at Lazula's home the following evening. Everyone was doing their part to collect intel. Mieruss had been back to the scene of his and Zinnnia's disappearance.

He had found the stone on which Lazula had laid the child. Mieruss looked for any carvings or markings in the stone. If there had been, they were gone now, worn away with time and the elements.

Unbeknownst to Lazula, Zinnia intended to sacrifice the baby. Zinnia had knocked Lazula out somehow. Whether she hit her or used dark magic remained to be seen.

The Dark Spirit wanted the soul, whether it was that of Solaura's or the Pure Soul.

"I told you I saw the Pure Soul escape. I believe I saw it dart into the Light." Mieruss confessed. " I have a feeling the Pure Soul did not stay there. I believe it went with Tovin's child. Whether or not it re-entered the child or Solaura's soul still resides in her is unknown. By what Krystle has told us, I still think it's the latter."

Tovin's reaction held a small glimmer of pain as Mieruss explained his theory. Aunt Cassie held Tovin's hand in a comforting gesture.

"Tovin, Flint, and I went to investigate the ancestral catacombs." Mieruss continued. "It took some time for the Glacial Falls over the cave entrance to thaw for us to gain entrance. We had found a cloth with a leather band on the ground. There were remnants of burnt incense and some dried crushed flowers."

"This links Zinnia to having been there to pay homage to the ancestors. It now stands to reason; this is indeed where she found the sacrificial dagger," Lazula confirmed. "I would not wager my sister to be so careless with any questionable relic. The Dark Spirit took advantage of her as she was already in an open spiritual state. She had unknowingly made herself vulnerable."

"This evil entity knows how to beguile people," said Mieruss. "I thought myself to be strong and resist its beckoning at first. We were amidst traumatic circumstances. I was in a heightened emotional state. I found myself quickly deluded."

"We need to determine its weakness!" I broached. "If it ever makes it to this world, we have to have a defense."

"We already know its current state," said Lazula. "It doesn't have the dagger. It can still manipulate the minds of others. We have an idea of its current form and how it may appear when the time comes. Lazula looked at Meiruss. "In all the time you were around Zinnia, was she ever able to change forms?"

"Other than aging in reverse, all she could do was disguise herself by artificial means. It was easy for her to prey upon compassion. She'd gain control by touch or looking into another's eyes." Mieruss explained.

"That must have been how she rendered Lazula unconscious," I said.

"I could not recall, but I believe this to be possible," said Lazula.

"So we must capture her without making physical contact," said Tovin.

"And we cannot look into her eyes. Sounds easy enough!" It reminded me of Medusa from Greek mythology without the whole people turning into a stone thing. Zinnia could seize the mind, which was a danger unto itself.

"Lazula, will there be any indication of the Light's next location?" Uncle Garreth asked. "Before Mieruss found me, I had maps. I had pinpointed the locations of the last several appearances on Earth. There was the beginning of a pattern, but I could only find information going back to the mid-nineteenth century. Mieruss was able to determine the next location. Perhaps we could do the same here."

"I only knew of each location as the Light arrived," Lazula admitted. "I have kept my records of passage, including a map." Lazula motioned to Clave. He ran upstairs, then returned with two scrolls, weathered with age around the edges.

Lazula carefully unrolled the scrolls and held them open with smooth stones. "I've already marked your arrivals." She pointed out three points on the map with our names written. Each occurrence had a name of a moon listed.

I observed the map—hundreds have crossed over the centuries. Most occurred during the Blue Pearlescent Moon. Only a handful had taken place during the Fire and Amethyst Moons. Only one happened during a Grand Glacial Moon.

I looked past the mountains to the East and found Beryl Beach. My name appeared along with Jasper's and Rhodin's. Mom and Dad's names were written in the middle of the Kaida Forest, west of the Aventurine Mountains. Garreth, Cassie, and Mieruss had arrived in a field near Euclase Forrest in the south.

"May I borrow these? I'd like to do some calculations and look for any patterns. I will be careful with the documents," said Garreth

"That will be fine," said Lazula. "If you need my help, don't hesitate to ask."

Garreth nodded.

"Where did your ancestors come through?" he asked.

"They came through the cave beneath the Glacial Falls. This is also the ancestral catacombs," said Lazula. "It was where they found freedom, so it made sense that it became their final place of peace."

"Uncle Garreth? Did you, Cassie, and Mieruss arrive together in the same spot?" I asked. "Jasper, Rhodin, and I were separated by a few miles when we arrived. Mieruss even said that Zinnia didn't find him till a few days later on Earth." I needed to know if this was consistent with each occurrence.

"We arrived in a large open field. I heard Cassie call out to me. Mieruss rejoined us shortly after. You think Zinnia will be separated from Taylin when they arrive?" he asked.

"Yes. That could be good and bad," I attested. "We'd only have an approximated area that could span out for miles. Taylin would have a chance to get away, but then so could Zinnia. Hopefully, Taylin realizes Zinnia is her foe and manages to break away. We have to be there first. We would either capture Zinnia or get Taylin to safety. The scenario could go in either direction."

Lazula spoke. "With this new information, I believe I should address the village as the time draws near. Everyone should be on guard. If Zinnia were to lure people to do her bidding, she could turn many against us. We'd have a great fight on our hands."

An intuitive feeling prompted me to present Rhodin and Hailey's stones. "Lazula, there is something you should see." Lazula gave me a curious look.

I set the bag of stones on the table. The map laid open still. The bag began to shake. The stones clattered with a pleading to be released. I opened the bag, and the stones rose into the air. They looked like asteroids floating through space. We watched the stones assimilate in arranged order before they snapped together instantaneously.

The pyramid hovered above the map. As soon as it reached Glacial Falls, it broke into pieces that tumbled and scattered. Each stone landed on one of the corresponding marks representing an occurrence within the last century. Garreth started listing off each area in order till he reached the last rock. It had no markings there.

"That was extremely helpful," he commented. "Saved me a lot of time."

"Quick, mark the spot," I insisted.

"That is thirty miles west of here," said Tovin. "It seems to be coming full circle back toward the Glacial Falls. Every dropped point had been within a fifty-mile radius. I'll go ahead and survey the area and come back with what I find."

"I'll come with you," said Garreth.

"Where did you find these stones?" asked Lazula.

"I didn't. Rascal, Hailey's pet mouse, dropped off one stone at a time each night over the past several months. I knew they formed a pyramid. The stones had needed to be arranged by hand before they snapped together. What we all just witnessed was an entirely new development."

I nudged at the stone covering Glacial Falls, and the rocks drew back together. The reassembled pyramid hovered up into the air once more. I held my hand open underneath. I could feel a flow of energy on my palm. A rippled current waved back and forth across my skin.

My Fire Moonstone warmed and glowed. It intensified as I brought the pyramid toward me, and the stone lifted off my chest, and the leather bind pulled at my neck. The stone pyramid slowly rotated, then came to a sudden halt. The Fire Stone snapped into place on the triangular wall that now faced me.

"That is what the empty spaces are for!" I looked on in amazement. "They're meant to hold the moonstones. The remaining three sides are for the Blue Moon, Amethyst Moon, and Grand Glacial Moon. I can feel an indent on the bottom of the base. I don't know if something is supposed to go there." The concave impression beneath felt perfectly symmetrical and smooth.

Lazula retrieved her bag of moonstones. She held them one by one up to the pyramid. The stones would glow, but they didn't connect. "This confirms a thought I had," she said.

"What is it?" I asked.

"It connected with your Fire Moon Stone. It stands to reason the other stones must come from the Chosen Pure Souls. You may confirm this theory. Gemma! Bring Garrissa here," said Lazula.

Mom rose with Garrissa in her arms. Garrissa bounced up and down. Babbled gibberish rolled off her tongue. Garrissa straightened her chubby arm and pointed at the pyramid. She giggled and squealed at the sight. Garrissa lurched forward as she strained to reach it.

The Grand Glacial Moonstone from her anklet began to light up. Mom loosed it from her ankle, and the stone flew from her hand. It snapped into the triangle opposite my Fire Stone. "That leaves the Blue Moon Stone and the Amethyst Stone," said Lazula. She motioned to Aura. As Aura approached, the stone on her ring lit up. She quickly removed the ring from her finger, and it flew and snapped into place.

"We don't have a keeper for the Amethyst Stone yet," I said. "Do you think it could be Taylin?"

"Only time will tell," said Lazula. "We won't know unless she gets here."

Garrissa reached out with both hands toward the pyramid. It lifted away from my hand and glided through space between us. Everyone in the room stared in astonishment. Garrissa twisted her torso. Mom positioned her facing forward.

Garrissa held her arms open and, aloft, ready to receive the object. She didn't grab on to it. She moved her arms up and down as her hands glided across the waves of energy. The birthmark on her head illuminated. She giggled adorably. It was music to our ears. The light from the stones responded and flashed along with Garrissa's laughter.

Giddiness bubbled up in my belly, and everyone bellowed joyfully. Contentment filled our beings and resonated throughout the room. Garrissa clapped her hands. The pyramid broke apart and tumbled into pieces on the floor. Garrissa's lips formed an "O," and she put both of her hands over her mouth. "Bu...Bo!" she yelled. It sounded like she was trying to say, "Uh, Oh!" She laughed again and clapped her hands like she was applauding a magic trick.

In essence, it all felt magical. Aura helped me gather the pieces and our Moon Stones. The puzzle stones went back into the bag. I retied my Fire Stone around my neck, Aura put her ring back on, and Mom tied the anklet back to Garrissa. I felt a residual energy course through me as the Fire Stone rested upon my chest once more. It made me feel light and wonderful.

"I felt the connection between the moons and the pyramid," said Lazula. "It was powerful. There is more to this. The capabilities of this object align with the connection between the moons and the Light. Once the final Pure Soul and the Amethyst Moon Stone surface, the power will be insurmountable. It will work great in our favor. Just like the dagger, we must keep this hidden and safe. Krystle, you must keep this with you."

I already knew the best place to hide it, within the confines of beasts and babes, which contained six fury guards and two small guardians.

Tovin and Uncle Garreth had set out the next day to scout the location. It was one-third of the way into Samarskite Ravine. They took Bax and Sierra with them in case something unexpected happened. The pair were excellent trackers, and they could find their way back home in case of an emergency.

Aunt Cassie forged ahead in her work with Mom. She wouldn't talk about anything that may or may not have happened with Tovin. She did smile whenever his name got mentioned. It was a good sign.

Lazula had agreed to let the Tucker's in on everything that had transpired over the past several months. I told them what was necessary, and this was under Lazula's authority. My hands had been tied. The rest of the village would find out when the time was right. In the meantime, everyone went about each day without any worry.

A few days later, Tovin and Uncle Garreth returned. Lazula came to our house for dinner, and they discussed their findings.

"This may be tricky. We may need to camp out near the ravine and keep watch weeks ahead of time. There are many places to hide within the gorge. We'll have to keep a diligent watch for the Light. We will need people to take shifts and further survey the area," said Garreth.

"We can bring more dogs to sniff anyone out of hiding," said Tovin. "This could work to our advantage in capturing Zinnia. She wouldn't be able to go far."

"We'll need a way to contain and transport her. We could construct a cage and cart it there," Garreth suggested.

"You have to blindfold her and bind her as well," said Mieruss. "As long as you don't make direct contact, you should be okay."

"I want to come along," I said. "Zinnia may be drawn to me. She never attempted to touch me during our interactions back at the resort. I had even looked into her eyes. It was off-putting, but I didn't feel any loss of control over my senses. I remember she had a hold of Rhodin when she led him to the cave that night. A moment before reaching the Light, Rhodin had managed to pull away from her. Jasper had grabbed her from behind and was able to contain her. I don't think he was affected at all. Rhodin said he and Jasper followed me immediately into the Light."

"I had seen this happen," said Uncle Garreth. "Jasper had dropped her in the water and charged in after you and Rhodin without a moment's thought. The Light seemed to implode immediately before Cassie and I reached it. I didn't know who the little girl was at the time. She got up and ran away without a word. At that point, I was too shocked to think anything of it. Cassie, Victor, and I tried to locate her the next day. She was nowhere to be found."

"Zinnia is extremely elusive," said Mieruss. "She's only gotten better at it over the years."

Lazula took a drink and set down her cup. "I remember when Zinnia and I were young. She always won at hide and seek. I always had the hardest time finding her.

She was a sweet child, and my dearest friend, I miss her deeply."

Aunt Cassie put her hand on Lazula's. Lazula looked at Cassie. "Your empathy is strong, child. You have the power to heal the mind. There's a richness to you like the most pleasant turnings of earth. The life your hand's touch grows earnestly to please you. You are very humble and loving. You are on the right path."

"Thank you, Lazula," said Cassie. She looked up and caught Tovin looking back at her. "I have a feeling I am on the right path as well," said Cassie. Tovin held her gaze. Cassie took hold of her cloth napkin and fanned herself. "I'm a bit flushed; I think I need some fresh air."

Tovin got up and pulled her chair back, "May I join you?"

Cassie blushed and nodded. He gestured for her to lead the way and followed her outside. Clave squeezed my hand under the table, and we grinned.

Lazula smiled as she tracked Cassie and Tovin's movements. "This was a wonderful dinner, Gemma! Thank you for inviting me."

"You're welcome, Lazula," said Mom. A mashed variety of colors covered Garrissa's face. She continued to shove little bites into her mouth and hummed approvingly.

"Is there something in the water around here?" Uncle Garreth's tone was complaining. "My new friend has turned into a lovesick puppy!"

"Just you wait!" Dad laughed. "Your day will come, brother!"

"Gah!" Garreth grumbled. "No time for all that right now. It's just a distraction." He went to pick up Garrissa. "I got my little squish bug here!" He lifted her into the air and blew on her belly. Garrissa started the giggle.

"You better watch it, brother, or she's gonna...too late!" Dad laughed.

Garreth handed her back to Dad. "I'm going to go take a shower. You'd think I'd learned my lesson from the last three kids." He took off his shirt and wiped gooey mush out of his hair. Clave and I were just holding ourselves together.

"She probably overate," said Mom. "Come here, baby girl, mama's going to clean you up while daddy does the dishes!"

Dad looked astounded by Mom's declaration. Lazula just said, "Sounds like a fair deal to me. Mieruss, are you ready to see me home?"

"Yes, Lazula." He helped her up. "We will see you all later. Thank you again for dinner." Clave and I walked them out. We sat in the swing together and enjoyed the evening. Out in the distance, we could see Tovin and Cassie walking together.

Has he made a move yet? I asked.

I'm sure he wants to. I think he's testing the waters, Clave replied.

Oh, he just took her hand! I squeaked.

Clave put his hands up to his cheeks, *O.M.G.!* He squealed like a girl. I folded my arms across my chest and glared at him. Chorus chittered at Clave.

Chorus said you should know better than to mock your lady. I thought you were mature. Your brain is going in reverse, I rebuked.

No…I really am just as excited as you are. Clave attempted to placate me with feigned innocence. When that didn't work, he quickly changed the subject. *You'll be eighteen on your next birthday. Any ideas on what you want?*

I can't believe I had almost forgotten my seventeenth birthday! Time is so different here, I admitted.

A lot has happened, said Clave. *You think so much about the well-being and happiness of others. That's why you need me around to remind you. Our students love you. Everyone here practically beams when they see you. You have become an integral part of many lives here.*

Thank you, Clave. The same applies to you. I kissed him on his dimpled cheek. *I don't need anything for my eighteenth birthday. It's not like a brand new car is going to show up in my non-existent driveway. I'm not going off to college, so I don't need anything for my non-existent dorm room.*

Do you feel like you're missing out on what could have been back on Earth? We can figure out ways for you to have those experiences here, said Clave.

No, I am really happy here with the way things are. This world is the way it should be. Unspoiled, clean, natural. People have meaningful interactions. Everyone is strong, healthy, kind, and unselfish. There are no bullies or social hierarchies. People don't have to party to forget their woes, relieve stress, or have meaningless physical interactions. They celebrate things worth celebrating. There is no condemnation for living the way we choose or believing what we want to believe. It's peaceful and beautiful here. Best of all, I have you here. I smiled and looked into his gorgeous gray eyes.

And I have you, Krystle. You're all I need. He stroked my cheek, leaned in, and kissed me—soft, tender, real. I felt the truth of his words in the bond we shared. I felt it with every touch, every kiss, every time we looked into each other's eyes. No, I wouldn't trade this for trappings of an existence with which I could no longer relate. I didn't feel like I fit there anyway.

I missed Taylin still, but I knew she would be happy for me. Knowing what I do now, it made sense how well we connected. I had connected immediately with Aura and Clave; I knew that I was meant to be a part of this family.

Chapter 21

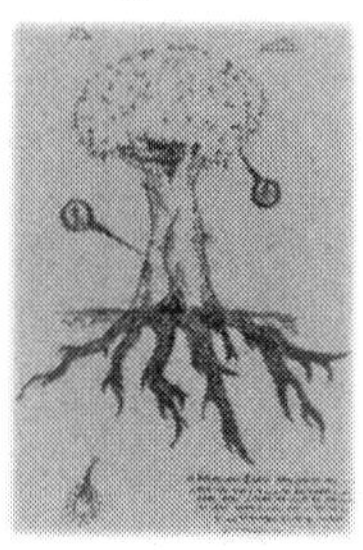

Dear Krystle,

I missed my chance! I could've kicked my own ass for missing the boat. I hope and pray Garreth and Cassie have found you. I wish there were a way for all of you to return. I can't wait to get out of here after graduation. I made sure they'd call your name in honorable mention. You may be lost from this world but haven't ceased to exist. Not to me or Maria. I haven't given up. I keep my promise to this very day.

My parents have been acting kind of strange. It's like there's something they want to tell me. I'm getting this negative vibe. They keep avoiding me. It's made me anxious. I need to get away from this mess.

Maria's family will be going to Brazil for the summer, and I'll be joining them! Maria says we'll spend our last summer of freedom on the beach. We'll be checking out all those hot chili peppers in tight speedos. My mind could use some positive distraction.

Your house has a big "For Sale" sign in the yard. Every time I drive by it, I want to cry. I've been working part-time at Cassie's shop. Lynn and Carol have been very kind, putting up with my shenanigans. They cut me some slack. They understand. They miss you and Cassie very much. They don't know what happened other than an unfortunate coincidence. Social media has noted that two more members of the same family have gone missing a little over a year later. Fodder for the conspiracy theorists.

Victor still manages the company. He realized Garreth and Cassie had found their way through the Light after a few days of zero contact. Garreth had told Victor he had a strong lead just days before. I'm pissed that nobody told me shit. Victor has instructions to take care of the company and employees if Garreth does not return within a specific time frame. Garreth pretty much signed it over to him and another guy he and your dad trusted.

Garreth had prepared a video statement for Victor to hand over so no implications would fall on him as a suspect. Garreth stated that he and Cassie would be traveling, and if anything happened to them, Victor nor anyone else would know what may have happened to them. So, the police think Garreth and Cassie went on a personal vendetta manhunt for Lattimier.

I had retrieved and hidden Garreth's maps. He had marked a new place a few hours south, somewhere around Austin. I'm guessing that's where they found their way through. I couldn't reach them on their phones. I found Garreth's. The sim card had been removed. His laptop had been wiped. I'm worried that Lattimier may have been following him. Garreth was trying to cover his tracks.

I wish I could have gone with them. I guess your uncle was trying to keep me safe. I'm kind of ticked about that too. This "GangStar" still knows how to handle herself.

Maria and I still watch the missing person chats and have added paranormal chat sites. People have mentioned strange light phenomena, but the descriptions didn't match up—all UFO lights in the sky and ghost bullshit.

Maybe the Light will find me one day. I still feel you calling out to me. Keep taking good care of yourself, Girlie!

I miss you still!

Love,

Taylin

The next Amethyst Moon was a few months away. Lazula urged me to call out to Taylin a few times beforehand. Taylin seemed to be in some sort of haze. I continued to warn her and send her my love. It seemed like she was somewhere else on Earth. I saw her on the beach with Maria, surrounded by people with gorgeous tanned bodies. I looked like a pale ghost.

The weather was warmer, so Clave, Tovin, Cassie, and I took Garrissa out in our favorite field. I wore a tube top and shorts. This pale body needed some color and vitamin sunshine. I laid back and closed my eyes, and enjoyed the warmth on my skin.

I could hear the shuffling of clothing. A small breath hit my belly before Garrissa had launched herself across my midsection. “Umphfff...Ohh... You little stinkerton!” I lifted her into the air. She giggled, and drool ran down her chubby fingers as she teethed on them.

Clave was watching our exchange. *Now that's adorable! I was enjoying a very delectable sight before that, but I'll accept the interruption for this little cutie.*

“Thanks for the heads up, Clave,” I squinted and stuck out my tongue.

Cassie laughed, “You had your eyes closed, Krystle. Clave couldn't have signed a warning to you.”

Tovin smiled and turned his head away. Tovin knew about our telepathic connection. Chorus landed on my forehead, and Garrissa grunted as she tried to reach out for him. Chorus chirped and chittered away.

I set Garrissa on my stomach, and her giggles turned into full-on belly laughs. “Chorus must be telling her some hilarious jokes.” My laughter had Garrissa bouncing up and down. Drool streamers were now hitting my chest.

“What's that?” Cassie's voice sounded panicked. I sat up, and Clave took Garrissa. I held my hand over my eyes and looked to where she was pointing.

“I saw something large moving in the trees. Are there bears around here?” She sounded frightened. Tovin stood up and walked forward a few paces.

A couple of faces peaked out. I knew who that was. I got to my feet. “Linger, Soorah,” I shouted. Cassie stood up and was hiding behind Tovin. She had her hands on his back. Tovin was smiling in a combination of testosterone and surety. He put his arm around Cassie, and she clung to him. I started walking toward Linger as he stepped out first.

Cassie started to scream but was quickly cut off by Tovin’s hand across her mouth. “Shh…you’ll scare them,” he said.

“Scare them?” I heard Cassie whisper shout.

“Welcome back, Linger.” I opened my arms, and Linger took to me into his and hugged me. “Hello, Soorah,” I signed. “Where’s Kyan?”

A little face peeked out from behind Soorah. “My goodness. Kyan has grown,” I signed to Soorah. She grunted softly and put her hand on Kyan’s head. They both stepped out with Linger. Kyan was the size of a five-year-old boy.

“Hello, Clave.” Linger greeted him as he slowly approached. “He is good, Soorah.” Linger told his mate. Soorah looked hesitant but remained calm. Linger pointed to Tovin and Cassie. “They are all good, Soorah.”

“Do you want to meet my Aunt Cassie and my baby sister Garrissa?” I signed and pointed. “It’s safe,” I assured Soorah and Kyan. “I was with your mama when you were born,” I told Kyan.

He seemed to comprehend as I talked to him. Kyan looked up at Soorah. Soorah nodded and signed, “Krystle, help,” Kyan nodded.

"Linger, my Aunt Cassie is new to this world. Please give me a moment to prepare her. She's a bit timid and shy."

Linger chuckled. Clave continued to stay with them as I walked back to Cassie and Tovin. Cassie looked terrified as she held Garrissa. Tovin still had his arm around her, smiling. I gave him an accusing look, and he just shrugged. *Opportunist!* I thought. Good for him, though!

"Krystle, who...what are those creatures?" asked Cassie.

"They are Yehati and our good friends. You should come to meet them, Cassie. Linger comes each year to trade with the village. Mom helped deliver their son, Kyan," I explained.

"Really?" Cassie was hesitant as Tovin guided her. I took Garrissa from her arms. "Krystle! Wait!" I knew she'd follow less reluctantly if I carried Garrissa ahead.

Garrissa was smiling with her two front bottom teeth on display. She reached out toward the Yehati like old friends. She was trying to launch herself out of my arms. I finally got to Linger and lifted her to him. He reached out to take her, and Aunt Cassie gasped.

"It's okay, Aunt Cassie," I told her. Garrissa fit entirely in the palm of Linger's hand. Linger held her tenderly up to his shoulder, and she grabbed onto his hair and leaned into him. She babbled while blowing little spit bubbles.

"Gemma's baby," Linger signed with his other hand. I nodded. "See, Soorah? Gemma's baby!" Soorah looked at her adoringly.

"Beautiful!" Soorah waved her hand over her face. Kyan raised his arms to Soorah, and she lifted Kyan to get a better look at Garrissa. Garrissa lifted her head and turned to look back. She put out one chubby hand and did her cute baby backward wave, signing the word, "more." She wanted to be friends with the Yehati family. Kyan reached out with a pointed finger and touched Garrissa's hand. Garrissa giggled, and Kyan let out a joyful sound.

"New friend," Kyan signed. Soorah smiled and nodded.

"This is my Aunt Cassie," I said.

"Hello," Cassie said in her small, shy voice. "Linger, Soorah and Kyan?"

"Yes," I confirmed. I pointed to Tovin, and Soorah looked at him. "Tovin, a good friend to Linger a long time. Your friend too," I told her.

Soorah nodded. We were making progress. "Want to see, Gemma," Soorah gestured.

"Okay, we will go get her and the Tuckers. All good. All safe," I told Soorah. Soorah began to look at ease. I reached, and Linger gently passed Garrissa back to me. "Do you want to come with us or wait here?" I asked Linger.

"Wait here, keep Soorah and Kyan calm," He signed.

I nodded. Linger, Soorah and Kyan stepped back into the trees as we walked back toward the village. “That was unreal!” Cassie huffed out in exasperation.

“I know, right? They will grow on you quickly, though,” I said.

We went and told Mom, Dad, Uncle Garreth, Rhodin, and the Tuckers. They were all excited and followed us back out to the field. I warned Uncle Garreth, Eric, and the Bens to stay calm because of Soorah and Kyan. When the Yehati’s stepped out from the trees to meet us, Uncle Garreth whispered in shock. “Well, I’ll be a son-of-a-gun! They really do exist!”

Mom slowly approached Soorah and Kyan. She held Garrissa, who was happy to see her new friend again. Mom smiled at Soorah. Soorah had Kyan on her hip and reached out to Mom. They both hugged. Soorah began to weep.

“Hi, Soorah.” Mom had tears in her eyes. “So, happy to see you and Kyan. Safe. Strong. Healthy.”

Soorah signed, “Thank you,” to her.

Rhodin and Hailey were hugging Linger. Eric patted Linger on the back, “Hello, old friend. How’s family life treating ye?”

Linger hugged Liv, and the Bens then responded. “Kyan gives me many new funny stories to tell,” we all chuckled. “Where’s my high-five buddy, Jasper?”

We all laughed as we remembered how Jasper had fallen on his rear when he high-fived Linger.

"Bonded with Aura now," Tovin signed. "New home, back at the village."

Linger's eyebrows rose. "Congratulations."

Tovin smiled and nodded.

"Yer here for yer haircut?" Liv asked. "It's a bit early, but I can fit ye in. Would Soorah like one? We will treat her extra gently."

"No, we will be back later in the season." Linger motioned. "Soorah wanted to see Gemma and her baby."

"Awe, I'm really happy about that," said Mom. "We are good friends now. Right Soorah?" Soorah grunted softly and nodded.

We all walked back together to our little picnic area from earlier. Kyan stood before Garrissa as she attempted to pull herself up while holding on to his legs. He crouched low and held his arms up to let her grab onto his fingers. He was very gentle with her. She pulled herself up to standing.

"Oh, look at that! She's standing!" I sat behind her in case she fell over. "Excellent, Kyan." I praised him, and he let out a happy huffing noise. Garrissa imitated the sound. They seemed to be carrying on a conversation in their own secret language.

Soorah and Linger were chuckling. Linger signed. "She can speak to us," he pointed at Garrissa.

Surely, it was just a coincidence. Babies make all kinds of noises as they learn to vocalize. But no, Linger, Soorah and Kyan seemed to understand her vocalizations.

They grunted, huffed, and cooed along. Garrissa looked up at Linger and Soorah and responded. The rest of us were astounded.

"Holy macaroni!" Aunt Cassie looked on in amazement.

"I agree with that sentiment," said Garreth. "Perhaps I should get my mental faculties checked."

"Welcome to the new world, brother." Dad patted Garreth on the back.

I went to talk to Lazula a few days later. "I have some interesting new information. Garrissa met Linger and his family. It turns out she can communicate with them."

Lazula looked surprised, "She can speak their language?

"She can speak it and understand what they say," I said. "We were all just as flabbergasted as you! I thought it was just a fluke. Babies mimic and vocalize in gibberish. It turns out gibberish is a big part of the Yehati language. Linger even confirmed they were making a clear, concise exchange."

"It's not just the Yehati. Animals come to her. Each time Clave and I take her out in the fields, wild animals approach. She giggles every time Chorus chirps. Clave can tell when Chorus is a jokester, and I think Garrissa understands the punchline," I concluded.

"She has an affinity toward animals and can communicate with the Yehati. She also has telekinetic control," Lazula commented. "The way she called the stone pyramid and commanded its' displacement with the clap of her hands proves as much. She may have more gifts yet to discover. Once she's older, she'll be more attuned with nature."

"How does she interact with you? Do you feel any heightened natural insight with her?" asked Lazula.

"I feel joyful and peaceful around her. I can feel it in the animals as well. Even with Clave and me near, they do not feel threatened," I explained.

"She is certainly a joyful child. More so than I have ever seen before," Lazula observed. "I feel younger in her presence. The whole village seems more exuberant with her around. Just knowing she's here. I believe she will be a great leader one day."

"Have you had any new visions or have called out to Taylin as of late?" Lazula questioned.

"I have tried. I think with everything new abuzz around here. I've been too distracted to concentrate. My feel on Taylin was kind of hazy. She should have graduated from school by now. A lot happens in a person's life at our age back on Earth," I admitted. "I haven't given up hope. I can only pray Taylin is safe."

"As do we all, child," Lazula agreed. "Did you ever show Tovin the picture you drew of her? I knew when I first saw it; her image reminded me of someone I knew!"

"Solaura," I acknowledged. "Tovin was taken aback when he saw the picture. He had said she looked so much like her mother. I had to draw another copy to give to him. I made one for Aura as well."

"That was very special," Lazula had a far-away look.

I looked at her questioningly. "What are you thinking?"

Lazula blinked. "The Grand Glacial Moon called your Mother because of Garrissa. The Fire Moon called you. The Pearlescent Blue Moon told me to give Jasper its stone as a gift to Aura. That just leaves the Amethyst Moon. I wonder if it intends to call Taylin. She seems to have a pivotal role in everything revealed so far."

"Do you think she has Solaura's soul?" I asked. "Did Solaura have any ties to the moons?"

"I do believe Solaura was born on the night of the Amethyst Moon." Lazula looked as if she was trying to recall this being a certainty. "I know little of soul transference from one being to another. In your world, they refer to it as reincarnation."

"I've heard of it! There are many different beliefs on the subject. I watched documentaries depicting children having memories from another life. I found it interesting."

"Did Taylin have any such claims of memories?" Lazula asked.

"No, she was just always feisty, brave, and funny. She always stood up for people against bullies. No one ever messed with her. She was well respected," I admitted.

"She sounds just like Solaura," said Lazula. "I used to keep an eye on Solaura when she was young. She could be defiant. She stood her ground for all the right reasons. She was the only woman who could challenge Tovin. Part of the reason he fell for her. Aura is like her in many ways as well."

"I noticed! From the moment I met Aura, I knew we would be instant friends." I confided.

"Yes," Lazula smiled. "Well, child, don't let me keep you all day. Clave waits for you. Please keep your eyes peeled and your gifts open."

We both got up and hugged. "I promise I will. Blessings and peace to you, Lazula."

"To you as well, Krystle."

I walked outside and saw Clave standing on the bridge where I had first laid eyes on him. Chorus flew down and landed on me. *Hello, beautiful!* I heard Clave speak through our connection.

Hello, stud muffin! Was it possible he got sexier every time I saw him? I realized he had heard my thought when he started flexing and posing. He did a sideways bicep curl pose and arched his eyebrow. I laughed so hard; my abs felt sore from the exertion.

He continued to make different poses like a bodybuilder and feign grunted as he spoke, *Would my lady love like to join her stud muffin for a nice tasty snack? I've got a side of beefcake I'd love to share with her.*

I was cracking up now. *Me thinketh I have created a conceited monster.*

Awe, babe! You had me all pumped; then you went and burst my bubble. He lowered his head and pouted.

Aww, I didn't mean to make you sad. We should eat, though, so I can have the energy to make it up to you later, I chimed.

Clave ran across the bridge and down around the tree on its spiraled steps. He swooped me up in his arms, and I yelped. He kissed me with his soft, delicious lips. *Lunchtime!* He called out. I continued to laugh as he carried me down to the river. He deposited me in a canoe. *We have a lunch date at Jasper and Aura's.*

Oh, they are finally receiving company? She finally had enough of my brother? I can't say I blame her, I teased.

Our life together will always be an adventure, Krystle. You'll never get tired of me, Clave declared. *Your brother, on the other hand...he's gonna have a struggle keeping up with Aura.*

We made it down the river. Aura and Jasper came out to greet us, "Ahtee, Krystle. Ahtee, Clave."

"Ahtee," I yelled back. I ran up the steps and hugged Aura, then Jasper. "Have you two finally decided to come out of hiding? I understand you're still honeymooners, but you still need fresh air sometimes."

"Just you wait, Krystle. You'll soon understand what all the fuss is about," said Aura.

"Number one, you're talking about my brother. And number two, eeww."

Aura laughed at me, “So I take it you’ll want no sisterly advice?”

“Not if it entails visualizing you with him!” I pointed at Jasper. He just rolled his eyes. Jasper and Clave did the brotherly man-hug with the pats on the back. They started walking ahead inside.

“It might take me a few to regain my appetite after that exchange. Thanks a lot, sister!” I walked alongside Aura. She waggled her eyebrows at me and laughed.

I entered their new home, much the same as most tree homes. Aura added some of her personal touches. The smell of fresh-baked goodness invaded my headspace, and I found my appetite had returned rather quickly.

We sat down at the table and ate. Clave and I had caught Jasper and Aura up on the latest developments with Garrissa. Both their jaws had dropped.

“That is amazing,” said Aura. “My sister speaks Yehati, and she’s still a baby! How can one so young be so comprehensive? She must be a genius!”

“She is most certainly gifted,” I agreed. “You saw what she was able to do with the stone pyramid! Lazula says she has telekinetic abilities and an affinity for animals and nature. Who knows what else she’ll be capable of as she continues to grow?”

“She’s a Genstone, enough said!” Jasper exclaimed.

Aura rolled her eyes. “Your brother went from being all: ‘I’m happy to be Mrs. and Mr. Otek-Genstone’ to ‘Jasper Genstone Rules!’”

"That's because it's what you said on the first night of our honeymoon, my beautiful thundercloud," said Jasper.

I dropped the bread from my hand, "Really? You two had to go there?"

Three against one were laughing now. "Clave!" I glared at him.

He had his hand to his stomach and was shaking his head. *Your reactions make it so easy. You are so funny to watch when you're shocked into reproach by such vile atrocities.*

"It's not vile or atrocious!" I defended. "It's just...I don't want to know about my brother's...sex life, okay?"

"One day, you'll laugh about this, sis," said Jasper. "You would never have acted this way if Taylin was dishing with you about some boy she'd made out with."

"That's different, Jasper. We're BFFs, and none of those boys was my brother." I voiced back.

"Ooh, my baby sister was getting some action. Go Taylin!" Aura lifted her hands in the air in a pump-praise.

"Taylin is always the action. She will always be my action hero. Damn, I miss her!"

"Awe, Krystle! I wish I had known her as you do. But I'm happy the two of you have each other." She reached over and wiped a tear from my cheek.

"Thanks, Aura. I could only imagine you two together growing up. You would have probably been butting heads all the time. You're both strong and proud in the best ways," I concluded.

"Taylin was always tough, and I was a hot mess," I confessed.

You're still hot, Krystle, Clave stated endearingly. *The mess part is only on occasion.*

I gave him a shocked look. Yet, I was internally high-fiving his impishness.

Aura reached over and slapped Claves arm. He rubbed it, *Ow, I keep forgetting not to tease when Aura's around. She hits harder than a man.*

Jasper exaggerated a sniffle, "I know how you feel, buddy. There's no help for me here. I have to tread carefully if she's in a mood." Aura gave Jasper the stink eye, and his chair slid back a good three feet.

"I'm sorry, my beautiful thundercloud. Have mercy!" Aura nodded in approval. It was all a playful charade. She looked at me and winked, then pointed to Clave and gave him the evil eye. Clave threw his hands up in surrender.

Oh, the antics of buffoons when they come together and make one their patsy. The stakes eventually make their rounds. Aura was the equalizer. I had to give her props for stepping up in my honor.

I lifted my cup in a toast, "To the Queen of the Otek-Genstone household. I do solemnly give my gratitude!" Aura lifted her head high in regal acknowledgment.

I looked at Jasper, who caught on after a momentary lapse. He quickly lifted his cup along with Clave. He cleared his throat and spoke with a brusque and burly tone, “Yes. To my queen, my love, my most gracious and magnanimous champion. She will always have my heart.”

“Here! Here!” I toasted and threw back a swig, then Jasper and Clave followed. We all enjoyed our juvenile collaborative exchange. I needed this moment of light-hearted banter to clear the weary fog in my head.

Clave looked at me and smiled. *I'm sorry if I've been too overt in my foolishness to see you've been holding in feelings of dismay, Krystle. We should talk about this. I'm here for you anytime you need me.*

“I know, Clave. We've been wrapped up in our little world—all the signs of an uncertain future loom over our heads. I just want the feeling of impending darkness to pass. I want to get past all this and survive to see this world and live fully. I want everything with you.” I drew in a breath and let it out.

He put his hand around my hair and kissed my forehead. *Me too, love.*

“We're all here for you, Krystle,” said Aura. “We will get through what lies ahead because we all have each other.” She and Jasper sat close together now. His arm around her shoulders in a display of solidarity. I felt so happy for them. I sent up a silent prayer for thanks and safety for my brother and sister.

Aura and I spent the rest of the time talking about Taylin. Jasper and Clave had gone outside to talk. When it was time to head home, Aura and I came out. The guys were still engaged in silent conversation.

"What are you two conspiring?" I stood and looked at my brother and Clave with my hands on my hips. Clave never cut me out of his conversations with others.

"We're not conspiring on anything," Jasper quickly shot back.

If you must know, it's about your birthday coming up, said Clave. *But, if you insist I spoil the surprise, then I'll let you in.*

Curiosity coursed through my brain, but I wanted to allow Clave his chance to do something special. It would bring him a feeling of knowing I had faith in our bond. "No, I can wait. You've been patient; I want to prove I can be patient as well. Do you have more to discuss?"

No, love. I believe Jasper knows enough. Shall I escort my lady home now? Clave asked.

"Yes, my love. I believe you still owe me a side of beefcake." I snickered.

"Eeww, sis! You two go before you make me barf," said Jasper.

"Ow, Aura!" Jasper rubbed his arm. "Krystle can make comments, but I can't?"

Aura smiled and waved. "Ahtee, sister! Peace and love to you."

"Ahtee Aura. To you as well. Later, brother!" I gave Jasper a flipped wave.

"Okay! Love you too, sis!" Jasper called. Sarcasm noted. Young adult sibling rivalry rears its head.

Clave and I walked home from there. He put his arm around me. I snuggled into his warmth.

Clave?

Hmm?

There's something I want to address. I don't know how you're going to feel about it. I stopped to look at him.

Whatever you say or feel, Krystle, know that I'm with you. We have a partnership. I'll always support you in whatever you want.

I know you want us to be bonded by ceremony soon. I was thinking about the after. I felt his Adam's apple bob up and down against my head as he swallowed.

Are you nervous about our wedding night? I promise I won't rush you. We can take things slow, said Clave.

Don't guys know, saying things like that makes girls want them more? Prince Charming and slow-burn romance are high heat-inducing, I said.

Really? Okay! So, are you talking about something else concerning this matter? Clave asked.

Yes, I admitted. *Clave, I want to be your wife, your bond. I want us to have a family together. It's just...*

Just what? He prompted.

It's just... I don't want to start a family right away. I don't want to pose any possible risks to myself or our child. We'll be together before the Light comes, and we're still not entirely sure what that will bring.

I want to wait till we're sure that the danger has passed. I want us to be victorious in our pursuit against the enemy. I want us to be able to accomplish that together. I won't be left behind while you take all the risk. As you said, we are a partnership, a team.

Clave stopped and faced me. *I agree with you, Krystle. I've had these same thoughts. I've seen how you have jumped in at every facet of this dilemma. You already have a plan in place. The details are unpredictable, but I know you will figure out the way. You have been brilliant in every step of this journey. I've never felt the need to intervene. I've always agreed with your input.*

Krystle, there will be risks with every aspect. We will do what we can to hold back as long as you wish with starting a family. I do want that with you when you're ready. If by chance, that happens before what may come, I'll do everything in my power to protect you and our child.

I know you will, Clave. But it has been prophesied that it is I who must fulfill this quest the Fire Moon has bestowed upon me. Lazula told me this the day I met her. I saw the look in Clave's eyes. It was determination and fortitude.

You have everything and everyone good surrounding you. I can't see any possible outcome besides victory. I'll be with you every step of the way. You drew me to you. We will always be together. For better or for worse, my love, my partner. He wrapped me up and lifted me, so our lips met. His kiss was like fire. It consumed me. Excitement built in me, knowing we'd soon be fulfilling our desire for one another.

Chapter 22

I thought it would be best if I talked to Mom at the clinic. I wanted to keep what I needed to say private. I was relieved to find her by herself in the back. She was journaling her finds as she had been looking through a microscope.

“Hey, Mom. I was hoping to catch you alone.” I sat on a stool across from her.

She looked up and smiled. “What can I help you with, baby girl?”

“The baby thing. Uhm...precisely.” I don’t know why I was nervous discussing this. She’s a woman, a doctor. It was the mother part that was getting to me.

“Clave and I have agreed to hold off on having a family right away, and I was wondering...? Is there something medically, naturally available to make that possible?” I swallowed nervously.

“I understand, Krystle. Hold on. I have something that will work for you.” She gave me a bottle of what she described as a natural plant-based solution and briefly explained how to use it.

"Krystle, you'll be a wonderful mother one day when you're ready! I'm happy for you and Clave. Love and enjoy each other. The physical bond between a couple in love is a beautiful and natural thing. Never feel ashamed or embarrassed by it." She pushed back my hair from my face and kissed my forehead.

"Thank you, Mom."

"You're welcome, Krystle."

I left feeling so much easier. I got home and went up to my room. I looked at the bottle and read over the label. "Here goes." I placed four drops under my tongue. It was a strange botanical flavor but not unpleasant. That was easy enough. I made a note on my mirror that said, "Don't forget to take your vitamins." I safely stored the bottle away.

The anticipation in the time that followed was close to maddening. I could feel Clave's nervousness. I almost wanted to talk to Aura about it. Almost! I found myself spying more on Cassie and Tovin. They were so adorable together. Tovin had opened up more. They laughed a lot. I heard him tell her the story about the waterslide of doom and our reactions. He described Jasper's high-pitched girlie scream. Cassie was cracking up. I had never seen her so happy before.

Later that evening, I finally spotted them kissing. Aunt Cassie returned home looking hot and bothered. "I'm going to take a shower. It was hot outside today." She walked past me. I could hear her singing 80's pop love songs. Dad was cooking dinner and started singing along in the kitchen.

When Cassie came out, Dad was still singing. He turned around and said, "Get it, girl!"

Aunt Cassie looked slightly embarrassed but quickly dismissed Dad's attempt to hold anything over her head. I think she was starting to assert herself and wasn't going to let anyone steal her thunder. Go, Aunt Cassie! I was proud of her.

"Your birthday's tomorrow," said Dad. "Anything special planned?"

I couldn't believe how fast the months had passed. Watching Garrissa grow and staying busy with everything else around me, it was a shock to realize my eighteenth birthday came so soon.

"Just cake and a little get-together," I responded.

Dad smiled and started whistling. By the look on his face, I knew that he knew something was up. I just pretended to be oblivious.

"Oh, yeah! I just remembered; Liv wants you to stop over tomorrow morning. She said she has something special for you," Dad waited for my response.

"Okay. Thanks for letting me know," I kept my voice monotone.

Dad continued to whistle. Aunt Cassie came back downstairs dressed in a simple t-shirt and shorts. She sat down next to me and grabbed a piece of fruit from the bowl on the table. She was playing it cool as well.

"Haven't seen Clave all day. What's he been up to?" She asked.

"Just working with the class on a project," I said.

"What project?"

"Something about nature and art. A field study is what he told me," I said.

"And you didn't want to participate?" Cassie questioned.

"Aura needed help with something," I lied. Before she asked another question, I asked, "How's Tovin doing?"

She smiled dreamily, "Oh, he's good. Very good!"

I had to bite my lips closed to keep from laughing. I looked at Dad. His back was to us, and he was shaking his head. I could tell he was struggling to keep his composure. He looked ready to burst and spill the beans.

After dinner, I went to take a shower. I was grateful Aunt Cassie didn't use much hot water. I needed it to relax the tense muscles in my neck. When I came out, I noticed it was still just Dad and Aunt Cassie. Everyone else was out late tonight. "I'm turning in. Good night, Dad. Good night, Aunt Cassie."

"Good night, Krystle," they returned.

I pulled my curtain and went to lie down. I felt drained from my brain, overly stimulated with emotions these past few weeks. I closed my eyes and fell asleep.

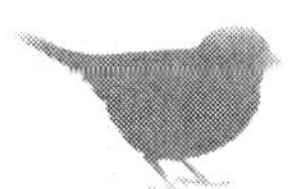

The following day, I woke refreshed. I'd had no dreams that I could recall. I felt pleasant, happy. Oh, yeah!

Happy eighteenth birthday, Krystle, I said to myself. I got up and looked in the mirror. Still the same face as yesterday, only this morning it included a significant case of bed head. My hair was a crazy mess. I brushed it and smoothed it out the best I could. I took my "vitamins" and took the slide downstairs.

"Good morning," said Mom. "Happy birthday!"

"Thanks, Mom! Where is everybody?"

"Where they usually go. Your Dad wants to get everyone together later to celebrate. I'm going to work on making a cake. Oh, and Liv said to come over whenever you're ready," said Mom.

"Okay. I'm just going to grab a quick bite to eat, and I'll head over." I toasted some bread and spread it on some fruit jelly. After I ate, I headed out the door. It was a beautiful day.

I knocked on the Tucker's door, and Bennigan answered. "Good morning, birthday girl! Come in, Mahm's expect n' ye."

"Oh, good! Come on! Get in here, Krystle," Liv yelled.

"Hey, Liv! Aura? What are you doing here?"

"Happy birthday!" Aura and Liv chimed.

"We're having a little dress-up slash makeup party for the birthday girl," said Liv.

"Yeah, it will be fun," said Aura. "I get to play with your hair, and Liv is gonna do your makeup."

"Oh, and I have a dress ye can wear," Liv said excitedly. She went to her trunk and pulled a dress that looked like something a proper lady wore back in the late 1700s. It had a white corseted bodice with small groupings of pink roses, a plunging scoop front that pushed up my cleavage, and short cuffed shoulder sleeves. The skirt was all white and flared out slightly, and reached my ankles. She added some simple white slippers.

Aura had put my hair up in the same loose French braid she had done once before. It was the day I met Clave. I smiled, thinking back on our first flirtatious encounter. Hailey came in with small white flowers in hand.

"Remember, Krystle. The day we were made into princesses? Ye really look like a princess now." She handed the flowers to me. "Happy birthday, Krystle!" She leaned in and kissed my cheek.

"Thank you, Hailey! Are you going to play dress-up with us too?" I asked.

"Yes, I have me a dress too. Mahm made it for me!" She left the room.

Liv put a light pink glossy balm on my lips and glittery light rouge on my cheeks. A natural touch of pale shimmery eye shadow and my face looked alive. My blue eyes popped. Aura added the little flower in my hair.

"Oh! Ye look beautiful, love," said Liv.

"Thank you, Liv and Aura. What about you two?"

"We're not finished having fun yet," said Liv. She started doing Aura's makeup in shimmering mermaid greens. It went perfectly with Aura's skin tone.

"Are we going to royal court? We seemed to have a centuries-old theme going on." I looked at their dresses, Liv in soft yellow and Aura in light green. Both long and corseted like my own. Hailey came bouncing in wearing light blue. Aura twisted Hailey's hair into springy curls and put Liv's hair back at the sides; the back kept long with soft curls at the ends.

"Well, this was fun," I commented. "Thanks for the dress-up party," I rose to get up. Liv stopped me.

"We're not just getting dolled up just to sit in the house, love. We're going on a picnic just like the royals did centuries ago," said Liv.

"We're gonna have a tea party, right Mahm?" asked Hailey.

"Indeed," Liv responded. "Our guys are gonna flip their lids when they see us strolling up!"

"Let's be on our way then, shall we?" said Hailey. She skipped ahead, and we headed downstairs. Two loud whistles came from the Bens.

"Good Lord almighty. What a vision ye ladies make," said Benjamin.

He and Bennigan were wearing crisp dress shirts and gray pants with suspenders. They looked handsome.

Their dress was more 1920's style. Benjamin offered me his arm, and Bennigan offered his arm to Liv.

"Shall we take a turn about the village, milady?" Benjamin asked.

"Yes, thank you," I said. We stepped out into the fresh, cooling breeze and started toward the river—people smiled as they passed. We came upon my students. They were all dressed up too.

Shane came up to me and signed, "Happy birthday, Miss Genstone."

"Thank you, Shane," I returned. "You all look dashing and darling."

They all beamed. "You are to follow us to the honeysuckle field, Miss Genstone." Shane signed. "We have a lovely picnic set for you."

We crossed the bridge over the river, and I saw the blankets and baskets set on the ground. Everything beautifully put together. All my family and close friends came out from behind the trees. Everyone had dressed from different eras. Mom held a cake, and everyone started singing Happy Birthday.

"Make a wish," said Dad.

I thought in my head, *I wish for happily ever after with Clave and everyone here.* I blew out the candle. Everyone parted, and Clave stepped out from behind a tree. I thought my heart had stopped. He was wearing all white: a crisp white dress shirt, pants, suspenders, and shoes. He was ridiculously gorgeous as he approached me with a smile. Chorus's bright red feathers popped out on Clave's shoulder.

Krystle, you take my breath away. Happy eighteenth birthday. He got down on one knee, pulled a white box from his pocket, and opened the lid. My hands flew to my mouth. A beautiful heart-shaped diamond sat in a gold band.

Krystle Alexandra Genstone! Will you do me the honor of being my wife, my bond, my forever? His gorgeous gray eyes shined up at me.

I nodded my head enthusiastically, "Yes, Clave! Forever, yes!" My hand shook as he took it and slid the ring on my finger. I threw my arms around him, and we kissed. Everyone applauded and cheered. He took my hand and led me to a spot I remembered well.

This is where we first kissed. I looked at him and nodded as tears were rolling down my cheeks. He pulled out a white handkerchief and dried away my tears.

This is where we will kiss again for the first time, as husband and wife. I heard everyone gather around behind us. I looked back at all their smiling faces. I listened to a motion from the trees.

Lazula stepped out in her ceremonial robe with a big smile on her face. "Are you two ready?" I looked at Clave. I already knew the answer was yes, for both of us. Lazula stood before us and said, "Good. Let us begin. Clave!" she motioned for him to speak.

He began to sign and speak through our connection. Those who knew of our telepathic connection could hear. Everyone else had to watch the movements of his hands.

"Krystle, you captured my heart and soul from the first moment I saw you. I just knew one day; you'd be my bond- my wife. I have dreamed of this day every day since then. You are all I hear in the wind and the rain, on the river, in the trees. You are my light. I will always find my way to you in the dark. The stars and moons do not compare to your beauty, both inside and out. I'm in awe of your strength and courage. Your genuine love and compassion guide me to follow you for all of our given days. I love you, Krystle Genstone. I bond myself to you in heart, mind, body, and soul."

Lazula looked to me, "Krystle!"

"Clave, you are my perfect match. My completion. I was a shy, uncertain girl before I came to this world. You walked up to me that first day we met, and I found my words. You drew a boldness I never knew before. I felt the embers, embers that burst into full flame. You ignited my entire existence. I knew of love before, but with you, I truly understand what love is. You have been with me every step of our journey. I can rest with you as if in the comfort of angelic wings. I want to be held in your arms forever. I want to continue to kiss you every day. I believe in happy ever after, and you are mine. I love you, Clave Frost. I bond myself to you in heart, mind, body, and soul."

Lazula placed the long golden chain around us. Aura handed me a gold band, and I slid it on Clave's finger. Jasper gave a gold ring to Clave, and he slipped it on below my heart diamond ring.

"With authority placed on me with humble acceptance from the four moons and spirits of our ancestors, I pronounce your bond as husband and wife. I introduce to all, Mr. and Mrs. Frost." Lazula placed a hand on each of our shoulders. “Congratulations. You will have a most blessed life together,” Lazula announced.

We kissed, and everyone cheered. Lazula removed the gold chain and hugged us. The Tuckers began to play the same music from my sixteenth birthday when I first arrived. Clave and I danced. Then I danced with my father. I put my head on Dad’s shoulder and cried. He stroked my hair. “I love you, baby girl,” his voice was ragged. We wiped each other’s tears.

“I love you, Dad.” Mom came in for a hug, followed by Aunt Cassie, Uncle Garreth, Aura, Jasper, Rhodin, Tovin, Azora, and Mieruss.

“Welcome to the family, daughter,” said Mieruss. “Azora and I are so happy for you and Clave.”

“Thank you, Mieruss.”

We had our picnic and tea, followed by a birthday/wedding cake. It started getting dark, and the lightning bugs came out in their beautiful dance.

The ground illuminated with our steps as the fire beetles made it to safety with each step—Mom, Dad, and anyone else who hadn’t witnessed the spectacular phenomena before looked amazed.

This whole day and night were magical.

“Ready to go home, Mrs. Frost?” Clave asked.

“Let’s begin our new life together, Mr. Frost.” I took his hand. We waved and said our farewells. Jasper and Aura waited for us in a canoe decorated with lanterns and white flowers. Clave and I sat together hand in hand. My head laid on his shoulder.

"That was perfect, Clave. I never was the kind of girl who dreamed of what her wedding would be. You managed to make it better than anything I could ever imagine."

It makes me happy to hear that you loved it. I've been planning this for a few months. It was all worth it. I lifted my head, and he put his hand on my cheek.

You look beautiful, wife. He kissed my lips with tender affection. We came to a stop at a tree home a few trees down from Jasper and Aura's.

"Welcome home, lovebirds," said Jasper.

"What? This is our place? Clave?" I looked up in surprise.

Everyone here loves you, Krystle. We now have our own home and can begin our life together. Clave took my hand and walked with me up the river bank steps.

"Catch you in a few days, neighbors," called Aura. "Have a good night!" She and Jasper pulled away.

It was just my husband and me now. Alone in the dark. He opened the door to our new home. I started to take a step forward when Clave hoisted me up in his arms.

Tradition! I've been looking forward to carrying my bride over the threshold. He stepped through the doorway then let me slide down to my feet.

I walked around and explored our new home, and he followed me from room to room. I went up the stairs and followed a trail of white petals along the floor and scattered atop our bed. Lanterns lit low, creating a romantic ambiance. I noticed my things made it to our new home and set in place.

It's perfect, I said.

Clave stepped up behind me. *You're perfect,* he said.

I could feel his breath on my bare shoulder. I pulled my braid aside. *Could you help me out of my dress, please?*

I felt his fingers work at the row of buttons between my shoulder blades and down to my waist. He slid the dress away from my shoulders, and it dropped around my feet. I took Clave's hand and stepped out from the dress.

I stood bare before him; my chest heaved in anticipation for his touch. He took in the sight of my pale canvas. His eyes trailed along my lines and curves.

Beautiful! Clave stared at me with the look of a starving artist lost in reverie. His fingers traced along my skin like brush strokes upon a treasured masterpiece. He licked his lips and leaned in to kiss me. I began to tremble.

Are you cold? he asked.

I shook my head. *No, quite the opposite.* A warmth akin to the Fire Moon Stone sparked and burned deep within me. Clave looked at me with those smoldering gray eyes. Our lips touched and opened. My soft palate felt the stoking of our tongues as they swirl around each other in a delectable symphony

I slid my fingers beneath the straps of his suspenders and pushed them over his shoulders. My fingers worked at the buttons of his shirt, and I pulled it open. Shade and light played off the hard planes of his magnificent tan torso. I placed my palms against his smooth bare chest, then ran my hands down his sculpted abs and back up to his chest. I pushed his shirt over his shoulders; my hands kept purchase over his strong arms. He pulled the shirt free and dropped it.

He removed his shoes and pants, and I took in the sight of his magnificent physique. Clave pulled my body flush against his. He was solid with yearning. The feel of his full arousal pressed against my soft belly. Our bodies pressed flesh to flesh stirred up a crescendo. The utmost beautiful colors sang to my soul.

You feel so good, Krystle, his voice was deep and appealing. I felt intoxicated with desire and need.

His lips pressed to the side of my neck as I leaned my head aside and hummed. Clave kissed along my jawline, then took my lips once more.

Clave, I need you. My body was trembling and longing for more. Clave lifted me and carried me to our bed. He laid me down on the soft flower petals then stretched out beside me.

He looked into my eyes. *Are you ready to be together, fully?*

"Yes, Clave. I'm ready. I need you so much!" I breathed out in my desperate plea.

I need you too, Krystle. Clave's voice ached with desire.

His kisses became more passionate. Our hands roamed one another and made way to our most intimate places. Clave moaned and shivered as I stroked him. I opened myself to him, and he settled upon me.

Clave, I'm ready. Just go slow at first.

I will, my love. He assured me. His thumbs stroked my cheeks tenderly.

Our lovemaking was slow and tender at first as my body adjusted to the new sensations. Once I was comfortable, Clave quickened his movements.

He pulled away from my lips and looked into my eyes. Our breaths were heavy. Outcries of rapture heaved out through my lips. I felt the warmth of the Fire Moon Stone on my chest and saw its red glow cast upon Clave's face. I could see love and passion staring back at me. A burst of euphoria crashed like a tidal wave and rippled through me. It collided with the rapid beat of my heart. Clave had frozen up then quivered. I felt him pulsing inside me as I tightened around him. Waves of bliss washed over me.

He stayed with me as my hands ran up and down his back. He held himself up on his elbows. Sweat trickled along our bodies. He slowly pulled away. I found myself craving more of him.

I can see what all the fuss is about now. I smiled.

Clave laughed. *Me too! Krystle, I want to do that with you again and again and again and...*

I kissed him. *Me too.*

We spent the next few days wrapped up in each other. We discovered all the ways we could share our love.

Clave continued to amaze me. He could bring me to the highest peaks, and I'd float back down on a feather.

We had become maddingly ravenous for each other. We christened every room and surface available throughout our home. We were drunken and giddy in sweet rhapsody. We laughed and loved until we had completely exhausted ourselves.

The window was cracked open enough for Chorus to make his escape and return as needed. We slept most of the day away, then got up to eat. We worked together in the kitchen to prepare our meal and sat down at our table.

If this could be the rest of our lives, I'd take it. Eventually, reality hits hard that there's still life outside our door. We talked about getting back to work with our students. I didn't want to think about anything else yet. I wanted this day together—one more day of bliss.

Chapter 23

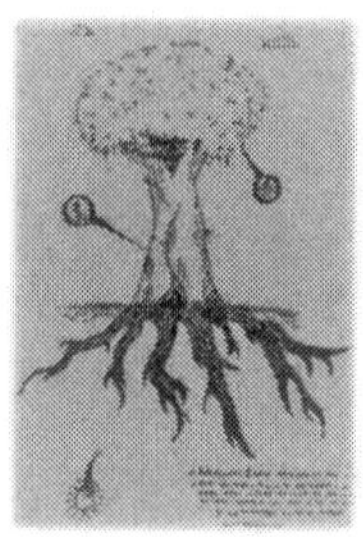

The next few months went by in a haze of happiness. We were welcomed back to the world and often asked how married life was treating us. The words amazing, phenomenal, fantastic, spectacular came to mind. But we just responded with, "It's been good!" Anyone who already knew understood what that meant.

Our students were growing up and moving on to the secondary teachers. Clave and I soon started anew with our next batch of post-baby phase grads.

Garrissa was hitting growth spurts and milestones faster than any of us could keep track. She was walking and talking months before average expectancy. She would often converse with the wildlife. We'd have to keep up with her as she approached the forest. She'd pet and talk to the deer, squirrels, and birds. I couldn't make sense of what she was saying, but the animals would still listen intently.

It was becoming difficult to hide Garrissa's abilities. Come planting season; it had become evident to everyone that Garrissa had telekinetic powers. She made simple motions with her hands, and the seeds would sow themselves into the ground. It started with a few. Then she had planted an entire row in an instant. Everyone had stopped their work and watched in fascination. There was nothing we could do to stop Garrissa at that moment. She was determined to be helpful.

Lazula was astonished. “It’s wonderful she’s able to help in such a way. But! We need people not to rely upon her abilities. They could become complacent. It could break the balance of community we share when we come together and teach each generation.”

“I agree,” said Mom. “We are trying to teach her not to overstep. It’s just she’s so willing to be helpful, she doesn’t understand how it can make others more dependent. I’ll try to redirect her.”

“Garrissa! Come to Mommy!”

Garissa turned and ran to Mom. She smiled and jumped up for Mom to catch her. “My little Opal Rose! Mommy is so proud of you. You are such a good helper.” Mom tickled Garrissa’s little tummy, and Garrissa giggled. “Let’s watch everyone plant the seeds, baby. It’s fun to touch the dirt and feel the seeds. They like our hands to work and feel. It makes the world happy and people happy. Understand?”

Garrissa nodded. “Come on, baby girl, let's do this together.” Mom walked with Garrissa to the fields. She pointed out the other mommies and daddies working with their small children. Garrissa observed the smiles on their faces as they went through each step of the process. Mom set her down, and Garrissa picked up the spade and scooped the dirt.

Mom had her smell the dirt and feel the texture. She handed her the seeds, and together they went through the different sensations and the feelings evoked. I could see the flash of Garrissa's birthmark just beneath her hairline. The Glacial Moon Stone lit up on her ankle.

Garrissa quickly understood the difference. It wasn't just about being helpful. The connection between each being and the natural world was necessary for growth. Nature and knowledge were prudent to survival. It was good to help, but everyone needed to learn their responsibilities.

As Garrissa grew over the next year, her interactions with nature flourished. She would bring Mom different things from the world and point out the elements from which they derived. It helped Mom tremendously in her research. Aunt Cassie's plants had taken on striking blooms and colors with Garrissa's aid. Animals would catch Garrissa's attention, and Clave and I would follow her as she went into the forest.

One day Garrissa picked up an injured bird and held it out to me. "Krystle, you can help." I looked down at the poor creature and its broken wing. It looked like it had been that way for some time. It lay weakly in my hands.

"I don't know how to fix it, Garrissa. Mom might be able to help," I said.

Garrissa shook her head. "No, Krystle. You can help." She pointed at my Fire Moon Stone. "You can help make it right."

Something occurred after she said those words. Lazula's voice echoed in my memory. "You have a great purpose! The Fire Moon rectifies wrongs." Then I remembered how she had pressed the stone to my arm, and it completely healed. Garrissa smiled and nodded at me as if she had seen the memories herself.

I lifted my necklace over my head and squeezed the Fire Stone in my hand. I could feel the warmth and see the glow from beneath my closed fingers. I gently pressed the stone to the bird's wing. The bird infused with glowing light. I lifted the stone away, and the bird wholly healed. I looked upon it, amazed as it stretched and flapped its wings fully. It cooed a few times then took off.

Garrissa laughed. "Della said thank you."

Garrissa looked at the Fire Moon Stone. I watched as it lifted from my hand, and the necklace was settled back in place around my neck. "Thank you, Garrissa." I beamed at her. She wrapped her arms around my hips and looked up at me with her big blue eyes.

"We're a team, Krystle." Her sweet little voice was so precious. She brought out a great joy in me. She lifted her arms to Clave. "Clave, hug bug!"

Clave lifted her, and Garrissa hugged him around his neck. He didn't even have to try and share his telepathic connection. Garrissa picked up on it quickly. I heard them both say, *Hug bug,* in my head. Clave put his arms around me. *Triple hug bug,* we all sang out.

Life felt as it should be. A part of me didn't want to accept what was due to happen eventually. I had to remind myself that it wasn't so long ago that I had endured many significant challenges and changes in my life already. It all led to being here and everything good my whole family had come to appreciate. We had to protect it: this world, the people, the generations to come. We were the generation chosen by the moons and the Light as keepers and guardians. We each had brought unique talent, knowledge, and wisdom.

We had established friendships and bonds of love. Reconnections happened, and emotional wounds healed. There was still one obstacle hanging over our heads. Lazula had told me I'd accomplish my mission by the next Fire Moon.

Uncle Garreth and I had reexamined the map and brought out the stone pyramid a few more times to confirm the place of the Light's arrival.

Tovin had notified our group of an emergency meeting at Lazula's. It seemed there was a new development.

"The timeline for the Light calling has changed. It will come sooner than we first anticipated," Lazula revealed.

"What does this mean?" asked Mieruss.

Lazula looked at Mieruss. "It means we have a few weeks before its arrival! You must prepare to leave by tomorrow. I must address everyone about what is to come."

"Has the location changed?" Tovin asked.

"It remains the same," said Lazula. "I need all here; please tell the village there's to be a meeting here tonight. Our people shall convene in the field behind my home."

We all set out immediately in different directions. We kept a calm composure as we told everyone we saw and asked them to spread the word. By that evening, everyone had gathered. Voices were asking questions. The people looked confused but ready to hear what Lazula had to say.

Lazula climbed up on the small platform and looked over her people. "Ahtee, my beloved people!" Everyone responded in kind. "There is a Light calling due to come very soon. We are certain it will bring goodness, but there is a development that has called to my attention."

Everyone listened as Lazula went over the story of their ancestral past. "We were certain we had completely escaped the Dark Spirit and its tyranny. It was discovered some years ago that an artifact had been brought through with the ancestors. This artifact contained the essence of the Dark Spirit. It had been masked through the Light by a Pure Soul unknowingly."

Everyone gasped; voices rose along with many questions. Lazula held up her hands to maintain silence. "I will address questions after I have finished what I need to say." Everyone quieted.

"This artifact was found by my sister Zinnia. She had become infected with the Dark Spirits' essence. She along with Mieruss had been displaced to Earth through the Light on the eve of Solaura's passing."

Everyone's faces looked troubled. I looked over to Tovin. He and Aunt Cassie held hands. She gave him the strength and continued peace to stand here now as part of his long past secret was revealed.

Lazula continued to speak as the people hung on her every word. “Since Mieruss’ return. He has been aiding me by providing information. It took time to figure out all the pieces. I now reveal this to you as we need to prepare. The Dark Spirit knows it can mask itself through the Light if it has a host. It is very deceptive and manipulative in convincing others to its aid. It intends to link itself to the next Pure Soul due to come to our world.”

“Everyone must remain calm,” Lazula urged. The voices began to stir once more; there was some panic. Mothers and fathers were clutching their children to them. “Please, listen,” Lazula commanded.

“We have a plan. The Dark Spirit is in a weakened state. It cannot take any souls whatsoever without the artifact, which is safely hidden. We have a team ready to set out to the location, and they are set to catch it upon arrival.”

“It still lives inside Zinnia, the woman we all know and love. But as she was held captive on Earth, something happened to her body. She looks like herself when she was a small child.” Lazula motioned me forward. I held up a portrait rendering of what she looked like from my memory, along with what Mieruss described.

“Mieruss has described her abilities as extremely allusive. She can render people under compulsion to do her bidding. We must prepare to evade direct contact with her if she were to escape. She will try to lure anyone weak of mind and turn them against everyone else. If she is seen, you must report it to anyone you see standing behind me.”

The Genstones, the Frosts, the Oteks, and the Tuckers stepped forward to be recognized.

"You must not engage Zinnia. On Earth, she had come to call herself Cynicca. The person she seeks is Taylin Luna Fuentes." Lazula prompted me again. I held up the portrait of a sixteen-year-old Taylin. My best friend.

"Solaura!" A few people cried out.

"Not Solaura," said Lazula. "Solaura and Tovin's child."

Everyone was startled at this. Their eyes flew to Tovin, and he stood tall and held their gazes. "My child was stolen from me on the night I lost Solaura. I was deceived. I did not know she still lived. I would have destroyed the Dark Spirit myself had I known." His voice carried fire and challenge, and the people bowed their heads in reverence and respect. Aunt Cassie stood unified by Tovin's side.

Mieruss spoke up. "The Dark Spirit held me captive for over sixteen years on Earth. I was able to save Tovin's child from its grasp. I hid her away, safe for all those years. She is a young woman now. Older than the picture you see before you. Her identity was able to be concealed until she reached adulthood. Krystle has been calling out to Taylin, trying to warn her what may come her way. I had kept track of the Light and its patterns during my time on Earth. Without a willing Pure Soul host, the Dark Spirit has been unable to enter our world. It seems now that time has run out. If Taylin falls victim to the Dark Spirits intentions, she will become its unknowing host into our world."

Lazula hushed the crowd, "The team will set out come morning. It will still be a few weeks before we know the outcome. I ask that everyone continue in their duties. Keep your eyes and ears open and watch over your family closely. We will reconvene in three moons' time. I will address any questions tonight and in the meetings to follow. Please do not interrupt the team as they prepare; time is of the essence. We must use this time to strengthen our resolve and keep our minds tempered from fear."

With a wave, Lazula had dismissed us. I could hear questions rise as we walked away. Each was things we had all discussed time and again. Lazula was capable of holding ground from here.

We had prepared for this moment for the past year. Our packs were ready to grab and go. Four canoes loaded with supplies and food and a fifth canoe held a small cage with wheels. Bax and Sierra, along with two of their pups, would come along.

Tovin, Aura, Jasper, Benjamin, Bennigan, Eric, Dad, Uncle Garreth, Mieruss, Clave, and I headed out early the next morning. We would make camp just outside the Samarskite Ravine. We got as close as the river would allow before we had to dock our canoes and unload. We unloaded the cage that was a lightweight metal wire. We put what could fit in the cage, and the dogs pulled it along. We each had a pack on our backs, and we continued on the second half of the journey.

By late afternoon we had arrived and started to set up camp. We pitched tents and gathered fire rocks and wood. After everything was organized, we all went together into the ravine along with the dogs. Uncle Garreth pointed out markers he and Tovin had etched into stones to find their way in and out.

Walls of stone washed smoothly with time towered over our heads. Paths split in multiple directions at each turn. Carved-out hollows and grottos were everywhere. It would be easy to get lost or hide in here. The place was a complete wonder, a natural labyrinth. There was a larger grotto with a clear pond of water at its base.

"This is the spot," said Uncle Garreth. "The Light should land here."

"But, as previously noted, the travelers could show up anywhere in the nearby vicinity," said Tovin. "We need to go out in pairs from here, and each takes a dog." Tovin pointed out markers from which we would start. Before each turn, we'd have to stop and make a new marker to direct us back to the path.

"It will be dark in a few hours, so we work our way out for an hour, then return here," said Uncle Garreth. He picked up a stone and scratched at the surface of a rock face. He made an arrow pointing back the way we came. Sable came with Clave and me, and everyone went their separate ways. It didn't take long for us to start marking.

About half an hour out, I needed to stop for a drink of water. I handed the canteen to Clave, and he took a drink. I held my hand out to Sable and poured some water for her to lap out of my hand. *Another half-hour to go before we need to turn back,* said Clave.

"We haven't run into anyone else this entire time. I wonder if we can hear each other if we call out? HELLO!" I yelled upward. My voice echoed.

"HELLO, KRYSTLE!" I could hear the Bens return my call. Other voices carried through the caverns as more of us called out. Chorus fluttered his wings and chirped vivaciously.

Sable whined and pawed the ground. *I think she's making a marking,* said Clave. *I wonder if she's picking up on an energy of some sort.* Sable stopped and ruffed, moving ahead. We followed her. She was moving too fast for us to stop and make more markers.

"Sable," I'd call out to her. Chorus flew back to us. He helped guide us through the twists and turns, and Sable continued ahead. "What do you think she's on to?"

I don't know, said Clave. We heard a bark, and we ran as we followed Chorus. Sable was sniffing inside a small hollow and began to whine. Clave held his hand out for me to stay back. I remained behind Clave wanting to see what was inside.

We both jumped when a creature leaped out and hurried away. It was a rabbit. I had grabbed my chest and took a few breaths to calm myself. Sable was still peering inside the hole. Clave got down on his hands and near. He gently backed Sable away to get a better look inside.

There's something in here, he said. He reached inside and felt around.

"Be careful, Clave. There could be something venomous in there," I said.

Got it! He lifted his arm out of the hole; I caught a glint of purple.

"It's an amethyst stone!" I declared.

Not just an amethyst stone, said Clave. *An Amethyst Moon Stone.*

"Lazula has a collection of Moon Stones. There's only been a couple of ways to determine if it is The Moon Stone. It's not glowing in your hand. Let me see it." Clave passed the stone to me. Nothing. I held it close to my Fire Moon Stone. The two stones glinted off each other but no glow.

"I think once it finds its keeper, it will glow." I put it in the pocket of the same shorts I had worn four years ago. The same pocket that I had placed my Fire Moon Stone. It resonated with me at that moment; this was not a mere coincidence. As for who the real keeper may be, it was yet to be determined.

Clave whistled to get Sable's attention. *We should start heading back now.* We held hands and watch Chorus lead the way until we found the last marker we had left off.

Clave pulled me to him, and he kissed my lips. His hands roamed down my back, and a strong desire built up inside me. I quickly looked around and listened for anyone who might approach. We were alone, aside from Sable and Chorus.

Sable just laid down and ignored us. Chorus took off. I guess we could be a bit much as far as he was concerned. Clave made quick work of removing only what was necessary. He lifted me; my back pressed against the smooth rock wall. Our breaths came heavily as our bodies rode the waves of passion. The echoes of my cries ricocheted into the canyon. Together we reached our peak. I looked up to the sky as I cried out Clave's name. He kissed my neck, my cheek, my lips. Then he lowered me down.

I love you, Krystle. Clave breathed in my scent.

"I love you too, Clave." I kissed his neck and jaw. I pulled myself together. It didn't take Clave as long. We laughed at ourselves for behaving in such a naughty manner. We were married. Why should we care what anyone thought?

We made it back to the meeting area. No one made eye contact with us except the Bens, who smiled and winked at us. "You go, girl," said Bennigan. Aura burst out laughing. Dad and Uncle Garreth were looking anywhere but in our direction.

Tovin cleared his throat. "Let's get back to camp. We'll eat and rest and resume in the morning."

I felt a bit guilty for sidelining with Clave on this vital mission, but who knew what might happen in the days to come. We would love each other come what may.

Everyone walked ahead. Aura came back to walk with me. She leaned over and whispered in my ear, "You're not the only ones," and pointed to Jasper. "Just try to keep it down a bit. You might scare the men off." We both burst out laughing.

I heard Tovin say, "Shiyavas!" I looked forward and saw him shaking his head.

When we made it back to camp, I revealed our find. The Amethyst Moon Stone was passed around. I was curious to see if the stone responded to anyone from our group. There was nothing. It didn't even flash when held in

Aura's hand with the Blue Pearlescent Moon Stone in her ring.

"Well, that settles that no one here is a keeper. We'll have to try when a person, hopefully, Taylin, comes through the Light," I said.

"I don't think this stone would do anything until it makes contact with its keeper. That seems to be how it has worked with my Fire Stone and Garrissa's Grand Glacial Stone. What about yours, Aura?" I look at her ring.

"It glows when I'm feeling heightened emotions," she responded. "I felt the pull from the pyramid. I was afraid it might pull my finger off with it."

We sat around the fire and talked for a while. I was feeling tired and ready to turn in. We had to take shifts watching the ravine and surrounding area. We were here early, but anything could happen at any time. Tovin and Eric took the first shift. There were enough of us to split it up over a couple of nights, so Clave and I would be on the first shirt tomorrow night.

It's been an interesting day, said Clave. We were on our sides facing each other inside our tent.

I smiled at him. *A few unexpected things happened. One, in particular, I can file away in my happy memories.*

I was happy to participate. I will be keeping that one too. Clave pulled me to him and kissed me. I lay my head on his shoulder. He stroked my arm, and...I closed my eyes.

I was riding down the highway in a convertible. "Whoo-hoo...Freedom!" a voice yelled next to me. I looked over.

"Taylin?"

"Hey, girlie! Long time no see!" Taylin was behind the steering wheel. We were flying down the desert highway. There were storm clouds in the distance.

"Hey, Tay! Uh, how have you been, and where are we going?" I saw lightning crackling across the darkened atmosphere.

"I am great! We are on our way, baby!" she shouted. "I finally got the coordinates. We're heading west on our way to Arizona. I can feel it, Krystle. It's calling me."

I pointed to the storm clouds ahead. "Better put up the top."

"Pftt...What do I care about a little rain? Bring it on!" Taylin yelled.

"Taylin, I know you're all about a little adventure, but we're bound to get electrocuted," I said.

"Krystle, Krystle! Always so cautious! Put on your big girl panties! You're my ride or die bitch, remember?" Taylin tipped her sunglasses up at me and wagged her eyebrows.

"Taylin, I thought you said that term had become too cliché." I pointed out. "That, and your bitch doesn't want to die today!"

Taylin just laughed and cranked up the radio. She started drumming her hands on the steering wheel to the raging guitar riffs from AC/DC's Thunderstruck.

We were under the thick, blackened clouds. A mighty crack of thunder had me nearly jumping out of my seat as electric bolts shot across the sky. Taylin held her hand in the air in a devil horns gesture. She started shouting "Thunder" along with the opening of the song.

This wasn't the Taylin I remembered. Rebellious, yes, but this girl was acting off the wall. I was about to climb to the back seat and pull up the top of the vintage Mustang. I glanced in the rearview mirror, and another set of eyes were looking back at me. I screamed, and the car started to swerve. We were about to crash.

"TAYLIN!" I screamed. I held my arms up in front of my face like a shield as I braced for impact.

A demonic voice came from behind me, "I'm just along for the ride!" There was a fit of malevolent laughter just before everything went completely black.

I sat up and screamed and put my hand to my chest. It was storming outside our tent. Clave sat up and put his hands on my shoulders and turned me to look into his eyes. *Are you okay, Krystle?*

My heart was in a tachycardiac fit. I caught my breath and nodded. "Bad dream."

He pulled me into his lap, then spread his legs, so I sat between his and massaged my shoulders. *Do you want to talk about it?*

"I was in a car with Taylin. There were eyes and an evil voice. We were about to crash." I shivered.

Sounds pretty intense, he commented. *What do you think it meant?*

"Taylin said she was on her way. She said 'IT' was calling to her. I think she meant the Light. The evil voice said it was along for the ride. Clave, I think we were accurate in our assumption about the Dark Spirit finding a host. And the host is, in fact, Taylin."

We're prepared, Krystle, Clave assured me.

"Who's on watch right now? How long has it been storming out there?" I tried to see outside the tent. It was dark aside from the occasional flash of lightning.

I'm not sure. I just woke because you did, said Clave. *Try to get some more sleep, Krystle.* We laid back down, and he enveloped me into a spooning position. I let the sound of the rain and now distant thunder lull me back to sleep.

"Krystle, wake up!" Aura was tugging on my feet. Ladies get to wash up first.

I sat up and squinted against the sunlight that cast an angelic halo around Aura's voluminous soft brown curls. She handed me a chuck of jerky and a piece of bread with fruit jam. I dug out my bottle of special vitamins. "Ah yes, thanks for reminding me," said Aura.

"Wait, I had wondered why there wasn't a little Otek-Genstone running around. You've been paying visits to Dr. Gemma Genstone as well," I said.

"We're still young, Krystle. I wanted to enjoy an extended honeymoon. Jasper and I are extraordinary together." Aura winked.

"Didn't need to hear that," I yelled as she left my tent.

"Yeah, well, we all heard you yesterday, Krystle," Aura retorted.

I heard the Bens chuckling outside. I slapped my hand to my forehead. Clave's and my little love tryst had echoed out into the canyon. My love operetta made it to number one on the top ten list.

After I ate and gathered up enough gumption to present myself to the rest of our crew, Aura and I headed to the main grotto in the canyon. She started stripping, and I turned to give her privacy as I slipped out of my clothes.

"Don't be shy, Krystle. We're grown women and sisters," said Aura. I turned to see her backside as she descended into the water.

"I've always been shy, Aura. Seeing you this way is giving me a complex about my physical self-esteem." Aura was flawless and self-assured. Her body confidence and care-free indifference were fully founded. It just made me more self-conscious.

"Krystle, you are beautiful. Own it," said Aura. I held my arms over my breasts and walked into the water. Aura splashed me and laughed.

"Argh, that's cold. At least let me get used to it." I scolded. I held my bar of fragrant clay soap and slowly inched my body down into the water. "It probably wouldn't be so cold if it didn't rain last night."

"Yeah, good thing we were up on higher ground. We could've been waking up in mud puddles," said Aura. "Clave told me you had a bad dream last night."

"Yes, I was with Taylin; we were about to be in a car wreck. It was storming in my dream. I woke to the thunder. I think the Dark Spirit is with her. She said she was on her way." I explained.

"Our timing is precise then," said Aura. "Lazula has taken great faith in your abilities to see into your dreams and callings. I also agree. We are but days away. It makes sense that you would have a dream so strong."

"I just don't like how literal this all feels. I'm scared for Taylin," I said.

"From what I've gathered, our sister is a bad-ass," said Aura. "I wouldn't be surprised if she had tricks up her sleeve."

"She was pretty bad-ass in the dream. I wonder if she's changed that much?" I questioned.

"You've changed quite a bit since I first met you, Krystle. You're more daring and confident. And if yesterday was any indication, you've become a lot less shy. You were singing to the world, girlfriend!" Aura stood and spread her arms wide.

Damn, sister's got it going on! Total boob envy!

"Aura, put those away," I shouted. "You're giving me an inferiority complex." Aura laughed and started splashing me again.

"It's on now!" I splashed back. We sounded like a couple of ditsy juveniles on spring break.

"You two better hurry it up." I heard Dad's voice call. "Your husbands are about to beat the crap out of the Tucker Twins for talking about spying on you two."

Aura and I looked at each other like two children busted for sneaking a cookie from the jar. "Just a few more minutes," I called. We quickly washed, dried, and dressed. We laughed as we walked hurriedly back to camp.

All the guys were walking around shirtless with towels slung over their shoulders. The Bens had acquired too much muscle, yet not enough brains to mention spying on Aura and me aloud. They walked past us and winked. Jasper and Clave waited behind with us so we wouldn't be alone at the campsite.

It would've been nice to let the couples take turns, but it seemed unfair to the rest of the guys. And, by the rest of the guys, I mean the twin dodo brains, said Clave.

It would also be nice to take advantage of the rest of the guys being gone for a few minutes. Too bad we've got to keep a lookout. We could've snuck away to somewhere more secluded, I said through our private connection.

Clave let out a seductive growl. *Maybe later, beautiful!*

I thought of all the times Clave, and I sat in a semblance of silence. During private conversations, Clave would say something funny or sexy, and I would laugh out loud. The Twin Bens would always ask what was up. They still hadn't a clue. I'd always come up with some nonsense response, and they'd chuckle along like they totally understood.

After everyone was ready for the day, we set off to explore the area. We placed more markers along the canyon walls. Hopefully, it would be helpful to anyone for future reference.

I started to feel a bit stir crazy after a few days. It was easy to lose track of time out here. At least it didn't rain anymore over the next few days. At night, Eric would tell ghost stories and play the flute or fiddle for entertainment. The Bens would tell jokes. Everyone was cycling through being on high alert, bored, melancholy, or slap happy. I'd had enough of hiking and marking trails.

Each night I felt sure that the Light would show. I'd see it flash somewhere in the ravine, and it would be GO time. I was holding on to hope. It had to be soon! I didn't have any more dreams. I was feeling too loopy to call out. At this point, I wasn't sure if I could reach Taylin anyway.

She was probably as caught up in anticipation as we were. I said a prayer for her safety. One thing I could always count on was the beauty of the night sky. I watched a shooting star and listened to the nocturnal creatures sing. It felt safe and peaceful out here.

Ready to rest, love? Clave asked. I looked to see Jasper and Aura emerge from their tent to take their shift.

I yawned. "Yeah, I'm so tired." I stretched and took my husband's hand. We settled in, and I was out in no time.

Chapter 24

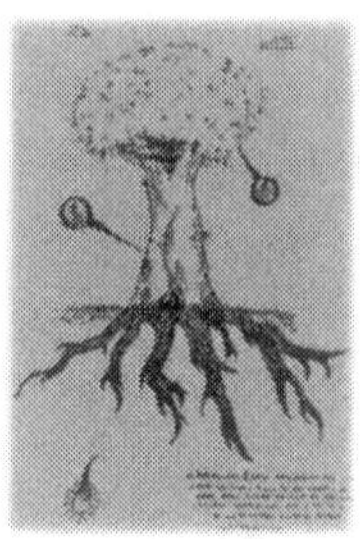

"Clave, Krystle, wake up." Jasper shook us. "It's happening!"

I shot up and scrambled out of the tent, followed by Clave. Jasper pointed to the sky northwest into the canyon. I could see the top ring of white light arched out above the tall rock formations. It was like watching an alien spacecraft landing.

"Let's get a move on." Uncle Garreth instructed. "It will be best to follow the individual paths each team marked out. You are already familiar with your directions."

The sun had just begun rising in the east. the ravine was still mostly cloaked darkness. My heart was pounding. "Taylin, please be there. Please be safe." We arrived at the grotto. The Light was gone. There was no one there. We split up and went along our designated paths. We carried lanterns to break up the dark trails ahead.

Clave and I walked quickly. Sable and Chorus led the way. If there was anybody else out there, I hoped it was within the proximity we had already marked. I started to call out, "Hello? Is anybody out there?"

We approached the turn where Sable had pointed out the hole where Clave found the Amethyst Moon Stone. A small voice creaked.

"Hello? Who's there?"

"It's Krystle. Who are you?"

"Krystle? Oh, thank mercy! It's me, Maria."

"Maria? Come on out, Clave, and I won't hurt you. We're here to help." A young woman, petite in stature, came out from behind a small boulder. I recognized her right away. Her hair was long and dark; it was difficult to make out all her features in the dim light. She did look a bit older than the last time I had seen her in my vision.

"Maria, Victor, is going to be so pissed off at you," I teased.

"You're not kidding," she said. "Have you seen Taylin?"

"Taylin came through?" I asked excitedly.

"Yes, she did," said Maria. She looked a bit foggy-headed. I could remember feeling out of it when I first woke up on the beach four years ago.

"Come with us. We have a search party looking throughout the area. Was there anyone else who came through the Light with you besides Taylin?" I asked.

"I don't know; my head isn't so clear right now. I'm having trouble remembering everything." Maria pressed her hand to her forehead and squinted.

"Don't push yourself, Maria. I remember when I came through. It was disorienting." I offered her my hand, and she accepted. Clave helped by placing her between us and putting her arms around us for support. We brought her back to the meeting point at the grotto. She sat down on a rock, and I offered her my canteen. She took a few greedy gulps and passed it back.

"I can't believe we actually found it after all this time. Taylin never gave up." Maria looked up at me. It looks like we've all gotten a little bit older. She looked at Clave. "Is this your boyfriend? He's hot!"

Clave and I laughed. "This is my husband, Clave Frost. Clave, this is Taylin's and my new friend, Maria Mehla."

"Awe, you remembered!" Maria smiled deliriously.

"Your dad was very kind to us. I would have loved to meet you sooner, but, you know!" I shrugged.

Aura and Jasper came running back from their direction. "Who is this?" asked Aura.

"This is Maria, Taylin's friend. She's been helping Taylin all this time. I trust her," I said.

"Wait, Maria, as in Victor Mehla's daughter, Maria?" asked Jasper.

"Yep, the one and the same!" Maria lifted her hand up and quickly dropped it.

"Krystle?" I looked up and saw Taylin as she stepped out from the direction the Bens had gone.

"Taylin!" I cried.

"Krystle! Oh my, God!" She cried out.

We ran to each other and embraced. We held each other tight and cried. "I knew I'd find you!" Tears ran down her cheeks. "I heard you! I felt your presence!"

"I've been calling out to you all these years, Taylin." My Fire Moon Stone began to glow brightly. I felt a cool sensation and looked down at my pocket. The Amethyst Moon Stone's glow was shining through. I reached into my pocket and placed it in Taylin's hand. She had been looking at my stone. And now, she was mesmerized by the purple stone glowing in her hand.

"What is this?" she asked. "What does it mean?"

"We have a lot to catch up on," I told her. "We found Maria. I pointed behind me."

"Maria, oh, thank God!" Taylin ran over to her, and they hugged. "Going through the Light was beyond an existential experience. I felt so out of it when I first opened my eyes. A couple of cuties found me; at least, I think it was a couple. I may have been seeing double."

The Bens came up from behind. "Nah, me brother and I found ye," said Benjamin

"It's a pleasure to make yer acquaintances, Taylin and Maria," said Bennigan. The brothers bowed like true gentlemen. This was new!

"Thanks for finding me," said Taylin. "I owe you a big kiss."

The Bens both smiled. "We look forward to it."

Taylin and Maria laughed. "They're cute!"

"Hubba, Hubba! Damn, girlfriend! Who's this hottie?" Taylin was checking Clave out.

"Taylin Luna Fuentes, I'd like you to meet my husband, Clave Frost."

Taylin's looked shocked. "Say what? Krystle, you're married? Holy frijoles, girl! Are all the guys around here smoldering?"

"Pretty much," said Aura. Jasper stood beside her.

Taylin's eyes widened. "Jasper? Is that really you? Life here has turned you into a damn fine specimen! Have they been feeding you some special kind of Wheaties or something? I gotta give props to whatever regimen you've been doing! Bring it in, brother!" She pulled Jasper in for a hug.

"It's good to see you too, Taylin." Jasper laughed. "This is my wife, Aura Otek-Genstone."

"Wow, your woman is pretty fine too. I don't swing that way, but I appreciate it. Nice to meet you, sister." Taylin pulled Aura in for a hug. Aura started to cry and squeezed Taylin to her. Taylin looked at me, confused.

"Wow, okay. This is a big moment, I guess." Taylin looked at Aura. "You, okay?"

Aura nodded and dried her tears away. "Yeah, just got a bit emotional in the moment, sorry."

"No probs," said Taylin.

"Taylin, I've got to ask you if anyone else came through the Light with you besides Maria? Maria is having a hard time remembering," I said.

"Yes, a little girl. She's five years old, blonde; her name is Zinnia." My face drained of color. "Did anyone find her?" Taylin asked. "She said she has family here. She lost her sister and has been trying to find her way back."

"Taylin, you may not believe this, but you've been played. That little girl is no little girl. She is a harbinger of something dark and evil. We need to find and capture her." My voice was serious and urgent.

"You're serious?" asked Taylin. "She helped get us to the Light."

"That's because she needed you to get her through. She couldn't do it on her own. The dark entity within her has come to finish what it started thousands of years ago."

"Krystle, you are trippin' me out. I need a minute for my brain to process this information!" Taylin pressed her fingertips to her temples.

"SOLAURA!" Tovin's voice boomed across the canyon. His eyes were imploring. His stance was precarious as his first steps toward us fumbled. Tovin stood and towered over Taylin as she gawked up at him.

"Holy!...Dude-a-saurus! Uh, hi. Nice to meet you. I'm Taylin. Krystle's friend." She held out her hand. Tovin took it and shook gently. He pulled her into a hug.

"Oh, Wow! Big, strong! Lots of muscles! Uhm, Krystle? Is everyone here this friendly?" Taylin gave Tovin small hesitant pats on his back.

"Pretty much." I smiled. "Maybe, we should get you and Maria back to the camp. We've got a lot of catching up to do."

“Uh, Tovin?” I looked at him. He was still holding Taylin and breathing her in. Taylin looked a bit uncomfortable.

Tovin released her and stepped back. “It’s nice to meet you finally, Taylin. You all go ahead. The rest of us will continue to search for Zinnia.” Tovin took one more look at Taylin and wiped tears from his face. He turned and walked away.

“That was a bit intense. What’s with the big guy getting all emotional?” Taylin asked.

“As I said, there’s a lot to catch up on. Let’s help Maria. She’s still struggling to wake up fully,” I said.

Once we got back to camp, we laid Maria down in a tent. Jasper and Clave were on the lookout while Aura and I talked to Taylin. Aura was on edge. She was waiting to see Taylin’s reaction to finding out they are sisters.

“Where did you come through on Earth? I had a dream about riding with you to Arizona.” I left out the rest. I had no idea if any of it was relative.

Taylin looked at me. “Krystle, I had a dream about you riding with me. I was sleeping, and Maria was driving. There was a storm, and rock music was playing.”

“We were connected,” I said. “It was the last time before you found the Light. It was confirmation for both of us.”

“All the times, I felt you near me, Krystle. It was really you?” Taylin lips were trembling.

"We never gave up on each other, Taylin. I've been reaching out to you all these years. There are more reasons than one why our connection is so strong," I said.

"Taylin, did your parents tell you anything important on your eighteenth birthday?" I asked.

She nodded at me. "Yes, I found out I was adopted. It didn't surprise me, though. I always had a feeling I didn't really belong. Don't get me wrong. I love my family. It was just I always felt I belonged somewhere different," Taylin explained.

"Remember how my mom and Aunt Cassie always told us to trust our intuition?" I looked at Taylin encouragingly.

"Yes," she said.

"Taylin. The reason you always felt the way you did is because there's the truth behind those feelings. You were born in this world. Aura is your sister, Tovin is your father, and my husband Clave is your cousin." I stopped and waited for it to sink in.

Taylin got up and started walking away. She stopped and paced back. She did this a few more times before she finally sat back down and looked at Aura, then again at me. "You know, this information is way out there, Krystle. I find out I'm adopted, and I'm like, eh- that's what I thought. But I wasn't expecting to hear what you just told me. I mean, I guess it makes sense. Are you saying this isn't my first trip down the rabbit hole?"

"That's exactly what I'm saying, Alice," I responded.

Aura looked confused, but I just waved her questioning look away. Where do I even start? It had to be the beginning, Taylin's beginning. So I told her the story of the night she was born. I brought her to her own light and revelations. Taylin's face went through a barrage of expressions as I gave her every detail.

I told her the history of the people and their ancestors, how they escaped the Dark Spirit to this world. I told her about the four moons and our purpose as keepers. She had been chosen as the keeper of the Amethyst Moon. I wasn't sure what that meant for her directly. Hopefully, Lazula could tell her.

She learned who Lattimier truly was and the role he played in saving her life. I revealed everything Mieruss had told us. His imprisonment under the influence of the Cynicca. Cynicca was Zinnia. A three-hundred-and-four-year-old woman, trapped in the body of a small child. She had become the Dark Spirits vessel when she found the dagger and unknowingly infected herself. We still needed to capture her and try to free her of the Dark Spirits' essence. We couldn't allow her to influence anyone else.

I told her about the Pure Souls, her soul, her mother's soul. Taylin took another look at Aura. "We have the same eyes. The more I look at you, the more familiar you seem."

Aura's eyes started to water. "I was only two years old when I lost our mother and you. I felt connected to Krystle the moment we met. You feel that connection, Taylin, just as I do. My heart was broken for so many years, as was our father's. I never thought this day would be possible. The moons and the Light brought the Genstone family into our lives. All this was meant to happen.

Everything! Life and family were stolen from us. We have a second chance. Not many people can say that. Are you with me, Taylin? My sister!"

Taylin's lips trembled. She jumped up and bowled into Aura's open arms. They cried together in a joyful reunion. Tovin and the rest of the men were coming our way. Tovin didn't hold back. He stood, and as he watched his daughters, he began to sob. Taylin and Aura and went to him. Aura stepped back just a moment to witness the recognition of beloved souls.

"Hello, old man," said Taylin. She looked up at Tovin with tears still raining down her cheeks.

Tovin looked down at her and smiled, "You know, your mother used to call me that." Taylin laughed and threw her arms around Tovin. He pulled her tight into his embrace. Aura watched for a moment as her hands swiped away trails of tears. Taylin and Tovin pulled Aura in, and they rejoiced in their continual embrace.

Everyone welcomed Taylin with open arms. She was excited to see Dad again. "Well, if it isn't the extraordinary Flint Genstone," Taylin smirked.

Dad chuckled, "Welcome home, Taylin."

Taylin looked at Uncle Garreth, "Thanks for bailing on me, Garreth, but I'm glad you made it here okay, even if it was without me."

He pulled her in for a hug. "Sorry, kiddo, I had to do what was necessary at the time. Forgive me?"

"Well, I'm here now. I have to give you some credit for helping with the directions," said Taylin. "I guess I can let it go." They smiled at each other.

Maria was finally lucid. She stood by my side. "If I ever make it back home, my mom and dad are going to be ticked. But, seeing this made it all worth it."

I put my arm around my new friend. "Before you ask, I'll have to let you know, the cell service here sucks. Actually, a better word would be non-existent."

Maria pulled her phone out of her pocket, "Well, crap! That bites! I told my folks I'd call them back tonight. That's the last thing I said to them. Not, I love you, or I'll probably never see you again."

"We're all here for you too, Maria. I just want you to know how thankful I am that you've been there for Taylin." I felt eternally grateful for Maria's help. But, with her doing so, she has also put herself in peril. She would feel more like a loner without her family here. Many more have come to this world as loners. It was supposed to have been me, but thanks to Garrissa, my family got a free pass.

Lazula was right, though! Everyone in my path is instrumental to the completion of my purpose. But isn't it the same for everyone? We're all connected in one way or another. There was still a mission to complete. And with that thought, I asked, "No signs of Zinnia?"

"No," Uncle Garreth answered. "We've been back and forth a few times. The dogs haven't sniffed anything out. She may not be anywhere near here."

"Which means we need to get back to the village A.S.A.P. to warn everyone," I said.

“We need to pack up and get ready to move out,” said Uncle Garreth. “We need to warn the village.”

We had everything ready to go in under twenty minutes. We made it back to where we had left the canoes, but only one remained.

“Do you think they washed away the night of the storm?” I asked.

“It’s possible but unlikely. We’re not all going to fit along with the dogs. Some of us will have to get back on foot,” said Tovin. “Flint, Garreth, why don’t you take the kids with you on the canoe.”

We began loading what we could when we all heard a scream. The dogs started barking and growling. We turned around to see Maria standing stark still with small arms around her neck, a knife pressed to her throat. I could make out legs wrapped around her waist from behind. The top of a dark head of hair peeked up with dark blue eyes.

“Zinnia!” Taylin shouted. “What are you doing? Let Maria go!”

Tovin started to step forward.

“Don’t take another step, Tovin.” The child’s familiar voice spoke with a warning. Tovin froze. A small trickle of blood ran from the blade around Maria’s throat, and she whimpered.

“Careful, Maria! Don’t drop me! This blade could slip across your neck, and you’d have a very bad day.”

“You’re not here for Maria,” I shouted. “Just let her go. I know what you really want.”

Those haunting deep blue eyes looked at me. "Hello again, Krystle Genstone!" Zinnia's voice took on a rasping sound. "The one who got away! I'll be collecting on that too!"

"What are you talking about?" I asked.

"Everyone back away from the boat. Contol your mangy animals!" Zinnia commanded. She jerked at Maria to move toward the canoe as we moved away. "She's coming with me, along with Krystle and Taylin." Maria stepped sideways; slowly, she made her way toward the canoe.

Zinnia looked at me. "Where's the Drosera blade?"

"Drosera blade?" I asked.

"The dagger, foolish child!" Zinnia shouted.

"I don't know. I speak the truth, Zinnia." I shouted back.

"Then you and Taylin will accompany me on this boat, and you'll take me to the person who does. More than likely, my sweet, humble sister, Lazula. She will give it to me, or your friend will meet her end," Zinnia's voice screeched.

"Climb aboard, Maria." Zinnia commanded. "I promise not to hurt you if everyone else cooperates."

"All you want to do is hurt everyone," I challenged. "You've been trying to get back here to finish what you started thousands of years ago."

"There's so much more to it than that, Krystle. We can have a little chat on the way back to the village. You and Taylin grab an oar. Let's get moving. NOW!" Zinnia shouted.

Taylin was looking at me, troubled. I started toward the canoe. Clave grabbed my wrist, and I looked back at him. *Go ahead and warn everyone. We will be alright.* I assured him. He saw the determination in my eyes, and though he looked worried, he let me go.

I looked at my dad. He looked ready to charge into the situation; repercussions be damned. I shook my head at him. I was not risking Maria's life. We still had options to defeat the Dark Spirit without risking casualties. In that moment of thought, Maria tried to play the martyr. She slipped and fell backward, flipping head first with Zinnia into the rushing river.

"Maria!" Taylin and I screamed. She had managed to break free from Zinnia's hold. They were both stuck in a current sweeping north. The Bens ran, and both dove into the water without a second thought. Benjamin had Maria and swam with her toward the shoreline. Bennigan had a hold on Zinnia's shirt. He tried to pull her back to shore when he screamed out. He cursed after he had let her go. She had drifted too far away. Before we knew it, she had escaped our sight.

We all ran to help them. Maria had a superficial cut along her neck. Bennigan had a cut along his forearm, which looked like it needed stitches. We got them to the canoe and began tending their wounds. "Holy nut rolls, that water's freezing," Benjamin chattered.

"Aye, brother, I think we won't be able to father any offspring after experiencing bollocks on ice!" Bennigan was shaking.

Taylin, Aura, and I helped Maria get out of her frozen clothing and put her in something dry and warm. I gave her a thermos of hot cider, and we gathered around her with a blanket.

The men helped the Bens get changed and warmed up. I looked at them and said, “Thank you.” They had been chivalrous, jumping in the face of danger to save our friend. They had a daring look that would convince a woman to take a chance on them. If only they were serious and dashing years ago, things might have gone differently when we first met. Perhaps they were becoming men worthy of earning a woman’s affections. Lazula had said their time would come. Maybe Taylin and Maria were their matches. Time would tell.

Now we had work to do. We double-timed our efforts to make it back to the village. We weren’t certain Zinnia would be found right away. There’s no way she would give up now that she’s here.

“Do you think her physical body is capable of surviving the cold rapids?” I asked Mieruss.

“I have seen her survive many things over the years,” said Mieruss. “As long as the Dark Spirit has possession of her vessel, it is capable of healing it. I’ve seen her pull through time and again while still maintaining control over my mind.”

Mieruss, Clave, Jasper, the Bens, Maria, Taylin, Aura, and me, and Bax and Sierra took the canoe back. Tovin, Dad, Eric, and Uncle Garreth went on foot with the Sable and Stoke.

"We have to warn Linger so he can get word to the Yehati. What effect might the Dark Spirit have on them?" I asked.

"I wouldn't know, but I agree the Yehati should be aware. We could use their help as lookouts to find Zinnia," said Mieruss.

I wondered what Zinnia had meant by; I was the one that got away. I did escape her clutches the first time. On the night, I came through the Light and woke up on Beryl Beach. I wasn't the only one, though. Rhodin, along with Jasper, went through that night. She said I was the one that got away, as in me only. At least that's what it felt like. Then Lazula had said, it was only supposed to have been me to have come here at first.

What is it about me that I'm missing? Pure Soul, check! Keeper of the Fire Moon Stone, check! My mission is to be complete come the next Fire Moon. I knew it had something to do with Zinnia and the Dark Spirit. I must help free the girl. The girl has once again flown the coop.

Lazula and I knew the dagger was the key. Would we just end up killing Zinnia in the process? I didn't want that to happen. We'd trap the Dark Spirit back inside the diamond in the daggers' hilt, then what? Would Zinnia just drift away to join the ancestors?

It seemed unfair to make her a sacrifice and still have the Dark Spirit in our midst. It would be trapped, but the people of this world would always be vulnerable. How do we destroy the Dark Spirit so there was no way it could ever return?

We had made it back to the village by the afternoon. We docked at Lazula's, and Mieruss ran ahead to alert her.

"Ahtee, children." Lazula looked bone-tired and weary. Aura and I brought Taylin and Maria inside. Mieruss gathered the guys and instructed them to alert the people to meet again. They ran out to accomplish their mission.

Once inside, we sat around the fire. Lazula took hold of Taylin's chin and looked into her eyes. Lazula smiled, "Welcome home, my child. You have been on quite a journey!"

"Yes indeed, ma'am," Taylin addressed Lazula respectfully.

"We are family, child. I am your great-grandmother. I wish you to call me Lazula as all my children do."

"Yes, Lazula. It's an honor to meet you finally," said Taylin.

"We've known each other before, Solaura." Lazula winked at Taylin.

"Excuse me?" Taylin looked confused.

"It is true that on the eve of your birth, the Pure Soul within you fled and escaped the Dark Spirit. Your mother, in the grips of death, bequeathed her soul to your form. I see her soul in your eyes, child." Lazula sat down.

Lazula looked at Maria. "I extend my thanks to you, brave one. You helped aid our daughter and sister home. You need not worry about those you left behind. Time will come that they, too, will find their way. Until then, we welcome you as our new family. You are an old soul but have much promise for this life you live now."

Maria bowed her head in respect. "Thank you, Lazula. I'm honored!"

Aura went about preparing some food for everyone. Mom came in with Aunt Cassie and Garrissa, followed by Liv, Hailey, and Rhodin. Rhodin ran to Taylin and wrapped his arms around her.

"Oh my goodness, Rhodin! You've grown so much," said Taylin.

"I'm happy you made it, Taylin. I've missed you," said Rhodin.

"I missed you too, Rhodin. Who is your beautiful friend?" Taylin asked.

"This is my best friend, Hailey Tucker," said Rhodin.

Taylin shook Hailey's hand, "Nice to meet you, Hailey."

"It's nice to meet ye, Taylin. We're happy yer here," said Hailey.

Taylin looked up. "Gemma! Cassie!" She hugged each of them. "Who is this precious little beauty?" Taylin looked to Garrissa standing by Mom's side.

"I'm Garrissa Opal Rose Genstone!" she announced. "You're my sister's BFF, Taylin. And you're Maria." Garrissa pointed out. "Nice to meet you both."

“Gemma?! I knew it!” Taylin slapped her leg. “I remember telling Krystle; I thought you and Flint were up to something. I was right!”

Mom laughed and smiled.

“Hello, Garrissa Opal Rose.” Taylin greeted. “I love your name.”

“I love yours too, Taylin Luna. You are the Amethyst Moon Stone Keeper. I can feel it. We are complete now,” said Garrissa.

Taylin looked surprised. Garrissa pointed, and the Amethyst Moon Stone rose out of Taylin’s pocket. Lazula held out her hand expectantly, and the stone floated to her. Lazula squeezed it, and it began to glow. Garrissa lifted her Grand Glacial Moon Stone from her anklet. I took off my necklace and held up the Fire Moon Stone. Aura took off her ring with the Blue Pearlescent Moon Stone. All four were glowing.

“Sisters,” said Lazula. “One of this world, one of this world taken and returned, one destined and born of another world, one pre-destined from another world and born to this world. All connected by spirit.”

There came a rattling sound. The bag containing the pyramid lifted away from Rhodin. The stones emerged from the bag and configured in the air. Then came the instant magnetic snap as they formed the pyramid. Lazula handed a polished square Amethyst Moon Stone back to Taylin. Garrissa raised her hand and motioned toward Taylin.

Taylin’s eyes held the glow of the Amethyst Moon Stone as the pyramid approached. The stone slipped from her fingers and snapped into place. Next was the Fire Stone, the Pearlescent Blue Stone, and finally the Grand Glacial Stone. Beams shot upward, and the pyramid turned slowly. The beams, like lasers, burned a scene far up into Lazula's ceiling.

"The four moons shall converge," said Lazula. "A great power is to manifest."

"Yes, Lazula." Garrissa agreed. My baby sister's voice, still sweet and youthful, carried a powerful edge. We all looked to Garrissa, and she waved her little fingers. The pyramid floated back to her and hovered in her palm. The moonstones dispersed and drifted back to each keeper. The pyramid stones returned to the bag. It floated back to Rhodin, who took it and tied it back to his belt loop.

"I knew I needed to bring it today," said Rhodin.

I looked at Taylin and then Maria, both their expressions stupified. "You'll get accustomed to seeing many new, strange phenomena. Heck, I'm surprised you're surprised after having come through the Light."

"Oh, and I'm sure you didn't have the same reaction when this first happened to you, Krystle," Taylin smirked at me.

"You got me, sister!" I laughed. "This world has been one adventurous discovery after another. Wait till you meet the Yehati."

Chapter 25

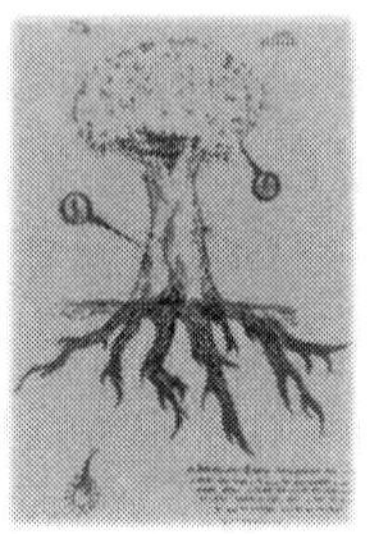

Clave and Jasper came back and assured Lazula that everyone was gathering out in the field. Clave pulled me into a hug and kissed me. I saw Taylin and Maria out of the corner of my eye, making celebratory gestures, and I laughed. Clave smiled and winked at them. Maria looked at Clave with adoring doe eyes. Taylin jested about being ticked off that she could no longer ogle Clave since they were related. She just chalked it up to awesome family genetics. I couldn't disagree with her.

"Did you see Zinnia at all?" asked Lazula.

"We did, in fact. She threatened Maria's life. She wanted us to bring her to you for the dagger. She called it the Drosera Blade," I said.

"Drosera is a carnivorous plant," said Aunt Cassie.

"That makes sense. The Dark Spirit being the eater of souls," said Lazula. "What happened then? She wanted to come, but she is not here?"

"Maria was being held hostage by Zinnia. She wanted to bring just me and Taylin. She said that I was the one that got away, and she wanted to remedy that. Maria slipped in the canoe, and they both went overboard. Then Zinnia got away," I explained.

"I suppose that is a good thing for now," said Lazula. "I've felt her return. Between that and the constant questions, I feel drained of energy."

Tovin, Dad, Eric, and Uncle Garreth came inside. "Lazula, you must rest," Tovin insisted. "We can address the village."

"I will be present while you do so," Lazula insisted. "No need for you to have to repeat everything. Then, I'll take my rest."

Lazula sat in a chair while Tovin told the village everything we knew. He asked for all to stay alert and recommended a curfew set till Zinnia was found. He asked for volunteers to head up search parties and reminded them of Zinnia's appearance and capabilities.

The Tuckers went on from there to find Linger and get the word out to the Yehati. We were all exhausted. Tovin and Aunt Cassie stayed with Lazula. The rest of us went home. I invited Taylin and Maria to stay with Clave and me. She would visit more with Aura and Tovin in the days to come.

"Everyone here lives inside these awesome tree homes?" Maria looked up and did a full circle. "This is so cool! The largest trees back home hold nothing on these."

"Pretty much everyone here in the village," I said. "The Yehati live out in the frozen no-go zone."

"I'm interested in hearing about that," said Taylin. "But first, I wanna know! My bio-dad and Aunt Cassie?

That is just, wow! I mean, it's cool. Way to go, Cassie! I'm happy for them."

"They had the hots for each other, but Clave and I had to give them a little persuasive push," I said.

"Is Clave always so quiet? You'd think being related to me and all, he'd be talking more. Strong and silent type, I get it," said Taylin.

Chorus flew in through the kitchen window and landed on the table. "Oh, what a cute bird!" Maria chirped. Chorus flew to her. She held up her finger, and he landed. He started his chittering flirt. "You are beautiful," she said.

"He knows it!" I exclaimed. "He's a glutton for compliments. Aren't ya, Chorus?"

"Chorus. Cool name," said Maria.

I looked at Taylin. "Clave is deaf, and Chorus helps him. Care to elaborate, hubby?"

Well, you know I had to wait till the coast was clear. Clave opened up his telepathic communication to Taylin and Maria.

"Okay, I can't say I'm surprised anymore!" Taylin emphasized a washed-out motion with her hands. "We're in this strange but fascinating world. Garrissa is a genius oracle slash telekinetic. So, I guess Clave is telepathic."

My cousin picks things up fast. Intelligence runs in the family. Clave smiled at Taylin.

"You're pretty cool, cuz! So, is little Chorus like your interpreter or something?" Taylin laughed like she was telling a joke.

Wow, you are good! That's exactly what he does, said Clave.

Maria looked up, fascinated, and Taylin slapped the table, "Ha! I'm on a roll today! I bet you can read minds too, can't you?"

Clave smirked. *Think of a number between one and three?*

Taylin and Maria laughed, then concentrated.

Clave drummed on the table with his fingers, then pointed. *Maria thought one and five-eighths, and Taylin thought two and one-sixteenth. You both took too much time concentrating, so I knew you wouldn't say two.* Chorus chirped repetitiously, and we all laughed.

"Krystle, you won the lottery, girlfriend," said Maria. "Your man is fine and funny."

"I know. I feel blessed." I looked at Clave. He returned a look of endearment and love.

"I want to find my el verdadero amor," said Maria. "Could you help me, little Chorus?" Chorus tilted his head a chirped. He flew out the window.

"Did he understand me?" Maria asked. "Did he just go to find someone?"

"He may have," I said. "He helped bring Clave and me together."

"Ah, that's so romantic," said Maria.

"A true love bird," said Taylin. "I'm happy for you and Clave, Krystle. I always wanted this for you."

“No luck for you two on Earth? Have men evolved at all since I left?” I asked.

“Just as douchey as ever,” said Taylin. “By the time they mature, they have so much baggage. You might as well wait till they're in their 60s before there’s a chance.”

Clave chuckled. Taylin looked at him. “So, communication is no go without Chorus around?”

“He can read lips and sign,” I said. “It’s something you’ll need to know around the village. Not everyone speaks the same language, but everyone learns sign language.”

There came a knocking at our door. Clave went to open it. Benjamin was at the door with Chorus on his shoulder. “Is everything okay? Chorus came to my window and was chirping insistently. Hi, Taylin. Maria.” Benjamin smiled. Maria blushed.

“Everything’s fine,” I said. “Chorus is just excited about everything.” I bailed Maria out. I owed her so much for helping Taylin. Perhaps we could make a love connection for the Bens after all!

“Come on in, Benjamin. We’re just catching up. Maria wanted to thank you for helping earlier,” I nudged her.

“Yes, thank you, Benjamin. You are my heart- I mean, hero!” Maria quickly corrected and blushed brighter.

Benjamin was beaming. “Yer welcome, Maria. You were very brave back there.”

"I wouldn't call falling out of a boat brave," said Maria.

"No, I could tell ye did it on purpose to shake that little demon off yer back. It's mighty brave of ye." Benjamin looked at Maria intently. "Maria, may I call upon ye sometime, for to get to know ye better?"

"Yes." Maria looked at Benjamin shyly. "I would like that very much."

"Thank ye, Maria. Are ye free tomorrow?" he asked.

Maria looked at me, and I nodded.

"Yes." She smiled.

"Great." Benjamin was keeping his cool. "I'll be by late morning. I know ye need to catch up on some rest." He walked back to the door. "I'll be seeing you. Good night." He closed the door behind him. He walked calmly past our kitchen window out of sight.

"Woo hoo!" We all heard him shout.

We all laughed. "I think he's really into you, Maria," said Taylin. "His twin, what's his name?"

"Bennigan," I said.

"Yeah," said Taylin. "You think they'd be up for a double?"

"Undoubtedly," I said.

Clave and I joined Maria, Benjamin, Taylin, and Bennigan on a walk along the river. We passed Tovin and waved. He looked at Taylin walking alongside Bennigan. I wondered what was going through his head.

"Clave and I are going to stop a moment. You all walk ahead, and we'll catch up." I pulled Clave's arm and motioned him toward the group of men Tovin had assembled for a search party.

"Ahtee, Tovin! Did your group find anything this morning?" I watched as the group broke up and went their separate ways.

"We've been keeping a perimeter around the village and areas where people work," He said. "I don't think she's come close, at least not yet."

"How are you feeling?" I asked. "About Taylin, I mean?"

"She is much like Solaura. I am proud of the young woman she has become. She knows what she wants and doesn't give up. She made it here after all," said Tovin.

"And, you're okay with her dating Bennigan Tucker?" I asked.

"Ahh, I see what this is all about now," said Tovin. "You're worried I'm going to jump down his throat for having an interest in my daughter?"

"No! Okay, fine! My curious mind wants to know what's going on inside your head," I admitted. Clave chuckled alongside me.

"She is my daughter, so of course I'll be concerned. But, I did not have the privilege of raising her. I did not have the same impact on her life as I had Aura. Taylin is now a young woman capable of making her own choices. But I'll be there for her if she needs me," said Tovin.

"How very forward-thinking of you, Tovin." I smiled. "Aunt Cassie has been a good influence on you."

"Yes, Cassie has," Tovin admitted. "She has been a great influence. We are very happy together."

"So, when are you going to pop the question?" I looked Tovin in the eye.

"Nosey much?" He chuckled. "Mieruss told me he overheard you saying that to Maria's father one time."

"Yes, I recall. I had actually finished speaking to Taylin on the phone when Victor mocked my conversation," I said.

"Anyway, Krystle. That information is on a need-to-know basis. And you will know as soon as Cassie knows." He winked at me.

"That sounds promising!" My voice came out in a sing-song. "See you later!"

"Enjoy your day," said Tovin.

We caught up to Taylin, Maria, and the Bens out in the field where Clave and I first met. They were sitting on a blanket, enjoying the sunshine. Benjamin had brought his flute and was playing a love melody. Taylin leaned her head on Bennigan's shoulder as they listened. Clave took my hand and spun me around, and we swayed together. Taylin and Bennigan got up and started to dance.

"I still owe you a kiss for saving me," Taylin said to Bennigan. She leaned in and pressed her lips to his.

Bennigan smiled, "I'm happy to have been the one to find ye."

I could see the look in Taylin's eyes. She was totally into Bennigan. The Bens had finally grown up. Now it was time for our fine young friends to leave the nest and fly. I had a feeling Taylin and Maria would teach them the rest of what they needed to know. I knew they'd also put them in their place if need be. Liv and Eric would be relieved.

"You all have fun," I told them. "Don't get too distracted and remember your curfew, kids." I teased.

"Thanks, Mom," said Taylin. "We'll be home in time for dinner!"

Clave and I laughed. We went home and spent some quality time together while we had the house to ourselves. Life felt so much more complete now—just one more hurdle to cross.

First, we had to find Zinnia.

By the time the villagers came together for harvest, Taylin and Maria had learned the ropes. They enjoyed being a part of the community. I'd seen more of the Ben's in the past few months than I had over the previous year. Liv and Eric were delighted that their boys had Taylin and Maria to keep them occupied. Liv had commented that the Tucker household had become much more peaceful and sang Taylin and Maria's praises.

Tovin and Taylin were having what looked like an interesting conversation. I watched from a distance as they talked and smiled. Taylin nodded her head enthusiastically l could read her lips just enough to make out the words "yes" and "happy for you." Taylin kissed Tovin on the cheek, and they hugged. I clutched onto Clave. I was getting excited because I knew what they were talking about.

Aunt Cassie looked confused as Tovin guided her out to the dance floor after the music stopped. Taylin, Benjamin, Clave, and I, watched with anticipation, and Taylin squeezed my arm. I looked at her, and she was beaming.

Tovin got down on one knee, and Cassie instantly cried out in surprise. "Cassie. Would you do me the honor of being my bond-mate and wife?" Tovin held up a rose gold ring with a rose quartz stone. The stone had a raised rose flower cut on the surface and was flanked with champagne sapphires.

"YES!" Cassie shouted. Her hand shook as Tovin slipped the ring on her finger. Cassie jumped into Tovin's arms, and they kissed. Taylin, Aura, Mom, and I were screaming like banshees. We all ran in and squeezed Cassie and Tovin. We bounced up and down like crazed hens. Tovin had to back up from the estrogen-infused frenzy.

Dad, Garreth, Mieruss, and Eric came up to give Tovin pats on the back. Garreth handed Tovin a celebratory drink, and the guys all said cheers and slammed their drinks back. Now, I only had to help Uncle Garreth find his special someone. I was beginning to get a reputation as the village matchmaker.

We spent the rest of the evening dancing. Garreth even took a few lovely ladies for a spin on the dance floor. He saved the last dance for Garrissa. She whispered in our Uncle's ear, and he laughed out loud. She was giving him tips on landing a new auntie.

Garreth had told us Garrissa was talking to him about Yehati courting rituals. The males would show off in competitive displays of prowess. She had told him he was already good at fishing, but to really impress a girl, he must catch as many fish with his bare hands as possible in an hour. Garreth told Garrissa that he wouldn't have any fingers or toes left because they'd freeze off in the icy river.

The next morning Garrissa asked everyone to come with her to the river. "Now, everyone, watch me and don't panic." Garrissa took off her shoes and jumped into the water. Of course, everyone panicked.

Garrissa's head popped up out of the water. "I said don't panic," she admonished us all in her little voice.

"Baby, come out," Mom pleaded. "That water is freezing!"

"It feels wonderful!" Garrissa cheered. "Now watch, Uncle Garreth; it's easy." We all watched on pins and needles as Garrissa swam with the agility of a river otter. Some came up to join her. “Awe, your babies are so cute.” She cooed at the mama otters with little ones on their bellies as they floated along. Everyone came to sit on the dock.

Garrissa dove under the water. We could still see her beneath the clear water. A school of fish stopped right in front of Garrissa. It looked like she was having a conversation with them. She swam up to us, and her head broke the surface. “Open your hands, Uncle Garreth.” She put a sizable fish in his hands.

“I promised Gurlo; it was a demonstration only. Sorry, Uncle Garreth, you’ll have to let him go,” said Garrissa. Uncle Garreth looked disappointed but handed Gurlo back to Garrissa. “Thank you, Gurlo.” Garrissa gave the fish a little kiss and released it. “See, Uncle Garreth! It’s just that easy!”

“I’ll play with you all later, she yelled back at the otters. My mom and dad are overly concerned about me,” Garrissa pulled herself up on the dock. She went and hugged Mom and Dad.

“The water coming off you is warm, and your warm,” Mom noted. I reached out to touch with Garrissa. She was warm.

“Flint, our daughter can acclimate to her environment. I think her body is capable of adjusting to different temperatures,” said Mom.

“She never breaks a sweat in the summertime. She always feels cool as a cucumber,” I added.

"Fascinating," said Dad. "You can swim with your friends, but someone has to be here watching. And you need to come out of the water every fifteen minutes so we can be certain you're okay. Understand, young lady?"

"Yes, Daddy. Thank you!" Garrissa threw her arms around Dad's neck, and he hugged her back. She turned around and yelled, "I can play! Here I come." She drove back into the water with the agility of an Olympic diver.

"Watch out for passing canoes," Mom yelled.

"I will," Garrissa shouted back. We all sat and watched her, mesmerized. Clave and I tried to put our feet in, but as soon as our toes hit the water, we retreated.

"That's a no-go for us regular warm-blooded folk," I said. "That water is colder than ice."

"Look at her go! She could beat a mermaid in a 25 k," said Uncle Garreth.

A few weeks later, on a cold morning, Clave and I went with Garrissa to meet up with Kyan. She would approach the tree line as usual and talk to the animals. This time something felt off.

I started walking closer and listening to Garrissa talking. "It's fine. No one will hurt you. Just come out," she said. I thought she might be talking to a shy Yehati, but then she said, "No, I will not allow that. You cannot have me!"

"Garrissa!" I started running to her. I heard Clave catching up behind me. "Garrissa, come away from there, now!" I yelled. As soon as I got to her, I saw a head of dark hair disappear behind a large tree. “Clave. Take Garrissa.” I swooped Garrissa up and passed her to Clave.

Krystle! Where are you going? Clave called out.

I made chase of the figure dashing deeper into the woods. “Zinnia!” I shouted. “I just want to help you!” I heard a little girls’ scream, then a large rustling and grunting. I froze in place. Clave held Garrissa in his arms. I motioned to silence them.

Linger came out from behind a tree in the distance. I breathed a sigh of relief. Linger walked toward us, hefting a bag full of Yehati hair. The bag was moving, and I could hear a muffled voice making protests and threats.

“You caught her,” I said.

Linger smiled and signed. “Yes. I bring Lazula a special delivery today.”

We walked behind Linger as we made our way down the river path to Lazula’s home. Clave dropped a disappointed Garrissa at the clinic with Mom and Aunt Cassie. Clave went to get back up.

Lazula came out from her home. “Linger! Krystle! How nice to see you both! I sense you have something, or should I say someone for me?”

Linger reached down in the bag. Linger grunted, pulled his hand out, and shook it. Little teeth marks were on his finger.

“Calm yourself, Zinnia. Linger means you no harm,” said Lazula. Lazula motioned to Linger, and he tried again.

He had a hold of her by the back of her shirt and pants. Zinnia screamed and writhed in protest.

"Put me down, you giant ape!" Zinnia kicked out in the air. Her arms flailed about, and she was spitting like a snake.

"He will put you down, but he will not let go. Yet!" Lazula motioned to the men approaching. Mieruss and Clave had gone around back and wheeled the cage around. Lazula nodded, and Linger set Zinnia inside. She sat and pouted.

"I do not intend to run away, Lazula. I just want to survive the winter. Then you will give me the Drosera Blade, and I will leave in peace." Zinnia spat again. "Damn Yehati hair! Don't you creatures bath anymore? It stinks in there."

Linger looked offended. I had to try hard not to laugh. Little Zinnia was a spitfire, that was for sure.

"And what do you intend to do with the dagger?" Lazula asked.

"I intend to remove this putrid essence from my soul and release myself to the ancestors!" Zinnia cried. "I'm tired and worn down to the bone, sister. With this moment of clarity, you'd better take me up on this offer. I don't want to hurt anyone else."

"Why wait till after the winter? If you're so set on killing yourself..." Lazula paused. "What if we can find a way to free you and keep you alive?" Lazula asked. "I've missed you, sister. I need you, us back together again. We are stronger together. We can accomplish much good."

"Yes, Lazula. We can accomplish much!" Zinnia's voice had changed. "Take my hand, sister, let me show you." Zinnia's hand reached out toward Lazula. Lazula looked hypnotized and stepped forward. She was reaching to take hold of Zinnia.

"Lazula, no!" I screamed. I lunged forward to intercede. Everyone shouted in panic, but it was too late! Zinnia had hold of Lazula in a locked grip. Lazula screamed and fell to her knees. A transformation took place before our eyes, and there was nothing anyone could do to stop it. We were all frozen in place.

Lazula was rapidly growing younger as Zinnia was growing older. My Fire Moon Stone lit up, and I found myself able to move. I quickly removed my necklace. I reached out and pressed the Fire Stone to Zinnia's hand. Her skin seared, and she screamed and let go of Lazula. Lazula fell back unconscious. Zinnia had pulled her hand back inside the cage. A young woman now stared back at me, huddled in the cage's corner with her hand pulled to her chest. Her deep blue eyes were wild yet clear. Her long dark hair was soft and healthy, and her body was young and supple. She was beautiful.

Lazula groaned and lulled back and forth. Tovin and the rest were freed from the spell holding them in place. He went to help Lazula sit upright. Lazula was a beautiful young woman, just like Zinnia. She looked down at her hands and blinked her eyes. "The demon tricked me," Lazula proclaimed.

Zinnia spoke, only this time it was no longer Zinnia's voice. "I wouldn't have killed you, sister. I would have stopped as you reached that of a small child. For once, you could feel as helpless as I have these past twenty years.

Thank you for the boost. At least now it will hold better in this world than it did on that retched Earth."

"Take that monster away from my sight," Lazula commanded. "Her physical needs are to be cared for, but she must remain locked up and guarded always!"

"Sister, I am sorry," Zinnia cried out. "It wasn't me! Kill me, please! Don't leave me this way!" Mieruss threw a cover over the cage. He and Garreth began rolling the cage away. Zinnia cried out and shook at the cage door. Lazula got to her feet. Tears ran down her cheeks. She looked at me. I was crying with her, for her and Zinnia both.

"Thank you, Krystle," said Lazula. "We will speak tomorrow. I need some time to rest." She turned to go inside her home and closed the door. Lazula had never closed her door on anyone before.

I turned and sobbed into Clave's chest. He held me tight and then turned me to head home. Linger dropped off the bag of Yehati hair in the village on the way. He was even downtrodden. He hugged Clave and me and told us he'd return to trade another day. We thanked him for his help, and he left.

Mom and Dad tried to ask me what had happened. I couldn't talk, so I let Clave explain. Tears streaked down Mom and Cassie's faces. Aunt Cassie stood with Garrissa at the doorway, and Garrissa listened calmly. It seemed the gears in her mind were turning, trying to problem-solve.

By nightfall, word had gotten out around the village. Everyone could breathe easier knowing we had Zinnia in captivity. Dad and Uncle Garreth had lined the inside walls of a smaller tree home in bars with more over the windows and door. Everything had multiple locks. The inside was childproofed, in case Zinnia got any ideas on harming herself. She couldn't just take her own life and be freed. As long as the Dark Spirit was inside her, she would be instantly healed. She needed the Drosera Blade to accomplish what she wanted.

The Dark Spirit held the forefront of her consciousness the majority of the time. It was just as Mieruss had said. It must have been torturous and maddening for poor Zinnia. It was heartbreaking to watch.

"I want to speak to her," said Garrissa. "I may be able to help. Something is missing. I could try to get the information needed."

"It's too dangerous, Garissa. She had control of all of us, even Lazula." I tried to reason with her.

"I know I can do something!" Garrissa cried. "We have to try!"

"You'll have to ask, Lazula," I said. "And even if she allows it, you're still a Genstone. You will need to get Mom, Dad, and Uncle Garreth to agree."

Garrissa huffed and pouted. That was the first time I had seen her do that. She was always happy, joyful, and full of laughter. I worried that the Dark Spirit's proximity was affecting her mood. All the more reason to keep her as far away as possible.

Clave and I had prepared everybody who hadn't seen the dramatic change to Lazula's appearance. We brought a prepared meal with us to her home. I breathed a sigh of relief to see her door open again.

It was hard to hide the women's startled looks as they took in Lazula's youth and beauty. Aura and Taylin went to her immediately and surrounded her in a loving embrace. The men all sat instead of standing as they usually did. They bowed their heads humbly in her presence.

"Oh, would you stop that already!" Lazula's voice was that of a young woman, but she still heeded authority. The men looked up. They all were swallowing nervously.

"We beg your pardon," said Uncle Garreth. "It's just we don't want to say anything that belittles your authority based on your current appearance. I realize that sounds sexist. It's just a dramatic change. We all must adjust."

"It's still the same old me," said Lazula. "Just speak to me as you always have." The men all bowed their heads.

"Forgive us, Lazula," said Tovin.

"There's nothing to forgive," she responded.

"Yes, there is," said Tovin. "We should have been more on guard with Zinnia's, or I should say the Dark Spirit's, ploys. Had we paid more attention, we could have prevented its reach upon you. We are most grateful to Krystle for saving you in time."

"Yes," Lazula agreed. "What's done is done. Now we know, first hand, how conniving the Dark Spirit can be."

I was waiting for someone to say something foolish like, "If it's any consolation, you look hot!" I looked at the twin Bens, but they were wisely holding their tongues. That was a relief.

Garrissa came up to Lazula. She put her little hand to Lazula's cheek and looked into her eyes. "I still see you. The beautiful soul that was always within." Lazula smiled at Garrissa and ran a hand down Garrissa's sweet face.

"You as well, Pure One." Lazula stroked Garrissa's cheek a few more times. "You wish to ask me something, Pure One?"

"I wish to speak to Zinnia," Garrissa stated boldly.

Lazula stared into Garrissa's soul. "We will arrange it. But, we must be cautious, okay?"

Garrissa nodded. She turned to Mom and Dad. "I know I can help," she pleaded.

"I will be with her," I stated. "The moons. They will protect us."

Mom and Dad looked hesitant but nodded.

"I will come as well," said Aura.

"Me too," said Taylin. "We're the four keepers, are we not? I figure all of us together is quadruple the protection. Am I right?" Taylin asked.

Lazula nodded. "I will be there as well. I know the signs to look for now after having experienced the Dark Spirit's touch. I will remove all if a situation should arise and pose a threat to anyone."

"I know what to watch for as well," said Mieruss. "I can help."Azora looked troubled, but Mieruss reassured her. "Worry not, love. She will not be able to harm me."

Garrissa turned her head, and the pouch containing Lazula's moonstones floated over and landed on Lazula's lap. The stones on a necklace floated from the bag and rested around Lazula's neck.

"We should bring her a treat," said Garrissa. "Something sweet." Tanna fruit seeds floated to Garrissa. "Can we go now?"

Chapter 26

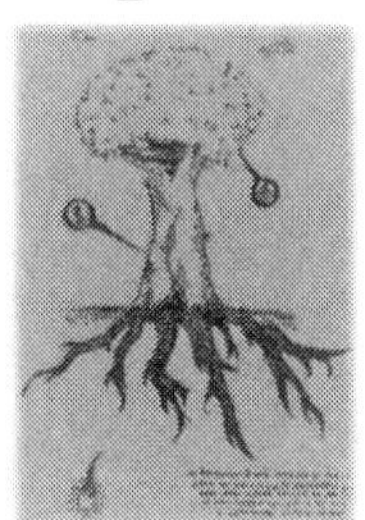

We approached the tree guarded by four people so no one could approach from any direction without being seen. It was sad to see the first-ever jail in the village. Mieruss pulled a key from a chain around his neck. He unlocked a small opening at the kitchen window. It was just big enough to slide a tray of food through it.

He placed the Tanna fruit on the tray and slid it inside. There was a quick tug on the tray, and Mieruss let go.

"Let's talk about the Drosera Blade," I said.

"What of it?" Zinnia asked.

"What becomes of the Dark Spirit if you use it to take your life?" I asked.

"Zinnia is set free, and I am trapped in the Drosera. Did you really think I would let her go? She's a fighter, and I enjoy a good battle," said the Dark Spirit.

"You've worn out her vessel. Wouldn't you like something new? Stronger?" said Garrissa.

"Are you offering up yourself, Pure One?" Zinnia's lips twisted up in a frightening smile.

"I already told you, you can't have me, demon!" Garrissa spoke with great authority. "What I offer you is a trip to a place filled with all the power you could ever consume. So many souls, you could have your fill for centuries to come," said Garrissa. The way she spoke made it sound like a place of wonder from a fairy tale story.

"Ah, but you didn't say Pure Souls, now did you, little one?" The evil entity returned.

"It's either what I offer or be trapped in the Drosera forever," said Garrissa.

"What do you know of this, sister? Have you heard of such a place? How do I know if it's not just another trap?" Zinnia's voice sliced like razor blades through our consciousness. It was starting to affect me. All our moonstones began to glow and drown out the dark influence. I stood with a strengthened resolve.

Mieruss had to motion the guards farther away. They had to redirect people to alternate routes and guard the pathways that crossed before and behind the tree. It had to be far enough for people not to hear the dark voice.

Zinnia laughed harshly. "It seems I have an even greater impact on the people in this world. Intriguing! I think I may stay awhile."

"Close the door," said Lazula. "That's enough for today." Mieruss came with a long pole and pushed the flap up. He quickly turned the key and moved away.

"She did not affect you?" I asked Mieruss.

“That voice grates on my nerves, but I did not feel any influence. Perhaps I have become immune in this world. I felt cleansed and refreshed when I came back through the Light.”

“Do you think we can put a protection on the people somehow?” asked Taylin. “I can feel the Light like a guardian, protecting me.”

“I’ve been through the Light too,” I said. “But I could sense the darkness. I was feeling an effect till my Fire Moon Stone lit up and drowned it out,” I said. “What’s the difference?”

“They’ve been through twice! Both ways! Body and soul!” said Garrissa.

“She’s right,” said Aura. “I was feeling the darkness affecting me too till my Blue Stone lit up. Krystle has been through once. I’ve never been through. I’m more vulnerable.”

“What of you, Garrissa?” asked Lazula.

“The ancestors sent my soul to Earth; I came back body and soul in my mom. It should apply to Krystle as well. She just needs to realize it,” said Garrissa. My baby sister did sound like an oracle. She keeps amazing me every day.

“How should it apply to me?” I asked.

I heard Zinnia’s voice murmuring from the closed window. I looked that way, but Lazula held up her hand. “Because you’re the one who got away,” said Lazula.

“Yes, Zinnia said that to me before. But, what does that mean?” I asked.

“Come back to my home. We will not discuss anymore in the dark presence.” Lazula turned to walk away, and we followed. Once we were inside. Mieruss had closed the door.

“The night Taylin was born, Mieruss said the Pure Soul had fled, and Solaura bequeathed her soul to Taylin,” said Lazula.

“Yes,” said Mieruss. “And I had seen the Pure Soul go with us into the Light. I was unsure if it went back into Taylin’s body or not. But, we can all see Solaura’s soul is in Taylin. The original Pure Soul that had inhabited her body found another life.”

“On Earth,” said Garrissa.

“Wait! Are you saying my soul was the Pure Soul? The one that was meant to be Taylin’s, but it escaped and took up residence in me?” I wanted to tell myself to catch up already because...

“That’s exactly what we’re saying, Krystle. You’re the Pure Soul that got away,” said Mieruss.

“But, when does a soul enter a body? Is it at conception? Is it just before birth? I can’t possibly remember myself!” My brain felt boggled.

“You already had a soul,” said Garrissa.

“Does that mean I have two souls?” I felt even more confused.

"No," said Lazula. "There was a switch in this world and your world. There had to be a balance."

Garrissa started giggling. "Like how Uncle Garreth likes to talk about trading baseball cards when he and Dad were kids."

"Someone, get to the point, please. I think I'm about to have a major brain malfunction," I pleaded.

"Oh, I get it!" Taylin cried out. "My soul was like, see ya, demon. Catch me if you can. Then I got traded with Solaura's soul. Krystle's soul was like, okay, Taylin's soul, you can crash here. But where did Krystle's original Pure Soul go?

Garrissa giggled again and raised her hand, "Hello! It's me! Catch up, ladies!"

"One, two, three...Like the points on a triangle," I said. "A triangle-like part of a pyramid!" I said excitedly. "I know what to do now!" I started jumping up and down.

"I do too," said Garrissa, "But we have to wait until then." She pointed up to Lazula's ceiling. We all looked up at the image the pyramid had burned into the wood.

"The four moons convergence," said Lazula.

I stepped out into the morning and felt the wind gusting. I put my hair back then took Clave's hand. We made our way down our daily path that had become our daily life together. We greeted familiar friendly faces and stopped to pick up Rhodin, Garrissa, and Hailey. Aside from the heavy gales blowing hair and clothing to frenzy, the sun still shined, and people still moved about their day as usual.

The air was cool, and I looked up at the beautiful blue sky. Birds were floating midair riding the currents. Clouds were large and moving; it seemed a storm might come, but I didn't see anything in the distance. We went about our day. We taught our class; we ate lunch, we took the children to play.

Clave and I, hand in hand, made our rounds to family and friends. We shared our daily anecdotes. We laughed, hugged, and told everyone we loved them. By late in the day, the winds increased. I was beginning to wonder if this world experienced tornados. Mom and Dad invited us to stay. It was a short walk home, but we could hear the wind howling. Outside everything had blown asunder. I looked out the window to see the benches and tables turned over. The last of the leaves of the trees were ripped from branches and swirling in the air.

The birds were no longer in the air; they had gone to take shelter. Everyone inside had piled and bundled together. The sound of branches snapping and tumbling started to concern everyone. Where else could we go? The ancient trees we lived in held firm to the root. There was the sound of breaking glass. Dad and Uncle Garreth went up the investigate.

"A branch hit and broke a window in Cassie's room," said Dad. Aunt Cassie's room had used to be my room. A knock came on the door. Uncle Garreth went to answer.

The door swung inward with force, and he had to muscle it under control. Tovin, Aura, and Jasper came in, and the guys pushed the door closed.

"We came to check on everyone," said Tovin. Cassie got up. Tovin came and wrapped his arms around her.

"We're okay," said Dad. "Have there been wind storms like this in the past?"

"None that I have ever experienced in my lifetime," said Tovin.

"It's frightening," said Cassie. Tovin held her and kissed her on the top of her head.

"Is Lazula okay?" Mom asked.

"She's shored up tight. Mieruss and Azora are with her," said Tovin.

Garrissa sat calmly between Mom and Dad. She was quietly concentrating. She seemed so zen it was almost relaxing to watch her. She began to hum. Not vocally, it was resonating from her entire body. Mom and Dad turned to her. "Garrissa?" They had both said her name.

"She's shaking," Mom cried. "I think she's having a seizure."

I approached Garrissa and put my hands on her. Our moonstones blazed alight. There was flowing, energetic movement within our stones' glow. Garrissa stopped, her eyes focused on mine. "The convergence is upon us. We must prepare."

As soon as she finished saying those words, a loud rumbling shook the earth. Everyone braced. I was on my knees in front of Garrissa. Clave had thrown his body around mine like a shield. Glass broke as things fell from the shelves. Mom and Dad huddled around Rhodin and Garrissa and stretched their arms out over Clave and me. I was breathing heavily. My head bent forward; I could see the glow continue from my Fire Moon Stone and Garrissa's Grand Glacial Moon Stone. They pulsated and hummed. I could feel the energy running through me. Deeper into my core. My soul recognized and welcomed it.

Everything stopped. It was so quiet, not even nature spoke. The wind ceased, and everyone lifted their heads slowly. We were all okay and in one piece. Clave helped me up. Garrissa took my hand, and together we walked to the door. She opened it with her mind, and we stepped outside. I looked up to the sky, and my breath hitched.

The Fire Moon hung large in the sky above. I reached up toward it, and I felt a mighty surge rush through me. A crackling glow ran across my skin. My whole body had become an electrical current. I looked to Garrissa, and she was experiencing the same. Only the crackling was white and shimmering. Aura came to stand beside us. She, too, had static bolts of blue and white running across her arms.

The door to the Tucker's home opened, and Taylin stepped out. She looked at us in awe. She slowly approached, and suddenly static purple charges snapped and surged across her skin. It all lasted for a minute then stopped. I looked up to see our family surrounding us, watching with bated breath and wild expressions.

"We have to get to Lazula's," said Garrissa. She looked at Rhodin. He didn't say a word. He just nodded his head and turned to run to the dog kennels. Garrissa pulled me by my hand, and we started to walk toward the river. Aura and Taylin follow. I could hear our family's footsteps as they trailed behind. No one said a word as we walked along the path.

Garrissa cleared fallen branches and debris before us with her mind as we continued forward. We stood out in front of Lazula's home. Her door opened, and she stepped out. Everyone looked up to the sky. The Fire Moon was in position east on the side of the river. The Blue Pearlescent Moon hung over the river to the north. The Amethyst Moon was over the river to the south. The Grand Glacial Moon was just behind Lazula's home to the west. All four held their position like standing soldiers awaiting orders.

Lazula beheld her four daughters, hand in hand. My sisters and I stepped forward in readiness. I felt our family gathered and standing behind us. I could feel Clave's need to be close and hold me. He recognized he must hold back.

"We must get her," said Lazula. We nodded in silent agreement. "Tovin, Mieruss, Garreth, go prepare her. Flint, take everyone else back across the river." I could hear Clave's protest. Lazula looked at him. "You cannot be of help here. Stand across the river and watch if you must. But you must go!"

My sisters and I turned to watch our families cross the bridge and gather to stand on the other side. We then followed the men down to the tree where Zinnia was held captive. Mieruss unlocked the wooden door, but the bars remained closed. Zinnia approached with a cocksure smile. She didn't say a word.

Mieruss held a cloth up for her to take. "Tie it tight around your mouth," He told her. She complied and tied the gag around her mouth. It parted her lips, and she pulled it taught and tied a knot at the back of her head. "Turn around, put your hands behind you, and place them through the bars, wrists together." She rolled her eyes but again complied. Mieruss put thick metal chained cuffs on her wrists, and locks clicked.

Zinnia pulled her cuffed wrists away from the bars. Mieruss unlocked the door, then grabbed her by the arm and pulled her forward. Tovin proceeded to put a blindfold over Zinnia's eyes. Mieruss marched her forward and passed up. Tovin and Garreth followed. Lazula and we sisters turned, and in silence, we followed.

It felt all too much like we were preparing for a ritual sacrifice. We were about to deal out a death sentence. As we approached, Lazula's dark clouds moved in overhead. The air grew cold and heavy. We came to stand at the highest stone platform above the riverbank. We were point center amidst the four moons above. They grew larger as a witness to what was to happen. The light they gave shone down together on the place where we stood.

I could hear the breaths of our loved ones from across the river. "Tovin! Garreth! You must go!" Lazula commanded. "You are now a liability if you stay!"

"Shit!" Uncle Garreth looked torn. He looked at me, and I nodded. His face morphed to anger as he stomped away, and we turned and watched as he and Tovin crossed the river. Only Mieruss remained. He had become immune to the Dark Spirit's calling. As soon as Tovin and Garreth's feet hit the ground across the river, Garrissa waved her hand in the air, and the ropes of the bridge snapped. It came tumbling down and splashed with heavy force into the water.

Our family started calling and crying out in anguished protest. Lazula held her hand up in the air. “SILENCE!” she commanded.

They all stopped. I could still hear troubled murmurs and cries. “We will need to concentrate, and that will not be possible with distractions. Do not stand crying and fretting in anger. Pray and find peace. Stand in a union as strong sentinels. We need all your positive energy!” Lazula stared them down.

I watch as hands clasped, heads bowed, and prayers for protection murmured from my family’s lips. The Genstones, the Oteks, the Frosts, the Tuckers stood together as a unified front.

The sky was completely dark now. The glow of the moons intensified, and it was a beautiful sight to behold. The Fire Moon moved like flowing lava. The Blue Moon pulsed, the whites and blues swirled in cyclonic patterns. The Amethyst Moon sparkled. The Grand Glacial Moon cast its glinting waves like a shining opal, catching light back and forth.

The stone pyramid floated across the river and came to hover before us. Zinnia tilted her head as she heard its approach. Aura, Taylin, Garrissa, and I took our positions. We each had our backs to the moon we represented as their keepers.

I felt the warmth of the Fire Moon at my back. I removed my Fire Stone from around my neck, Aura her ring, Taylin her bracelet, and Garrissa her anklet. The stones floated away from our hands. They rose into the air high above our heads along with the pyramid. They didn’t immediately snap into place. My mind was puzzled as to why all was in a holding pattern.

I looked around at my sister's. All but Garrissa had looked up, then back down and about at one another. Garrissa was concentrating. She must have been holding everything in place. Waiting...

Lazula began to pray in her native tongue. Zinnia, held in place by Mieruss, began to thrash. The gag around her mouth muffled her screams. Lazula reached into a bag and pulled out the dagger still wrapped in cloth. She continued to chant as she unwrapped the blade. The diamond in the hilt glinted as the light hit it.

Lazula grasped the hilt and approached Zinnia. She stood, her back to us now, and continued her prayer. Zinnia's cries had become desperate, then morphed into a low, deadly growling. Her head swung back and hit Mieruss, and he fell backward, unconscious. Lazula's voice seized up. She held the dagger above her head. Zinnia lunged into her. Her hands had broken free from their constraints as she and Lazula crashed onto the ground. Zinnia had quickly pulled her blindfold and gag. Lazula struggled with the dagger in her hold as Zinnia reached and pried it from her sister's hand.

We were all frozen in place as Zinnia screamed out a guttural demonic roar. She kicked Lazula in the stomach. Lazula lay on her side with her hands clutching herself in pain. Zinnia had the dagger in her grasp. Her eyes shot up at me. "You're the first on my list!"

She charged for me, and I felt my feet drag backward. Zinnia screamed. The dagger in her hand lunged toward my chest. Everything began to move in slow motion. I heard Clave and my parents scream my name from across the river. I felt the tip of the dagger impale my chest and just hit my sternum. Hands reached around Zinnia and pulled her back.

I could feel a pull. My soul felt like it was being ripped from my body. I screamed in agony. Soft tendrils of my essence pulled toward the dagger. Then I felt a force push my body backward. My eyes widened; my arms shot forward, hoping for somebody to catch me before I fell off the precipice. My dream from years ago shot to the forefront of my mind. This was me falling to my death.

I felt the shocking cold as my back hit the water. I began to sink as its frozen embrace enveloped me completely. I could hear Clave screaming, *KRYSTLE!* in my mind. The pull from the dagger on my soul had been severed. My body continued to drift downward. I was in shock, unable to move to save myself. I saw the light of the four moons. My head felt heavy and hazy.

My eyes began to droop and blink in and out of the darkness in a slow lull. I heard the sound of a body diving into the water. I saw a figure swim toward me as I closed my eyes for the last time.

I felt odd as I broke the water's surface. I floated freely upon it then began to rise above it. I felt weightless in the air. I looked up to the four moons and smiled. I was so close; I could reach out and touch them. The Light opened before me. It was different this time. I drifted toward it, and voices called to me. Bright glowing hands reached out for me, and I wanted to go to them. I reached for them. "Krystle...Krystle...Krystle..." They called and beckoned me. I felt like I was coming home.

My life flashed before me like pages of a sketchbook flipping at full speed between finger and thumb. I saw my hands drawing each page in lightning-fast motions, and a scene appeared on each piece of paper. My mother's hands held me, my father's, Cassie's, Garreth's, Jasper's. My hands holding Rhodin. My hands holding Garrissa. My hands embracing Taylin as we and laughed together. My hands helping Aura get ready for her wedding day. My hands held in Lazula's as we bowed our heads together.

My hands passing out food and drinks to young starving children. My hands as I picked up a red stone and water rushed around my feet. My hands gripping a rope squeezing to hold on for dear life as I rushed down a raging slide. My hands holding a small red bird as my fingers stroked its head. My hands signing and teaching as little smiling faces looked upon me. My hands rested in the hands of a gentle giant. My hands swaying to music.

My hands as I watched a ring slip on my finger. My hands touching Clave's face, his body. My hands as I gripped the Fire Moon Stone to my chest. My hands...My...hands...My hands...reached out and touched others now. They pulled me home. Swirls and orbs surrounded me, and I could see smiling faces within.

One orb elongated and took the form of a man. He smiled as he approached; he wrapped me in his arms.

"Krystle!" He said my name. "I am Nole. I want to apologize to you for the problems I have caused."

"What do you mean?" I looked at Nole. He was a young man. Not much taller than me. He had short dark hair and amber eyes. "Come, I'll explain." We sat on a soft unseen surface. Orbs and Wisps floated about, whispering kind, loving encouragements.

"You know the story of our ancestors," Nole began.

I nodded.

"When we escaped, I wanted to make sure no one would be hurt ever again. Had I the foresight, I would've left the dagger behind. But, in my youthful, arrogant certainty, I thought taking it was the best solution. I wrapped it in a cloth and tied it. When our people passed through the Light into the cave of the new world, I thought it best to hide it there. I had buried it under a rock. I thought it would remain there. Safe. I didn't know it contained the dark essence inside. My Pure Soul had cloaked it as I had passed through the Light."

"I see," that was all I could say at the moment.

"I'm so sorry for Zinnia," said Nole. "For you and your family."

"I'm free!" I heard Zinnia's voice cry out.

Nole and I looked up. Zinnia stood shining before us. She came to me and wrapped her arms around me. "Krystle, I'm so sorry for all the pain I caused. Please forgive me."

I hugged her back. “I forgive you, Zinnia. It wasn’t your fault.”

“It was mine,” said Nole.

“I forgive you, Nole. You thought you were doing the best thing for our people,” said Zinnia. “I was the one! Foolish! I felt the negative energy from the blade. Yet, I was weak. I picked it up and accidentally cut my finger on the blade.”

“What happened to free you?” I asked.

“Lazula, she fought past her fear of losing me and used the Drosera Blade to free me,” Zinnia cried. “I feel whole and happy for the first time in decades!” She threw her hands up and yelled again. “I’m free!”

“Yes, you are,” said Nole. He smiled. I could hear the calls of the ancestors rejoicing. I felt happy, giddy with joy.

“You are free from the Dark Spirit,” said Nole. “But, you are not finished with the world yet, Zinnia. Nor you, Krystle.”

“But what need is there of I that I must return?” asked Zinnia.

“You must go back to your sister. You must help teach the next generation of keepers. True love awaits you. You still have much to fulfill,” Nole told her. Zinnia stood quiet in contemplation.

Nole turned to me, “Krystle, you have to complete your destiny. You must go back. There are many things you must still accomplish. Look and see.”

Nole stood and stepped aside. Two bright orbs hovered before me- Pure Souls. I looked at them. I could see beautiful little faces. Scenes appeared within them like looking into a crystal ball. A baby girl with dark hair and big blue eyes bounced on Clave's knee. My hands reached out for her, and she lifted her arms to me. "Mama!" she cried out and laughed.

The next orb showed me sitting up in bed, and I held our newborn son wrapped up in a soft blue blanket. Clave sat beside me with our daughter in his lap. She held her hand out, and tiny fingers wrapped around hers. We were all smiling in contentment. The scene faded, and the orbs floated on.

I felt a force like a pull on my soul. There was a pushing sensation, like hands pushing against my heart. A little red bird flew toward me.

"Chorus?"

"It's time to go, Krystle," said Nole. "We'll meet again someday," he smiled.

"Follow the bird, Krystle. He's never led you astray."

Nole faded away. I watched as his soul shot off, his mission complete.

I didn't see Zinnia anymore. I walked toward the little red bird. It flew, and I started to chase it. I saw a glowing ring of fire before me. My Fire Stone was showing me the way. My steps hastened with echoes of thunder, and I pumped full speed ahead and dove through its center.

My lungs drew in pure oxygen, and my heart raced like the galloping of wild stallions. My ears picked up muffled sounds and echoed cries filled my consciousness. My eyes lids fluttered open. Strong arms wrapped around me. Deep shaking sobs accompanied their embrace. Warm tears dropped upon my face. My hands rose up, and I took hold of those arms.

Krystle! Clave cried. I reached up to touch his tear-soaked face. *Krystle!* He cried again. He began to kiss my face all over, then my lips. I wrapped my arms around him, and he pulled me tightly to him. *Krystle, my love.* He kept repeating my name in cadence between kisses. I squeezed my arms around him. He was shivering, wet, and cold. I realized I was as well.

I could hear my family shouting my name from across the river. My mom and Aunt Cassie were crying and shouting. “Oh, thank God!”

I looked around me. Lazula was on the ground cradling Zinnia’s limp body in her arms. Total anguish consumed her.

“Help me up,” I told Clave.

Krystle, love... he began to protest.

“Help me up, Clave! Please!”

Clave stood and lifted me by my arms. He held me till I felt steady on my feet. Aura, Taylin, and Garrissa stood in place. Tear tracks stained their faces as they looked me over with relief. I saw the Drosera Blade cast aside several feet away. The dark presence swirled within the diamond. It struck out at the inside surface, desperate to escape. I took in the Dark Spirit’s anguish. “Sucks, doesn’t it?” I smirked.

Garrissa spoke up. “It has to be you, Krystle! You are the only one who was ever supposed to be.”

I finally understood those words. It didn’t apply to me being the only one to come through the Light to this world. I was the one who had to go through everything I experienced to make it to this point. It all made sense now!

I reached down and picked up the dagger carefully by its hilt. The pyramid held its place above. The four moonstones waited just outside their designated positions. I walked beneath the pyramid and held the dagger in the air. It pulled gently away from my hand.

I stepped back and watched as the diamond containing the Dark Spirit broke free from the hilt. The dagger crashed to the ground and broke into pieces. The diamond hovered below the pyramid, just under the round concave indent in the base. The diamond and all four moonstones instantly snapped into place. The pyramid began to spin like a centrifuge as beams of light cast down from the four converging moons.

The pyramid halted. The moonbeams held a connection to their adjoining stones. The diamond had emptied, clear once more. One brilliant beam shot up into the sky from the pyramidion. The Dark Spirit screamed in agony as it was rushed toward the heavens then exploded.

Ash rained down upon us. A starburst of white glowing orbs rushed through the air like fireworks. The dark clouds parted, and the Light opened and received the freed Souls.

One stray orb was left behind as the Light closed in on itself. Down it drifted, then settled into the limp body lying in Lazula's arms. Zinnia woke with a gasp. Lazula howled out cries of joy as she and Zinnia embraced. "Sister!" They cried into one another's shoulders.

The pyramid crumbled to pieces. It, along with the diamond, crashed to the stone ground. The diamond shattered into thousands of tiny particles.

Clave put his arm around me as we watched the moonstones return to their keepers. My fire Moon Stone settled around my neck once more. "Hello, again, my friend!" It pulsed warmly in reply, then faded back to its dormant state.

My sisters rushed upon us, and we huddled with arms around one another. "I love you all," I cried.

"We love you too, Krystle," they all responded.

I put my hand on Garrissa's cheek. She smiled up at me. "Good job, Krystle!"

I laughed, "You too, little stinkerton."

We all went over to Lazula and Zinnia.

"Thank you! All of you!" Zinnia cried. She and Lazula still had their youthful appearance. They looked like they were in their mid-twenties. If anything, it was one nice perk, I suppose. Not worth having an evil entity in one's body. But, they deserved their second chance and a fresh start.

Garrissa raised the bridge back up. Our family came rushing back across to meet up with us. Joyful tears, hugs, and love pulled us all together. Lazula invited us all inside. Mom, Liv, and Cassie worked together with Garreth, Dad, and Eric to make a feast. Tovin and Mieruss stood in a huddle with Azora, Lazula, and Zinnia, singing an old ancestral song. Bennigan was holding Taylin in his arms as they sat next to Benjamin and Maria. Jasper was kissing Aura. Rhodin, Hailey, and Garrissa played and laughed themselves silly.

I sat in Clave's arms as we watched our family. The joy I felt in my heart overflowed. I tilted my head up to look into Clave's gorgeous gray eyes. *I love you,* I said to him through our connection.

I love you, too! He responded.

Where's Chorus? I looked around. I didn't see him anywhere.

I don't know, said Clave. He sat up and looked around. *I don't feel him nearby.*

Clave, I can still hear you!

And I hear you, my love, he smiled at me. *I guess Chorus has completed his mission too.*

Remember what you told me about people going on spirit journeys with their animals? I asked.

Yes, said Clave.

I believe, Chorus guided me home! Tears sprung from my eyes. *If he's really gone...*

We will see him again one day, Clave promised. *We still have much to do in this world.*

We do, I agreed. Clave kissed me. I melted into him. With him, I was home.

We had said our goodnights and made it back home in record time. We pushed through the door and ran upstairs hand in hand. We created our little bit of heaven over the next few days as we made love with fervent passion. It was time to live again, and we were making the best of it.

In the days that followed, the entire village had come together to clean up the aftermath of the storm. The moons had gone back out into their orbits, and nature was singing once more.

Epilogue

A few weeks later, just before the first snowfall. Tovin and Cassie had their bonding wedding ceremony. It was beautiful, as was Aunt Cassie. She had confessed to being extremely nervous about her wedding night referencing once more to size difference and body logistics. Mom and I laughed and assured her she would be fine. Mom insisted that Cassie would be more than fine and told her to enjoy her long winter honeymoon. She and Tovin didn't stay long at the reception.

Dad and Uncle Garreth had sent them off, yelling, "Get it, girl!"

The winter had come and gone, and I sat in Clave's lap as he rubbed my growing belly. Aura and Jasper would visit often. Aura and I would compare our bellies. Aura's was looking much bigger even though we were within the same time frame of our pregnancies. Mom confirmed two heartbeats for Aura. She and Jasper were to have twins.

The Bens were in love with Taylin and Maria. A few months later, the Light brought the rest of the Mehla family to this beautiful world. Maria was beyond ecstatic as she reconnected with her family.

Everyone welcomed them. Victor's eyes popped when he saw my belly bulge. He and Lee congratulated us. Maria's younger brother, Tobias, found some friends, and many young ladies were interested in him immediately. Victor wasn't all too fancy at first about Maria and Benjamin, but he finally came around.

So many new and exciting things were happening. It was hard for my hormonally-addled brain to keep up. Ceremonies, celebrations, births all started happening in a short time.

Zora Noelle Frost was born on an Amethyst Moon. Her head full of thick dark wavy hair and big blue eyes stole every extra piece of me. She was going to be a daddy's girl for sure.

Her cousins Gazer, a boy, and Honor, a girl, were born a few weeks later during a Blue Pearlescent Moon. The village had a massive celebration at the news of their birth. They looked a lot alike with thick dark curls and gorgeous azurite blue eyes.

Lazula and Zinnia yipped for joy. They confirmed the twins to be the new Four Moons Keepers and began arguing about what would happen first.

One Year Later

Everyone was bustling. Little Zora sat on my hip as I watched women hovering around the bride. I left the room to check on the groom. Dad was teasing Uncle Garreth like he always did. I passed Zora Noella to Clave and rubbed my little belly bump. Yes, number two was in the oven.

"Dad, would you cut Uncle Garreth a break! Do you know how long it took Clave and me to get him to cut ties with bachelorhood? Don't make him regret it and back out."

Uncle Garreth looked up at me, "Krystle, I'm not getting any younger, and neither is my bride-to-be. We are so very ready. If either of us run, you have my permission to knock me upside my head."

"I can't help teasing your uncle! He's a forty-eight-year-old man getting ready to marry a three-hundred-and-six-year-old woman." Dad chuckled.

"A mighty fine-looking three-hundred-and-six-year-old woman," Garreth added.

"Well, I'll give you that," said Dad.

"Everyone, out already! It's time," said Taylin.

Everyone took their places, and Lazula waited between the ceremonial totems. The music began to play. Taylin and Aura stood to one side as bridesmaid and maid of honor. Dad was Best Man with Tovin and Mieruss beside him. The bride emerged. She was beautiful in her white flowing gown. She smiled, looking straight ahead, and everyone's heads turned toward Garreth. His eyes shined with love as he smiled back at his bride. The two walked toward each other and met in the middle before Lazula.

Lazula looked at the couple standing before her. She greeted the guests and spoke her words of blessing upon the union. She then turned a stern eye on Garreth and said, "Garreth, speak your vows to my beloved sister Zinnia. And they had better be good!"

Weeks later, Lazula had invited the Genstone-Otek-Frost-Tucker clan to her home. A large covered object stood upright in her front yard. It looked to be eight feet tall by five feet round.

"I had this in the works over the past few months, and I'm excited to show it to you all today," said Lazula. "As you see on my home behind me, the carvings of our ancestral history fills the entire surface, so there was no more room to tell the story. So, it stands before you all now on stone."

Lazula grabbed the cloth with both hands. "Before I unveil this, I want you all to know many generations have come from Earth and since moved on to the Light. All have contributed in many good ways. Many made strong, lasting impressions with their contributions. I wanted to honor this generation. This generation has brought the greatest contribution by far. This generation has laid a strong foundation from which we build anew with gratefulness in our hearts. The ancestors will sing your praises for all time. I present to you, Generation Stone!"

She pulled the cloth away. A tall pillar of stone stood with faces carved all around. From the top, our story was told and read downward-moving back in time. At the very bottom, a family was standing hand in hand as a unified front. Their bodies encompassed the entire circumference around the stone pillar.

Their shoulders were the foundation the story was built upon. Names were carved above the heads. Flint, Gemma, Jasper, Krystle, Rhodin, Garrissa. The surname cast boldly above.

GENSTONE

The End

About the Author

Misty Tackett lives in Texas with her husband of 26 years, their three children, one spoiled dog, and a little budgie bird. She enjoys reading and writing fiction, romance, adventure, supernatural, and mystery. She also dabbles in poetry.

Generation Stone, Revelation Light Calling is her debut into the world of literature. She is aiming to write and publish more stories in the near future. Dreams are her inspiration. As such, she has created Dreamscape Writing and can be found on Facebook.

She lives by "One day at a time" to get through what life throws her way. And she holds dear her mother's words, "Life is a test. As long as you keep trying, you're going to pass."

Made in the USA
Columbia, SC
07 July 2021

41434156R00290